"*DOME CITY BLUES is a smart,* ~~.~~ *...~~mystery thriller set in a~~ future reminiscent of Blade Runner. Edwards combines the mind-twisting surrealism of Philip K. Dick with the hard-boiled characters of Elmore Leonard. His writing is clean and vivid, with cliff-hanger plot twists, and an edge-of-your-seat mystery. I can't wait for the next one!*"

— **JAK KOKE,** Bestselling author of '*THE EDGE OF CHAOS*' and '*THE TERMINUS EXPERIMENT*'

"*Fresh and surprising at every turn, DOME CITY BLUES by Jeff Edwards delivers first-rate adventure, high-thrills, and a vision of the future that will keep you fascinated. With this book, my only advice is enjoy!*"

— **GAYLE LYNDS,** New York Times bestselling author of '*THE BOOK OF SPIES*'

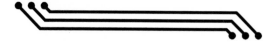

"*Take the intelligence of a Neal Stephenson novel, add a heaping helping of Richard K. Morgan kick-ass, fold in a cup or two of real world technical knowledge and an eye in the future, and then put the result in a noir dystopia bleak enough to make Philip K Dick and William Gibson shed a few tears. Bake at 2000 degrees. You now have an idea of what Jeff Edwards has in store for you in DOME CITY BLUES.*"

— **PATRICK HEFFERNAN,** Mysterious Galaxy Books

"*Ex-private detective David Stalin inhabits a world you might not want to live in, but you definitely want to visit. Whether or not you'll survive the trip is anybody's guess... but you won't stop flipping the pages until you're done. An impressive achievement!*"

— **JEFF MARIOTTE,** Author of '*THE BURNING SEASON*,' and '*CITY UNDER THE SAND*'

DOME CITY BLUES

DOME CITY BLUES

Jeff Edwards

STEALTH BOOKS

DOME CITY BLUES

Copyright © 1994, 2011 by Jeff Edwards

Stealth Books

www.stealthbooks.com

ISBN-13: 978-0-9830085-6-9

Printed in the United States of America

To Don Gerrard,
who has been waiting for this book *far* too long.

When you live inside a plastic bubble,
Hidin' from the sky.

You know that this ain't livin',
But you ain't got sense to die.

The air you breathe comes from machines,
It kills your soul and steals your dreams.

And you think you might be human,
But you can't remember why.

Rusty Parker — *Dome City Blues*

CHAPTER 1

The City Planners called it Los Angeles Urban Environmental Enclosure 12-A. Those of us who lived there called it the *Zone*. By either name, it amounted to a geodesic blister of translucent polycarbon fused to the east side of LA Dome #12 like a Siamese twin joined at the hip. It lacked the graceful sweeping arcs of the domes that covered the rest of the city. It was ugly, but then it was never designed to be pretty. It was an afterthought, thrown together after the inhabitants of East LA had made it violently clear that they didn't appreciate being left outside under a sky that pissed acid rain and streamed dangerous levels of solar ultraviolet.

I leaned against a wall and pried a Marlboro out of a squashed pack. The lettering on the box said, "crush proof." It wasn't. The box, like the cigarettes it contained, was a Brazilian knockoff—one of a hundred offshore counterfeit brands that had sprung into existence after the collapse of the American tobacco industry.

I stroked the wrinkled cigarette a few times to straighten it. It was still pretty rumpled, but it didn't look too mangled to be useable. I touched the tip against the black circle of the ignition patch on the bottom of the box. It took two or three seconds for the catalytic reaction to light the tobacco. I took a longish drag, and blew a gout of smoke into the air.

The last rays of the sun were starting to crawl up the tops of the buildings. Night was coming to the Zone. I watched as it crept over the decaying structures, hiding the sandstone texture of crumbling cement and rusting steel under a humid cloak of shadow.

Holographic facades flickered and appeared across the faces of most of the buildings: glamorous mirages that concealed graffiti-covered walls behind idealized projections of fairy tale palaces and pirate ships under sail. Here and there, enough sunlight still filtered through to weaken the holograms, leaving patches of drab reality visible through the bright fabric of illusion. In a few minutes, when the sun dropped a little farther, the holographic facades would become seamless, and the illusion would be perfect.

Above the street, triggered by the failing light, holosigns winked into phantom existence. Neon colored lasers woke up and began painting nightclub logos on the underside of the dome.

1

Two meters above the main entrance to Trixie's, a hologram of a naked woman crackled to life. The woman writhed suggestively through a ninety-second loop of canned video data. A glitch in the software caused the dancer's left leg to vanish in a smear of video static for the last few seconds of the loop. Lately, the glitch seemed to be spreading to the upper slope of her right breast.

Somebody tried to tell me once that the dancer was Trixie herself, the hologram built up from video footage shot when she was young. I've seen Trixie up close. I don't think so.

When half of the cigarette was gone, I ground it into the cracked sidewalk with my shoe and started walking again.

The strip was still mostly deserted, people just beginning to filter in. Four or five early-bird whores staked out their turf. A small knot of sailors cruised the bar fronts, waiting for the action to start. The inevitable sprinkling of tourists wandered around goggle-eyed, too ignorant of street-level protocol to realize that their chances of making it home safely were dropping with the sun.

A nocturnal creature, the Zone hibernated during the day and came to life when the sun went down. After sunset, even LAPD Tactical didn't venture through in less than squad strength.

I passed a pair of muscle-punks leaning against the carcass of a vandalized police car. They were decked out in the severely retro fashion popular in the Zone: black jeans, Gestapo boots, and synthleather jackets with too many zippers.

Both had peroxide white hair shaved close on the sides, left long on the top, and combed into crests like exotic birds. Their well-used leathers reeked of old blood and chemical reflex boosters. They watched me closely as I walked by, predatory eyes sizing up my potential as a target. Some signal passed between them and they decided to leave me alone.

I crossed Santa Fe Avenue, and walked in the front door of Falcon's Nest. I waited a few seconds for my eyes to adjust to the dim illumination, and then scanned the room. I was looking for John Hershell, a friend I was supposed to be meeting for drinks.

John and I were technically cousins on my mother's side, through some geometry that had been explained to me once and then promptly forgotten. We had been buddies right up through our teens. We'd even ended up in the Army together.

John wouldn't be hard to spot. He was strapped into a powered exoskeleton, compliments of a perimeter defense laser that our squad had tangled with in Argentina. The laser had sliced through his spinal cord, leaving his body pretty much null and void from the chest down. Turns out, he was one of those lucky one-in-a-million people who are allergic to the DNA modifying retrovirus that stimulates growth of spinal ganglia.

John wasn't here yet.

Unfortunately, Preacher *was* here, sitting at the bar, and he was in full cry. I slid into the booth farthest from his stool and signaled for my usual: Cutty Sark on the rocks.

Preacher's real name was Robert Treach, and he was an expert on everything. As usual, he was talking loudly to everyone within earshot.

"Natural selection," he was saying. "You can't wipe out disease. You just can't do it. They tried it in the Twentieth Century, right? Antibiotics, vaccines, miracle drugs, all that. Wiped out polio, smallpox, measles, and a bunch of other diseases."

Someone in his general area must have asked the obvious question.

Preacher squeezed a swallow from his tube of beer and shook his head. "Hell no it didn't work. It *can't* work. Not in the long run. Nature always figures out a way to restore the balance. When the population gets too high, natural selection kicks in and a new disease shows up, usually something real ugly. Where do you think AIDS came from? And then AIDS II, and AIDS III? Too many people bumping into each other, that's where. It's not healthy. Nature had to cull the herd. Worked too, didn't it? Culled the hell out of the human race."

I ran his words around in my head for a second: *"Culled the hell out of the human race."* Only Preacher would choose such a banal phrase to describe the disease that had ultimately wiped out a third of humanity.

"It'll happen again too," Preacher said. "Nature will keep on weeding out our weak bloodlines until we wise up enough to do it ourselves."

He downed another squirt of beer and nodded in response to something I couldn't hear. "That's what I'm telling you," he said. "Compassion is not a pro-survival characteristic."

I tuned him out just as he was spouting some nonsense about Darwin.

Falcon's Nest was a dark and cozy little blues bar. As far as I knew, it was the last one left in Los Angeles, maybe even the world. It was an anachronism, with its exposed beam ceilings, dark Portsmouth paneling, and worn leather upholstery. The owner, Rico Martinez, had kept it as true to the traditions of his grandfather as possible. It remained an island of quiet sanity in a sea of designer drinks, psycho-rock, and holo-neon.

When Rico finished pouring my drink, he shooed the waitress away and brought it to me himself. Watching him hobble across the room made me wish I'd sat at the bar.

His round face split into a huge grin as he slid the drink across the mahogany table. "You've finished a piece, haven't you?"

I pushed an ice cube around the top of my scotch. "What makes you say that?"

Rico's grin got wider. "You *bastard*, you *have*, haven't you?"

It was my turn to grin.

He slapped the table. "I knew it! When do I get to see?"

I took a sip of scotch. "I'll probably shoot a couple of holos tomorrow. I'll drop you a copy in a day or two."

"Is this piece as good as the last one?"

I shrugged. "You'll have to be the judge of that."

Demi, the latest in a long line of temporary waitresses, slipped up behind Rico and whispered something in his ear.

He glanced back toward the bar and nodded. "Duty calls, Amigo. I have thirsty customers and the booze must flow."

I lifted my glass and toasted him silently as he limped back to the bar.

Rico doesn't talk about it, but rumor says—when he was a kid—his mother sold the musculature in his left leg to a black market organ clinic. I don't know if that's true, but I've seen the leg. From the knee down, it's not much more than skin stretched over tendon and bone.

I asked him once why he's never gotten a muscle graft to replace the missing tissue. But Rico had given me a sad smile, shaken his head, and told me that you never can be sure whether organ donors are volunteers, or victims.

Lonnie Johnson's *Low Down Saint Louis Blues* found its way out of the speakers. I took another sip of the scotch and settled down into listening mode.

"Getting started without me, Sarge?"

I looked up into John's grinning face.

"You're late," I said. "There is scotch to be drunk, Johnny Boy, and you are not carrying your end of the load."

John eased himself into the booth; the servomotors that drove his exoskeleton bleated softly as they bent his unresponsive lower body into a sitting position.

"A problem that can be quickly remedied," he said. He waved Demi over and ordered a drink.

John wore dark colors as usual, slate gray pants and a pleated black jacket with flyaway shoulders. The dark color scheme was supposed to hide the narrow gray ribbing of the exoskeleton. Under the dim lights of the bar, it almost worked; the exoskeleton was nearly invisible.

"What's the big news?" I asked.

"My R&D team is getting close to a breakthrough on the neural shunt," he said.

The neural shunt was one of a hundred crazy schemes that John had cooked up in his drive to free himself from the exoskeleton. I didn't understand most of the technical details, but the shunt was basically an attempt to wire around the damage to John's spine, sort of like jumpering around a bad circuit.

It consisted of a custom-designed microchip implanted in his frontal lobe. The chip was supposed to interpret synaptic firings from John's brain, and transmit the signals through a fiberoptic strand that ran down his spine to a second chip implanted below the injury. It had been an ugly piece of surgery, and it hadn't really done the trick.

"You're going to try that crap again?"

"Of course I'm going to try it again. That's why I built Neuro-Tech in the first place. Owning a medical R&D team isn't exactly my life-long dream. If anybody else would work on the problem for me, I'd sell the company in a nanosecond. Until that happens, I'm going to have to keep trying myself."

I took a swallow of scotch and tried not to frown. "I thought the neural shunt was a dead-end."

John shook his head. "So did I, but my engineers have worked up a new angle on it."

"John, you told me yourself, every time you power up that chip, you go into a full-blown seizure. You've got to stop screwing around with your brain."

John tapped a fingernail on the carbon laminate ribbing of his exoskeleton. "I've got news for you, Sarge. My brain is about all I've got left to screw around with."

I set my glass down a little too hard. "Damn it, John. You know what I'm talking about."

John nodded. "I know," he said. "And I appreciate your concern. I honestly do. But I'm going to be okay, Sarge. *Really*. This is going to work."

I bit back the obvious comment. When it came to getting his legs back, John's weird projects were always 'going to work.'

It was his quest, his single-minded obsession. In an age where medical technology could cure cancer, transplant organs, and rewrite DNA, John was just about the only crippled person left. He wanted out of that exoskeleton, and he didn't care how many fortunes he had to spend to get there.

"What about the seizures?" I asked.

"We're getting a handle on that," John said.

I gulped down the rest of my scotch and signaled Demi for another.

When it came, she waved away my money and jerked her head toward a woman in the next booth. "Already paid for," she said. "Your secret admirer." Her nasal accent made it sound like *saykrit admoyra.*

I glanced at the woman for a second and then felt my eyes drawn to her again. She definitely had the goods. She was also definitely a hooker.

Her hair was a tousled auburn mane falling well past her shoulders. She had opaline green eyes with improbably long lashes. Her lips were a deep glossy red, with a swollen bee-stung look that suggested she had just climbed out of bed. The soft prominence of her cheekbones tapered to a pointed chin.

A skintight bodysuit of dark green synlon clung to her as if sprayed on. The fabric was photo-active, oval cells of the material cycling to transparency, revealing her white skin in sharp contrast to the dark green synthetic cloth.

Tiny windows of nudity drifted slowly across her body like clouds being chased by the wind. I tried not to stare as one of the transparent patches flowed diagonally across her rib cage and up around the curve of her breast, revealing the cinnamon-toast brown of her nipple.

Cinched tight around her waist was a broad black belt with leaves of ivy embroidered in metallic green thread. Her shoes were those impossibly high stiletto pumps that street kids call *fuck-me shoes.*

She was beautiful; as beautiful as surgical boutiques and DNA-modifying viral cultures could make her.

Beautiful. Perfect. Artificial.

"Wow," John said softly. He tipped his drink slightly in the woman's direction and then took a sip.

A second later, the woman stood beside our table. She looked at John. "Are you David Stalin?"

John hooked a thumb in my direction. "There's your man..."

The woman turned toward me and held out one of my old business cards. "I called your office," she said, "but the number is out of service. I tried the address on your card, but it looks like they've turned that whole building into a pump shop for commercial steroids. If you'll tell me where you've moved your office, I'll be glad to drop by during business hours."

Her perfume was delicate, but overtly sensual. It must have been packed with pheromones, because it was down-loading sexual imperatives to my reproductive system on a frequency that I barely managed to ignore.

"I didn't move my office," I said. "I closed it."

I took another sip of scotch, and paused while it ran down my throat. "I'm out of the business."

John watched me, nodding his head slightly as if encouraging me to somehow take advantage of the situation.

The woman's shoulders slumped a little. She stared down at the table top. "I need your help Mr. Stalin."

"I'm sorry, Ms..."

She glanced up. "Winter," she said. "Sonja Winter."

"I'm sorry Ms. Winter, but I don't do that kind of thing anymore."

Her eyes were glassy, as though a tear might find its way down those long lashes any second. "I need your help," she said again. "I've run out of options. You're the last hope I've got."

As I stared into her eyes, I realized that her eye shadow and lipstick were not makeup. They were tattooed on.

I cleared my throat softly. "I'm not anybody's last hope. There are a thousand private detectives out there that are as good as, or better than I ever was. All you have to do to find one is walk to the nearest public terminal and access the business directory."

The entire situation was right out of an old Mike Hammer vid, but even the bizarrely cliché quality of our conversation didn't stop me from feeling like a totally heartless bastard as the first tear rolled down her cheek.

"If you'll let me tell you..." Her voice trailed off. "If you'll please just... reconsider..."

"Cut her some slack," John said. "It might do both of you some good."

"There's nothing to reconsider," I said. "I'm out of the business, and I'm not going back."

The woman closed her eyes for a long second. The first tear was joined by a second, then a third.

She swallowed heavily. "It's my brother," she said. "He's been... he was murdered."

"Then you've definitely got the wrong guy for the job," I said. "You need to call the police."

She opened her eyes and brushed her fingers across her cheeks, wiping away tears. "The police know all about it," she said. "They're not interested in finding the killer."

Out of reflex, I nearly asked the only logical question. I caught myself just in time, and shut my mouth. She was a smart one. She was dangling the bait right in front of my lips. A murder had been committed, and the cops had decided not to investigate. The very idea suggested either ineptitude the part of the police, or some kind of cover-up. What detective (or even ex-detective) could resist finding out which?

I took a swallow of scotch. If I asked that first question, I'd have to follow it up with another one, and then ten more after that. Before I knew it, I'd be up to my neck in this woman's problems. I wanted no part of that.

John nudged me under the table.

I glanced at him out of the corner of my eye. He was nodding nearly imperceptibly, urging me to go for it.

I turned my eyes back to the woman. "I don't know anything about your brother," I said, "but I'm sure the cops have their reasons. I'm not going to second-guess them."

The white skin of her cheeks took on the slightest hint of pink. She swallowed, and then nodded slowly. "I'm sorry I troubled you, Mr. Stalin. Thank you for your time."

I nodded.

She started to turn away and then turned back. "Your new career, do you mind if I ask what it is?"

Her voice was quiet, her carriage dignified. Somewhere behind eye shadow tattoos and fuck-me shoes was a woman with character.

"I'm a sculptor," I said. "Metals."

A feeble smile tugged at the corners of her lips. She dropped the old business card on the table and walked away.

When the door closed behind her, John reached across the table and pressed his fingertips against the inside of my wrist. His lips moved, as though he was counting under his breath.

I stared at him. "What are you doing?"

"Checking for a pulse," he said. "After you let a gorgeous thing like *that* walk out the door, I was afraid you might be dead."

I tugged my arm away.

John raised his eyebrows. "You sure weren't like this in the old days." He grinned. "How about that gun-ship pilot you hooked up with in Porto Alegre? The Nordic blonde with legs up to her neck?"

"I remember," I said.

I picked up the business card and turned it over. The front was iridescent silver with our old logo in blue 3-D capitals.

```
┌─────────────────────────────────┐
│                                 │
│      CARTER AND STALIN          │
│                                 │
│    PRIVATE INVESTIGATIONS       │
│                                 │
│    M. CARTER   D. STALIN        │
│                                 │
└─────────────────────────────────┘
```

The holographic lettering seemed to float two or three centimeters above the card. Across the back was a data strip containing the office's address and phone number.

I'd never liked those cards. They were too flashy and too expensive. I'd voted for black printing on white cardboard. Maggie had loved them, though. She'd liked the final batch best of all, the ones where her last name had been *Stalin*, instead of *Carter*.

John reached out for the card. I handed it to him.

He whistled softly through his teeth. "I still can't believe you didn't go for that," he said. He read the card and then tapped the edge of it on the top of the table three or four times. "I'll bet you haven't seen one of these in a long time."

"A *long* time," I echoed. I downed the last of the Cutty in a single gulp and called for another.

John put his hand on my forearm. "Take it easy, Sarge. We've got all night, buddy."

When my new drink came, I closed my eyes, leaned back into the red tucked leather upholstery, and let the voice of Billie Holiday carry me away.

CHAPTER 2

‖‖ ‖ ‖ ‖‖‖‖‖ ‖ ‖ ‖‖ ‖ ‖ ‖‖ ‖ ‖‖ ‖‖‖ ‖‖ ‖ ‖ ‖‖‖‖ ‖ ‖‖ ‖ ‖‖ ‖‖

"David, wake up."

I opened one eye and fought to drag the green digits of the clock into focus. The clock won the first round, its readout remained blurry and danced in dizzying circles.

"David, wake up. There is someone at the door."

I opened the other eye and rubbed them both. "Okay, House," I grunted. "I'm awake. What's up?"

"There is a visitor at the front door, identity unknown."

I sat up and stretched, my lower back making unpleasant popping noises. "House, give me half lighting and a picture of our guest, uh... one-way visual, far wall, life-size, no audio."

The room lights slowly faded up to half brightness and the wall across from my bed sizzled to life.

I was starting to wake up. The image on the wall screen wasn't nearly as hard to focus on as the clock had been. It was the woman from the bar: Sonja something... Sonja... Winter. Yeah, that sounded right.

The insides of my teeth felt fuzzy. "House, let me have two-way audio, please."

A soft chime told me that House had enabled the connection.

I cleared my throat. "Good morning, Ms. Winter. To what do I owe the pleasure?"

She looked directly at the camera pickup. "I need to talk to you. Can I come in?"

I squinted at the clock again; it was a little after noon. I climbed out of bed and stumbled toward the bathroom. "Sure, just a minute. House, audio off."

Again the chime.

"House, run a hot shower and start some coffee. Scan the lady for weapons and then let her in. Oh, and keep an eye on her."

"Of course, David."

The sound of the shower starting told me that House was on top of things.

Fifteen minutes later, I was clean and reasonably awake.

10

After a stop in the kitchen to grab two cups of coffee, I went in search of my guest. I could have asked House where she was; he knew to within a millimeter. I preferred to find her myself. It gave me a little extra time to think.

I knew what my uninvited visitor wanted, and I wasn't prepared to give it to her. I was going to have to disappoint this woman for the second time in as many days.

I found her in the loft, examining one of my sculptures, a hammered-iron casting of a pair of woman's arms reaching up through a plate of blackened steel. The iron fingers were curled and grasping, as though the unseen woman in the sculpture were trying to claw her way up out of some dark pit. I called the piece *The Quest for Air*.

Ms. Winter was dressed more conservatively than she had been the night before: brown slacks and a cream pullover sweater. Gone were the porn queen shoes and pheromone perfume. Only her eye shadow and lipstick tattoos spoiled the girl-next-door image.

She turned around and caught me staring at her.

I handed her a cup of coffee. "I hope you like cream and sugar."

She took a tiny sip. "This is perfect. Thank you."

Her eyes swept the room, taking in the polished oak decking and vaulted ceilings. "This place is *huge*."

I nodded. "It used to be the local LA-Trans office. We bought it for a song when they pulled the MagLev trains out of the Zone."

Her eyes turned back to the sculpture. "I like this. It's, I don't know... dark. It sort of... broods. Is it one of your pieces?"

"Yeah. An old one. I never have decided if I like it."

She reached out to touch it, glancing at me sideways to see if I objected. She gave a little gasp of surprise when her fingers passed through it. "Oh! It's a hologram. But it looks so real."

"The projector is built into the pedestal," I said. "I keep the lighting soft in here, to make it hard to see the scan lines."

She looked around the room at the other dozen-odd pieces. "Are the rest of them holograms too?"

I pointed. "That one's a holo. So is that one, and those two over there. Most of the rest are real. When I sell one, I shoot a holo of it before I let the original go. Silly I guess, but they almost feel like my children. I hate to let them go entirely."

She nodded. We stood without talking for a few moments. It became a stalemate, each of us waiting for the other to break the silence.

I gave in first. "How did you get Rico to give you my address?"

She raised one eyebrow.

"Come on, Ms. Winter, the business card you handed me is four years old, and there's nothing in the data strip to link me to this address. In my book, anyone good enough to follow a trail that cold doesn't need to hire a detective. You got the card and my address from Rico, didn't you?"

She nodded. "He said you were the best."

"Rico exaggerates," I said. "He's a great guy and a damned good bartender. But that doesn't exactly make him an expert on the private spook business. I'm tired; I'm out of the game, and I'm not going back. Rico knows all of that."

"I've tried other detectives," she said. "They think I'm crazy. Rico said you would at least give me a chance to explain. He also said something about you needing to get back on the horse."

She tilted her head slightly to one side. "What do you suppose he meant by that? I've never even seen a horse. They've been extinct since before I was born."

I rubbed the stubble on my chin, and realized that I had forgotten to shave. "It's an old cliché. It means that Rico thinks it's time for me to come out of retirement."

I shook my head. "Rico is starting to sound like John. Both of them seem to think they know what's good for me."

She watched me without speaking.

A good detective or attorney knows how to use silence as a tool. Most people can't bear more than a few seconds of silence at a time. When conversation lags, they feel obligated to say something, *anything* to fill the void. If you let them babble long enough, they will eventually slip up and say something they don't want you to know. Ms. Winter would have made a good interrogator. She remained silent long enough to put the ball back into my court.

Once again, I found myself breaking the stalemate. "All right, I'll listen to whatever you have to day. But don't get your hopes up. I have no intention of changing my mind."

The woman followed me into the den. I climbed into my favorite chair, an overstuffed brown wingback from another age. She chose the couch. I lit a cigarette and wiggled into a comfortable slouch; it was my house and she was an uninvited guest. I had no reason to be on my best behavior.

A plume of smoke left my lips, blossomed and then darted toward the ceiling as House reconfigured the ventilation system to draw my smoke away from our guest. The bastard. His manners always had been better than mine.

Ms. Winter sat stiffly erect, as if she were afraid that I would read something sexual into casual body language.

I settled back and took a healthy swallow of rapidly cooling coffee. This time it was her turn to break the silence. I wasn't going to coax her. She had come here to tell me something. Now she would either tell it, or she wouldn't.

She inhaled sharply, steeling herself to say something she didn't want to say. The breath held for a second, then two, then three. "My brother was Michael Winter... *the* Michael Winter."

The words came out in a rush, as if they were a bad taste in her mouth and she wanted to spit them out.

"Obviously you expect me to know who *the* Michael Winter is, or was... I believe you told me last night that he'd been murdered. I have to confess ignorance. I don't have a clue who you are talking about."

The look on her face was pure surprise. "Don't you watch the vid? Scan the news sites?"

I shook my head. "I stopped paying attention to that stuff a few years ago. The stories don't really change, just the faces and names. What is, or was, this brother of yours? A vid star?"

Her voice was a tense near-whisper. "A serial killer."

Try as I might, I couldn't come up with a clever response. I was still working on it when she handed me something. It was a data chip, the flat fingernail-sized kind, like they use in holo-cameras.

"Here," she said. "Play this. Then I'll explain."

I stood up and walked across the den to the little Queen Anne table that held my holo-deck. The table was one of Maggie's many 'discoveries.' She'd rescued it from a dusty curio shop in West Hollywood. It was supposedly a genuine antique, but we'd never gotten around to having it authenticated.

The holo-deck was a fat lozenge of matte black plastic; its streamlined profile played sharp counterpoint to the inlaid ivory and dark wood of Maggie's table.

I hadn't used the deck in so long that I wasn't even sure if it would work. I plugged in the data chip, punched the power button, and walked back to my chair. The air above the unit snowed video static until I found the remote and punched the *play* button.

A seedy hotel room coalesced out of the snow. The walls were painted hot pink and the paint was peeling badly. One entire wall and—from the looks of it—most of the ceiling, were covered with cheap plastic mirrors. Bolted to the wall just inside the door was a blood-scanner, the kind that used to be standard fixtures in hotel rooms before over-the-counter AIDS III tests hit the market.

The camera had one of those circuits that superimposed the time and date of the recording over the image. It appeared in the lower right hand corner of the picture in electric blue alphanumerics. The very first time code read **11:42 p.m./14APR2063**.

The scene wobbled, as though something had jarred the camera, and then someone walked directly in front of the lens. The image was blurry for a second as the camera's microprocessor compensated for the change in depth of field. When it focused, a man was sitting on the bed. The image was poorly framed, the man well to the left of center, as though he had miscalculated the camera's field of view.

He was young, perhaps twenty-five. His face was familiar. I knew I'd never seen it before, but I had seen another like it: Sonja Winter. Their features shared that too-perfect quality that people like to describe as 'aristocratic.' I revised my opinion of Sonja; maybe her beauty hadn't come from surgical boutiques after all.

The image made it hard to judge scale, but he seemed to be about medium height, well built. His clothes looked European: khaki slacks, too-white shirt, dark blue yachting jacket, black leather shoes, and a matching shoestring belt with silver buckle.

He turned toward the camera, his eyes a familiar shade of blue-green. "I am Michael Winter," he said. "This video chip is my last will and testament. It is my legacy."

He brushed at a stray lock of hair. It was a coppery shade, lighter than his sister's.

"You probably don't know me. It doesn't matter." He smiled, his teeth white and even. "I'm certain that you know my work."

He leaned forward, the image of his face growing larger in the hologram. His features contorted, leered, as if some malevolent creature hiding behind his eyes had decided to reveal itself.

He pulled something out of the right pocket of his jacket: one of those Japanese kitchen knives like they advertise on the vid, the kind that cut polycarbon and still slice tomatoes.

Tilting the knife back and forth, he watched the light run up and down the blade. Narrow bands of reflected silver strobed across his face.

"I cut Kathy Armstrong's heart out with this," he whispered. "Her soul made the most beautiful sound when I set it free."

I heard a squeak behind me. Ms. Winter's face was pale, sickly. Her eyes glistened as tears welled up. But she never cried. Her brother's ghastly recital was tearing her apart, but she never quite let herself cry.

Obviously, she had seen the recording before, so the contents weren't a surprise, but that couldn't have done much to deaden the pain.

I took a last drag off the cigarette and stubbed the butt out in an ashtray.

Kathy Armstrong wasn't the only name that Michael mentioned. Miko Otosaki... Felicia Stevens... Annette Yvonne Laughlin... Charlene Velis... Amy Lynn Crawford... Linda Joan Brazawski... The list continued. All teenage girls, thirteen to fifteen years old. All dead. All butchered by a maniac who carved open the chests of his adolescent victims and ripped out their hearts.

Virginia Mayland... Carmen Rodrigez... Paula Chapel... Jennifer Beth Whitney... Marlene Bayer... Christine Clark... Tracy Lee...

Fourteen girls. Michael Winter described the death of each in grisly detail, complete with dates and addresses. If half his claims were true, he was a one-man slaughterhouse.

When his recitation wound to a close, he sat in front of the camera. His breathing was ragged, his face flushed. "I am finished now," he whispered. "Not because I fear capture; I do not. You could never catch me. I have *seen* the bridge. I have *crossed* the bridge. I have touched the face of God."

His hand slid into the left pocket of his jacket. "He is calling me now. I can hear him. He is close..."

The left hand reappeared, wrapped around the butt of a large-caliber automatic pistol; it looked like a Glock.

"He is touching me now... I can feel his angels dancing in the spaces between my atoms." The left hand brought the gun up level with his head, the muzzle touching his scalp just forward of his left temple. "My work is done..." His finger tightened visibly on the trigger. "I am finished..."

The slug slammed his head to the side. A large chunk of the right side of his skull blew off in a cloud of pink mist.

I swallowed a rush of bile as I watched his head come apart. His body fell to the bed, a marionette with its strings cut. The gathering pool of blood showed hardly at all on the dark red sheets. A gobbet of flesh clung to the mirrored wall for a second and then began a leisurely slide toward the floor, trailing a red smear.

The scene remained unchanged for about four more minutes before the chip ran out. The last time code read **12:12 a.m./15APR2063**.

I pointed the remote at the holo-deck and pressed the *off* button. The image above the unit vanished as the deck powered down.

I lit another cigarette and drew the smoke deep into my lungs. "Let's cover the obvious first. Are you certain that the man in the recording is... *was* your brother?"

A nod. "The police compared DNA structure, dental work, and retinal patterns. The body in that hotel room was definitely Michael."

"Okay. Do the times, dates and circumstances of his confession agree with the police files?"

Another nod.

I swirled the last of my cold coffee around the bottom of my cup. "Is there any physical evidence, other than the recorded confession, to link your brother to any of the murders?"

"I don't know," she said. "When the police found Michael's body and saw the recording, they closed the case. The files are sealed; I don't know why."

"Did Michael have an alibi for *any* of the crimes?"

"Nothing that would stand up in court."

I sighed. "Okay, Ms. Winter, I'm confused here. Just what is it that you want me to do?"

Her gaze locked with mine. "Find out the truth. Prove that my brother was innocent. Find the real killer."

I suddenly understood why all the PI's thought she was crazy. But, I had promised to hear her out.

"You said you were going to explain," I said. "I assume that you have some reason for thinking that your brother was innocent."

"Michael was with me on the eighth of February."

I searched my memory. "Christine Clark?" Michael Winter had confessed to killing Christine on the afternoon of February eighth.

"Maybe he got the dates mixed up," I said. "Maybe he did Christine Clark on February ninth, or seventh."

"Uh-uh, I checked the news sites. They all quote the police as saying that Christine Clark died on the eighth at about 3 p.m. Michael had breakfast in my apartment at about 9 o'clock in the morning, and we spent the day together. He didn't leave until just before six that evening, when I had an appointment with a client."

The look in her eye dared me to react to her use of the word *client*.

I tried to blow a smoke ring. The modified air currents pulled it apart and snatched it into a vent on the ceiling. "Are you sure about *your* dates? The day you spent with Michael could have been the eighteenth, or the twenty-eighth. Remember, we're talking six months ago."

"It was a Saturday," she said. "I do a lot of business on Saturdays. Mike usually worked Saturdays too. When he called and asked me to spend the day with him, I had to reschedule several appointments. There are notations in my date book. It was most definitely the eighth of February. Harmony remembers it as the eighth too."

"Harmony?"

"The Artificial Intelligence that runs my apartment."

"Is Harmony tapped into DataNet? If she is, there should be a time signature stamped over any footage shot by your apartment's security cameras. Your brother may have an airtight alibi locked up in your AI's data core. For one of the murders, at least."

"No good," she said.

"You're not on the net?"

"I'm on the net all right, but my apartment doesn't have any video cameras. My clients tend to be rather jealous of their privacy. All of Harmony's interior sensors are either infrared or Doppler sonar. Good enough to chase burglars or keep house by, but not good enough for an ID that would stand up in court."

I sucked a lung full of smoke and put out the cigarette. A crumb of tobacco stuck to the tip of my tongue. I bit the crumb in half with my front teeth and blotted the pieces off the end of my tongue with a finger. "Let's say you're right. Let's say that your brother was at your apartment during Christine Clark's murder. He still could have killed one of the others. Or *all* of them."

"You're looking at it from the wrong angle, Mr. Stalin. If my brother confessed, in vivid detail, to *one* murder that he didn't commit—maybe he didn't commit *any* of them."

My stomach rumbled. It was starting to forgive me for exposing it to Michael Winter's suicide. It was starting to think about breakfast.

I stood up and wandered over to one of my favorite pieces, a tall, asymmetrical piece of twisted black grating that I called *Broken Concrete by Moonlight*. "Why is it so important to clear your brother's name? Is there an inheritance, or are you just interested in justice with a capitol *J*?"

She answered from the couch. "I admit that I have an ulterior motive."

I waited. My stomach growled again.

"Michael was a software engineer," she said, "a good one. He specialized in high-speed data compression and retrieval. Several of the big companies tried to seduce him into a contract, but he wanted to stay independent. He wasn't getting rich, but he was living pretty well.

"About four years ago, he started having these fainting spells. I finally convinced him to see a doctor. It turned out to be a brain tumor, and the tests showed that it was malignant. He needed a major operation and he didn't have nearly enough money. I had a few marks stashed away, but nothing like the kind of cash he needed. A big Eurocorp called Gebhardt-Wulkan Informatik ended up fronting Mike the money. He had to indenture himself to them for ten years. He was pretty screwed up physically, and I guess the company execs were afraid that he would die before they got their investment out of him. I had to co-sign his indenture.

If Michael died or skipped out, I'd have to work off the remainder of his contract.

That's the bottom line. If I can prove that Michael was murdered, his life insurance will pay off his indenture. If the official cause of death remains suicide, I end up working off the indenture in GWI's Leisure Department. Since their girls get paid bottom-scale, it will probably take me about fifteen years."

I scratched my jaw and thought about trying to crack my neck. "So all I have to do is prove that your brother didn't commit the fourteen murders that he confessed to, find out who *did* commit the murders, and figure out how someone murdered Michael while making it look like a suicide. Sounds simple enough."

I walked toward the kitchen. "You want some breakfast?"

She got up to follow me. "Breakfast? It's after one o'clock."

"I had a late night."

She pulled a small stack of pictures out of her purse and handed it to me.

Most of them were trids, but a few were old two-dimensional photographs. I thumbed through them quickly. "What are these?" I asked.

"Just some pictures of Mike."

"I already know what your brother looked like, Ms. Winter; I saw the vid."

"That video is a fake. I don't know how it was done, or who did it, but my brother did not do those things." She pointed to the stack of pics. "The real Michael Winter is in *there*, Mr. Stalin. I just wanted you to know a little bit about him."

She stood with her arms crossed. The look on her face said she expected me to disagree.

"Okay," I said. "I'll look at your pictures."

She exhaled and uncrossed her arms. "Will you take the case?"

"I'll think about it."

"You will?"

I started rummaging through the kitchen cabinets, looking for my favorite skillet. House knew where it was, but I wasn't about to ask him.

"I'm retired, Ms. Winter. Your story intrigues me, but I really *am* out of the business. I promise to give your request honest consideration, but if I decide against taking the case, you'll have to accept my decision. Agreed?"

She extended her hand. I shook it. Her grip was firm. Her hand was warm, fingers long, nails unpainted. "Agreed."

CHAPTER 3

||| || | || ||||| | || || | | || | ||| ||| ||| | || | ||||| || | ||| | ||| |||

The next evening, I left the Zone and rode the westbound Lev to Dome 15, West Hollywood.

Nexus Dreams was a specialty bar on Santa Monica Boulevard, catering to jackers, wannabe's, and techno-groupies.

The club's holo-facade was a live video feed of the street outside the front doors, pumped through a processor and rendered in simple polygon graphics. The result was a cartoonish video-mirror of the street scene in which all people and objects within about fifteen meters of the bar appeared as computer icons.

I watched my own icon grow larger as I approached the front of the club. My head appeared as a truncated pyramid, my body as two rectangular boxes (a short one for my pelvis, and a taller one for my trunk) and my arms and legs were jointed cylinders.

I walked past my polygon doppelganger, and into the club. The decor inside was intended to suggest a jacker's-eye view of the DataNet: matte black floor, walls, and ceiling divided into neat one-meter squares by low intensity florescent blue lasers. The tables and stools were transparent acryliflex, edge-lit in bright primary colors. Slash-rock pounded out of hidden speakers, an abrasive, atonal barrage masquerading as music.

At twenty after nine, the club was packed: a shoulder-to-shoulder swarm of human beings that seemed to writhe and pulsate in time to the arrhythmic beat of the music.

I fought my way to the bar and wedged myself into a narrow opening between a muscle-boy with florescent tattoos on his face and an androgynous albino dressed in black wet-look osmotic-neoprene. The albino's fingernails were black acrylic, long and pointed like tiny obsidian daggers. His/her features and complexion were flawless testimonials to the possibilities of elective surgery.

When I finally got the bartender's attention, I tried to order a Cutty on the rocks, and received a blank stare in return. I looked at the neon-colored drinks everyone else was having and decided that a beer was my safest bet.

The beer came in a purple octagonal squeeze-tube with raised Chinese characters on the label. I squirted some into my mouth; it tasted like cold aftershave.

I scanned the room. I was looking for Zeus, a data-jacker who had hung out here once-upon-a-time, back when Stalin and Stalin Investigations had still been a going concern. We'd hired Zeus several times, when our need for computer-skullduggery had overreached Maggie's talents.

Zeus's real name was Orville Beckley, a fact that he went to great lengths to conceal. I'd found that out as a result of a bet that Orville had made (and ultimately lost) with Maggie. He'd boasted of having erased every trace of his real name from the net. True to his prediction, Maggie hadn't been able to catch even a sniff of his birth records in the net. But he hadn't reckoned with Maggie's tenacity. She'd gone on to teach him three simple facts:

#1 Hospitals are bureaucracies.

#2 Bureaucracies are paranoid.

#3 Paranoid bureaucrats keep duplicate records of *everything*... in hardcopy... in file cabinets.

I could still remember the look of stunned disbelief on Zeus's face when Maggie had whispered the *Orville* word in his ear, the certain knowledge that his secret was not dead after all. The memory brought me a smile.

I looked around again. As far as I could tell, Zeus wasn't in the bar, but I did catch sight of a face I recognized. I threaded my way through the crowd until I came to her table. Her handle was Jackal; I didn't know her real name.

She wore a baggy maroon jumpsuit with a couple of hundred pins and badges stuck to it. I remembered her as thin. Now she looked anorexic.

Her hair was a thick black mop that ended suddenly just above the tops of her ears. It looked as though someone had dropped a bowl on her head and shaved off everything that stuck out. Her eyebrows were shaven as well. As she craned her neck, I saw two, no, *three* gold alloy data jacks set flush into the back of her head. One jack held a program chip. A thin fiber-optic cable ran from the second jack to a box clipped to her belt. The box was about two-thirds the size of a pack of cigarettes, molded from charcoal gray plastic, covered with flickering LEDs. The third jack was empty.

She looked up at me, a bare glimmer of recognition in her eyes. She knew she had seen me before; she just couldn't remember where. She reached into the right breast pocket of her jumpsuit and pulled out a small handful of data chips. She selected one and plugged it into the empty jack.

Her eyes closed for a second. When they opened, her expression was totally changed. She gestured toward a stool. "Stalin, right? Long time."

I took the offered seat and faked a sip of the almost-beer. "Yeah, it has been a while. You still calling yourself Jackal?"

"*THE* one, *THE* only," she said.

She took a swallow from her tall green drink. "Are you looking for Zeus?"

"Yeah," I said. "Have you seen him?"

Jackal shook her head. "Not in a couple of months. The last I heard, he snooped Ishikawa Audio for some pretty fancy technical specs. If he fenced them through the Cayman Islands, like he usually does, he's probably off spending his bankroll in the skin-bars in Bangkok. We probably won't see him for at least another six or eight weeks."

I nodded, and studied Jackal's face. As near as I could figure, she must have been about twenty-eight. She looked forty.

Jackal returned my stare. "Are you looking for Zeus for social purposes, or are you here on business?"

We had to lean close to hear each other over the crowd and the music.

"Business, actually," I half-shouted.

"What have you got? Maybe I can hook you up."

I thought about it for a second. I didn't really know her. I'd seen her hanging around with Zeus from time to time, but I had no idea whether or not she was any good.

She obviously had the skull modifications, and she knew how to talk-the-talk. But, when it came time to ride the data grid through somebody else's security software, could she slip in and out without a trace? Or would she leave a trail of bread crumbs through the net that some AI could follow? Or, worse yet, tangle with a neuro-guard subroutine that would reach through the interface and fry her brain?

My gut instinct told me that she could cut it.

I leaned close to her ear. "I've got two jobs, if you're interested. The first is a protected database. Are you up to that?"

"Depends. Whose?"

"LAPD. Homicide Division. I need a complete data pull on a closed murder investigation. The files are sealed."

Jackal rummaged through her pocket full of chips and selected one. She popped a chip out of one of her jacks, and plugged the new chip into the empty slot.

"The Boys in Blue have good security," she said. They just upgraded their AI about four months ago. Not cutting-edge, but real good stuff."

Her eyes went vacant for a second as the chip continued to download arcane technical data into her brain. "I can crack that base," she said. "Not easy, but I can do it." She looked back at me and smiled. "Also not cheap."

I nodded. "I didn't think it would be."

She pushed her drink around the table top leaving a smear of condensation on the clear surface. "You mentioned a second job."

"A personal database," I said. "It probably has fairly standard consumer-grade protection. Shouldn't be too difficult to penetrate."

She smiled again. "If it's as easy as all that, I might just throw it in as a bonus. But if it turns up any surprises, it's going to cost you."

We talked for another half-hour: price, time schedule, data format.

I elbowed my way out of the bar and caught a hovercab to the eastern perimeter of Dome 12. The cab was a beat-up old Chevy with a patched apron and a wobble in the left rear blower that threatened to loosen my teeth.

The driver was an attractive African woman, her proud cheekbones decorated with the inverted chevrons of ritual tribal scars. Over her shoulder, I could see the tattletales on the taxi's liquid crystal instrument panel. Every few seconds, one of the status bars would blink from blue to red. When it did, she would tap the display with her right index finger until it blinked back to blue.

She dropped me off at the corner of 55th and Fortuna, a couple of blocks short of the barricade. Nobody's been dumb enough to drive a cab into the Zone in years.

The MagLev doesn't run through the Zone anymore either. People kept stealing the superconductor modules out of the track, maybe for the resale value, maybe for the hell of it.

A few years ago, somebody stole five modules in a row. Ordinarily that wouldn't have been a big problem; the computers at LA Transit Authority are smart enough to spot damaged track and stop the train. Unfortunately, the thief managed to bypass the track sensors and trick the LA-Trans computers into thinking the track was safe. A Lev derailed, killing twenty-nine people and wiping out a half dozen buildings.

Now, unless you actually have your own car, the only way in or out of the Zone is on foot.

The cops at the barricade let me through with a quick wave of their scanner and a token pat down. It was a formality. They don't much care who or what goes into the Zone. They're worried about what gets out.

The Fearless Leaders of our fair city like to keep most of their bad eggs in one basket. Don't get me wrong, they have crime in the other domes too, but not like we've got it in good old Urban Environmental Enclosure 12-A.

I should have moved ages ago. Just stubborn I guess.

When I got home, I laid down on the couch with my eyes closed and told House to play some blues. House responded with Blind Willie Johnson's *Lord, I Just Can't Keep From Cryin'*. I tried to lose myself in the music, but even Blind Willie's gently gruff voice and sensuous slide guitar couldn't distract my racing brain.

After a few minutes, I stood up and lit a cigarette. I couldn't even pretend to relax.

I kept telling myself that there was nothing to get keyed-up about. I didn't have to take the case. I hadn't promised Sonja anything.

No, that wasn't true. I had promised to give her case serious consideration. But I was doing that, wasn't I? Hadn't I hired Jackal to scope the police files on the case? When I got access to those files, I would go over them in detail and prove to myself what I already knew: that Michael Winter was guilty.

I would be off the hook. I could stay snuggled up in my little cocoon, listen to ancient blues, drink scotch, smoke bootleg cigarettes, and weld pieces of metal together in patterns that amused my simple mind. I could tell Ms. Sonja Winter that her late unlamented brother was a murderous psycho-pervert, who deserved to have his brains blown out.

Except...

I didn't want to do that. I didn't want to tell Sonja that her brother was a killer. I didn't want to tell her that she was going to spend the next fifteen years as a corporate sex-toy.

Maybe a lot of people wouldn't appreciate the difference that would make in her life. She was a whore, right? So what if she had to punch a time clock for somebody else instead of set her own hours? She still made her living flat on her back, right?

The difference was in *control*. As an independent call girl, Sonja could select her clientele. She could take a day off if she wanted. She could say *no*.

It was the difference between freedom and slavery.

Still, none of that was my problem. I had troubles of my own. I didn't need to shoulder someone else's burden.

I jump-started a second cigarette off the butt of the first and then ground out the butt in an ashtray.

I wanted a drink. There was a bottle of Cutty hidden somewhere in one of the kitchen cabinets. I went looking for it.

On the counter next to the refrigerator was Ms. Winter's little stack of pictures.

I picked them up. The picture on top was a dog-eared photograph of Michael Winter as a boy, twelve, maybe thirteen. He was skinny, his hair a much brighter red than it had been in the video. On his left hand, he wore a baseball glove; a bat was draped across his right shoulder.

I paged through the stack slowly. A trid of a high school graduation, Michael and two other grinning teens in caps and gowns. Michael in his early twenties, sprawled on a couch with a huge tabby cat sleeping on his chest. The shot had probably been taken a year or two before North America had been hit by the genetic plague that made cats an endangered species.

I flipped to the next picture, another flat photo, Michael at four or five, in a bathtub full of bubbles. An obviously staged trid of an adult Michael surrounded by electronic equipment and wrapped in a tangle of test sensors and wires.

The last trid in the stack caught my attention. Michael as an adult, his arm around the shoulders of a pretty young woman dressed in orange surgical scrubs. The woman carried a data pad and had a stethoscope strung around her neck; she was obviously a doctor or nurse. It took me a couple of seconds to recognize the woman as Sonja Winter; the holo had been shot before she'd gotten the eye shadow and lipstick tattoos.

I wondered if the surgical getup was a Halloween costume. If so, why wasn't Michael in costume as well?

I dropped the pictures on the counter and opened the door to a cabinet. The Cutty was around somewhere. I closed the cabinet and opened another.

As I reached up to rummage through the shelves, I realized that my hand was trembling.

Maybe a drink wasn't such a good idea. I closed the cabinet and went to bed.

I had the dream again...

I am in a dark labyrinth of rusty steel walls and worn cement floors. The tops of the walls and ceiling are lost in shadow. Somewhere, I can hear water drip slowly into a stagnant pool. The air is damp and has a weird echoing quality that makes me think of indoor swimming pools. The darkness is interrupted by irregular patches of light.

I hear a series of muffled thumps. Someone is pounding on a wall. I don't know how I know it, but I'm certain that it's Maggie. She's in some sort of danger. I have to find her! I listen carefully to the pounding, trying to figure out where it's coming from. I can't tell. I touch first one wall, then another. It's no good; I can feel the vibration through all the walls.

The pounding becomes faster, more urgent.

I start to run through the maze, taking turns at random. I've got to find her! I will goddamn it, I will!

I run faster, my feet skidding through puddles of water, stumbling over unseen debris. Sometimes I lose my balance and bounce a shoulder painfully off one of the walls or sprawl headlong on the floor. When that happens, I scramble to my feet and take off again, rushing blindly on through the labyrinth.

The pounding grows weaker, less frequent.

Every time I turn a corner, I promise myself that Maggie is just around the next one. At each new corner, the promise turns into a lie.

The pounding is very weak now. I have to stop running to hear it over my own footsteps. She hasn't got much time left. Oh God, don't do this to me... PLEASE God... I'll do anything...

I found myself sitting up in bed whispering "Please God..." over and over as the tears streamed down my face.

I knew better than to try to stop it. I just let it out in great wracking sobs that left me gasping like a fish on dry land.

When it was over, I felt wrung out. I laid down and listened to the sound of my own breathing until I drifted off again. If I dreamed, it wasn't anything worth remembering.

The next morning, I was in the shower when House played that pleasant little chime he uses to get my attention. I paused in mid-scrub. "Yeah House, what have you got?"

"As you requested, David, I have downloaded the morning news feed."

I resumed scrubbing. "Great, check the Personals for any messages addressed to Igor."

The *Igor* thing was Jackal's idea. I guess jackers have an obsession for code names.

"There is one message addressed to Igor," House said. "Shall I read it to you?"

"Please."

House made a quiet throat clearing sound. It was an obviously superfluous gesture, since he didn't actually have a throat. I guess something in his programming told him that it was an appropriate sound to make, prior to reading aloud. "To Igor, From J — The job is done. Come see me."

"That's all?"

"Yes."

"Thanks, House."

"Don't mention it, David."

Nine hours later, I walked to Dome 12 and caught the Lev to West Hollywood.

Nexus Dreams was every bit as crowded as it had been the night before. One end of the room had been cordoned off into a makeshift stage. The attraction was a computer performance artist who billed himself as "Insanity." The performer's long black hair was slicked back and pulled into a point, giving his head a sort of teardrop shape.

He wore a white synthleather trench coat that hung to his knees. His entire act appeared to consist of a table top full of computer equipment jacked into a hologram projector. The rig generated an animated hologram of the artist's own face. The holo was enlarged to about five times its normal size, so it could be easily seen from all over the room. It floated over the heads of the crowd, its features contorting themselves through a range of weird expressions as it alternately screamed and whispered bizarre epithets.

"Night is the contrivance of solidified truth!" it shouted. "I am the crystal blood-mist of hyperbolic fuel that mummifies the secret organs of the gods..."

The holographic face ranted ceaselessly, never making an iota of sense.

I watched the thing whimper and rave. At first, I thought it was just a simulation, a vid recording of the artist's face that had been doctored by video morphing software to create bizarre facial expressions. But I began to realize that it was more than that. There was something hypnotic about it, as though the hologram were a living thing instead of a weirdly distorted digital recording.

Somehow, from across the crowded bar, the hologram's gaze met mine. I found myself staring into its eyes, and I saw an agony reflected there that nearly staggered me.

"I can't stop them," the hologram said. "Leaves of corruption are falling on my face, burrowing their way like insects down into the empty chasm of my heart, and I CAN... *NOT*... STOP... THEM..."

It suddenly seemed possible that I might stand there forever, crucified by the power of the holo's gaze. Then the tortured eyes flicked away from me, and began wandering the room again. The spell of pain was broken.

I tore my eyes away and stared at the floor. It took me a couple of seconds to remember why I'd come here. Finally, I lifted my head and started scanning the crowd for Jackal.

I found her sitting at a table at the end of the room opposite *Insanity*. Seated next to her was a kid I'd never seen before. He was augmented cybernetically, *heavily* augmented. Enough of him was hidden behind hardware implants to make it difficult to read his age, but my best guess was about seventeen. He was definitely too young for the bar scene, but no one seemed to be interested in scanning his ID-chip.

Where the kid's eyes should have been, cylindrical electroptic lenses protruded from his eye sockets like the barrels of twin video cameras. His camera eyes whirred softly as the lenses spun to bring me into focus. His right hand looked normal, but his left was cybernetic, an articulated alloy skeleton that made me think of robotic bones. His head was shaved, his scalp tattooed with intricate patterns of circuit runs. The servomotors in his cybernetic hand emitted sporadic electro-mechanical whimpers whenever he moved his fingers. He stared at me for a second and then shifted his electroptic eyes back to Insanity's performance art.

I turned to Jackal. If anything, she looked thinner than she had the night before. In place of the jump suit, she wore blue stretch-pants and a white sweatshirt with the sleeves ripped off. The front of the shirt was a photo-active trid depicting a famous cartoon mouse sodomizing his cutesy mouse girlfriend in lurid 3-D. The mouse appeared to move in and out when Jackal turned her body.

Jackal motioned me to a seat.

I sat down without ordering. I didn't intend to be there very long.

Jackal started to say something, but Cyber-kid interrupted her. "They think that shit is funny," he said.

His voice was gravelly, obviously generated by a speech synthesis chip. I was struck by the certainty that he'd had his own larynx removed, just so he could speak with the voice of a machine.

"They're too stupid to know what they're doing," he said. "Either that, or they're too stupid to care."

Jackal took a swallow of her bright green drink. "It's no big deal," she said.

"That asshole is torturing it," the kid said in his metallic voice. His camera-eyes were locked on the performance artist's floating hologram. "And everybody thinks it's funny."

I forced myself to look down the length of the bar room at the hologram, ready to jerk my eyes away the instant I felt the touch of its electric gaze. From this distance, the face's jabbering voice was hard to hear over the murmurings of the customers.

"It's like it's alive," I said. "At first, I thought it was just a vid recording, but it's more than that, isn't it?"

"It's a Scion," Jackal said.

"A Turing Scion?" I asked.

"Yeah," the kid said. "A digital image of a human mind. And Asshole over there is driving it crazy, on *purpose*."

I knew a little something about Turing Scions. The concept had been around since the nineteen forties, the brainchild of Alan Turing, the British mathematician who'd invented digital computer logic, Artificial Intelligence, and the so-called *Machine Mind*.

Turing had predicted that technology would eventually permit a human mind to be recorded in digital form. Thought, personality, idiosyncrasies, prejudices, the whole ball of wax. Turing had been right; technology had caught up with his ideas in less than a hundred years.

"How can you drive a Turing Scion crazy?" I asked.

The kid turned his electroptic eyes toward me. "Leave it plugged in," he said.

"That doesn't make any sense," I said. "Turing Scions are *supposed* to be plugged in. That's what they're designed for."

"True," Jackal said, "but they're only intended to be active for short periods of time. If you leave one plugged in too long, it goes crazy."

"I still don't understand," I said.

"Look," the kid said. "The entire point behind the Turing Scion is to preserve the knowledge base of our so-called civilization. In the past, if a brilliant engineer died, his knowledge and his creativity died with him. His thought patterns, his ideas, his personal methods of problem solving ... *everything*. All gone forever. That's the way things worked for most of human history. Then, along comes the Turing Scion and changes all the rules. Now, if our hypothetical engineer has a Turing Scion, his knowledge doesn't disappear when he dies. If we have a problem that only Mr. Hypothetical Engineer can solve, we just plug his Scion into a computer node and start asking questions."

"But you can't *leave* it plugged in," Jackal said.

"Why not?"

The kid stared at me like I was an idiot. "Scions are sort of like software," he said. "They're only active when you plug them into a computer node. Unplug one, and it's just an anodized box full of dense-pack memory chips. It can't talk. It can't think. It can't do *anything*. It's inert. Asleep, if you prefer."

"But when they *are* plugged in," Jackal said, "they have dynamic memory, just like AI's. They continue to think, and learn, and grow."

"How does that make them go crazy?" I asked.

"Think about it," the kid said. "Even a low-end computer can process information three or four hundred times faster than a human brain can. For every hour of real-time that passes, an active Scion would experience four hundred hours. That's about sixteen days. Not sixteen days for some piece of artificially intelligent machine code that only *thinks* it's alive. Sixteen days for a human mind who has memories, wants, aspirations."

I nodded.

The kid looked back toward the performance artist's Turing Scion. "Asshole over there has kept his Scion plugged in for over a year. Try to imagine that. Four hundred years trapped inside a machine."

"It's not like it's a real person," Jackal said.

"It *thinks* it's a real person," the kid said.

I looked across the bar at the anguished face of the Scion, and suddenly I couldn't bear the thought of being in the same room with it. I cleared my throat. "This is all very interesting," I said, "but I have business to attend to." I looked at Jackal.

"Sorry," she said. "I got a little sidetracked." She pulled a data chip out of her pocket and slid it across the transparent table top.

I reached into my pocket and pulled out an envelope. "Cash," I said. "As agreed."

We traded.

I wouldn't be able to verify the contents of the chip until I got home. Jackal knew this; out of courtesy, she didn't open the envelope until I was gone.

Outside the bar, I waited for a cab on Santa Monica Boulevard, and tried not to think about Turing Scions. I'd seen one years before, and I hadn't liked it anymore than I'd liked the one inside Nexus Dreams.

John had talked Maggie into letting him make the recording. She'd been excited by the idea: her mind, her *personality* stored in a digital module. All you had to do was plug the Scion into a computer and presto, Maggie in a can. Sort of the electronic version of immortality.

She was in there, all right, or at least an incredibly accurate computer approximation of her personality was. Her memories were in there too, current up to the instant when John had slipped the sensor network over her head.

Maggie had tried to talk me into making one. She and John both had. I'd refused, a decision I had never regretted for a second. Man is not meant to be factored into logic algorithms.

The Scion had just been a novelty to John and Maggie, an interesting trinket. Every once in a while, they would drag the module out and plug it into John's computer. They'd talk to it for hours, giggling over it, like children playing with an amusing gadget. Then they'd unplug it, and it would go back on the shelf.

It might still be there somewhere, gathering dust at the back of one of John's closets. I made a mental note to ask him about it. If the damned thing was still around, I wanted it erased.

The past was dead, and nothing that was recorded on a stack of memory chips could change that.

CHAPTER 4

The computer in the den was concealed in the mahogany surface of my desktop. I plugged Jackal's data chip into a hidden slot in the right edge of the desk and thumbed the power switch. A holographic display field unfolded in the air above the desk, the translucent blue rectangle empty except for a slowly flashing cursor. The keyboard was a hologram as well, projected over a grid of infrared sensors that read the position of my fingers in relation to the imaginary keys.

I called up a file menu.

I would put off the actual crime-scene recordings until last. I'm not usually squeamish, but the fact that the victims were all children, or practically so, added an unpleasant dimension. I wanted to work myself up to them slowly.

I started with the text files. Most of them I just skimmed. It takes a while to read every report generated during a single murder investigation. I had files from fourteen murder cases. Fifteen, if you counted Winter's suicide.

The first murder had occurred in 2061 on the thirteenth of August. The victim: a fourteen-year-old girl named Kathy Lynn Armstrong.

Twenty-four days later came Miko Otosaki, thirteen years old.

Some time after the death of Felicia Stevens, the third victim, an over-educated desk sergeant had started calling the killer *Huitzilopochtli*, in honor of an Aztec God whose thirst for human sacrifices demanded a regular diet of hearts.

Since none of the rest of the cops in the station house could pronounce Huitzilopochtli, they'd quickly shortened the killer's nickname to Aztec. The media had picked up on the title immediately.

The last of the killings attributed to Aztec was a thirteen-year-old named Tracy Lee. Tracy had died on the twenty-ninth of March in 2063: a little over two weeks before Michael had put a bullet through his own brain.

Fourteen victims stretched out over nineteen months. The shortest interval between killings had been four days. The longest had been ninety-eight days. That made the average about forty-five days.

I checked my watch. Aztec hadn't killed in 133 days, not since Winter's suicide.

None of the murdered girls had been penetrated orally, vaginally or anally. The police had never found a trace of semen or foreign saliva on or near any of the victim's bodies.

Christine Clark's file I examined in detail. Sonja was right about the date; Christine had been murdered on the eighth of February. The coroner's best guess was 3 p.m., plus or minus a half-hour. LAPD's AI estimated time of death at 3:07:21 p.m., plus or minus two minutes.

So if Sonja was telling the truth—if Michael really had been with her that day—then he couldn't have killed Christine.

But a check of the physical evidence files put another nail in Winter's coffin. The LA coroner had positively identified the knife found on Winter's corpse as the weapon used in all fourteen Aztec slayings.

I backed out of the LAPD files and logged onto the other file.

The second data pull consisted of one file: twenty-four hours of data recorded by a household AI.

Ten minutes of random sampling told me what I wanted to know. Still, the data could have been edited. I had the desktop computer run the entire file at a compression ratio of 3600 to 1, verifying each DataNet time code recorded. In twenty-four seconds I had my answer: there were exactly 86,400 seconds worth of sequential time codes. None were missing and there were no extras. That didn't totally eliminate the possibility that the file had been edited, but it made it damned unlikely.

One thing was clear: on the eighth of February, 2063, an adult male answering to the name of Mike had spent the better part of nine hours in Sonja Winter's apartment.

Until I could prove that he was Michael Winter, I decided to call him Mr. X.

Since Sonja Winter's apartment wasn't equipped with video cameras, there was no identifiable footage of Mr. X.

The man appearing in the security system's IR imagers could have been anyone of the proper height and weight. A person's heat patterns are as individual as fingerprints, but Michael Winter had probably never been thermally mapped. Since thermal mapping only works on warm living tissue, it was too late to map Michael now. Without a reference map on file, there was no basis for comparison. Those heat patterns might have belonged to Michael Winter. Then again, they might not have.

So, scratch visual, and scratch infrared. What did that leave? Audio.

There were three voices in the recording, two female and one male. One of the female voices I recognized as Sonja's. The other female voice was easily attributed to Harmony, Sonja's AI. The male voice belonged to Mr. X.

I captured three random samples of Mr. X's voice and compared them to the police file copy of Michael Winter's suicide recording. The voiceprints matched. The voice in Sonja's apartment on the day of Christine Clark's murder belonged to Michael Winter.

The court wouldn't buy it, of course. The District Attorney would rationalize it away.

No two voiceprints are ever perfectly identical. The DA would call in a half dozen voiceprint experts, all prepared to testify that the minuscule variations between two samples made absolute positive identification impossible. The voice in Ms. Winter's apartment *might* belong to Michael Winter. Then again, maybe not.

Or, the DA might be willing to concede the possibility that Michael had an alibi for the murder of Christine Clark. Which didn't alter the fact that Michael had confessed to the other thirteen killings.

LAPD and the District Attorney's Office had a solution that made them happy. Fourteen murders were solved and the killer was dealt with. They certainly weren't going to call a press conference to announce that fourteen murder cases were being reopened and a killer was still running rampant.

According to the case files, before his suicide, Michael hadn't been a suspect. In fact, the police hadn't even been aware of his existence. His confession had taken them by surprise. Coming—as it had—complete with the murder weapon and a suspect who knew intimate details of the crime, the whole package must have seemed a Godsend to the police. All of which felt just a little too convenient.

I was a long way from being convinced that Michael Winter hadn't killed Christine Clark, but—for the sake of argument—what if he hadn't? What would it mean?

By Sonja's extension of logic, if he was innocent of one murder, then he hadn't killed any of them.

I wasn't ready to make a leap that large. He might very well have killed one or more of the others. I didn't know yet.

Damn. So much for the easy way out. I wanted the bastard to be *obviously* guilty. Then I could walk away from this whole mess with a clean conscience.

But there was a glimmer of a possibility that Michael Winter was innocent. If so, he had paid the price for someone else's crimes. And his sister would go on paying for years.

I stood up and reached for a cigarette. My pack was empty. I crumpled it up and tossed it into the recycling bin on my way to the kitchen.

I rummaged through the kitchen drawers. No smokes.

"House, where are my cigarettes?"

"There are two packs of cigarettes in the top drawer of the nightstand in your bedroom. There is a partial pack in the right pocket of your tan jacket in the hall closet. There are three full cases and one partial case in the storeroom. There are..."

"Okay, okay. I've got it." I walked into the bedroom and grabbed one of the packs from the nightstand.

I peeled the foil wrapper off the top of the pack. A neat little disclaimer paragraph printed on the foil reminded me to keep my cancer immunizations up to date, so that I could continue to enjoy the flavor of a good cigarette without serious risk to my health. I opened the pack and lit one. I knew it was going to be a long night, so I asked House to make some coffee.

A few minutes later, I returned to the den with a cigarette in one hand and a cup of coffee in the other. I sat back down at the computer and started reviewing the crime scene reports.

Half a pack of cigarettes and two pots of coffee later, something caught my eye. It was an inventory of items found in the hotel room where Michael had killed himself. Except for the gun (I had been right, it was a Glock) and the Japanese kitchen knife, there was nothing unusual in the items found on the body. Six key chips on a shark tooth key ring, a packet of breath mints, a spray can of solar block and a wallet containing five wallet-sized trids, two credit chips, an address chip, two condoms, and 205 Euro-marks in cash.

The police had found no cigarettes on the body, or anywhere in the hotel room. So what had given me the idea that Winter was a smoker? I was certain that Sonja hadn't mentioned it, but somewhere I had picked up the impression that the man had smoked.

I loaded the recording of Winter's suicide, fast-forwarding until I came to the part I was looking for. I froze the picture just as Winter was reaching into the right pocket of his jacket for the knife. I advanced the recording, one frame at a time. *There.* The front of the jacket was bloused open, revealing a stretch of expensive white European shirt. There was something in the left breast pocket of the shirt; something the size and shape of a pack of cigarettes.

I punched a few keys, dragging a green wire-frame box around a portion of the image. Another keystroke enlarged the boxed image until the holographic projection floating over my computer consisted entirely of the man's pocket and a little of his shirt front.

The object in the pocket was a brightly colored box. I keyed a command for digital enhancement into the computer. The resolution of the image increased slowly. By the time the machine beeped to signal maximum enhancement, I could read the brand name off the pack: *Ernte 23*. German cigarettes. I saved the enhanced image under a separate file name, and backed out of the recording.

It took me a few minutes of searching to find what I was looking for: the report by the cops who had discovered Michael's body.

According to the report, at 12:10 a.m., LAPD Tactical had received a report of gunshots from the Velvet Clam Hotel. Two uniformed officers were dispatched to check it out. They arrived on scene in about ten minutes. Witnesses pointed them to room 216. They knocked on the door and got no answer. They were about to kick the door in when the night manager showed up with a pass chip. Officers Reba Brock and Victor Matawicz entered the scene of the crime at 12:22 a.m. Their report said that they exited the room, touching nothing, and guarded the scene while they waited for a homicide team.

The night manager's statement backed them up. The door was locked when they arrived, and no one touched anything in the room from the time the door was unlocked until the homicide team was on scene.

I ran the sequence of events through my head, trying to get things to click. At about eight minutes after midnight on the fifteenth of April, Michael Winter shot himself in the head. The video camera continued to record for four minutes after he was dead. Ten minutes later, or fourteen minutes after the gunshot, two uniformed cops arrived to secure the scene.

Where had the cigarettes gone? In the ten minutes from the end of the video recording to the arrival of the police, someone had removed that package of cigarettes from Michael Winter's left breast shirt pocket.

It could have been Brock or Matawicz, but why would they chance it? Why would one or both of them risk ending their careers and possible felony charges for a pack of cigarettes? Besides, the night manager, William C. Holtzclaw, stated that neither officer had touched anything in the room.

By the time the homicide team arrived, it would be impossible for anyone to snag something out of the pocket of the corpse without being seen by a dozen people.

The conclusion was unmistakable; in the ten minutes from the end of that video recording to the entrance of Officers Brock and Matawicz, someone else had been in that hotel room.

I decided to carry my thinking one step farther. According to the clock, it was a little after midnight. Too bad. I punched up Sonja Winter's number.

She answered on the third ring. Her face wasn't puffy and her hair was perfect. She hadn't been asleep. Somehow I found that annoying.

"Ms. Winter, was your brother a smoker?"

She shook her head.

"Never? Are you certain?"

"I'm positive. Michael hated cigarette smoke. He thought it was disgusting." Her tone told me that she agreed with him.

"Thank you." I reached to terminate the connection.

"Wait." She looked puzzled. "Why is that important? Have you discovered something?"

"Nothing concrete. Just a notion I'm kicking around."

"Does this mean you're on the case?"

"It does not mean that I'm on the case. It means I'm giving your request fair consideration, as promised. Goodnight Ms. Winter, or rather, good morning."

"Good morning." The look of puzzlement on her face deepened as I terminated the call.

The autopsy report on Michael Winter confirmed it. Except for some evidence of scarring from childhood asthma, his lungs had been clean. He was a non-smoker.

Who would break into a hotel room and rifle a corpse's pockets to steal a pack of cigarettes? Or had they broken into the room at all? Someone might have already been in the room, outside of the camera's field of view. In the bathroom, perhaps.

I exited the autopsy file and stood up and stretched. It was time. I had been putting it off for long enough; I had to look at the crime scene footage.

I found my simulator gear in the top of the hall closet: a pair of Nakamichi wraparound data-shades molded from iridescent high-impact plastic, and two gray Kevlar data-gloves, each studded with tiny octagonal sensors. A long thread of ribbon cable with a three-way splitter on one end connected the gloves to the data-shades. The free end of the cable was wound several times around the entire package. I pulled the bundle down, began unwinding the cable, and walked back into the den.

Technically, it was an arcade setup, designed for kid's games, but the graphics resolution was excellent and the audio was state-of-the-art, a VRX bone-conduction rig with active noise reduction.

The connector on the end of the cable looked clean. I blew it out anyway, inspected it for bent pins, and plugged it into the interface port in the edge of the desk, next to the slot that held Jackal's data chip.

I pulled on the gloves and slipped the shades over my eyes. It took me a few seconds to adjust the audio conduction pads against the bones behind my ears. I spent another few seconds getting the focus just right on the test pattern that appeared in the eyepieces, making unnecessarily minute adjustments. I was stalling, and I knew it.

I punched the phantom space bar, and the test pattern disappeared, replaced in the eyepieces of the shades with the computer's menu display. Green three-dimensional representations of the data-gloves floated in the foreground, superimposed over the menu.

I curled the fingers of my left hand in that peculiar fashion that means *browse*. The iconic representation of my hand repeated the gesture in instant synchronization, and a highlighted selection bar scrolled down through the file menu. I stopped when the highlighted selection read:

► CLARK, CHRISTINE, L: CRIME-SCENE: 08FEB63/5:21p.m. ◄

Five twenty-one. The footage had been shot roughly two hours after her death, probably very shortly after the homicide team had arrived on scene.

I took a breath to steel myself, and pointed the index finger of my right hand at the highlighted entry. The sim recording blossomed in front of my eyes.

I found myself in a smallish room, powder blue wallpaper flocked with Victorian carousel horses and royal blue ribbons and bows. Pinned to the walls were at least a dozen holo-posters of what I took to be young rockers and vid stars.

The furniture was small and delicate, burnished blonde wood cut with intricate curves and inlays. The dresser and bureau tops were lined with porcelain dolls in frilly dresses. It was the bedroom of a little girl who was almost ready to be not so little anymore. Now she would never get the chance.

A block of bright yellow text covered the lower right hand corner of my vision: temperature readouts, humidity, the time, the orientation of my point of view to true north. When I turned my head, the color of the data readouts changed so that they always contrasted with the background.

I reached out with my virtual hand and picked up one of the dolls from the top of the bureau. When I moved the doll, the computer drew a yellow wireframe outline around the part of the image where the doll had been. It was the computer's way of reminding me that the picture inside the wireframe wasn't part of the actual recording. The camera had never actually seen the wall behind the doll, so the computer's imaging software was taking its best guess, based on what it had seen of the rest of the wall. A flashing red disclaimer appeared at the bottom of the text readout, reminding me that the images inside the highlighted areas were extrapolations and were not admissible as evidence.

I turned the doll around. The backside looked real and natural, but the computer flagged it with a wireframe as well. Another best guess. I put the doll back on the bureau.

I turned my head again. My field of view passed over the mirror on the vanity. I could see the reflection of the panoramic sim camera and its tripod standing in the center of the room like one of the three-legged alien machines from H. G. Wells' *War of the Worlds.*

Past the reflection of the camera, on the other side of the room, I could see the reflection of a four-poster canopy bed. The pastel blue canopy and the wall above the headboard were flecked with dark spots.

I decided to get it over with. I turned my head quickly, and took in the other half of the bedroom. The blood that peppered the canopy and wall was just the beginning. The bed sheets and pillows were doused with great gouts of blood, turning glossy black as it dried. Christine lay sprawled on her back in the middle of the black slick.

The size of the data readout doubled as the computer began to throw in potentially relevant information on the body: skin temperature (based on surface thermographics), height, width, and estimated weight, coordinates and attitude as measured from three fixed points on the walls and ceiling.

She was dressed in a tight green sweater jersey and white French-cut plastic pants that were probably supposed to make her look grown up. The blood had beaded up on the slick plastic of the pants, still oddly red and liquid in contrast to the dark pool drying on the fabric of her sheets and sweater.

The hole in her chest was larger than my fist, the edges ragged, reddish-black and wet looking. The killer had cut directly through her sweater.

Enough blood had sprayed her face and matted her mousy brown hair to make it difficult to make out her features, but the look in her still-open eyes burned itself into my brain.

I spent twenty more minutes in Christine's virtual bedroom. Then I checked out the crime-scenes of three more of the killings at random.

The MO was identical, variations on a theme.

I pulled off the data-shades at a little after two in the morning and shut down the computer. I was tired of looking at files and recordings. I wanted to ask some questions of my own.

My brain must have been on autopilot. Halfway out the door, I caught myself strapping on the shoulder rig for my 12mm Blackhart. Surprising how old habits could still sneak up on me.

They weren't my habits. They were the habits of a David Stalin who no longer existed. I put the automatic and shoulder holster back in the desk drawer.

I was not that man anymore, and hadn't been for a long time.

CHAPTER 5

The decor of the Velvet Clam Hotel was no more tasteful than its name implied. The central theme was retro-Art Deco sleaze, the vision of a designer who had obviously made no attempt to reign in his or her baser impulses. The front counter was a thick oval pane of smoked acryliflex stretched across the naked back of a kneeling woman, rendered in the style of the chrome angels that used to decorate the hoods of cars in the nineteen thirties. The woman was painted a tarnished gold, the paint scaled and flaking, brassy chips of it flecking the gray fake-marble tile. The door frames, the columns flanking the main entrance, and the wall sconce candelabras all had the same cheesy look about them.

At 3:12 a.m., there was no one in the front office. From the customer's side of the counter, I could see through a half-open door into the back. There, in a worn-out easy chair, a man sat reading a book. It was a real book, not a data viewer, but an actual hardcover with pages. From my vantage point, it looked like Kipling.

Presumably, the man in the chair was the night manager, William Holtzclaw. If so, he defied any preconceptions I might have had about what sleazy hotel managers should look like. He was in his mid-fifties, tastefully dressed and had the sort of indefinable good looks that people call distinguished. Any self-respecting talent agent in the world would have cast him in the role of a college professor.

I pressed the service button and a bell rang in his little office. He looked up, set down his book and joined me at the desk.

His voice and gestures were as refined as his appearance. "Will it just be a room, or will you require a lady? We can provide an excellent selection of companions."

I shook my head. "No. No ladies. I..."

He interrupted smoothly. "We can also provide gentlemen companions."

"No. No thank you. I just want to ask you a few questions." I reached into my breast pocket.

Holtzclaw tensed, possibly expecting me to pull out a badge, or worse. He relaxed when he saw the sheaf of Euro-marks in my hand.

I dropped a twenty on the scratched acryliflex surface of the counter and slid it toward him. "Michael Winter. You were working the night he committed suicide?"

Holtzclaw nodded and made the twenty disappear.

I replaced it with another €m20. "You checked him in yourself?"

Another nod and another disappearing act.

I slid a third €m20 bill across the counter. This one I hung on to. "Tell me about it."

He rested his fingers on the other end of the bill. "Not much to tell, really. Mr. Winter checked in at a bit after eleven that evening. Perhaps an hour later, I heard the gunshot and called the police."

"Was he alone when he checked in?"

"Yes. I offered to provide a suitable companion, but he declined. I assumed that he had made his own arrangements."

"Did he have any luggage?"

"Hmmm... I believe that he was carrying a small case. Smaller than a briefcase."

"Could it have been a video camera case?"

Holtzclaw considered it for a few seconds. "It might very well have been."

I looked around and spotted an ashtray at the far end of the counter. I relinquished my hold on the twenty and reached for the ashtray. As I lit up, out of the corner of my eye, I saw the bill disappear. "Could someone else have been in the room with Winter?"

Holtzclaw produced a pipe and began the elaborate ritual involved with packing and lighting it. "Someone could have been. I cannot say with certainty." He looked thoughtful.

"Are your door locks electronic?"

"Of course."

"Are they monitored by your office computer?" I indicated a desktop machine visible through the door to the back office.

Holtzclaw hesitated. I dropped another twenty on the counter.

"They *are* electronic," he said. He motioned for me to slip around the end of the counter and I followed him into the back office.

The book wasn't the only antique in the office. The computer was a gravely misused relic. The holo display was badly skewed; the characters on the left were two or three times larger than those on the right, giving the impression that the text trailed off into infinity. I leaned my head to the side in hopes that it would make the display easier to read.

Holtzclaw looked at me expectantly.

I straightened my neck. "Call up April fourteenth and fifteenth."

He stroked a few keys and the projection changed to two columns of data: time/date stamps on the left, and five digit alphanumeric codes on the right. There were only three types of code entries: 00216, 00000, and PPPPP.

I pointed to the column of code entries. "What do those mean?"

Holtzclaw poked the stem of his pipe at a line that ended in 00216. "This indicates that the door was unlocked using a key chip. Entries ending in five zeros mean the door was opened without a key chip, from the inside."

The entry for 12:14 ended in zeros. Someone had opened the door to Room 216 from the inside, four minutes after Michael was dead.

"What about the two records marked PPPPP?"

"That's the system's way of showing that the door was opened using a pass chip. That first record would have been Housekeeping opening the door just before noon to clean the room. The second entry was from when I let the police in, after Mr. Winter shot himself."

Twenty marks bought me a chip with a copy of the door lock files. For another twenty, Holtzclaw agreed to let me into room 216.

"Consider yourself fortunate," he said, as he led me down the hall. "Two sixteen has been extremely busy of late. We were afraid that Mr. Winter's death would adversely affect business, but quite the reverse has been true. Apparently, a great many people find death sexually stimulating. Instinct, perhaps. The reaffirmation of life in the face of one's own mortality."

From behind a closed door, I heard the crack of a whip and a scream. Agony? Ecstasy? Either way, it didn't sound much like the reaffirmation of life to me.

"Right."

On the stairs, we passed a tall brunette in a skintight red latex skirt and heels that made Sonja's stiletto pumps look like flats. The top of her outfit seemed to consist entirely of a coating of oil and a sprinkling of glitter across her nipples. She pursed her lips at us and raised one elaborately arched eyebrow. Her lipstick and nail polish were the exact same glossy shade of red as her skirt. Holtzclaw winked at her and shook his head once as we climbed past her.

When we were in the hall, and out of earshot, he nodded back over his shoulder in the direction of the stairs. "That young lady's name is Kenya," he said in his pleasant voice. "Surgical hermaphrodite, both sets of sexual organs. Nobody's really quite sure which set she was born with, and which came from the clinics. Personally, I don't believe I care to know."

He stopped in front of a door and slid a key chip through the lock sensor.

Room 216 looked pretty much like it had in the holo. Large irregular areas of the red carpet were stained a darker shade of red. Someone with a flair for theatrics had created those stains. There wasn't that much blood in the human body. Besides, Winter had fallen on the bed, so the mattresses and sheets would have absorbed most of the blood. The management of the Velvet Clam was obviously playing up the scene-of-the-crime angle.

The air had a strange scent, a bizarre combination of raw sexual musk and cinnamon air freshener.

I walked around the room for a few minutes, trying to reconstruct events in my head. The camera would have been about here, facing the bed. Winter had sat there, on the bed.

From this angle, I could barely see my own reflection in the mirror on the left wall. I couldn't see myself in the mirrored ceiling at all. I took a small step backwards and disappeared from the wall mirror. The camera had been here. Someone had positioned that camera carefully, to insure that it didn't appear in any reflections. Anyone behind the camera would have been similarly screened from reflection.

"Someone was with you, Michael," I said quietly. "Someone stood here and watched you pull the trigger. Someone leaned over your body, took a pack of cigarettes out of your pocket and calmly let themselves out the door."

"It's a pity that the video chip didn't run longer." Mr. Holtzclaw stood in the hall just outside the room. His voice startled me. I'd almost forgotten him.

"I'm sorry?"

"I was just thinking what a shame it is that the camera wasn't loaded with a longer chip. If some unknown person disturbed the body before the police arrived, as you seem to believe, a longer running chip would have recorded them. Caught them in the act, so to speak. As it is, the camera shut itself off well before the police arrived."

"Good point. That probably wasn't an accident."

Holtzclaw nodded. "My thoughts exactly." He looked around the room. "Are you about finished in here?"

"In a minute. I want to get a look at the bathroom and the closet."

The closet was empty, except for six of those steel coat hangers that stay locked to the rod, and a few dust bunnies.

The bathroom was no more helpful.

After one last look around, I thanked Mr. Holtzclaw for his help. I didn't have any business cards, so I wrote my name and phone number on the inside of a Velvet Clam matchbook, and asked him to call me if he thought of anything I might find interesting.

He closed the matchbook and slipped it into a trouser pocket. "Are you a detective, Mr. Stalin?"

I thought about it for a second. "It's starting to look that way."

CHAPTER 6

Outside, I stopped under the hotel's sign to light a cigarette. The sign was predictable: an animated hologram of a cartoon clam slowly opening and closing. Its fleshy pink lips were overtly vaginal. The words Velvet Clam in bright red cursive lettering endlessly orbited the sign at a forty-five degree angle.

My gaze wandered until I found myself staring through the dome at the night sky. It was one of those rare nights where the air was clear enough to see the stars. A three-quarter moon hung low over the western arc of the dome. The transparent polycarbon panels of the dome facing repeated the moon's image hundreds of times, a brilliant collage of ghostly silver orbs. Each image was slightly different, the distortions growing more pronounced in the reflections farther removed from the single perfect moon at the center.

This eerily beautiful collage reminded me that there was an entire world outside the domes. I hadn't been out there since the night Maggie died. I wondered how many other people were caught in the same rut, going through their daily routines without ever considering the world outside. How quickly the rats become accustomed to the cage.

I yawned and started walking toward the Melrose Avenue Lev station.

By the time the sun was dragging its hundred reflections up the eastern panels of the dome, I was in bed.

House woke me up less than two hours later with his *someone's-at-the-door* routine.

"Who is it?"

"Two persons, identities unknown."

I asked House to throw a projection of my visitors on the bedroom wall. No real help. One woman, one man. She was in her early thirties and looked like a professional body builder. He looked like an aging used car salesman. I didn't recognize either of them, but their body postures and off-the-rack suits said "cop."

"House, scan them for weapons."

"Both persons are armed with semi-automatic hand guns, stun wands, and handcuffs, all of which appear to be standard police issue. The gentleman is carrying a briefcase-sized object that is emitting low levels of electromagnetic energy, consistent with active electronics. If you like, I can run a signature-analysis of the electromagnetic emissions, and attempt to identify the contents of the briefcase."

"No thank you."

I was pretty sure that I already knew what was in the briefcase: a Magic Mirror. That was the street slang for it, anyway. The technical jargon was a string of polysyllables about a kilometer long: Multifaceted-Electro-something-something-something.

"Uh... give me two-way audio."

I waited for the chime. "Can I help you?"

The woman turned her head and stared into the camera. "David Stalin?"

"Who are you?"

She leaned toward the camera. Forced perspective made her image seem to grow larger and closer. It's a good trick if you do it right. It feels threatening, even when you know it's a projection. She did it right.

"Don't fuck with me," she snapped. "*Are* you David Stalin? Give me visual. I want to see your face."

Her partner pulled out a badge. "Los Angeles Police Department. We're here to..."

The woman glared at him. "We're gonna kick this fucking door down."

I took a hit off the cigarette. "I wouldn't. My house is equipped with an extensive anti-intrusion system. Starting from stun level and escalating to lethal-mode in ten seconds. All registered, and all perfectly legal."

She flipped out a badge, flashed it at the camera for a millisecond and put it away. "We need to..."

"Name and badge number?"

She glared at the camera. "Detective P. L. Dancer, Alpha Two Seven Six One."

Her partner leaned in. "Detective R. Delaney, Alpha Two Nine Two Four. We'd like to ask you a few questions."

"Do you have a warrant?"

For a second, I thought Dancer would explode. Then she visibly swallowed and spoke in a tense voice. "No, we do not have a warrant. I can have one transmitted to me in about five minutes. Is that what you want?"

"I don't think that will be necessary."

I told House to open the front door and start a pot of coffee.

I met them at the door and led them into the living room. "Sorry there's no coffee ready; I'm just getting up. I've got a pot on now."

Detective Dancer scowled. "We're not here for tea and biscuits. We're here pursuant to a murder investigation."

I motioned them toward chairs. Delaney sat down. Dancer did not.

I sat in my favorite wingback. "I thought the investigation was closed."

Dancer arched her eyebrows. "Closed? What in the hell are you talking about?"

"The Aztec investigation. It's formally closed, isn't it?"

Dancer's brow furrowed. "Aztec? What does Aztec have to do with this?"

Delaney pulled an audio recorder out of his pocket and loaded a fresh chip. "Are you David Stalin?"

"Yes," I said. "I'm David Stalin."

"For the record, Mr. Stalin: do you object to our recording this interview?"

"What if I say yes?"

Dancer tried to stare a hole through me. "Then we get that warrant, and things start to get ugly."

I shrugged. "No, I don't object."

Delaney punched the *record* tab and put the little unit on the coffee table. Then he set his briefcase on the table and opened it. The lower half of the case was packed full of electronics modules and the anodized louvers of heat sinks. The inside of the lid was a flat-screen crystal display with an integral keypad. It was a Magic Mirror all right.

Dancer smiled a hard little smile that had no joy or amusement in it. "You know your rights, Mr. Stalin?"

"Why? Am I accused of something?"

Delaney pulled a worn plastic card out of a small pouch inside the case and began to read. "This is a Multifaceted Integrated Electroencephalographic Response Analyzer and Recorder. It measures physiological changes that take place in response to certain visual stimuli. It incorporates..."

"I know what it does," I said. "It's a Magic Mirror. An electronic mind-probe. You can skip the dissertation."

"This is just a little EEG scan," Dancer said. "You give us any shit, we'll drag you down town and wire your ass up to the *Inquisitor*. Then you'll find out what a fucking mind-probe is."

Delaney paused for a second, to see if we were finished interrupting, and then continued to read. "It incorporates four dermal sensor pads that measure electrical brain activity, galvanic skin reflex, and fluctuations in skin thermography."

I noticed that his pupils stayed locked on one spot of the card as he talked. He wasn't reading; he was reciting from memory.

"Although you are not currently accused of a crime, it is our intention to interview you regarding an on-going homicide investigation."

He flipped the card over and continued to pretend to read. "You have the right to terminate this interview at any time. If you refuse this procedure, we reserve the option to take you into physical custody and transport you to the nearest Police Forensic Electronics facility for questioning under controlled conditions. You have the right to have an attorney, real or virtual, present during this, and any subsequent interviews. If you desire an attorney and cannot afford one, you will be granted real-time access to a fully cognizant Artificial Intelligence attached to the Public Defender's office."

He looked up at me again. "Do you understand your rights as I have read them to you?"

"Whose murder are we talking about here?"

"Just answer the question, Mr. Stalin. Do you understand your rights?"

"Sure," I said.

"Do you wish to have an attorney present during this interview?"

"Not really."

Dancer peeled off her jacket. Underneath, she wore a cross-draw shoulder holster strapped over a light blue short-sleeved shirt. Even through the shirt, I could see that the muscles of her arms and upper body were impressive. She could probably bench press me a couple of dozen times. She tossed her jacket across the back of a chair. "Are we done with the formalities?"

"We're done," Delaney said.

"Good," she said. "Then hook him up to the fucking machine."

Delaney slid the briefcase down to my end of the coffee table and unreeled a set of electrical leads. He plugged one end of each of the leads into his machine, and connected the other ends to self-adhesive sensor pads. He turned toward me, the sensor leads dangling from his left hand. "I'm going to connect these to your forehead. They will not hurt, and the adhesive is hypoallergenic. Do you understand?"

Dancer had angled well to his left. It struck me that she had taken off her jacket to clear the way to her shoulder holster. She was ready to draw on me if she had to.

"Yes," I said. "I understand."

Delaney stuck two of the pads to the skin above the outer edges of my eyebrows. The adhesive was cold and had a cloying fake-lemonade smell about it. Delaney glued the remaining pair close to the center of my forehead, just below the hairline. He was careful to stand to the side, out of Dancer's line of fire.

I was equally careful not to move while he was close to me. The last thing I wanted was for Dancer to show me her quick-draw routine.

Delaney turned back to his briefcase and thumbed a switch. The screen of the analyzer came to life, the electro-tropic crystal wafer strobing with shifting rainbow abstracts for a second or two before blooming into a full-color high-definition display. Two internal cooling fans spun up, each emitting a tone that nearly harmonized with the other.

Delaney sat down and punched a few buttons on the keypad and a data window popped open in the upper right corner of the screen. A series of jagged waveforms appeared in the window, complex, constantly changing, and looking very much like the scribbling of a small child. Presumably, between them, they described my skin temperature, electrical conductivity, and some component of my brain waves.

Delaney gave Dancer a thumbs-up and turned the briefcase to an angle that hid the display from me.

Dancer nodded. "Do it."

Delaney pulled a stack of trids out of the pocket of his jacket. He handed me the first one: a picture of a building that I didn't recognize. He watched the display. "Miss."

He handed me another: the Eiffel Tower lying in ruins, the shot that had become so famous after the European Liberation Front had tried to nuke Paris back into the Stone Age. "Hit. Irrelevant."

...a young woman eating a slice of pizza. "Miss."

...a storefront with broken windows. "Miss."

...a pair of brown shoes. "Miss."

...a front view of my house from the street. "Hit. Irrelevant."

...the lobby of the Velvet Clam Hotel. "Hit."

Dancer and Delaney exchanged glances.

...an overflowing dumpster. "Miss."

...a matchbook from the Velvet Clam, enough of the inside visible to reveal the last three digits of my phone number. "Hit."

Dancer flexed the fingers of her right hand slightly. What in the hell was going on here? Was she expecting me to try something?

...a man's body sprawled on a floor, a lake of blood congealing around him on the tile. "Miss."

Dancer stepped toward the coffee table. "What do you mean, *miss*?"

I stared at the image. The man's throat had been cut. Not just sliced, but hacked open as though someone had been trying to take his head off.

"Have a look," Delaney said. He pointed to something inside his briefcase. "This is what Mr. Stalin's recognition-characteristic looks like. He definitely did *not* recognize that image."

I continued to stare at the trid. The man was older, somebody's grandfather. There was something familiar about him. "Oh Jesus," I whispered. "It's Holtzclaw."

Delaney pointed to the screen again. "Hit," he said. "Delayed."

"Goddamn it," Dancer said. "Are you sure?"

"I'm certain," Delaney said. "Mr. Stalin recognized the victim, but he was clearly not aware that Mr. Holtzclaw is dead."

"When was he killed?" I asked quietly.

"Some time around four thirty this morning," Delaney said.

Dancer snatched her jacket off the back of the chair and jammed her left arm down a sleeve.

"Who killed him?" I asked.

"That's a stupid fucking question," Dancer snapped. "If we knew that, we wouldn't be dicking around with you, would we?"

She wrestled her right arm into the other sleeve and looked back to Delaney. "Pack it up, Rick. Let's get out of here."

I peeled the pads off my face and handed them to Delaney. The skin where they had been felt cool and prickly.

Delaney rolled up his leads and closed the case.

Dancer began buttoning up her jacket. "Let's slide, Rick. There's a killer out there somewhere."

CHAPTER 7

||| || | | |||||| | || ||| | | || | ||| ||| ||| || | ||||| || ||| | ||| |||

I stepped into the shower stall; the door slid shut silently behind me. I didn't feel like going back to bed, and a hot shower seemed like the next best thing.

"What will it be this morning?" House asked.

"Let's go with Program Six," I said sleepily.

"Starting program now. Enjoy your shower, David."

"Thanks, House."

The walls and ceiling of the shower stall cycled from featureless high gloss white to shifting patterns of mottled green and then, with a rapidity that was almost startling, the projection snapped into focus and I was standing in the middle of a rain forest. The footage had been shot in the eco-modules in Dome 7, and the trees and foliage were a lush and vibrant green. Vines hung in fat loops from the branches overhead. The shower floor under my feet was the only flaw in the illusion; it remained its usual white porcelain, rectangular self, a safety feature designed to keep me from walking into the walls or shower doors that were now invisible behind the projection.

I could hear birds singing in the distance, the chittering of monkeys, and wind blowing through the leaf canopy. House added those parts himself; there were no monkeys, or birds, or wind in Dome 7.

A fat drop of water hit my left shoulder, followed a couple of seconds later by another drop that struck me square on the top of the head. Suddenly, drops were falling all around me, gaining in speed and density. Except for the temperature, which I kept as hot as I could stand, it was as much like an actual squall in a forest as I could imagine.

No, that wasn't quite true. I'd been caught in several downpours, in a real rain forest, at Iguazu, in Argentina. But that was an experience so far removed from the make-believe forest in my shower as to seem like something from another planet.

At Iguazu, we'd worn snow cammies, because the dappled grays had blended in with the dying vegetation better than green jungle camouflage. The sky had been the color of old concrete and the dead leaf mulch had been thick under our boots. We'd slathered our skin with protective ointments against rain with a pH factor so low that it bore little resemblance to water, and we'd been damn careful not to swallow any.

A psychiatrist would probably say that Program Six was my way of denying Argentina, or that showering in a rain forest signaled my refusal to face the realities of our ruined ecology. Personally, I think it was simpler than that. I think I just liked it.

After my shower, I was half way through shaving when I decided to call Ms. Winter. I was naked except for a towel around my neck and shaving cream on half of my face, so I selected voice-only for my end of the call.

It took her about six rings to answer.

She had a wild, disheveled look. Her hair was mussed, her cheeks were puffy, and her eyes were rimmed with red. For a second, I was afraid that I'd caught her with a client. I reached for the disconnect, thankful that she couldn't see my face.

She let out the tiniest sniffle and I jerked my hand back from the button. This wasn't the aftermath of passion; she'd been crying.

She tried to focus on the phone, her eyes bleary. "Who is it? Can I have video please?"

"It's David Stalin. You can't have video, I'm naked."

She sniffed again and tried to smile. "Is this an obscene phone call, Mr. Stalin?"

"No. I called to invite you to lunch. My place, around one... If you like seafood."

This time she did smile. "A call from a naked man who wants me to come over to his house. This *is* an obscene phone call. My day may be looking up."

I angled the camera so she could only see me from the waist up and switched it on. "If I'm going to make an obscene call, I want to get it right."

She smiled as soon as she saw me. "I didn't know that anyone still shaved that way."

I touched my cheek and grinned when I felt the smear of shaving cream. "I'm a little old fashioned."

Her grin matched mine. I was glad to have chased her tears away, even if only for a few moments.

"You're not old fashioned, Mr. Stalin. I think you like to do things the hard way."

"About that lunch..." I said.

She ran her hands through her hair. "Are you asking me out on a date, Mr. Stalin?"

"No," I said. "Not at all." I paused for a second. "I've got a friend coming over, and I thought you might like to join us."

It was her turn to pause for a second. "Okay," she said. "One o'clock? Do you want me to bring anything?"

I shook my head.

"One, then." She hung up.

I washed the rest of the shaving cream from my face and punched up John's number.

The phone screen filled with the logo for Neuro-Tech Robotics: the winged staff and entwined serpents of a medical caduceus laid out in drab green and striped with shiny foil runs like a circuit board with no components attached. Hundreds of tiny data chips flew in from random corners of the screen and affixed themselves to the circuit board until the letters NTR were spelled out in silicon.

"Good morning, Neuro-Tech Robotics, how may I help you?" The voice was flatly artificial. It belonged to the AI that ran John's company offices on Hawthorne Boulevard. John had never bothered to give the AI a name, or even the rudiments of a personality. As far as John was concerned, his research needed every byte of memory that could be squeezed out of his computer's data cores. When he had to address the machine, John just called it *Mainframe*.

I didn't bother with niceties, because I knew that Mainframe was programmed to ignore them. "Let me speak to John," I said.

"One moment, please."

Ten seconds later, the NTR logo was replaced by John's face. He smiled when he saw me. "Hey, Sarge! *Que pasa?*"

"I'm just getting ready to throw a pan on the stove. Got time to join me for lunch?"

John looked back over his shoulder at a partially disassembled surgical robot. "I'm kind of in the middle of something here. Can I take a rain check?"

I gave him an exaggerated grimace. "I'd rather you didn't. I've got a guest coming, and I don't want her to think I'm hitting on her."

John's eyebrows went up a millimeter. "A lunch guest? It's about time you let a woman into that mausoleum. Who is she?"

"Sonja Winter. The woman from Falcon's Nest the other night."

John's eyebrows went up again.

"I know what you're thinking," I said. "And she's probably thinking the same thing. But it's not like that."

John grinned. "You need a chaperon?"

I sighed, and then grinned myself. "Okay," I said. "If that's what you want to call it. I just want to make sure that she doesn't think I'm trying to get into her pants."

"Here's a stupid question for you," John said. "Why *aren't* you trying to get in her pants? That woman is a knockout!"

"Fine," I said. "She's a knockout. Are you coming to lunch, or what?"

"I think I can make a window in my schedule," said John. "What time?"

"About one o'clock."

John narrowed his eyes as though trying to look past me. "Did you call her just before you called me?"

"Yeah," I said. "Why?"

He nodded at something over my shoulder. "Ask her how she liked the show."

"What show?"

John winked at me. "See you at one, Sarge." He reached out to terminate the connection.

His image was replaced by static. What show?

When I turned around, I saw what John meant. My camera-angle modesty was a failure. The sliding doors on my shower stall were set to mirror-mode. By looking over my shoulder, Ms. Winter would have had a clear view of anything she wanted to see.

Had she looked? Probably not, I thought. In her line of work, she saw a lot of male flesh. I wasn't vain enough to think mine was anything special.

I busied myself in the kitchen, digging out spices that I hadn't used in ages.

House had come up with a couple of dozen tiger prawns, each the size of a child's fist. They'd probably come from the tank farms in Dome 16, but I didn't ask. House was in charge of procurement. I just handled the consumption end of things.

I timed it so that the first handful of prawns went into the pan at one o'clock. They were just beginning to sizzle when Ms. Winter showed up at the door.

House had to let her in; by then I had my hands full with the prawns. They tend to smoke a bit when you cook them the way I do, and you have to be really careful not to scorch the butter.

She walked into the kitchen wearing a hound's-tooth jacket over a champagne-colored jersey dress. Her hair was pulled back and around so that it spilled over her left shoulder like a dark waterfall. The effect was simple, but stunning. She set her purse on the kitchen counter and smiled. "Hi. Am I early?"

"Just in time," I said. "Lunch is almost ready."

She looked around. "Am I the first to arrive?"

"John will probably be late," I said. "He usually is." I smiled. "You met him at Falcon's Nest the other night. He was late then too. Don't worry; we don't have to wait for him."

She looked surprised. "Won't he think we're rude?"

"Not at all," I said. "It's the only way to get him to show up."

Her eyebrows narrowed.

"Really," I said. "It's a cause-and-effect relationship. Like lighting a cigarette to call a bus. That one works, by the way. If you're ever in a hurry, and you don't want to wait for a bus, just light a cigarette. The bus will show up within about thirty seconds and you'll have to put the cigarette out. It's a natural law, I think."

"I don't smoke," she said.

"It works for the shower too," I said. "If you're ever lonely and you want someone to call you, just climb in the shower. As soon as you're soaking wet and your hair is full of soapsuds, your phone will ring. Cause and effect. You can't stop it."

Ten minutes later, we sat down to ice-cold pasta salad, piping-hot Cajun garlic prawns *a la* Dave, and a fairly good bottle of wine.

House was kind enough to serenade us with a little Robert Johnson.

I watched Ms. Winter's face carefully when she first tasted the prawns. Her look was one of total surprise. "What's in this?"

I grinned. "Garlic, butter, onions, cayenne pepper, lemon, a dash of wine. The rest of the ingredients are a family secret, handed down to me by my grandmother. Do you like it?"

"It's wonderful!"

I laughed. I can be modest about most things. My cooking isn't one of them.

I speared a prawn and was in the act of raising it to my mouth when House played a little chime and announced John's presence at the door. I smiled and set my fork down. "Told you. It's cause and effect."

"Shall I let him in, David?" House asked.

"Of course, House. And tell him we're in the dining room."

"Are you always right?" Ms. Winter asked.

"I'm usually right about John," I said. "Not so much about other things, but I've pretty much got John pegged. We've known each other since we were kids."

The quiet whining of John's exoskeleton preceded his entrance into the room by about two seconds. "Starting without me, Sarge?"

"Not me," I said. "It was Ms. Winter's fault. I begged her to wait for you, but she flat-out refused."

"Please," she said, "call me Sonja." She motioned John to a chair, and rewarded me with a mock steely-eyed glance. She lifted a fork full of prawn. "And since we've already established that I have unspeakably bad manners, I have nothing to lose by eating like a pig."

John's exoskeleton eased him into his chair. He picked up a fork and tasted the garlic-prawn. When he had swallowed, he nodded in my direction. "I'll bet Sarge here told you that he cooked this, didn't he?"

John shook his head. "Not a word of truth in it. Sarge has a two-headed dog-boy locked up in the cellar. The wretched little creature does all the cooking, while David here gets to invite beautiful women over for lunch and take all the credit."

Sonja laughed. "Is *that* how it works?"

"I don't have a cellar," I said. "I keep the poor creature up on the roof, like a gargoyle."

"I have to ask," Sonja said. "Where on earth did you find a two-headed dog-boy?"

"Actually, it's John's twin brother," I said. "Dog-boy got all the looks in the family, and John was so jealous that he sold the poor fellow into slavery."

John nodded. "At least we *think* it's my brother. It could be my sister. I asked Sarge to check, but I'm not altogether sure that he knows how to tell the difference between boys and girls."

Sonja laughed again. She pointed her fork at John. "Why do you always call him Sarge? Are you guys ex-cops? Is it *Sarge* as in *Police Sergeant*?"

"Not cops," John said. "The Army."

Sonja turned to me. "You were a sergeant in the Army?"

"I was never a sergeant," I said. "Just a plain old mudfoot, Private First Class."

Sonja put down her fork. "Okay," she said. "Now I'm really confused."

"There used to be a kid's cartoon," I said. "Sergeant Steel. Huge muscles, scar down his cheek, ran around with a rocket launcher in one hand, and a machine gun in the other, blowing the enemy-of-the-week into bite-sized chunks."

Sonja touched a finger to her chin. "Was he the one with the tattered uniform that showed off his biceps?"

"That's the guy," I said. "John named me after him. Just a joke, really."

"Right," John said. "Now tell her *why* you got the name."

Sonja's eyes widened a fraction. "Well?"

I took a bite of prawn and pretended that I hadn't heard.

John winked at Sonja. "He hates it when I tell this story."

I swallowed. "I don't hate the story," I said. "I've just heard it too many times."

"Well I haven't heard it," Sonja said.

John leaned back in his chair. "Iguazu Falls," he said. "Misiones Province. Our squad was running flank and cover for a demolitions team. It was an easy job; the demo squad was supposed to slip a few kilos of plastique into the hydroelectric plant, and all we had to do was cover their butts. If we pulled it off, half the radar sites in Northeast Argentina would be without power."

He took a sip of wine. "The forest must have been beautiful once, but when we were there, you could see that it was dying. The trees were gray, and the ground was covered with rotting leaves. The only real color was from patches of the stickiest red clay you ever saw. It was almost the shade of blood that isn't quite dry yet."

"Okay," I said. "You've established a suitable air of melodrama. Now, finish it off and let's talk about something else."

Sonja's eyes were locked on John's face. She fluttered a hand in my direction without looking at me. "Ignore him," she said.

"Always do," said John. "Where was I?"

"The laser," I said.

John looked at Sonja. "He's rushing me," he said. "But I guess we can humor him; he *is* getting old, you know."

"The laser," I said again.

"Right," John said. "The laser." He clapped his hands and rubbed them together. "It was a perimeter defense unit, a big tripod mounted thing with a robotic control loop. Chinese-built, probably. Stacked plastic armor, photo-active camouflage, infrared-suppression, and enough electromagnetic razzle-dazzle to give it the radar cross-section of a grape. According to our intelligence reports, the locals weren't supposed to have anything *like* that kind of technology. But the local boys apparently hadn't bothered to read our intel."

He smiled a thin little smile. "So the first we knew about it was when Bad Suzi Jabarra went down. I just thought she had tripped over a root or something. I bent over to help her up, and I was just realizing that she'd been hit, when the laser nailed me. I don't know how powerful the beam was, two hundred and fifty—maybe three hundred megawatts, but it cut through two layers of woven carbon armor like it was nothing and punched a hole right between my shoulder blades."

He took a sip of wine and looked down at his glass. "Actually, this story goes better with beer than with wine."

He raised his eyebrows and shrugged. "Then I was on the ground, and my legs didn't work. I remember being surprised that there wasn't any pain. People were screaming and diving for cover, and the laser kept reaching out like the finger of God, burning everything it touched."

John looked at me and grinned, the way he always did when he came to this part of the story. "And then I saw him."

Sonja cocked her head to one side. "Saw who?"

John nodded toward me. "You should have seen him, running through the trees toward that damned laser. His helmet was gone. His flak vest was half open and flapping in the breeze. He was screaming at the top of his lungs, his M-279 blazing away. And you should have seen his face."

John laughed and shook his head. "I swear to God... Davie here looked just like Sergeant Steel from the cartoon. He would have made a perfect cover for one of those animated comic books."

Sonja waited a few seconds for John to continue, and then asked, "what happened?"

John skewered a prawn and raised it half way to his lips. "Tell her, Sarge."

I shook my head. "It's your story."

John laughed again and turned his eyes back to Sonja. "He took it out."

"The laser?"

"Yep," John said. "The crazy bastard went toe-to-toe with an automated perimeter laser, armed with nothing but a couple of grenades and a smart-rifle. And he took it out. He blew that laser all to hell. And that's how he got the nickname."

Sonja stared at me. "Is that true?"

I felt my ears burn. "John exaggerates a bit," I said. "But the truth is hidden in there somewhere."

"That makes you a war hero," Sonja said.

I shook my head. "I was young and stupid. And I'm damned lucky that I got a chance to be *old* and stupid."

John leaned toward Sonja and whispered, "don't let him kid you. He's a hero."

I sighed. "Are we done with Story Hour yet?" I stared at them both. "Good. Let's eat."

After lunch, I led John and Sonja to my workshop. Before I let them in, I had House darken the room except for the pedestal supporting the new piece.

The sculpture consisted of twenty-eight bars of stringer-steel, welded together into a climbing arch that resembled a section of struts and rafters from the roof of an old partially collapsed building. I had chemically stained the steel to give it a weathered look.

Sonja walked around it slowly, her eyebrows drawn close together. "City of shadows," she said.

"What?"

"I don't know," she said. "Just some words that came to me when I first saw it. City of shadows." She looked up at me. "Maybe that's what you ought to name it."

"I've already named it," I said. "It's called *No Resurrection*."

John just stared at the piece in silence for a long time. Finally, he shook his head once and looked up at me. "It's still there," he said.

"What do you mean?" Sonja asked.

"There's a common thread that links all of David's work. Sort of an aura of... desperation. It's nothing I can quite put my finger on, but it's always there."

"I like it," Sonja said. "It bothers me somehow, but I like it."

We stood around discussing the piece, the two of them ooh-ing and aah-ing, and me aw-shucksing until the wine in our glasses ran low.

Eventually, we wound up in the den, comfortably draped over my fat brown pit sofa, our glasses freshly brimming with wine.

"So tell me about this great mystery of yours," John said. "Especially the part where Sergeant Steel here comes to your rescue."

Sonja stared into her wine glass without speaking.

John's smile faded. "I'm sorry," he said. "I get so used to running my mouth that I don't always know what's going to come out. I didn't mean any disrespect to your... It was your brother, wasn't it?"

Sonja looked up. "It's okay. I'm starting to get used to the idea."

I wondered if she believed her own lie.

"The police aren't having any luck?" John asked.

"They aren't even looking," Sonja said. "They're convinced that it was suicide."

John looked at me. "How about it, Sarge? Have you got any good leads yet?"

Sonja traced figure eights in the condensation on her glass with the tip of her right index finger. "He hasn't decided whether or not he's going to take the case."

"What is she talking about? Of course you're going to take the case, aren't you Sarge?"

I didn't say anything. My eyes were locked on Sonja's fingertip as it continued to sweep tiny eights on the surface of her wine glass.

"Come on, Sarge. The woman needs your help. *You* need this too. You need to get out of this damned house and get back to work."

My attention stayed riveted on the motions of Sonja's fingers. Wheels spun in my head. Fingers... fingers... something about fingers.

I set down my glass and slid across the couch to sit beside Sonja. "Let me see your hand."

She looked at me strangely, then extended her left hand. Her palm and fingers were cool and damp from the wine glass. I took it in both of mine, touching it, turning it over, examining it. Something...

My brain was straining to make a connection. I could feel an idea struggling to fight its way to the surface of my mind. Hands... fingers...

"Now, the other one."

She transferred the glass to her left hand and offered the right. I examined it the same way. Something... damn it! Something! What was it?

I ran my fingers over the backs of hers.

I stopped, looked up. Sonja and John were staring at me. Sonja's skin was soft... smooth... except... except for a small callus on the side of her middle finger. A writer's callus, from holding pens and pencils.

I had one too, in the same spot. I was right handed.

It clicked. The photograph of Michael as a boy, the one with the baseball bat and glove. The glove had been on his *left* hand.

"Sonja, was your brother ambidextrous?"

"No," she said. "Michael was right handed."

"Did you ever see him do *anything* left handed?"

She frowned. "I don't think so. He ate with his right hand, wrote with it..." Her voice trailed off.

I took a swallow of wine and reached for my smokes. "So, if Michael was right handed, if he ate that way, and wrote that way, and threw a baseball that way..." I looked at Sonja. She nodded. "Why did he shoot himself with his left hand?"

Sonja sat bolt upright. "My God! You're right! I wonder why I never noticed."

"That's why you hired a detective," John said.

Sonja looked at me. "Have I? Hired a detective?"

I took a sip of wine. If I was going to bow out, now was the time.

The case intrigued me, no doubt about that. I didn't know whether or not Michael Winter was innocent, but I knew that his death had been more than a simple suicide. I nodded slowly. "I guess I'm on the case," I said.

Sonja closed her eyes. After a second, a single tear ran down her left cheek.

I started to say something when I realized that Sonja was sobbing softly. "They called me this morning," she said. Her eyes remained closed.

"Who?"

"Gebhardt-Wulkan. Or rather, their law firm called me. I have until the end of this month to pay off Michael's contract. They have a court order requiring me to report for duty on September the first if the contract isn't liquidated."

Jesus. No wonder she'd been crying when I called this morning. She must have just gotten off the phone with those bastards.

"Don't give up yet," I said. "I've got a few leads and a few ideas."

She looked up with a sniff. "You do?"

"Of course he does," John said. "Our David is one of the best PI's in Los Angeles."

"I wasn't all *that* sharp when I was in the business," I said. "And now I'm rusty as hell."

John stood up, the servos in his exoskeleton throbbing heavily as they lifted him to his feet. "Got to get back to work, boys and girls. I've got a series-three articulated surgical remote lying in pieces back at the lab." He looked at Sonja. "Don't worry. Sarge has a tendency to sell himself short."

"So I'm discovering," said Sonja.

"He's good," John said. "You'll see."

"I'm glad he's good," Sonja said. "He'll have to be. The police have Michael's files sealed, right along with the rest of the Aztec case."

John nearly flinched. "Aztec? Your brother was *that* Michael Winter? He was Aztec?"

"Michael was *not* Aztec!" Sonja snapped. "The police are wrong!"

John looked at me. "I'm sorry," he said. "I understood that it was an airtight case. I didn't realize there was any room for doubt."

"There isn't any doubt," Sonja said. "My brother was not a killer." Her voice was thick. She was on the verge of tears again.

"Once again, I apologize," said John. "I spoke out of turn. What little I know of your brother's case, I learned from the news media: not exactly an unimpeachable source."

He gave Sonja a sad little smile. "I hope you find your brother's killer. I really do."

Sonja sniffed and tried to smile back. "Thank you," she said. "I didn't mean to snap at you. I guess I'm a little sensitive about the whole thing."

"Rightly so," John said.

He looked at me. "Come on, Sarge. You can walk me to the door."

I stood up and followed him out of the room. When we were out of Sonja's earshot, I said, "what do you think?"

"She's gorgeous," John said. "If you have any sense, you'll lock her up on the roof with my two-headed sister."

We stopped at the front door. "What do you think about the case?" I asked.

John sighed. "On the one hand, I'd really like to see you get back to work. It would be good for you..."

I could hear it in the tone of his voice. "But not on this particular job?"

"You need a case that hasn't already been solved," he said. "I was being polite back there. Your lady friend is distraught. She can't come to grips with the truth, but the fact of the matter is, her brother was a killer, plain and simple. He knew it. The cops knew it. The press knew it."

John leaned his head in the direction of the den. "Probably everybody in the world knows it, except for her."

"And me," I said. "I'm not sure one way or the other yet."

John smiled and turned toward the door. "Okay, Sarge. You go chase the bad guys. I have to get back to work."

"Thanks for coming," I said.

"Any time, old buddy."

Sonja was still pretty upset when I got back to the den. I spent ten minutes calming her down and then another hour bringing her up to date on the case: what I knew, what I could prove, what I suspected. I owned up to raiding her apartment's database. I ended with Holtzclaw's murder, and my morning encounter with Dancer and Delaney.

Sonja pulled a tissue from her purse and dabbed at her eyes. "Is there any chance that Mr. Holtzclaw's death is related to the case?"

"I don't know," I said. "I hope not. I'd hate to think that I led the killer to him."

Her eyes widened. "The killer? You're saying that the killer is still out there somewhere?"

"Maybe," I said. "If Michael was innocent, and I'm still not convinced that he was, the real killer is still running loose."

"Well, at least he can't afford to keep killing. I mean, the police would find out that he's still alive, wouldn't they?"

"Not necessarily. If the killer is smart, he could change his style, move to another city, and start another spree next month, or tomorrow."

I watched the awful possibilities register in her eyes.

"Or yesterday, or last week," I added.

Sonja inhaled sharply. "He could be killing again? Already?"

I nodded. "Worse. The Aztec spree may not have been his first time out of the box. He may have played out this scenario two or three times, using different MO's, in different towns. If he has, there's no telling how many people he's killed."

We sat in silence for a few minutes.

I used the time to turn over the implications of the things we'd discussed.

I found my thoughts drifting. The wine, my full belly and the soft couch conspired to remind me of how little sleep I'd had. I closed my eyes for a second.

A hand shook me gently. "David."

I cracked one eye. The lighting in the den was low. I closed the eye again.

An unseen hand ran gently down the side of my cheek.

"Mmm..."

"Come on, David. You need to get off this couch and crawl into bed."

I struggled to a sitting position, ran my fingers through my hair and yawned so hard that my ears rang afterward. "What time is it?"

"After seven."

"Jesus, why did you let me sleep?"

"You needed it. Besides, I enjoyed watching you."

"I've got work to do." I stood up.

She stood up with me and gave me a gentle shove in the direction of the hall. "You're going to bed."

"Uh-uh."

She crossed her arms and cocked her head to the side. "Do you have an appointment?"

"No, but I..."

"Anything you can do after seven o'clock, you can do after nine. You need at least a couple of more hours. House, wake David up at nine o'clock."

"David?" House sounded doubtful. He wanted to be polite to my guest, but he wasn't prepared to take her orders unless I confirmed them.

I sighed. "Yeah. A couple of hours won't hurt. Wake me up at nine."

Sonja smiled. "Want me to rub your back? You could probably use it after that couch."

I stretched. "No, I'm okay."

Her eyes flashed. "That offer means exactly what it says. A back rub. I was *not* offering anything more horizontal."

I nodded sleepily. "A back rub sounds great."

"You go climb into bed and I'll be right in."

I muttered an unintelligible acknowledgment and shuffled toward my bedroom.

I was in bed with the sheets pulled up to my waist when she appeared in the doorway and knocked on the frame.

"Come in."

She set a glass on my night table and sat on the bed next to me. "House told me where to find it. Cutty on the rocks, right?"

I reached for it, took a sip.

She took the glass from my fingers. "Roll over."

I did, keeping the sheet pulled over my butt. When I was settled comfortably on my stomach, she handed me the drink.

John and I had caroused a few massage parlors in our Army days. The girls all seemed to operate from the same script. Cursory, unskilled kneading of a few muscles and a lot of 'accidental' contact with some of my more obvious erogenous zones. When the expected erection appeared, the masseuse inevitably offered to correct the problem for a small tip.

Sonja hadn't read that script. She dug her fingers far enough into my muscles to elicit little grunts of pain. I stiffened, raised my head off the pillow.

She shoved my head back down. "Lie down. I knew you needed this. You're way too tense."

I tried to lay still, but her probing fingers seemed determined to find every little pocket of pain hidden in my muscles. Gradually I became aware that she was good, I mean really good. The occasional painful twinge notwithstanding, she knew exactly how to soothe the kinks out of my tired muscles.

I'm not sure what I was expecting, but this wasn't it. It was totally non-sexual and somehow, intensely sensitive and personal.

Occasionally I would stir just enough to sneak a sip of scotch. After a while I gave up even that and let myself drift toward sleep.

I was almost totally under when I felt her weight shift. She stood up. Her voice was almost a whisper. "I'm leaving now, David. Goodnight."

I spoke softly, eyes closed, trying not to interrupt my own gentle transition to the dream state. "You can stay here if you want. I have a spare bed..."

She sighed softly. "I can't. I have... a client. Rest now. Call me tomorrow, please?"

I listened to the sound of her leaving and pretended to be asleep. After a while, I was.

CHAPTER 8

‖‖ ‖ ‖ ‖‖‖‖ ‖ ‖‖ ‖‖‖ ‖ ‖‖ ‖‖ ‖‖‖ ‖‖‖ ‖ ‖ ‖‖‖‖‖ ‖ ‖‖ ‖ ‖‖ ‖‖

"David, wake up."

Both eyes came open easily. I felt rested and refreshed. "House, run a shower and start a pot of coffee. I'm going out and I'll probably be gone all night."

"Very well, David. Would you like me to download the morning news feed?"

That stopped me. Morning? I felt the first stirrings of suspicion. "What time is it, House?"

"The time is nine-oh-one a.m."

"It's after nine in the morning?"

"Yes, David."

I felt a rise of annoyance. "House, I told you to wake me up at nine *p.m.*"

House remained quietly unperturbed. "You did not specify a.m. or p.m. Just before she left, Ms. Winter assured me that you intended to sleep all night. Is there a problem, David? Have I made an error?"

I climbed out of bed and threw the sheet on the floor. "No, House. You didn't screw up, but someone did."

I showered, and dressed at a leisurely pace. My schedule was shot in the ass. Most of the people I wanted to talk to were night crawlers. They wouldn't be out and about for hours.

Despite the lack of hurry, I wasn't relaxed. I was nurturing a little spark of annoyance, trying to fan it into genuine anger, and frustrated by the knowledge that it wasn't working.

I broke out the Blackhart and the cleaning kit. I fieldstripped it over the kitchen table. When it was down to base level components, I lit a cigarette and called Sonja.

I knew the second she answered that I'd finally caught her asleep.

I jammed a brush through the barrel of the Blackhart and blew smoke out the side of my mouth. "I'm glad to see I'm not the only one sleeping the day away."

She smiled sleepily. "Morning..."

"Morning my ass, it's practically afternoon. Why did you lie to my AI?"

66

She stretched and yawned lazily. "You needed the sleep."

Even with my carefully pitched scene, I had to concentrate to keep the edge in my voice. "There's a killer out there somewhere. Sleeping isn't going to catch him."

"That's where you're wrong," she said. "In the shape you were in last night, you were definitely no match for him. Now, you're pissed off and overly dramatic, but your mind is alert."

"Goddamn it! That wasn't your decision to make."

"Did you ask my permission to raid my personal database? Or did you use your best judgment and do what you thought was best for me?"

To my credit, I didn't actually stammer. "I'm a detective," I said. "I get *paid* to snoop. It's what I *do*."

"I'm a call girl," she said. "I get paid to make people feel good. It's what *I* do. You were feeling like shit. I fixed it."

She moved in for the kill, still smiling. "Besides, two days ago, you swore most solemnly that you were *not* a detective. How did you become so fanatically dedicated to your profession so quickly?"

She was grinning.

I ground out the butt of the cigarette and grinned back at her. "I surrender," I said. "You win."

"I don't want to win," she said. "I want breakfast. You cook."

"I've already eaten."

She faked a pout. "You don't have to eat; just cook. I'll handle the eating part."

"I offered to cook you breakfast the other day. You turned me down."

"It was the middle of the afternoon. Anyway, I didn't know that you could cook, then."

"Your mistake," I said. "You have scorned my breakfast once. You won't get a second chance."

She wrinkled her nose, stuck her tongue out at me and hung up.

I laughed and started reassembling the automatic.

I slipped on my shoulder rig and shoved the Blackhart into the holster. On the way out the door, I realized that the call hadn't gone even remotely according to plan. I laughed again and pulled a windbreaker over the Blackhart.

I walked to the barricade and caught a hovercab to Dome 11.

Nearly half of the dome was dedicated to corporate enclaves.

The Gebhardt-Wulkan Informatik enclosure was a carefully landscaped park. At least thirty acres of meticulously manicured grass were spread like a lush green blanket over a half-dozen gently rolling hills. Evergreen trees were sprinkled here and there with a carefully calculated randomness. The air had a sweet headiness about it that was rich with natural unfiltered oxygen from the trees and grass. It smelled like the forest eco-modules in Dome 7, only more so.

At the center of the park-lawn stood the Gebhardt-Wulkan building, a towering pyramid of gold-tinted glass that reached nearly to the underside of the dome. The outer skin of the twenty-five bottom floors was photo-active, making the lower half of the building an enormous electronic video screen. I'd seen that kind of thing before: animated billboards around town, crawling with commercial vid clips for everything from Italian sports cars to Asian herbal tea. The technology was superior to holographic facades because it was unaffected by daylight. It was also a lot more expensive.

Gebhardt-Wulkan Informatik wasn't using its giant photo-active surface to sell sports cars. Instead, each side of the pyramid was plugged into a live video-feed from the opposite face, showing what you would have seen had the building not been there. The effect was stunning; the lower half of the building was invisible, or nearly so. If I really tried hard to focus on it, minute distortion of scale made it possible to spot the edges of the building, but I really had to work at it. As soon as I stopped concentrating, my eyes would glide over the minor discontinuities in the image, and the building would vanish again.

The fact that the upper twenty-five floors were *not* invisible made the image even more powerful. The visible half of the pyramid appeared to hang in the naked air.

Just looking at it gave me a touch of vertigo. Intellectually, I knew how the trick was done, but on a gut-level, my instincts insisted that it was impossible. A tiny part of me held its breath and waited for gravity to pluck the golden pyramid out of the sky and hurl it to the ground.

The entrances to the pyramid were marked by a pair of triangular archways, made of the same gold-mirrored glass that covered the upper floors. People moving into the building appeared to vanish as they passed through the archways, while those leaving the building apparently materialized out of thin air.

There were several smaller buildings in the enclave, all hidden from casual sight by strategically positioned hills and trees, to avoid marring the park-like scene that showcased the pyramid.

According to Sonja, Michael had worked in 6-B, one of the outbuildings. I had the cabbie drop me off out front.

Building 6-B turned out to be one of those single story prefabs assembled from cubical modules like a child's building blocks.

It was a low security building, so I didn't have a lot of trouble swapping a few crisp €m20 bills for a guest pass.

I wandered up and down a dozen identical modular hallways until I found a door labeled, "DATA PROTOCOL RESEARCH." Under the engraved plastic label, someone had taped a hand-lettered sign reading, "HOME OF THE DATA SQUASHERS."

I shouldered the door open and stepped into a large room full of computer work stations, matrix generators, holovid projectors, and racks of memory modules, all connected by about fifty kilometers of optical cable.

Eleven programmers were working at computer terminals, six women and five men. Each of them wore an elastic headband set with neural sensors. Slender loops of ribbon cable linked their headsets to matrix generators. None of them reacted to my presence; they were all jacked into the DataNet. They were operating on another plane of reality, one in which I didn't even exist.

Except for the movement of fingers on keyboards, they were practically motionless, giving the scene a sense of lethargy. I knew that it was a false impression. Behind their vacant eyes, their minds were blurring through logic matrixes at speeds I couldn't even imagine, shooting down corridors of shifting data, making thousands of decisions a minute.

I wove my way through a maze of equipment and cabling until I found a man and a woman huddled around another computer workstation in a back corner.

The man was thin, balding and fortyish. He waved a length of hardcopy around and jammed a finger at it.

"You're crazy," he half-shouted. "If you try to tokenize the seed variable, you're going to end up with a whole series of cascading encryption errors."

The woman shook her head. "You're not listening to me, Frank. We can't tokenize the entire data stream and leave the seed variable unencrypted. We'd never be able to retrieve. We *have* to tokenize the seed. All we have to..."

Frank shook the printout. "You're the one who's not listening. You can't pull an encrypted variable out of a five-deep compression wafer and decode it in real-time. You can't do it!"

The woman snatched the printout and stomped in my direction.

I turned sideways to let her squeeze past.

Frank looked up at me. "Who the hell are you?"

I stepped forward, grabbed his empty hand and shook it vigorously. "Bertram Tyler," I said. "True Crime Video. We're thinking about shooting a piece on Michael Winter, the Aztec Killer. I understand you used to work with him?"

"True Crime?" Frank snatched his hand away. "If I didn't talk to the legitimate media, what makes you think I'm going to spill my guts to the tabloids?"

I smiled my best snake-oil smile. "Because the legitimate media doesn't make it worth your while. If *we* decide to shoot this piece... Well, let's just say that we know how to reward our sources."

Frank turned toward his workbench. "Whatever you're offering, I guarantee you don't pay enough to make it worth losing my job."

"We can quote you off-camera as a confidential inside source," I said. "Mind you, it doesn't pay as much, but the money still isn't bad. Or..." I snapped my fingers a couple of times.

"Or what?"

"We could do an on-camera interview, one of those things where we electronically disguise your voice, and distort the picture to hide your face."

I nodded quickly, as if I was warming to the idea. "People love that sort of thing. *Brave Citizen Takes on the System to Bring you the Truth!*"

"Takes on the System?" Frank didn't look crazy about that idea.

"Don't worry about it," I said. "It's all hype. It pushes the ratings up. There wouldn't be any real risk at all. When our camera boys get done monkeying around with the signal, your own mother won't recognize you."

Frank rubbed his left earlobe between thumb and forefinger. "What would I have to do?"

"That depends on whether or not there's even a story in this," I said. "First, we kick around a few easy questions, and see if we have anything to work with here."

Frank nodded cautiously.

"Let's start with the basics," I said. "How long did you know Michael Winter?"

"A little over two years, I guess."

"From the time he came to work here until the night he committed suicide?"

"Yeah."

"How would you characterize the quality of his work?"

Frank sneered. "His work? His work was a *joke*. Winter was supposed to be some shit-hot code jockey, but you sure couldn't prove it by me."

Frank's voice got a little louder as he warmed up to the idea of criticizing his former co-worker. "Winter was unreliable. Some days he wouldn't even bother to show up, and I'd have to cover for him. I carried my workload and his too. I'll characterize the quality of Winter's work... It *sucked*. Everybody knows that Winter was hired because..."

"Because what?"

Frank looked away. "Never mind."

"It doesn't work that way," I said. "I can't get a camera crew in here for 'never mind.' Why was Michael Winter hired?"

Frank lowered his voice. "Because of Rieger. The Board of Contract Indenture would have turned Winter's application down cold if it weren't for Rieger."

"Why? What was wrong with Winter?"

"He had some kind of brain rot. A tumor or something. The Board wanted no part of that shit. Rieger stepped in and personally approved the contract."

"Who is this Rieger, and why did he approve Michael Winter's indenture?"

"Kurt Rieger. He's the head of Information Systems Research. He approved the indenture to get at Winter's sister."

"Sister?"

"Yeah. I've never seen her, but she's supposed to be some kind of hot."

"What does that have to do with Kurt Rieger?"

Frank coughed nervously. "The word on the work-floor is: Rieger tried to hire Winter's sister a couple of years ago. She turned him down. I guess she's some kind of call girl, but apparently she's choosy about her customers. Anyway, Rieger wants her. If she ends up indentured to Leisure Division, he plans to requisition her for his personal use. She better hope that doesn't happen."

"Why?"

Frank looked around. "I thought you were doing a shoot on *Aztec*. What do you care about Winter's sister? I knew the man, the killer. When are you going to ask me about *that*?"

I pulled out a cigarette. "Mind if I smoke?"

He shook his head, so I lit up. "Who might have wanted to kill Michael Winter?"

"He killed himself."

"Humor me," I said. "Who had a motive for killing Michael Winter?"

Frank looked thoughtful and shrugged. "Nobody that I know of. Maybe the parents of one of those little girls he killed."

"Okay, let's table that for now. I'm going to ask you for a gut reaction. Do you believe that Michael Winter was a killer? Do you truly believe that he was capable of butchering little girls?"

Frank shook his head slowly. "No. He pissed me off, and his work wasn't what it should have been, but Mike was a good boy. I know that he must have killed those girls. He *did* confess, didn't he? But I sure have trouble seeing him as a killer."

There was a wistful, faraway look in Frank's eyes.

I took a hit off my cigarette. "Did you ever see Michael smoke?"

"Uh-uh. He hated cigarettes."

"Hmmm... Do you smoke?"

"Gave it up years ago."

"Have you ever heard of Ernte 23?"

"Ernie what?"

"Ernte 23. It's a brand of German cigarettes. Does anybody around here smoke German cigarettes?"

Frank turned and started fiddling with a data keypad. "Probably half the people here; this is a German company."

"Does this Kurt Rieger smoke?"

"Yeah," Frank said. "I think so."

"German cigarettes?"

Frank shrugged. "I have no idea. And just to save time, I don't know what brand of toothpaste he uses, or what kind of starch he puts in his shirts."

"Did Michael ever talk to you about his social life?"

"No. He made it pretty clear that it was none of my business."

"Did he ever..."

"I've got work to do," Frank snapped. "If you guys decide to shoot a piece on Winter, you come see me. I could use the money. But that's all the freebies you're getting out of me."

"Okay," I said. "Thank you Mister..."

"Franklin. Arthur Franklin."

"Thank you Mr. Franklin. You've been most helpful. If we decide to shoot the piece, we'll be in touch."

"Aren't you going to leave me your card or some shit?"

I patted my pockets. "Sorry, I'm out of business cards."

I could feel him staring at my back as I walked out.

The woman caught up with me as I was crossing the neatly landscaped lawn. She was overweight and breathing heavily when she fell into step beside me. "Frank's an ass," she said, "but most of what he told you is true."

I stopped walking and stared at her. She was dressed in a baggy black pantsuit that might have been intended to make her look thinner. A name tag pinned over her left breast identified her as Lisa Caldwell.

She looked toward the evergreen trees that concealed building 6-B. "When I stomped out, I didn't go very far."

She looked down at her feet, then looked back up at me and grinned. "I stood on the other side of the power supplies and listened. I heard every word."

I lit a cigarette. "Which part was a lie?"

She frowned. "Just about all of it was true. Except about Michael's work. Michael was good, I mean he was *really* good. Frank's not bad either, but he's not as good as Mike was."

"Would you say that Frank was jealous of Mike's work?"

"Not really," she said. "Frank's ego wouldn't let him see that Michael was a better coder. Frank was..."

She fixed her gaze on the floating pinnacle of the GWI building. "Mike was an attractive man. Frank was..."

"Attracted to him?"

"Well, yeah."

"And Mike rebuffed his advances."

Lisa scrunched up her pudgy little nose like a rabbit as she tasted the idea. "It wasn't really like that. Michael didn't actually shoot down Frank's advances. It's more like he didn't even notice them."

"Mike was hetero?"

She looked at me like I had just insulted the entire female half of the species.

"I take it that's a yes," I said.

She didn't say anything.

"So, Frank was blowing smoke when he said he always had to cover for Mike?"

"No," Lisa said. "There was some truth to that, sort of. Frank was right about one thing, Mike didn't always show up for work. We had to cover for him sometimes."

She cocked her head to one side. "Are you going to buy me lunch, or what? I know a quiet little cafe that serves the most scrumptious seafood."

I wasn't really in the mood for seafood two days in a row, but I allowed her to steer me to her favorite restaurant.

The 'quiet little cafe' turned out to be a dingy little hole in the wall. The decor was make-believe nautical, complete with fishing nets, lighting fixtures shaped like ship's wheels, and trids of fish on the walls. The signs on the restroom doors read 'Buoys' and 'Gulls.'

I ordered the steamed dungeness crab. Lisa ordered the same, the grilled halibut, the fried shrimp and two appetizers.

In all fairness, the crab was pretty good. I swallowed a bite and pointed my fork vaguely in Lisa's direction. "What do you think about Frank's theory? Did Kurt Rieger hire Michael just to get at his sister?"

Lisa shrugged. "It's a rumor."

"But not a rumor that *you* believe?"

"It could happen," Lisa said. "I've seen her around a few times. She's a beautiful woman, and Mr. Rieger's certainly a healthy male."

"You don't sound convinced."

She did the rabbit thing with her nose again. "The way I hear it, she might be a bit too old for Mr. Rieger. I understand that he likes his ladies a little younger."

"How much younger?"

Lisa shrugged. "A *lot* younger. Maybe younger than the law allows."

A chill ran down my spine. "That can't be an easy itch to scratch. Especially for a respected business man."

Lisa made a production of squeezing lemon over her halibut. "I've heard that there are places in the Zone that cater to that sort of thing."

I was reasonably certain that there weren't any places in the Zone that fit the bill. I hoped not anyway, but I didn't see any profit in arguing with her.

Something touched my right leg just above the ankle. It was a pudgy, stocking-clad foot. I took another bite of the crab and tried to ignore it.

"You're not really a reporter, are you?"

"What makes you say that?"

Her plump toes slid under the hem of my pants leg and began to trace circles on the bare flesh above my sock. "You don't *feel* like a reporter."

"How so?"

She frowned a little and her toes paused in their wandering. A second later her features relaxed and her toes resumed their journey. "Because you're not going to sleep with me. If you were really a scout for one of the tabloids, you'd do whatever you had to do to get the story. You'd even sleep with a fat woman that you care nothing about, no matter how distasteful you found it."

Her fork speared a chunk of my crab and flicked it into her mouth. She swallowed before continuing. "You have... principles."

"Can't a reporter have principles?"

"I doubt it," she said, "not a tabloid reporter. Anyway, you care too much. You ask the wrong sorts of questions. I don't believe you're scouting for a vid shoot. I think you're trying to find out who killed Michael. I can't see you as a cop, and that makes me wonder why you're doing this. Were you a friend of Michael's?"

"I'm more of a friend of his sister."

"Oh." Lisa's toes retreated. "I certainly can't compete with *that*."

"If it makes you feel any better, I'm not sleeping with her either."

Lisa smiled. "I'm not sure I believe you, but it's nice of you to say that."

We ate in silence for a few minutes.

Lisa blotted her lips with her napkin. "Why don't you think that Michael killed those girls?"

I debated with myself for a moment and decided that the truth wouldn't hurt. "He had an alibi for one of the murders."

I noticed that Lisa's eyes were unfocused, like she was staring off into infinity. "I almost wish that the bastard would kill somebody else."

She looked up quickly. "I'm sorry; I shouldn't have said that. I shouldn't even be *thinking* it."

"Why do you want Aztec to kill again?"

"Because it would prove that Michael was innocent. I know that's a terrible thing to wish for. I just want the world to realize that Michael wasn't a killer."

"Aztec may have already killed again," I said. "He's probably stalking young girls in Atlanta, or Houston by now and the news feeds are calling him the Reaper, or Scorpio, or something."

I made a snap decision. "You're a programmer, right?"

"That's what it says on my contract," she said.

"You can help me catch him," I said. "Maybe we can clear Michael's name."

She sat up and squared her shoulders. "What do I have to do?"

I grabbed a paper napkin with pictures of whales on one side. I rummaged through my pockets for my pen, flipped the napkin over and started a list on the blank side. "I think the killer may have done this whole thing before, maybe in another city. I want you to run a search of all serial murders in the U.S. in oh, say the last ten years. Eliminate any that are unsolved. I want only cases in which the killer confessed and then somehow committed suicide."

"It's not that hard to run a search," Lisa said. "Just call up your favorite search engine, and start punching in search terms."

I shook my head. "I'm not completely helpless around computers, but they're not exactly my strong suit. I'd rather give the job to someone who knows how to do it properly."

Lisa nodded. "Fair enough, I guess. But why do you want me to concentrate on only the solved cases?"

"Just a hunch," I said. "I'm beginning to think that the killer—whoever he is—likes to leave a patsy to take the blame for his crimes. With the patsy dead, the police mark the case as solved and close it. Everyone stops looking for the murderer and he's free to move on to another city."

Lisa shuddered, sending ripples of revulsion through her ample flesh. "Don't the police already have databases that track that sort of thing?"

"They do," I said. "And some of their software agents are incredibly effective. The problem is that the police AI's may be *too* smart. They're programmed to eliminate known-dead criminals from their data searches. It shortens search times considerably, and it keeps the police from trying to track down criminals who are already dead."

I added my phone number to the bottom of the napkin. "You can reach me here, if you find anything."

Lisa took the napkin, glanced at it and slipped it into a pocket.

"What do I call you? Your name obviously isn't Bertram Tyler, or whatever it was that you told Frank."

I took her plump hand in mine. "My name is David Stalin. I'm honored to make your acquaintance."

Lisa giggled. "You have an old fashioned streak about you, David. I think it's charming."

I smiled at her.

She returned it. "You're still not going to sleep with me, are you?"

I shook my head.

She stood up. "Then you can get the tip."

CHAPTER 9

▌▌▐▌▐▐▐▌▐▐▌▌▐▐▌▐▐▌▐▐▌▌▐▐▌▐▐▌▐▐▌▐▐▌▌▐▌▐▐▌▌▐▐▐▌▐▌

Like just about every other stationary object in LA, Lev depots collect a lot of graffiti. The Central Avenue depot didn't have any. I don't mean *not much*; I mean *none*. A tribute to the fanatical effectiveness of corporate security groups.

Perhaps the people who worked in Dome 11 found it comforting to be wrapped in an invisible security blanket. It made the skin between my shoulder blades itch.

I suppressed a shudder and tried to take my mind off it by concentrating on the people. At two in the afternoon, the platform was nearly deserted. A young couple snuggled and played kissy games. Two middle aged women in severe business attire conversed in low tones. An elderly Asian man with an immaculate black suit stood with a strangely shaped package at his feet. Judging from his formal samurai haircut, he was probably Japanese. His package appeared to consist entirely of colored washi paper, each origami fold crisp and precise.

The Lev slid up to the platform exactly on schedule. The electromagnetic cushion that kept it hovering ten centimeters above the track made the hair on my lower legs stand up.

I felt a surge of perverse pleasure when I saw that the streamlined carbon-laminate cars were mottled with graffiti. I don't usually condone graffiti. I've always considered it a sign of social decay, but suddenly, it seemed like a breath of freedom—a sign that this train traveled to places beyond the sterile confines of Dome 11, outside the playground of corporate security Nazis and industrial ninjas.

I ended up in the second car from the rear. It was empty except for three teenage boys crammed into one seat at the back. They all wore electrostatic necklaces that made their hair stand on end, crackle, and emit sparks. The old Japanese gentleman followed me in and took a seat in the middle of the car.

I slid into a spot near the front, and leaned back in my seat as the Lev glided out of the station. The Lev accelerated smoothly, reaching its cruising speed just as the corporate enclaves of Dome 11 gave way to the stacked apartment modules of Dome 12.

There wasn't a lot to see in the way of scenery. Rectilinear concrete walls rocketed by my window at 150 kilometers an hour.

My attention drifted to the graffiti that peppered the inside of the Lev car. Most of it seemed to be the usual gang symbols, boasts, and epithets.

I spotted one in yellow paint-stick that I'd never seen before: two curved lines, arcing upward like ski-jumps, and crossing each other near the top. At first I took it to be a stylized 'X', but then it struck me that the two arcs looked more like statistical distribution curves than a gang symbol, as though two mathematical variables tracked over time were destined to intersect and create some sort of critical condition. Below the X-curves, the tagger had written *'Prepare for the Convergence'*, in the same yellow paint-stick.

The Convergence? What in the hell was that?

I glanced up at the ceiling into the friendly electroptic eye of a security camera. A blue LED next to the lens told me that the camera was on-line and that my fellow passengers and I were safe under the watchful gaze of LA-Trans Security. Of course, the cameras hadn't stopped vandals from scrawling graffiti all over the inside of the car. Probably, they were only monitored at random intervals.

I closed my eyes and leaned my head against the window.

The world exploded just to the left of my head. Not really, but it certainly felt that way to me.

I know enough about physics to realize that all of the things that happened next must have been so nearly simultaneous that the human brain couldn't possibly distinguish the timing.

Screw physics. My brain captured those events in a certain sequence, and every time I drag out the memory and replay it, everything happens in exactly the same order: *a flash of red light, bright enough to be seen through my eyelids, visible to both eyes, but much stronger in the left. A wash of heated air over the left side of my face. A pinpoint of searing pain in the fleshy part of my left ear. The distinct odors of singed hair and burnt meat: mine.*

Laser!

I'd seen enough of them in the Army to recognize one when it trimmed the edge off my ear.

It took me about a nanosecond to cram myself down between my seat and the front wall of the car.

My heart shifted into high gear and my adrenaline level skyrocketed as my body kicked into fight-or-flight mode.

I had three major problems...

#1 — I didn't know if the guy with the laser was in front of me or behind me. The window set in the sliding door at the front of the car was transparent enough for the laser to have passed through it like sunlight through water. If the shooter was in the next car, he could have fired through the window without leaving a mark on it.

#2 — I didn't have a clue what the mystery person looked like. Male? Female? Old? Young? Tall? Short?

#3 — I couldn't get to my gun.

As tightly as I was jammed into the small well between my seat and the wall, no amount of wiggling was going to get my fingers on the butt of my Blackhart. The closest I could manage with my right hand was about ten centimeters. To get any closer, I'd have to bust a hole in the shell of the Lev or voluntarily dislocate my right elbow. My left arm was pinned against the seat.

I listened for a few seconds, trying to catch some kind of clue to the location of the shooter. I could hear the muffled chattering of the teenage boys at the back of the car. I hoped they were smart enough to take cover. I couldn't hear anything from the old Japanese guy at all. He might be hunkered down behind his seat in silence. Or he might be lining up the laser for another shot at me.

I strained to hear any sounds from the next car. If the shooter was up there waving a laser around, people might be screaming. For the first time in my life, I regretted the quality of the soundproofing in MagLev trains.

The sound of my own heart pounding swelled until it filled my ears. I tried to think…

If the shooter was in front of me, in the next car, he could only see me through the windows in the doors between our cars. The laser could shoot through the windows too, but at least his field of vision would be limited. I could crawl out of my hidey-hole, pull the Blackhart and jockey for a better position. As long as I stayed below window level, I'd be safe.

However, if the shooter was behind me, he'd burn me the second I tried to move.

I tried to remember what I knew about lasers. They need power. A lot of it. The big swivel mounted jobs (like the one that had sliced up John's spine in Argentina) were usually plugged into a good-sized generator, or a major power grid. The little hand-held types had to depend on battery packs. Most of the ones I'd seen were reasonably bulky, small enough to fit into a backpack or a large purse, but much too large for a pocket. Which meant that my shooter was probably carrying a largish bag or package.

Who did that leave? Somebody already on the train? Uh-uh. No one could have possibly known exactly which Lev I would catch. Whoever it was had followed me to the Lev station and boarded when I did.

The two business women were probably out; neither had carried a briefcase or purse.

The Japanese man, with his origami package, was a strong candidate. That would put the laser behind me.

The young lovers were also a possibility. I couldn't remember whether the woman had been carrying a purse or not. If it was the young couple, the laser would be in front of me.

My attempts to reason my way through the problem had taken me full circle. I still didn't know if the laser was in front of me or behind me.

If I were a vid detective like Mike Hammer, I'd have pulled the foil wrapper off a stick of gum and used it as a mirror. Then I could have spied on the Japanese guy behind me from the safety of my hiding place. Or, if the laser were in the next car, I could have used my foil mirror to reflect the deadly beam back into the killer's face. No muss, no fuss: Bad Guys dead in time for the commercial.

I didn't have any gum, and I couldn't have reached it if I had.

Come to think of it, Mike Hammer wouldn't have dived for cover anyway. When the shooting started, he'd have whipped out his automatic and shot it out with the Bad Guys on the spot.

This entire line of thinking took place in the ten seconds following the first laser shot. That left me with two minutes and change before we pulled into the 52nd Street depot.

All I had to do was wait. The killer was bound to take off as soon as the doors opened.

Two things changed my mind. First: it occurred to me that, on his way out, the killer might just decide to ease up to the side of the train and shoot me through the nearest window. Second: my right arm was beginning to fall asleep.

I mentally tossed a coin. It came up heads.

I threw myself sideways, uncoiling my body until I was stretched most of the way across the aisle. If that nice Japanese gentleman happened to have a laser, I was now a perfect target. I snatched the Blackhart out of the shoulder rig and rolled over, ready to spray 12mm slugs toward the rear of the car.

The Japanese man was still sitting up. There was a neat round hole the diameter of a cigarette in his forehead. The laser had taken him just over the left eyebrow.

I touched the half-moon shaped notch in my left ear. The flesh was cauterized, no blood, but it stung like hell. I was alive by an accident of geometry. If the beam had been a few centimeters to the right, it would have been me sitting there with a hole in my forehead, instead of that poor Japanese man.

I scrambled to a crouch and turned forward, most careful to stay below window level.

I spotted a crumpled sheet of hardcopy on the floor. I carefully reached for it, picked it up, and rolled it into a cone. I poked it above the lip of the window for about a second.

The laser fired again, cutting perfectly circular holes through both sides of the paper cone.

Two shots. A hand laser on batteries was only good for about five shots at maximum power, and that one certainly seemed to be cranked up to the limit. Which left the killer with three more shots, four at the outside.

A totally irrational urge came over me. Suddenly, I wanted to pop up like a jack-in-the-box and start pumping 12mm slugs through that window. I couldn't do it; I knew that. The killer wasn't alone in that car; there were people in there with him, people whose only crime was riding the wrong train at the wrong time.

The Lev braked suddenly, taking everyone by surprise. Levs *never* brake sharply unless there's some type of emergency. Thrown off balance, I lurched forward out of my crouch.

My head and left shoulder slammed painfully into the door. Somehow I managed to hang on to the Blackhart. The body of the Japanese gentleman pitched forward, bounced off a seat-back, and fell sideways into the aisle. Behind me, I could hear fumbling and cursing; the teenagers had gotten banged around a bit too. I knew that everyone else on the train had suffered similar fates. Everyone except my friend with the laser, that is.

I had no doubt that the killer was expecting this, and had prepared for it. He was probably the only person on board not nursing a few new bruises.

Now that I thought about it, it made sense. Even if no one was monitoring the security cameras, probably two-thirds of the people on the train were carrying phones. At least two dozen passengers had called the police by now. When the Lev pulled up to the platform at the 52nd Street depot, the place was going to be crawling with LAPD Tactical.

The killer would have foreseen this, and planned for it. It was a perfect recipe for hit-and-run murder: follow Stalin until he gets on a train, boil his brain with a laser, stop the train suddenly (well short of the next depot), and run like hell. It would have worked too, had I not leaned my head against the window at the last second.

The doors hissed open on both sides of the car as soon as the Lev came to a stop.

My options were limited. I couldn't fight back with innocent people around. So I had to lure the shooter to a place where I *could* fight back. I had to get the killer off the Lev.

On hands and knees, I scooted across the floor to the door at the left side of the car. A quick look both ways told me that the killer was either still on the Lev, or had gone out the other side.

I gathered my body into a crouch and threw myself out the door.

The ground came up hard and fast. I rolled with it and came up running.

A pencil thin finger of ruby light flashed by the right side of my head. I swerved suddenly to the left and kept running.

Three shots. Which meant the laser was down to two charges, maybe three.

I changed course every few seconds, darting to the right or left with intentional randomness, trying to make myself a difficult target. I was angling toward a trash dumpster behind the closest of the apartment stacks, about twenty meters away.

The ground under me was cracked plast-phalt, littered with broken glass that crunched beneath my shoes as I ran.

I made the edge of the dumpster, and darted behind it, breathing hard. Up close, I saw that the dumpster was an old orbital cargo module, no doubt reduced to trash duty after its seals could no longer hold pressure against the vacuum of space.

I peeked over the top of the dumpster, the Blackhart in my fist outstretched like an accusing finger. My pursuers had covered maybe a third of the distance between us. It was the lovers, moving toward my position in sort of a weird half-walk/half-stumble. The man was in front, the woman with her left arm around his neck.

The woman raised the laser over the man's right shoulder and fired in my direction. The beam scorched a line of paint across the top of the dumpster. Four.

The man was struggling and it was throwing off her aim. She was using his body as a shield.

The hostage thing might be a ruse. They'd gotten on the Lev together, been huggy-kissy at the depot. They were probably working together. On the other hand, his struggles obviously weren't helping her aim.

I had a couple of brief opportunities to take her with a head-shot, but I passed them up. It had been a long time since I'd even pulled the trigger. I certainly wasn't ready for trick shooting.

She pointed the laser at me again, then changed her mind and jammed it against her hostage's right cheek. He stopped struggling, and started cooperating with her.

She pulled him to the side, angling away from me. What was she doing?

She moved cautiously, careful to keep her hostage's body between us. I was equally careful to keep the dumpster between us.

They were moving toward an alley between two of the apartment stacks. She was probably down to one shot, and had decided to abort the hit while she still had enough firepower to get away.

They broke and ran into the alley.

I took off after them.

The Blackhart led the way around the corner into the alley. I could see them up ahead. I was gaining on them.

A flight of steps was coming up: a good tall one, maybe twenty-five steps high.

They hit the steps about four seconds ahead of me and I was still gaining fast.

I took the steps two at a time. By the time I was halfway up, they were at the top. I expected them to keep running. Instead, they paused at the top and turned to face me.

I froze on the steps, my automatic pointed up at them. We looked at each other.

The woman shoved her hostage down the stairs and ran.

The young man came bouncing down the concrete steps in a jumble of arms and legs. I don't think a professional stunt man could have taken that kind of fall without breaking a few bones.

I could have jumped out of the way and let him tumble past. Lady Laser was expecting me to stop and help the poor bastard. I had a split second to decide. I stepped to the side and lowered my center of gravity. When he rolled by me, I reached out and grabbed him. His momentum dragged us both down three or four steps. For a half second, I thought we were going to end up careening down the steps together. Then, thankfully, we ground to a stop.

I could hear the woman's footsteps receding in the distance. There was still time to give chase.

One look at the young man's battered face made up my mind for me. He was badly injured, maybe critically. I let the woman go and tended to her victim.

His pulse was weak and rapid, but he never stopped breathing and his heart never stopped beating. He undoubtedly had several broken ribs. If I'd had to use CPR, he'd have died for sure.

Two grunts from LAPD Tactical found the bottom of the alley after about ten minutes. One was female, one male. Both were decked out in riot armor, carbon-glass helmets with full HUDs and enough firepower to depopulate a small town.

I left the Blackhart about five steps below us and kept my movements carefully non-threatening. When they got close enough to hear me, I pointed up the stairs. "The Bad Guy went that way."

They ignored me. Tarzan covered me with a mini-gun the size of a small refrigerator while Tarzana recovered my automatic.

They obviously weren't going to chase the nice lady with the laser. I tried Plan B. "Listen, you'd better call for medical assistance. This man is dying."

Twenty-five minutes later, I sat in an interview room at Southwest District Headquarters.

A thoughtful police sergeant brought me coffee in one of those plastic bulbs that come from vending machines.

I twisted the button-shaped top off and felt the bulb start warming in my hand as soon as the air hit the thermo-chem coating on the inner layer of plastic. The coffee smelled like charcoal. I drank it anyway.

I thought about a cigarette, but someone had taken them, along with everything else in my pockets. A plastic sign reminded me that smoking was forbidden in Municipal buildings. There were about forty cigarette burns in the sign and a hundred more on the top of the only table in the room.

Just as I was settling in for a long wait, the door opened and my good friends Dancer and Delaney walked in.

Delaney sat in a chair across the table. This time he didn't ask my permission before he started his recorder.

Dancer tossed my cigarettes on the table.

I pointed to the sign and raised an eyebrow.

Dancer glanced at the sign. "Screw em'."

I lit up.

Dancer scratched the side of her nose. "Holy shit, Stalin. Two bodies in three days. People are just dropping dead all around you. If that asshole who fell down the stairs happens to flatline, you might be three-for-three."

"I didn't kill any of them."

"I know that," Dancer said. "If we thought for a second that you *had*, we'd have been up your ass with a microscope by now."

I took a hit off the cigarette and waited.

She leaned forward and rested her hands on the table. "We also know that the Jap on the Lev..." She snapped her fingers several times.

"Takamura," Delaney said. "Joseph Takamura."

"Right. Takamura was zapped by a Caucasian female perpetrator armed with a military surplus hand-laser. Harvey Miller, the guy you danced with on the stairs, managed to talk for a little while before USC Medical sedated him. He claims the perp walked up to him out of nowhere and offered to get naked and horizontal."

Dancer rolled her eyes. "I guess this woman is supposed to be nice looking, and Miller is kind of a zero. Naturally, the stupid bastard went for it. They were supposed to be riding the train to her apartment, when she whipped out a laser and started frying shit. Miller tried to hide behind a seat like everybody else. The perp found him and grabbed him for a hostage. You know the rest."

I nodded. "How is he?"

Dancer shrugged. "Last I heard, he was pretty fucked up, but the Trauma Unit said he was probably going to make it. Frankly, he's not my problem until he flatlines."

I took another drag off the cigarette.

Dancer straightened up and stretched. "Are you going to tell us what in the hell is going on here?"

"What do you mean?"

"Don't play stupid. We've talked to seven or eight people who were on that Lev. They all say the woman was shooting at you, and *only* you. The witnesses also said that, when you got off the Lev, she followed you.

"We got a preliminary readout from LA-Trans; looks like their mainframe was crashed by a virus, just in time to stop the Lev and let our female perpetrator get off. The virus also slicked the vid recordings from every security camera on the Lev. No other Levs were affected, just *that* one. Hell of a coincidence, wouldn't you say? That was an attempted hit, Stalin. You know it, and I know it."

My turn to shrug.

Her face clouded. "Don't try to hand me that strong silent shit! You've got somebody pissed off at you, Stalin. Somebody bad enough to pull a whole lot of heavy kink down on your ass. I don't want any more fucking bodies! I want some fucking answers! What in the hell are you messing around with?"

I followed the grand tradition and ground out my cigarette on the table top. "Can I have my gun back now?"

Delaney said, "obstructing an investigation is a crime, Mr. Stalin. We could charge you..."

Dancer snorted. "Don't try to play the badass, Rick. You're not equipped for it. Okay Stalin, you can pick up your gun at the Property Desk. I think you're a goddamned idiot, but that's not against the law. I promise you, though: if you turn up any more corpses, I'll shoot you myself."

I stood up and walked to the door. I stopped and turned. "Dancer, what was in the old man's package?"

"The one with the fancy Jap paper? It was some sort of Kabuki doll. I guess it's his granddaughter's birthday."

I searched Dancer's eyes and wondered what it had taken to create the streamlined shell that armored her against feelings and compassion. How much time spent staring into the ugly guts of human nature had it taken her to transform an elderly and dignified gentleman like Joseph Takamura into a *dead old Jap with fancy Jap paper?*

Dancer returned my stare, something glinting like ice behind her eyes. I started to say something, and then changed my mind. I turned and stepped through the door.

I heard it slide shut behind me.

CHAPTER 10

‖‖ ‖ ‖ ‖ ‖‖‖ ‖ ‖ ‖‖‖ ‖ ‖‖ ‖ ‖‖ ‖‖‖ ‖‖‖ ‖ ‖ ‖‖‖‖ ‖ ‖‖ ‖ ‖‖ ‖‖

Dancer had a squad car drop me off at the barricade. It wasn't even four-thirty yet. I still had time to take care of an errand I'd been wanting to run.

I stopped by my house just long enough to grab the vid chip with Michael Winter's suicide recording, and to print out a copy of his credit reports from the LAPD case-files.

According to the records, Michael had made three credit transactions on April 14, 2063, the day of his death. One had been the room rent at the Velvet Clam; the other two were purchases made from Alphatronics, a retail electronics outlet on Hudson Avenue, at the southern end of Dome 14.

When the hard copies were finished printing, I walked to the barricade and caught a cab to Hudson Avenue.

Luckily, Alphatronics turned out to be a small, family business. If it had been part of a big chain, my chances of talking to the right person would have been slim.

The owner was a hulking Samoan named Henry Mailo.

I introduced myself and told him what I wanted.

He glanced at my hardcopy of the credit transaction and stuck his head through a curtain covering a doorway behind the counter. "Hey Tommy, get up here."

A few seconds later, a slightly scaled-down copy of Henry powered through the curtain like a tank. Tommy looked about seventeen and already he had the classic Samoan walk, that utterly self-confident swagger that suggests that even walls would do well to get out of the way. "Yeah, Pop. What's up?"

Henry showed him the printout. "Did you sell this camera?"

Tommy furrowed his brow. "Pop, that was four months ago. How am I supposed to remember?"

Henry looked at the printout again. "A Hitachi 1250. We don't move a lot of those. Are you sure you don't remember?"

"Oh, the H-1250. Yeah... I remember, now. That was the guy who made me swap the recording chip."

I leaned on the counter. "What do you mean?"

"The H-1250 comes with a blank recording chip in the box," Tommy said. "All the good holo-cameras do. The 1250 comes with an ultra-high grade Hitachi Platinum series. That's a five-hour chip. But, this guy didn't want the Platinum. He wanted to swap it for a twenty-minute chip. I tried to tell him that he was losing money on the deal, but he didn't care. He wanted the twenty."

"Did he buy anything else?"

"Yeah. A camera tripod."

I nodded. "Do you remember what the man looked like?"

"Yeah, now that I think about it. He was slender, about your height, kind of muscular. Red hair. A pretty-boy."

I showed him a trid of Michael.

"That's the guy, alright."

"Was there anyone with him?"

"No, I don't think so."

"Were there any other customers in the store?"

"There was a woman in the shop too. Dark hair, kind of pretty, I think. I didn't pay her a lot of attention."

I wished I had a holo of the woman on the Lev. Could it be the same woman?

I looked around for security cameras; there were four, one in each corner. "Do you keep recordings from your security cameras?"

"Sorry. We only hold the chips for seventy-two hours. After that, we reuse them."

Damn.

"The dark haired woman and the man who bought the camera, did it look like they were together?"

Tommy shrugged. "Hard to say. I'm pretty sure they didn't talk to each other or anything. On the other hand, she didn't buy anything and I think she left about the same time he did."

"Did the man act funny? Could the woman have been holding a gun on him?"

Tommy shook his head. "I don't think so. The guy didn't seem nervous. He seemed distant, disconnected. Like maybe he was scattered."

"Scattered?"

"Yeah, scattered. You know, fragged. On drugs."

I nodded slowly. "Thank you very much, Tommy. You've been a great help."

I turned back to his father. "Henry, who's the best video-jockey you know?"

"Tommy." He said it without hesitation.

I motioned for Henry to step closer and lowered my voice. "I've got a video clip that I need to have picked apart, frame-by-frame. It's a recording of a suicide. It's not pretty. I don't think you want Tommy to see it."

Henry pointed toward the entrance to the shop. "I got a lot of nice equipment in here. Every once in a while, somebody wants to take some of it home. Last summer, two punks came in waving guns. I was on the wrong side of the counter and couldn't get to my 10 millimeter. Tommy stood behind the curtain and blew both of them away with a pump shotgun. It wasn't pretty. You grow up fast around here, Mr. Stalin."

"David."

"Okay, David. If you want somebody to look at your chip, Tommy's your man."

I nodded.

Henry called Tommy over and explained the situation.

I showed him the chip. "Can you duplicate this and analyze the copy? I'm going to need mine back."

Tommy took the chip. "Not a problem."

He loaded the chip in a holo-deck, plugged a blank chip into a second deck, and connected the two units with optic cable. His finger paused above the play button. "So this is serious stuff, huh?"

"It's pretty ugly."

He punched a code into both of the decks. "I'm going to dub this at high speed: ten to one. It'll be done in two minutes. Less chance of scaring away a customer, if one happens to walk in."

He pressed *play* on one deck and *record* on the other.

An image of Michael appeared in the air over the source deck. He pranced and capered at impossible speed and then blew his brains out and threw himself to the bed in an instant. At increased speed, the scene felt cartoon-like.

Tommy ejected my chip and handed it back to me. He pocketed the copy. "I'll look at this on my rig in the back. I'll give it the works, but it would help if I knew what I was looking for."

"Start by checking for any indication that the recording has been altered."

"Do you think it has?"

"I doubt it, but check anyway."

"Anything else?"

"Yeah," I said. "Look for any evidence that someone else was in the room at the time of the suicide." I handed him a hundred marks.

He took it with a surprised look on his face. "What's this?"

"A retainer."

"What if I don't find anything?"

"According to your Dad, if you don't find anything, there's nothing to find."

I thanked them both for their help and left them my name and phone number on a scrap of paper. I was doing that a lot lately; I really needed to have some business cards printed up.

I caught a cab to the 1600 block of 55th Street, and walked the last hundred meters to the barricade. The sun was all but gone by then, submerging the Zone in rapidly deepening twilight.

Unlike the rest of the city, where holo-facades were common on houses and businesses, in the Zone most of the holographic glitz was reserved for the bars and massage parlors over on Santa Fe Avenue.

The buildings along 55th Street were old and tired looking, with only the gathering darkness to hide their decaying faces.

An instant after I turned the corner onto Alameda Street, an incredibly bright light hit me in the eyes, half blinding me.

My reflexes kicked in. I threw myself to the right, and came up in a crouch behind a parked car. I snatched the Blackhart out of its holster; in the Zone, most surprises are nasty ones.

I tried to peek through the windows of the car. I had to use my peripheral vision, because afterimages of the light hung in front of my eyes like irregular purple blobs.

"Back off!" a voice said. It was gravelly and loud, a man's voice through an amplifier.

I could see a van across the street. A bank of high-powered flood lamps stretched across the van's roof, lighting a wide swath of the street to a silver-white intensity. Tendrils of milky vapor spilled out of the open rear doors of the van.

I realized that I must have turned the corner just as the lights had come on. Bad timing. I'd caught them full in the face.

"Back off!" the amplified voice said again. "Back the fuck off."

I continued trying to scan the street through the corner of my eye. There were bodies, four or five of them, sprawled on the street and sidewalk near the van. Judging from their clothes, they were bangers: gang soldier-boys.

My eyes were beginning to adjust. I could make out two shapes, men in police-style riot armor; they were throwing a body into the back of the van. A third man, also in armor, stood between me and the van, silhouetted by the bright light behind him. His fat combat rifle was leveled at the car that I was hiding behind. His voice amplifier kicked in again, "Listen up, Dickwad. We are a registered organ recovery unit and this is an authorized salvage operation. So why don't you just get your ass out from behind that car, and get the hell out of here?"

Organ poachers. Probably not licensed, no matter what they said. The Zone was a fertile hunting ground for them. On any given night, the gangs would leave enough meat lying in the gutters to keep an industrious team of freelancers in business.

The two men in the background swung another body into the back of the van. A cloud of displaced nitrogen vapor gushed out of the doors.

"What's it going to be, asshole?" the amplified voice asked. "You can walk away now, no harm, no foul. But, if you want to try something fancy..."

The implied threat hung in the air.

I didn't trust him, but I didn't really have a lot of choice, either. I couldn't spend the night hunkered behind that car, and I had no reason to even think about trying to shoot it out with them.

I slid the Blackhart into its holster. "Okay," I said. "I'm walking away." I stood up slowly, keeping my hands in view.

His rifle tracked me as I walked back the way I'd come. Despite his assurances, the muscles in my back didn't relax until I had safely turned the corner.

I had to circle three blocks out of my way to get back around to Alameda and headed toward home again.

My detour took me close to Wong's Italian Pizza. I decided to stop in for dinner. Wong doesn't look very Italian, and neither does his pizza. But looks aside, his pepperoni and mushroom is a work of art. I ordered a medium. I could eat half tonight and maybe half for lunch tomorrow.

At one time, Wong's building had been a soy-burger restaurant, part of a now-defunct fast food chain whose trademark decor emphasized white ceramic tile framed by flamingo pink neon. A few of the neon tubes buzzed and flickered feebly, making the cobwebs in the corners of the ceiling look like tufts of cotton candy.

When the pizza was ready, I tucked the foil vacu-therm pouch under one arm and headed toward home.

I couldn't help thinking about the dead gang-bangers as I walked, the organ poachers ready to scoop up bodies before they even hit the sidewalk. Los Angeles was perfectly happy to kill you the second you took your finger off the button. And if LA didn't get you, some maniac like Aztec would gladly fill in.

He was out there somewhere, planning the next move in our little game of chess. That idea scared the hell out of me. The last move had left Joseph Takamura lying dead on the floor of a Lev, and Harvey Miller laid up in a trauma ward trying to breathe through a tube. I had no way of knowing for certain if William Holtzclaw's murder was part of this, but I strongly suspected that it was.

The body count was climbing, and a suspicion churning deep in my gut told me that it was going to get a lot uglier before this case was over. I shook my head and tried to think of something else.

About a block from home, the feeling hit me. Someone was following me.

I turned a corner without warning, plastered my back against the wall of a building, and drew the Blackhart. I set the foil pizza pouch on a windowsill, to free up my left hand.

The footsteps slowed as they approached my position. They stopped just short of my alley.

I wheeled around the corner and shoved the automatic into the face of my pursuer.

We stood for a second, both frozen.

It was Sonja.

She drew a deep breath and released it slowly. "It's generally considered bad luck to shoot the person who signs your paycheck."

I lowered the gun. "You haven't signed any paychecks yet."

Sonja smiled tentatively. "You haven't sent me a bill."

I slid the Blackhart into the shoulder holster. "An oversight that I can correct."

A frown crossed her features for a second. "Umm... could we go to your place now? I think I need to change my panties."

I retrieved my pizza and started walking toward the house. "What are you doing here?"

She took a couple of quick steps to catch up and fell into step beside me. "I wanted to talk to you."

"Why didn't you just call?"

"You never gave me your phone number. Besides, I was kind of hoping that you'd cook me dinner."

There was a hurt tone in her voice. I stopped walking and turned toward her. "Listen, I've had a really bad day."

"You're trembling." She stopped and turned to face me.

"What?"

She stepped closer and touched my cheek with the palm of her hand. "You're trembling."

I turned my face away and stared off toward the house. "Were you not paying attention just now? I came very close to blowing you away."

Sonja's hand touched my chin and guided my face back around toward hers. "You haven't carried a gun in years. Why are you suddenly ready to shoot at your own shadow?"

I broke away and started walking toward the house again. "Someone on the Lev tried to kill me today."

"Kill you?"

"A woman tried to drill a hole in my head with a laser. She missed and killed some poor old man instead."

I stopped at my front door and waited for House to scan me, a ritual that always reminded me of letting a dog sniff your hand. Half a second later, satisfied with the results of his ID scan, House opened the door and let us in.

I made a beeline for the kitchen, set the pizza pouch on the counter and started pawing through cabinets.

"In the cupboard over the sink." Sonja stood leaning against the sill of the door to the dining room.

"Thanks."

I opened the cabinet over the sink and retrieved the bottle of Cutty. It was two-thirds full. I unscrewed the cap and knocked back a healthy swallow. The warm scotch burned a furrow of heat down my throat. I took another swallow. "House, play some music."

"What would you like to hear, David?"

"I don't care. Pick something."

House's answer took the form of the opening strains of Jimmy Reed's *Bright Lights Big City*.

I started to hit the bottle a third time when I noticed that Sonja was reaching for it. I handed it to her. Her swallow was every bit as healthy as mine had been. She lowered the bottle. "What are we drinking to?"

"Who is Kurt Rieger?"

She handed me the bottle. "He's head of Information Systems Research at Gebhardt-Wulkan Informatik."

I set the bottle on the counter beside the pizza and lit a cigarette. "Do you know him?"

"I've met him," she said.

"Did he use his influence to get GWI to accept Michael's indenture?"

"What does this have to do with anything?"

"I don't know yet," I said. "But I'm going to find out. You could save me some time by telling me yourself. Did Rieger influence the decision to accept Michael's indenture?"

Sonja nodded once.

"Why would he do that? What was so special about Michael that Kurt Rieger would pull strings for him?"

"I told you, Michael was a topnotch software engineer. Rieger wanted him."

"Bullshit," I said. "GWI's Contract Indenture Board was scared of Michael's brain tumor. They were avoiding him like poison."

I drew a lung full of smoke and exhaled loudly. "Rieger wanted to sleep with you, didn't he?"

She met my stare. "What if he did? I'm a whore, remember? I sleep with people for money. In case you haven't figured it out, that's what whores do. And, if I can do it for money, why shouldn't I do it to save my brother's life?"

She jerked her gaze away from mine. "What do you care, anyway?"

Good question. Why *did* it bother me so much? She was entitled to screw anybody she wanted.

"So you did go to bed with Rieger?"

"You're goddamned right I did. I fucked his brains out. Are you happy?"

"Well, that blows one theory."

She picked up the bottle and unscrewed the cap. There was ice in her voice. "What theory?"

"One of Michael's coworkers is convinced that Rieger prefers his girls a little younger."

Sonja took a deep swallow and shoved the bottle toward me. "What does that make me, an old lady?"

"No," I said. "I mean a *lot* younger."

She made a face. "You mean little girls? That's sick."

I took a swallow and nodded. "Can't argue with that. Doesn't matter though. If Rieger's attracted to you, his tastes are probably pretty healthy."

"Is that supposed to be some kind of sideways apology?"

I handed her the Cutty and opened the refrigerator. "What do you want with your pizza?"

She pushed the door of the refrigerator closed in front of my face. "You do that a lot, don't you?"

"I do what?"

"You change the subject when somebody asks you a question you don't like."

I pushed her arm gently to the side and reopened the refrigerator. "How about a salad?"

She sighed. "Sounds wonderful."

"Good. Will you toss it? I need a shower."

She nodded.

"Everything you need should be in the refrigerator. If you have trouble finding anything, ask House."

Sonja nodded absently. She was staring at me.

"What's wrong?"

She pointed to my left ear. "Is that from the laser?"

I touched my ear. The cauterized edge of the missing crescent of flesh stung like hell when my fingertips brushed it. "Yeah."

She turned away quickly. "Oh David, I'm sorry. I had no idea it was going to be this dangerous."

"Well, you can't expect Aztec to sit quietly and wait for me to track her down."

"Her? You think that woman who tried to kill you might have been Aztec?"

"I don't know," I said. "There was a woman in the video store when Michael bought his holo-camera. From her description, she might be the same woman who tried to kill me on the Lev today."

Sonja looked thoughtful. "Aztec, a woman?"

I pulled off my jacket and shrugged out of the shoulder holster. "Of course, even if it was the same woman, we can't overlook the other possibility."

"Which is?"

"That the woman is working with Aztec. And, if there are two of them, there might be five. This thing could be bigger than we thought."

CHAPTER 11

Between the pizza, the shower and fresh clothes, when I left my house two hours later, I felt pretty human again.

Sonja decided to wait for me. I left her curled up on my sofa, exploring an extinct style of music called the Blues.

When I walked out the door, she was trying on John Lee Hooker's *The Motor City is Burning*. She was beginning to appreciate the difference between notes strung together by expert software agents, and music written by men and women who felt it in the marrow of their bones. I envied her contented smile of discovery.

At twenty after nine, the Zone was in high gear. I worked my way through the street crowd on Santa Fe Avenue, watching the hookers closely, looking for the youngest face that I could find.

"It's comin'!" a voice screamed. "The Convergence is comin', and woe be unto us if we ain't ready!"

I looked in the direction of the voice. A scarecrow of a man lurched and staggered up the sidewalk, shaking his bony fists and spraying saliva as he shouted.

I'd seen him before, dozens of times. He was easily in his seventies. No one knew his real name, but everyone called him Nostradamus because he predicted death, destruction, and earth-shattering conspiracies on something approaching a three-minute cycle.

Wherever he went, the crowd parted and let him through. I couldn't blame them for that. I'd been close to him before; he reeked of dried urine and sweat. I watched him wobble up the street, yelling dire prophecies until his manic cries faded into the distance.

The Convergence... Where had I heard that before? It took me a couple of seconds to figure it out. The graffiti on the Lev. *Prepare for the Convergence.* Pretty much what Nostradamus had just been shouting. If he was picking it up, it was probably something weirdly religious.

I turned my attention back to my search for the youngest hooker on the street.

She turned out to be extremely pretty and about sixteen years old, seventeen at the outside. She flashed me a smile. Her teeth were perfect. "Hey Mister, you wanna try something really different?"

"What do you have in mind?" I asked.

The top two buttons on her turquoise blouse were open. Every few seconds, I flicked my eyes down to glance at her cleavage because that's what she'd expect a potential john to do.

She pulled long honey-colored hair back from her right temple. There was a platinum alloy jack set flush into the side of her head.

"Neural feedback loop," she said. "I can plug you right into my sensorium. You'll feel everything I feel. Ever wonder how good you are in bed? There's only one way you can find out for sure. When I get off, you're gonna know it."

Suddenly, I got a really powerful visual: young Ms. Perfect Teeth lying in an alley with a hole carved in her chest where her heart used to be. She couldn't be more than a year or two older than Paula Chapel, the oldest known victim. Two years ago, when the killings had started, she would have been just about the right age to attract the killer's attention.

I shook my head. "I like my girls young."

She cocked her pretty head to one side and pursed her lips in a pout. "How old do I look? I'm only sixteen."

"Sorry," I said. "You're at least two years too ripe for my tastes."

"I've got a friend," she said. "Her name is Jenny. I think you'll like her. She's almost thirteen and she *loves* older men."

I suppressed a shudder. It wouldn't be in character with the slime-ball I was portraying.

Ms. Perfect Teeth was looking over my shoulder, scanning the street for better prospects. "I can introduce you," she said absently. "For a price."

Again I swallowed my revulsion. I wondered if Ms. Perfect Teeth thought she was doing her friend Jenny a favor.

"No good," I said. "I like variety. I prefer to pick my girls."

I pulled out a wad of Euro-marks and slipped her a fifty. "You know of any clubs or houses that could provide a selection of girls the right age?"

"Not for fifty marks, I don't. For another fifty, maybe I know something."

I slipped her another bill.

She leaned close to my right ear and whispered. "There's a place outside."

"Outside?"

"Yeah. A club, outside the Domes, a couple of klicks east of South Lock. It's called the Poison Apple. Tell Teddy, the guy at the door, that you're *hungry for some candy*. It's sort of a code-word."

"Anything else?"

"Are you paying for something else?"

I shook my head.

"Then that's all."

She turned and walked away, switching her rump back and forth in an exaggerated fashion intended to make me regret having declined her hired affections.

I hadn't been outside the domes in so long that I'd gotten out of the habit of carrying protective gear. I'd have to stop somewhere and pick up supplies.

I walked South on Santa Fe, and turned left at Clarendon.

There was a 24-hour convenience store about two blocks from South Lock. It was one of those places where they don't actually let you inside. I stood in a booth and looked at the merchandise through a bulletproof plastic window. As I spotted the items I wanted, I read the code numbers off the attached placards and punched them into a menu keypad. Eye drops, ear drops, nose filters, and a can of solar block. I thought about contact lenses, but the generic one-size-fits-all type give me a headache after about five seconds. I decided on a pair of mirrored sunglasses instead. It might be dark now, but I had no way of knowing how long I was going to be outside.

I punched the *TOTAL* key. The purple LEDs at the top of the keypad read €m41.67. I punched the *BUY* key.

An old Vietnamese man appeared from behind a partition and glided around the store, gathering my selected items. He wore a gray carbon-laminate flak vest over a black silk robe. A well-used riot shotgun hung barrel-down across his back. Despite the cumbersome armor and shotgun, he moved with a boneless grace that suggested that gravity and inertia didn't apply to him.

We traded money for items through one of those bank-style sliding drawers that only open on one end at a time. The money went through first.

At South Lock, I sprayed the solar block on my exposed skin and squirted protective drops in my ears. I waited till last to do my eyes. I hate giving myself eye drops. I always blink at the wrong time and end up with half the bottle running down my cheeks. This time was no different.

I stood around wiping eye drops off my face and blinking myopically until my vision cleared up.

South Lock isn't really an airlock. It's more of a pollution trap: three short tunnels strung end-to-end through the concrete skirt of the dome's foundation, each tunnel beginning and ending with a revolving door.

The graffiti in the first tunnel was built up in layers, like geological strata; the cave paintings of modern culture.

The air in the first tunnel had some bite to it, a hint of things to come.

The graffiti in the second tunnel wasn't as heavy because the air was worse.

By the third tunnel, graffiti was scarce and the air was harsh enough to make me put in my nose filters.

I stepped through the final door and stood under the naked sky for the first time in years.

Even with the protection of the drops, the air stung my eyes. I made the mistake of breathing through my mouth. Once.

From somewhere to my right came the whine of an air filtration station, the high pitched scream of the wind-rams cutting through the theoretically soundproofed enclosures. Under the blue-white radiance of the dome's halogen-arc perimeter lights, the turbine enclosures looked like hundreds of huge cement coffins.

The ground vibrated with power as each of the fusion-driven turbines rammed a continuous column of air through five meters of staggered permeable-membranes, forcing filtered air into the dome.

Originally, the dome system had been designed as a closed loop ecology. Hydroponics tanks full of algae, the forest eco-modules, x-number of square kilometers of grass, and bushes, and trees. It was all supposed to generate enough oxygen and recycle enough carbon dioxide to keep our fair city humming along.

The air filtration stations had been installed later, after it had become clear that the system wasn't going to keep up with the demand. We needed the filtered air that the wind-ram turbines forced into the domes, because we needed to flush our air supply constantly.

The turbines were symbols of our inability to learn from our mistakes. It was not enough that we had fouled our planet and driven ourselves under the cover of plastic bubbles; we continued to pollute the air inside our domes with everything from chemical solvents to cigarette smoke. Even with clean fusion power at our fingertips, we continued to pollute.

A kilometer wide perimeter around the domes had been bulldozed flat, a featureless no-man's land broken only by the wind-rams. Outside the perimeter lay the rotting carcass of old Los Angeles. It bore little resemblance to the radioactive desert that had become so popular in late twentieth-century fiction. No savage mutants here, no sword-wielding telepathic warlords, and no huge-breasted Amazon warrior-women in steel brassieres. Just a dead city: houses, shopping centers, donut shops, garages, and office buildings, all gone to ruin.

People still lived out here. Not many, but some. Dropouts mostly, on the run from some corporate security group or other. It couldn't be much of a life, hiding from the sun, breathing tainted air, scrabbling for food.

I walked out past the brilliance of the perimeter lights and waited for my eyes to adjust to the darkness.

Gradually, details faded out of the shadows until I could see by the light of the stars, not well, but enough to keep from tripping over things. There were no street lights out here, just the occasional cooking fire on the other side of no-man's land.

The stars were brighter than I remembered and, somehow, colder.

I thought about going home for my night goggles, but decided against it. I wasn't planning anything serious; I just wanted to check out the Poison Apple and find out a little about Kurt Rieger's supposed hobby.

I put my back to South Lock, picked a fire in the distance that was more-or-less east of me and started walking.

Just on the other side of no-man's land, I found a paved road leading into the dead area. I followed it to the fire I was using as a landmark.

The fire turned out to be the carcass of a mini-van sitting in the parking lot of a gutted convenience store. It was an old style van, the kind with wheels.

Someone had packed the van full of old rubber tires and set it on fire. The burning tires gave off an oily black smoke. The smell was nauseating. From the looks of things, that van had been burned a lot of times. Maybe every night. Was it some kind of signal? A territory marker?

On the side wall of the store, someone had sprayed graffiti in red glow-paint. Huge scrawled letters assured me that the Headhunterz were going to eat my brain.

I didn't much like the sound of that. It might just be some idiot screwing around. Then again, it might be some three-meter tall psychopath with a machete.

I pulled out the Blackhart. Maybe a bit of an overreaction. Then again, maybe not.

I followed a side street in an easterly direction and tried sincerely to grow eyes in the back of my head. I'd been out here before, but not in years and never alone at night.

A couple of blocks farther on, I came to another fire. A car this time, packed with burning tires just like the van. I kept moving.

Periodically, I heard things in the darkness, sometimes close to the street, sometimes not.

I drew an imaginary grid in my brain and tried to pinpoint the position of each sound, so that I could shoot if I had to.

Four blocks and two car fires later, I found the Poison Apple.

The building had started life as a fire station. The front wall was an enormous expanse of brick, interrupted by four huge metal garage doors and one smaller door at the extreme right end. The entire structure, including the doors, was covered by an airbrush mural of a primeval forest, perhaps intended to suggest the Garden of Eden. Woven into the forest tapestry were numerous scenes of graphic sexual acts, unvaryingly showing adult men and women coupling with little boys and girls.

A concealed laser painted the words 'Poison Apple' on the brick above the entrance door in glowing apple-green letters.

The entire area around the club was brightly lit, an island of electric light surrounded by an ocean of darkness.

To the left of the building was a large fenced-in parking lot. The fences were topped with razor wire. I could see at least three guards patrolling the lot, all of them armed as conspicuously as an LAPD Tactical Squad. There were enough high priced hover-cars and limos parked inside to warrant the expense.

I stood in front of the club and tried to swallow. My mouth was as dry as cotton. I suppose I must have suspected that places like this existed, but I had never been slapped in the face with the reality of it before.

Coming here had been a bad idea. I didn't know if I could walk in that door and hobnob with a bunch of child molesters. I became intensely conscious of the butt of the 12mm cradled in my right palm. I don't know how long I stood there fighting the urge to walk into that club and shoot every one of those sick bastards. I'd be doing future generations a favor by cleaning up the gene pool.

Eventually, I slowed my breathing to something resembling normal, put away the Blackhart, and walked up to the entrance.

To my surprise, the door wasn't locked. I opened it and stepped through into a short hallway ending in another door. The hall was a combination buffer zone/pollution trap. Two huge vents exchanged outside air for filtered inside air.

Standing between me and the second door was a two-and-a-half-meter tall homicidal maniac wedged into an off-the-rack suit. The suit made no attempt to conceal either of his two shoulder holsters. This must be Teddy.

He looked at me expectantly.

I realized that my mouth was nearly too dry to speak. "I'm ah... hungry for some candy," I said.

Teddy looked at me like I was an insect to be stepped on, but he stood to one side and opened the inner door for me.

I stepped past him into the club.

The Garden of Eden motif was continued inside. Ten circular dance platforms were equally spaced around the outer walls. Male and female dancers in varying stages of undress bumped and ground on the platforms to the throbbing rhythm of a psycho-rock tune with a driving beat. The oldest of the dancers was about thirteen, the youngest perhaps eight.

A chill ran down my back. I shook it off and tried to smile. I was supposed to be enjoying myself. The false grin felt wooden on my face.

I sauntered over to the horseshoe-shaped bar and ordered a gin and tonic. They were well stocked with Cutty, but I didn't want to indulge in any sort of personal pleasure in this place. I hated gin. Maybe I was symbolically punishing myself for belonging to a species capable of supporting a fetish this demented.

The drink was tiny and cost €m50. I took a little sip and tried not to cringe.

I looked around the room. There were about forty customers. Most were men, but there were a few women. At a guess, I'd say there were nearly twice that many children, counting the dancers.

I tried to burn the faces of each of the customers into my brain. God help any of them I ever caught in a dark alley.

There were no empty tables, so I stayed at the bar. I made eye contact with a girl of about twelve, and patted the top of the stool next to mine.

She bounced across the room and plopped down on that stool with the same gangly lack of grace you'd expect to find in any twelve-year-old. Her pink baby-doll nightie and pigtails were no doubt meant to paint a picture of prepubescent innocence. Just the right kind of bait to attract the pedophile crowd.

She gave me her best little-girl smile. "Hi, I'm Minda," she said. "What's your name?"

I swallowed a sip of gin and tonic. "Pete."

Minda dropped her hand to my knee and squeezed. "You need some company?"

I tried to keep smiling. "Okay."

Minda said, "I've never seen you before."

"It's my first time."

She showed me her dimples. "Do you think I'm pretty?"

"Very," I said.

She glanced around the room. "Prettier than the other girls?"

I nodded. "You're the prettiest girl in the room."

"Do you think I should wear makeup?"

"No."

To her mind, we had apparently made enough small talk to constitute an introduction. She slid her hand a little farther up my thigh and squeezed again. "Want to go see my room?"

"Maybe in a few minutes."

"Don't you like me?"

"I like you a lot," I said. "But right now, I'm looking for Mr. Rieger. Could you point him out for me?"

Minda's body tensed. "Who?" Her attempt at a casual tone of voice was markedly exaggerated.

I watched her. I couldn't be certain if she was reacting to Rieger's name, or to the fact that I was asking questions in a place where none were supposed to be asked.

"Mr. Rieger," I said. "Has he been in tonight?"

Minda's eyebrows went up in an overstated display of innocence. "Don't know him."

"Are you certain?"

"I'm sure," Minda said. She narrowed her eyes. "Are you a cop?"

"No," I said.

"Do you have a gun?"

I decided to tell the truth. If Minda wasn't too shy to fondle a strange man's thigh, she definitely wouldn't balk at feeling around for a gun. "Yes," I said.

"Can I see it?"

"Not right now."

Minda exhaled through her nose. "I think you are a cop. I'm gonna have to call Teddy. It's the rules."

I shook my head. "I'm not a cop. I promise."

She turned her head and looked at me out of the corner of her eye. "Can you prove it?"

"How do I do that?"

She tugged the neckline of her nightie away from her chest and held it out like a tent, exposing the tiny swellings of her breasts. "Touch my titties."

She had me. If I refused her offer, it would prove to her that I was a cop. Not only would I not get any of the answers I'd come for, but I'd almost certainly have to take on Teddy the Gorilla just to get out of there alive.

I tried to wiggle out of her trap. "I don't like to touch," I said. "That's not what I'm into. I like to watch."

"Sure," Minda said. Her voice had that all-knowing tone that only children can generate. "You can't touch me, can you? That would be against the law, because I'm under age."

Well, it wasn't like I would be violating a virgin. This was a path that she'd been down many times. I slid my hand into the opening she'd created in her nightie. Her skin was cool, still padded with baby fat.

When my fingers brushed her nipple, she closed her eyes and pulled my hand tight against her breast as though it was the most delicious sensation she'd ever felt. Her performance was way over the top.

I left my hand in place for a few seconds and then pulled it away. "See?" I said. "I'm not a cop."

She opened her eyes and let the neckline of her nightie fall back into place. Her left hand dropped to my lap and gave my crotch a squeeze. "I'm glad," she said. "Are you mad at me for saying that?"

"No."

Minda grabbed one of her own pigtails and held the end of it under her nose like a mustache. She giggled. "Are you sure? It's okay if you're mad. I know I've been a bad girl. Does Papa want to spank?"

"Let's talk about Rieger first."

Again, Minda seemed to flinch at the sound of his name. "I told you, I never heard of no Kurt Rieger."

"Then how did you know his first name?"

She squinted. "What?"

"I never mentioned his first name," I said. "You filled in that blank yourself."

She scanned the faces of the other customers. "I have to find somebody to take me up to my room. I don't want to get in trouble."

I pulled two twenties out of my pocket and tucked them into the neckline of her nightie. "You don't like Mr. Rieger very much do you?"

Minda stared at me without speaking. I added two more twenties.

She made a face and shook her head. "He's scary," she said. "He likes..." Her voice trailed off.

"He likes what?"

"He *hurts* his girls. Bad sometimes."

I took a sip of gin and didn't even try to pretend that I liked it. "I take it we're talking something a little rougher than *'Papa spank'*."

She nodded. "And he doesn't like scar-babies either."

"What's a scar-baby?"

Minda looked at me like I was incredibly naive. "Somebody that *likes* to get hurt." She nodded across the room toward an even younger girl wearing a corset and fishnet stockings. The girl's arms and shoulders were striped with welts. "Kimberly's a scar-baby." She pointed to a young teenage boy wearing only a cowboy hat and chaps. "Trevor is too."

"You're not a scar-baby, are you?"

Minda grimaced. "Uh-uh. Spank and tickle is okay. But I don't like the scary stuff."

"Does Rieger want you?"

She nodded. "I'm scared of him. He likes that. And I don't want to get hurt. He likes that too."

She looked into my eyes and squeezed my crotch again. "Can we go play now?"

I lifted her hand off my crotch and stood up. "Not tonight, Minda. I have to take care of some business."

I handed her another twenty and walked out. Lisa Caldwell's nasty little rumor was grounded in truth.

CHAPTER 12

Sonja was asleep on the sofa when I got home, an open book lying across her chest. I lifted the book gently, and read the gold-leafed Frankfort lettering down the spine. It was one of Maggie's favorites: a tattered old hardcover edition of *Frankenstein*, by Mary Shelley.

Sonja had already plowed through the first quarter of the book. I turned it so that I could see the pages she'd marked. My eyes picked a passage at random:

> *The different accidents of life are not so changeable as the feelings of human nature. I had worked hard for nearly two years, for the sole purpose of infusing life into an inanimate body. For this, I had deprived myself of rest and health. I had desired it with an ardour that far exceeded moderation; but now that I had finished, the beauty of the dream had vanished, and breathless horror and disgust filled my heart.*

I closed the book and set it on the end table near Sonja's head. I started to wake her up, and tell her that it was time to go home, but I stopped short. I smiled to myself. Let *her* oversleep for a change. And if she happened to miss an appointment, well...

I dug out a light blanket and spread it over her. She mumbled something softly and snuggled into a more comfortable position.

I shed my jacket and the shoulder rig, hung them in the hall closet and headed for the showers. I could still feel the chemical sting on my skin from the air outside the dome.

Fifteen minutes later, freshly scrubbed and bone tired, I looked in on Sonja again. She was still in the same position.

I stopped in the hall bathroom to make sure that the toilet seat was down, and told House to leave the bathroom light on at half-intensity so that Sonja could find it if she needed to.

I crawled into my bed and drifted off myself.

And dreamed...

I peek around the corner of an up-ended trash dumpster. Even by moonlight, I can see that the warehouse has been deserted for years. About a third of the corrugated steel roof panels are missing, leaving a rusted skeleton of rafters. Two stories above street level, a bank of small windows runs the length of the outer walls. The glass is gone from most of the frames, giving the building the look of a mouth with missing teeth.

A huge sliding door in the west wall is open, allowing me a glimpse inside. Moonlight streams through the missing roof panels, mottling the darkness inside the warehouse with irregular pools of light. Puddles of stagnant water speckle the cracked cement floor. A few meters inside the door, to the right, is a mound of rusted steel that might have once been a forklift. The floor surrounding the forklift glistens with the rainbow sheen of ancient oil on damp pavement.

The air is cool, swollen with the promise of rain. The damp wind blows through holes in the corrugated steel walls, making sounds like a pipe organ.

Somewhere, a door or window slams open and closed rhythmically in the wind.

"I'm in position." Maggie's whispered voice crackles softly in the left earphone of my commset. She is crouched in concealment behind an abandoned car on the east side of the building.

I key my throat mike. "Ready when you are, Magpie."

Her voice carries a lilt of amusement. "You're ready again? So soon? I thought we had solved that problem, for a while anyway. Hmmmm... come to think of it, I'm ready too. What say we have a quick talk with our Mr. Rubac first?"

I chuckle softly. "On your signal, Princess."

Somewhere inside the warehouse is Martin Rubac. Every once in a while I can hear a splash and a muffled curse as he finds another stagnant puddle in the darkness.

By now, he has undoubtedly learned that the warehouse has only two doors. I've already checked two sides of the building. There are a lot of holes and cracks in the rusty steel, but none large enough for a man to crawl through, especially a fat man like Rubac.

Maggie has checked the other two sides.

Mr. Rubac is bottled up. He's only got two exits and we have them both covered. He's trapped and that makes him dangerous.

Dangerous, not the first word I would ordinarily choose to describe a short, fat Certified Public Accountant. Still, he's trapped and even timid animals lash out when their backs are in the corner.

I run my left hand over the 12mm Blackhart in my right fist, ensuring that the slide lock and safety are disengaged. I don't expect to use it, but I prefer to hedge my bets.

"Three... two... one... Go!" Maggie's voice in my left ear urges me out of concealment.

I cover the distance to the open door in seconds, slide around the frame and plaster my back to the wall, my automatic tracing a protective arc in the darkness.

Rapid footsteps on cement tell me that Maggie has done the same on the opposite side of the building. "I'm in."

I key my mike. "In."

Nothing but silence. We wait.

"Mr. Rubac?" Maggie's voice is loud enough to be heard anywhere in the warehouse. "Mr. Rubac, we're not here to hurt you."

Her voice is soothing, sincere. No answer. Somewhere, water drips slowly into a puddle.

"Mr. Rubac, my partner and I just want to ask you a few questions. You don't even have to show yourself, just talk to us."

No answer.

"Mr. Rubac, we represent Chang and Kellerman. They don't want to hurt you either. They just want to know what happened to the Ginnsburg files."

No answer. I imagine that I can hear labored breathing in the darkness.

"If you return the files, they won't even press charges."

Something moves in the north end of the warehouse. A scraping, metallic sound.

"Advance slowly." Maggie's voice is a whisper in my ear.

I move carefully toward the northern end of the building, straining in the gloom to see debris that could trip me up, or puddles that could give away my position.

Another noise, still north of me. It seems to come from above eye level. He might be climbing something. I start to include the ceiling in my visual survey. If Rubac is trying to climb out through a window or the roof, maybe I can catch his silhouette against the moonlight.

"Hold." Maggie's whisper in my ear again.

I stop, still straining to see in the near darkness.

"Mr. Rubac, theft of information is a crime. You could go to jail, maybe even get brainlocked for this. Just tell us where the Ginnsburg files are, and we can all go home."

Another sound overhead and to the north. No answer.

"We are not the police, but we will turn you over to them if we have to."

No answer. This time I really can hear his breathing. He is definitely above us and close.

I whisper into my throat mike, telling Maggie.

"I know," she says. "Stay where you are. I'm going to circle to the right."

I wait.

A few seconds later, there's a noise to my right: a sort of clang that echoes through the empty warehouse. I hear Maggie stumble.

I abandon the mike and speak aloud. "Maggie, are you okay?"

"I'm all right. I tripped, that's all. I'm standing on some sort of grating." She's still using the commset.

From my right, I hear a subtle creaking as Maggie takes a few experimental steps out onto the grating. It reminds me of the groaning you hear in the rafters of an old house when it settles.

I key my throat mike. "Maggie, get back on the cement."

"No, I'm all right," she says. "It seems to be pretty sturdy. I think it'll support my weight."

"What is it?"

"I don't know. Maybe the cover to some sort of grease-pit or something."

I don't like it. "Get off of it," I say. "Get back on the cement."

"No, it's okay. I'm..."

The creaking gets louder, growing in pitch and intensity until it becomes a continuous wail.

"Maggie! Get out of there!"

The wail rises to a shriek, as tortured metal begins to give way.

"Maggie!"

I cram the Blackhart into my shoulder holster and run toward the sound. Rubac is forgotten. I trip, over some unseen obstruction, sprawling headlong on the wet cement.

The left side of my face and the knuckles of my right hand sting viciously. The fall has cost me some skin. I hear the commset clatter away somewhere into the darkness.

I ignore it, find my way to my feet and start running again.

"David!"

A splash, from somewhere in front of me, then several more. From the sound of it, the grating is disintegrating, large sections falling into water somewhere below.

"Oh my god! Daviiiid!!!"

The fear in Maggie's voice scares me more than anything; I've never known her to panic before.

I am close to the ragged edge of panic myself. For the first time in my life, I understand the meaning of the word "helpless." Something is happening to my wife and I can't even find her.

A splash, followed by thrashing as Maggie hits the water and tries to struggle back to the surface. Two or three louder splashes tell me that several pieces of grating hit the water a split second after Maggie.

I'm close enough to see the grating in the darkness. The pit seems to be about ten meters wide. The far side is lost in shadow; I can't tell how long it is. Most of the grate panels are tilted at crazy angles. A lot of sections are missing entirely. I can't see Maggie at all.

"Maggie!"

I grab the closest grate and use it to slide down into the pit.

The water is hot; a coating of oily scum covers the surface.

Somewhere down there, Maggie is struggling, churning the water.

My feet don't touch the bottom. I have no idea how deep this thing is.

I slosh through the hot soup, pulling myself along hand-over-hand, using what pieces of the grating I can. Some of the panels support my weight. More than once, I have to thrash out of the way of a grate that breaks loose and crashes into the pit.

I should be close by now. Maggie can't be very far away.

The oily sludge burns my eyes so badly that I can barely keep them open.

I reach for another handhold and then jerk my hand back as a ragged piece of steel slices my left thumb nearly to the bone.

Maggie is below me now, I can feel the turbulence she's causing.

I take a breath and dive, both hands extended to feel for Maggie and to protect my head.

I swim blindly; visibility is zero. I find nothing but pieces of grating.

Lack of air forces me back to the surface. I repeat the dive again and again.

My third or fourth time down, something slips neatly between my groping hands and strikes the right side of my forehead a glancing blow. Somehow, I manage to surface without drowning. My head is reeling. My lungs feel raw from the polluted air I've been breathing in great gasps.

I dive again.

I'm about to turn toward the surface when I realize that something has snagged my left pants leg. I reach down to free the snag and find Maggie's fingers wrapped tightly around the fabric of my pants.

Maggie! Frantically, I pull her hand loose from my pants and try to follow her arm down to the rest of her. I'm stopped at her wrist by a grating. She's trapped under it.

It's time to surface for air. I ignore the burning in my lungs and feel my way to the edge of the grate. When I get to the edge, I try to slip under but I run into the wall.

I try to shift the grate. It won't budge; it's wedged against the wall by several other pieces of wreckage. I try to brace against the wall and gain a little leverage.

It's not going to go.

I increase the power to my arms.

It's still not going to go.

More power, I don't know where it comes from. Something gives in my left shoulder and I begin to see colored fireworks inside my eyeballs. I'm totally out of air now, but the grate is starting to move. A little... a little more... Come on, you Son of a Bitch, move. Farther...

The opening is big enough. I dive under it and grope around in the ink black water until my questing fingers latch onto Maggie's jacket.

Her body has gone totally limp. I wrap an arm under her breasts and try to fight my way back to the surface.

I don't know what keeps me from passing out before we get there. Every grate and twisted metal stanchion in the pit manages to sneak between us and that lovely slick of oily scum that marks the boundary between water and air. My lungs can't even remember what oxygen feels like.

I'm losing it.

Maggie. Concentrate on Maggie. Do it for Maggie, boy. She's been without air a hell of a lot longer than you have.

We're not going to make it. We're not going...

My head breaks the surface and I gulp down a huge gout of air. Polluted or not, the stale air or the warehouse is the most delicious thing that I have ever tasted.

I fight to get Maggie's head above water.

It seems to take forever to pull both of us out of that hellish hole. The entire time, I'm extremely conscious of the fact that Maggie isn't breathing.

I lay her limp body on the cement as gently as I can and check for breathing or a pulse. She has neither.

I give her mouth a quick sweep for foreign objects and then start CPR. Come on girl, you can do it. Come on.

She's not responding. Come on Maggie, breathe. Do it for me, baby.

Oh God, don't do this to me. PLEASE God...

"David. Come on David, wake up."

I kept my eyes closed, trying to will Maggie to life. "Please God... Please..."

"David, it's just a dream. A nightmare. Open your eyes."

I felt warm fingers on the side of my face, felt them smear the hot tears that squeezed out from between my tightly shut eyelids.

Recognition filtered slowly into my brain. Sonja. She drew me into her arms, pulled my head against her chest and rocked me gently, the way a mother soothes a frightened child.

I lay there, clinging to her, listening to the quiet rhythm of her heartbeat.

My eyes stayed closed. Somehow, if I didn't open them, the dream wasn't over. And if the dream wasn't over, it might not be too late to go back and do something differently. I didn't know what, but *something*. If I could do something differently, the *right* thing, the dream wouldn't end the way the reality had: with my wife lying dead in my arms on the floor of an abandoned warehouse.

Eventually, the feeling faded and I became self conscious about crying in the arms of some woman I barely knew.

I opened my eyes and stared at the ceiling. "I need a drink." I started to sit up.

Sonja pulled me back down onto the bed. "You do *not* need a drink. You need to finish crying."

"I'm finished." I stifled a sniff.

"I don't think so," she said. "You're not going to be finished crying until you cut it loose. You've got to let her go, David."

"I *have* let her go," I said. "She's dead."

"Then why haven't you been able to say good-bye?"

"I can't say good-bye," I said "I couldn't. I wanted to, but I couldn't."

"Why couldn't you?"

I realized that I was on the verge of breaking down again. I had to stop this. I couldn't let this person, this stranger, so far inside my guard. "Look, Maggie is dead, okay? She's gone. It doesn't matter anymore."

"Please don't do that, David." Sonja's voice was gently insistent. "Don't slip behind that wall that you've built for yourself. Right now, you're close to something, maybe closer than you've been in years. Don't run away from it. Face it. It's a question you need to answer. If not to me, then at least to yourself. Why couldn't you say good-bye?"

Fresh tears welled up in my eyes. I squeezed them shut again. "They took her from me. The bastards took her away."

"Who took her?"

"I carried her," I said. "I could barely walk; my hands were sliced up; one of my ankles was twisted, but I carried her. I don't know how, but I carried her from that... from a warehouse about three klicks Northeast of Dome 10, all the way to the Humboldt Street Lock."

I stopped, swallowing several times before continuing. "A taxi rushed us both to the hospital. I had a concussion. I'd taken a pretty good knock on the head. I guess I passed out in the cab on the way to the emergency room. I woke up in a hospital bed three days later, ranting and raving, demanding to know about Maggie. Eventually, one of the doctors worked up the nerve to tell me what I already knew: Maggie had been dead on arrival. I could have dealt with that. I could have *learned* to deal with it, but they... they..."

"What, David? What did they do?"

I lay there breathing heavily, trying to gain control of my voice.

"They said it wasn't their fault. It was a computer virus. Maggie... Maggie's body was on ice, in deep freeze. Her file was supposed to have been marked 'hold.' But they said the virus scrambled a lot of their data. Somehow, Maggie's file got re-flagged."

"Re-flagged?"

"For... organ barter. An organ clinic bought her whole body while I was lying unconscious in that hospital bed. I tried to track it down, but the clinic broke up her body and sold it for parts before I got there."

Sonja hugged me tighter. "Oh, David. I'm so sorry."

"They wouldn't even give me the names of the organ recipients. They said it would be illegal. The hospital was terrified that I was going to sue, or drag their name through the media. They offered me a big settlement. I didn't want their damn money, but their lawyers kept after me until I accepted it. I didn't want their goddamn money. I wanted to say good-bye to my wife and the bastards even took *that* away from me."

I was sobbing uncontrollably now.

Sonja rocked me until my sobs faded into quiet breathing.

After a long while, I slipped into the temporary oblivion of dreamless sleep.

My room was still dark when I woke again. I followed a slow path up the mountain from oblivion to waking. Someone was touching me. I had an erection. A gentle scraping of teeth on skin and the feather light flicker of a hot tongue told me that Sonja was also awake.

I heard the hissing rush of waves washing up on a beach, quietly at first, but growing until the sound became the pounding of surf.

Sonja's fingers danced on my skin.

The walls of my room cycled slowly from darkness to an indigo suffused glow. The projection unfolded until the bedroom was invisible behind a starlit beach.

I felt a sharp pang in my chest. House was running our favorite program, Maggie's and mine. The one she'd always liked to make love by.

I mumbled something, trying to tell House to stop the program, to shut it off, but I was not quite awake enough to speak.

"Shhhhhh..." One of Sonja's hands came up to cover my mouth. "Go back to sleep." Her weight shifted as she moved to straddle me. Her hand slid away from my mouth. Her lips replaced the hand.

The tip of her tongue parted my lips and slipped into my mouth at the exact instant that she impaled herself upon me. She froze for a second, totally motionless and then her body shuddered almost as strongly as mine did. She began to rock back and forth, slowly to begin with, then gathering speed.

At first, I attempted to match her rhythm, meet her thrusts with my counter-thrusts, but she used her thighs to clamp my legs to the bed.

The message was clear. This was *her* ride. I was a passenger.

I experimented and discovered that Sonja's unspoken rule against movement didn't seem to apply to my hands or mouth. I began a journey of exploration across the unknown landscape of her upper body.

My hands discovered and cherished a myriad of wonderful things: the tiny ridge of bone between her shoulder blades, the shallow dimples at the small of her back.

Her nipples awoke and hardened under the attentions of my tongue and fingers.

It couldn't last long; there was no way. I hadn't been with a woman in years. Besides, she was a professional. Surely her techniques and instincts would coax an orgasm out of me faster than any amateur could.

But it did last, longer than I would have dreamed possible and then, longer still. She wasn't teasing me; she was trying with all her heart to push me over the edge, but something in me resisted. I couldn't quite turn loose. She kept me dancing on the razor's edge for longer than I would have dreamed was humanly possible.

Her own breathing became faster. She began to make little self-concerned grunts, the kind of sound you never make when you think someone else can hear you.

She didn't squeal when she came, or yell, or moan, or any of the things you'd expect from someone whose job depended on a flair for theatrics in bed. Instead, she gripped me tighter than I have ever felt before and continued to ride me as she ran through a series of unbelievable contractions.

Then, she leaned down and bit my shoulder. *Hard.*

The dam gave way. Four years of sexual repression reached up and broke free like a butterfly tearing its way out of a cocoon.

Her lips fused themselves to my mouth as we both rode our orgasms down to a dizzying stop.

She lay her head on my shoulder and fell asleep on top of me. In a little while, I drifted off for the third time that night.

CHAPTER 13

Sonja stood in the doorway to the kitchen, leaning against the frame. She yawned and rubbed the sleep from her eyes. She was wrapped in one of my old robes. Her hair was a mess, her face swollen. She looked beautiful.

I tried to smile. "Morning, sleepyhead. What are you doing up?"

She stretched languidly. "I smelled bacon frying." She yawned again. "What time is it?"

I forked a couple of strips of bacon out of the pan and onto a plate. "Breakfast time. Why? Got an appointment?"

She shook her head, throwing her mop of auburn hair into artful disarray. "I don't do appointments anymore."

"What does that mean?"

She picked up a slice of bacon, looked at both sides of it and nibbled the end off. "It means what it sounds like."

She swallowed the bacon. "I figure it like this: you're either going to solve this case, or you're not. If you *do*, Michael's insurance will pay off his indenture. With my savings, what's left over should be enough for me to retire on, if I'm careful. If you *don't* solve the case, I'm going to have a steady job for at least the next decade, so there's no point in maintaining my clientele."

She shrugged. "I'm betting on you. I think you can solve this thing." She took another bite of bacon.

I picked up both of our plates and moved them to the kitchen table. "I appreciate the vote of confidence. Would you grab a couple of glasses and that pitcher of O.J. from the fridge?"

While Sonja poured the orange juice, I went after coffee and silverware.

We ate in near silence. A half-dozen times I thought of something to say, only to chop it off a second before I opened my mouth.

What was she? A client? My boss? A new friend? A lover? How was I supposed to feel towards her? How should I act?

The heat of her body burned fresh in my mind, the flutter of her eyelashes against my cheek. Half of me wanted to rip that robe off her and screw her brains out on the kitchen floor.

116

The other half of me whispered that what had happened last night had been a betrayal, an act of unfaithfulness to Maggie's memory. And that this woman had no right to be sitting in Maggie's chair, wearing my robe the way that Maggie would have done.

Sonja watched me from across the table, chewing slowly. She swallowed. "I have some things to take care of this morning. Can I come by later? Say, early evening?"

I had a mouth full of egg. I nodded and swallowed. "Of course."

I hesitated a second, then made a decision. "House, Sonja has the run of the place when I'm not here. Store her in your permanent files."

"Certainly, David."

Sonja looked startled. "You don't have to do that."

"What if you show up when I'm not around? This isn't exactly a good neighborhood. I'm not worried; House is smart enough to keep you out of serious trouble."

She looked up at the ceiling. "I won't give you any cause for alarm, House. I promise."

"I appreciate that, Ms. Winter."

"Call me Sonja. Please."

"Very well, Sonja."

I stood up and went in search of cigarettes. My quest led me to the hall closet and my jacket. When I returned, I leaned against the kitchen doorframe the way Sonja had earlier.

I lit a cigarette. "I'm not sure what my plans are this morning. At this stage of the game, I'm basically waiting for a couple of people to return my calls."

Sonja started carrying dishes to the sink.

"Don't worry about those," I said. "House will get them. Won't you House?"

"Of course, David."

The door to a service alcove slid open and House's kitchen drone rolled across the tile on soft yellow neoprene wheels, and began clearing away the dishes and loading them into the dishwasher.

The drone looked nothing at all like the anthropomorphic metal-man robots in adventure vids. It was about three-quarters my height, topped with two vid cameras mounted on a gantry crane. Its tubular alloy arms were long and multi-jointed. I'd always thought that it looked clumsy, but House guided it through its work routines with an economical grace that rivaled a zero-g ballet.

Sonja stared at the remote. "House is quite the talented fellow."

"Absolutely."

"Are there more of those around?"

"Several."

Sonja's eyebrows drew together. "Why haven't I seen any before now?"

"House is programmed to keep his drones out of sight. Unless I tell him otherwise, he's very careful to clean rooms only when they aren't occupied. If you did happen to walk into a room where one of his remotes was working, House would stop it where it stood to avoid distracting you."

"Why did this one come out now?"

I shrugged. "House probably interpreted my last remark as an order to get off his butt and do the dishes now."

House spoke up. "I'm sorry, David. Have I misinterpreted your instructions? Shall I put the drone away?"

I shook my head. "Don't sweat it, House." I put out the cigarette. "I'm for the showers."

Sonja looked at her watch. "I need to get dressed and get going."

We were both making excuses to put some distance between ourselves. There was an awkward tension between us that needed time to iron itself out.

Something had happened last night, something important. I had closed a few old doors and, maybe, opened a few new ones. I just wasn't sure that I was ready to take out my soul and examine it in the bright light of day.

After Sonja had dressed and collected her things, I walked her to the door. "Thank you."

She looked up into my eyes. "For what?"

"For last night," I said. "For understanding. For a lot of things."

She kissed me lightly on the lips and smiled. "Any time, David. Thank *you*."

The instant the door closed behind her, I realized that I didn't want to be alone after all. I stared at the door and listened to the soft click of her heels against the sidewalk, a gentle cadence fading into the distance. There was still time to catch her, to ask her to come back.

She would come; I was almost certain of that. She didn't have any appointments; she'd already told me so. Her list of things-to-do was a polite fiction, intended to give me the solitude she'd seen me groping for.

I tore my eyes away from the door. There were things to do. Not big things, or important things, but things that would keep me busy. With any luck, I could occupy myself enough so that I wouldn't feel the emptiness she'd left in my house.

I skipped my shower and spent the morning shooting trids of *No Resurrection.* I chain-smoked two-thirds of a pack of cigarettes while House played Wolf Cooper's *Iron Horse Blues* over and over again. The alternating growl and croon of the old man's voice was loud enough that I couldn't hear the sound of my own breathing.

When I finish a new piece, I usually shoot a dozen or so trids, and forward a couple of the best to Susan Blayne, at Blayne Galleries. This time, I couldn't seem to stop. I would shoot seven or eight frames, shift my position, and then shoot another set. When I'd shot from every angle I could think of, I would order House to adjust the lighting, and I'd start again.

The electronic bleat of the holo-camera's discharging condensers punctuated Wolf's syrup-coated sandpaper vocals.

"Whoa... Cold steel rails..." [BLEAT]
"Takin' me for one last ride..." [BLEAT]
"Lord, I just can't stop cryin'." [BLEAT]

I shot a chip full of images, loaded another chip in the camera and kept going. My shots started coming faster, closer together, until they began to lose any semblance of composition, or planning.

Some part of me heard the phone ringing over the pounding of the blues tune and the staccato bleating of my camera. I ignored it.

I orbited the sculpture like a predator circling wounded prey. The button beneath my finger became a trigger. I fired the holo-camera at my helpless target again, and again, and again.

Some unknown time later, I found myself sitting cross-legged on the floor of my workshop. The holo-camera dangled from my right wrist by its strap. At least a dozen data chips lay scattered across the floor. Some of them were damaged, crushed and ground into the tile by the heels of my shoes during my insane little dance around the sculpture.

My ears were ringing from the unaccustomed silence. The music had stopped. At some point, I must have told House to shut it off, but I couldn't recall having done so. The skin on my cheeks was stiff from the salt of dried tears that I didn't remember crying.

I climbed to my feet; my knees were a little unstable at first. I walked out of the workshop without looking at the piece on the pedestal. "House?"

"Yes, David?"

"Take care of the mess in there, will you?"

"Of course, David."

"And sort through the data chips on the floor. Some of them are damaged, but you should be able to salvage the others. Have a look at the trids that I shot and see if you can find two or three good ones. Don't worry about composition; just look for shots that are well lit, well focused, and are close enough to being centered that you can crop the edges to center them up."

"Of course, David. Anything else?"

"Yeah, transmit holos of the best shots to Susan Blayne. Maybe she can sell that damn thing and get it out of my house."

"Of course, David."

Susan was pretty much a one-horse setup, but she seemed to have a knack for finding buyers for my pieces. My work never sold enough to make me rich or popular, but it sold often enough to make me feel like an artist. Susan had worked pretty hard for me in the past. She deserved better than whatever House could rustle off the floor, but I didn't want to look at the piece anymore.

I might never look at it again. I recognized it now for what it was: a symbol of my own weakness; tangible evidence that I couldn't lay my past to rest.

"By the way, David, you have a phone message. Shall I play it back?"

"Not right now. I'm heading for the showers. You can do something else for me, though. When you're transmitting those holos to Susan, shoot copies to Rico Martinez at Falcon's Nest. I think the piece is garbage, but I promised Rico that he could get a look at it."

"Very well, David. What shower program shall I run today?"

"No program, House. No illusions. Just turn on the hot water. My brain can use a dose of reality for a change."

CHAPTER 14

After my shower, I fixed myself a cup of coffee. I had puttered away the morning feeling sorry for myself. Now it was time to turn my attention back to the case. I decided to start with the phone message. I asked House to play it back, and project it on the wall. John's image appeared, a grin on his face. "Sarge, I was hoping to catch you at home. You've got to come see me... today!" His grin got even bigger. "I'm serious! When you get this message, drop what you're doing and come see me. I've got something to show you."

He reached out to terminate the connection. My wall sizzled with static.

I left the Zone and caught a taxi to Dome 17. Neuro-Tech Robotics occupied a five-story office block on Hawthorne Boulevard. Almost exactly as wide as it was tall, the building was a nearly featureless cube of cement. Its windows were small, widely-spaced rectangles of bulletproof polycarbon, designed for industrial security rather than beauty.

The overall effect was not just boring, but *industrial-strength* boring. John had tried hiring an architectural firm to give the building a face-lift, but the simulations for every design proposal came out looking like a cube with fancy do-dads glued on.

John often cited it as proof of one of the basic truths of life: You can't polish a turd.

Short of huge investments and major construction, during daylight hours, Neuro-Tech's headquarters would remain a big, ugly cube. After the sun went down, it was a different matter entirely. Holographic-facades were cheap; once John had projectors installed, changing his building's image became a simple matter of swapping software. At night, it could become Cinderella's castle, if he wanted it to.

Right now, though, the sun was up and John's building was as ugly as a mud fence.

I walked through the front doors and into the lobby. It was very nicely furnished: plush emerald carpeting, and teak furniture with brass fittings. John's attempt to compensate for the building's dowdy exterior, I guess.

121

Ms. Carlen, the receptionist, sat behind a curved teak counter. She looked up when I walked in, smiled, and waved me straight through to the elevators. "Good afternoon, Mr. Stalin. He's in his apartment, if you'd like to go up."

I nodded and smiled as I walked by. "Thank you."

I stepped into the elevator and asked it to take me to the top floor.

As expected, I was greeted by the flat mechanical voice of Mainframe, John's AI. "You have requested access to a controlled area. Please stare at the black glass data plate set into the wall to your left. There will be a brief flash of red light. You will feel no pain or discomfort."

I complied.

The burst of red laser light startled my eyes. You can brace your body for a punch, but there's no way to steel your pupils against a sudden change in lighting.

"Retinal imaging and pattern matching are satisfactory," the computer voice said. "Please place the palm of either hand against the glass."

I put my left hand against the panel and the laser behind the glass flared again briefly.

"Mr. Stalin, my hard object scanner has detected a handgun on your person. I must advise you that any attempt to discharge your weapon inside this building will bring an immediate and lethal response from installed security systems. Please understand that this is a statement of security posture and is not intended as a threat. Our insurance coverage requires a verbal acknowledgment. Do you understand the preceding warning?"

"Yes."

The doors whispered closed and the elevator ascended rapidly. "Thank you for your cooperation."

"You're quite welcome," I said.

The elevator sighed to a stop and the doors opened. I stepped through into the foyer outside John's apartment.

A sentry robot stood watch over the carved hardwood doors leading to John's chambers. The robot was an armored, industrial-strength version of one of House's service drones, with some kind of air-powered Gatling gun thrown in for good measure.

The doors opened almost immediately. I couldn't see John, but I could hear his voice. "Sarge, come on in."

The carved doors swung shut behind me a second after I stepped through them into John's suite.

The decor was distinctly modern. Eggshell white walls, plush carpets in muted blues, and ergonomic furniture done in smoked glass, gray kid leather, and chrome.

"I'm out on the balcony." John's voice came from an intercom speaker near the front doors.

I walked to the sliding glass door that led to the balcony and slid it open.

I was about to step out onto the balcony when I caught sight of a picture sitting on an oval glass table to the left of the sliding door. It was a trid, a shot of Maggie that I'd never seen before. I found myself staring at it. Her chestnut brown hair was pulled around to one side of her neck and cascaded over her right shoulder gypsy fashion. Her chin was raised ever so slightly, making her pug nose seem turned up at the end. She'd been looking directly into the camera, and I couldn't shake the feeling that she was staring at me.

Her wide almond-shaped eyes were a deep shade of brown that lightened to golden amber near the centers. This gave them a beautifully feral quality that never failed to take my breath away.

It had been her eyes that I'd spotted first. John and I had been carousing, alphabet drinking our way up the bars on Sunset Strip. It was about three months after Argentina, and we were still war heroes and the lords of all creation.

We were somewhere around the *G's*, or maybe the *H's*, when I caught sight of the most incredible eyes I'd ever seen from across a crowded room. I was fast approaching that critical threshold where not falling down becomes an act of concentration, but this woman's raw animal gaze cut through the fog of my alcohol like a laser. I felt my mouth go dry.

I could hear John staggering around behind me, the servomotors that powered his exoskeleton whining crazily as the microprocessor strapped to his waist tried to interpret the addled signals coming from his alcohol-soaked brain.

He had still liked the exoskeleton back then. It was a symbol of his bravery, a dueling scar, something for bragging, and for raising the maternal instinct in women. And best of all, it was temporary. He was still confident that the Army's bio-tech labs were just around the corner from repairing the notch that the perimeter laser had carved in his spinal cord. It was still a joke to him.

That would change.

He lumbered up behind me and threw an arm around my shoulder. "Sergeant Davey, what kind of drink starts with the letter *'I'*?"

I didn't answer; I couldn't. I was hypnotized.

John struggled to locate the object of my stare. He spotted her and made a show of craning his neck to get a better look.

"Good eye," he said, and elbowed me conspiratorially. "I think I'm going to get me some of that."

No, I thought. No, you're not.

"Hey Sarge, are you lost?" John's voice came in from the balcony.

I wrenched my eyes away from Maggie's picture and stepped through the sliding door.

The balcony was a huge sundeck stretching across the west face of the building: John's only real addition to the exterior architecture. It was bright out there; I stood squinting until I found my mirrored sunglasses and slipped them on.

John's chair was stationed about three meters from the railing, to the right of the door. He wore a blue kimono made of raw silk. His gold-rimmed mirror shades looked a lot like mine, only his frames were probably real gold.

I walked across the balcony and stood by his chair. "Okay Wise Guy, what's this miraculous thing that you can't wait to show me?"

John handed me a trid. "Check this out."

The trid was a digital artist's conception of a dark castle: a shadowy stone fortress, complete with crumbling walls and twisted battlements. It was a dead-on rendering of the haunted castle from a B-horror vid. All that was missing was the werewolf or mad scientist of your choice.

I handed the trid back to John. "What's this?"

"It's my new holo-facade. I just got the software this morning. That ought to give this place some atmosphere when the sun goes down, don't you think?"

I shrugged. "Beats the hell out of that Taj Mahal thing you've been running lately."

I pulled out a cigarette and lit it. "That's not really what you called me up here to see, is it?"

John tried to look hurt, an attempt made unsuccessful by the fact that his grin was almost as big as his head.

"Come on," I said. "Out with it. What's the big surprise?"

John stood up and walked to the railing. "No surprise," he said. "I just wanted some company." He raised his hands in a depreciative gesture. The blue silk of his kimono stood out in sharp contrast to the pale skin of his legs.

It took a second to hit me. When it did, the cigarette fell out of my mouth and bounced off the floor of the balcony. His legs... They were bare. No carbon-laminate ribbing. No exoskeleton. He was standing without his exoskeleton!

"Holy shit. You're..."

"Walking?" he asked. He nodded vigorously. "That is a fact."

"What happened to your exo?"

"The Beast is in the closet, where it belongs."

"This is great. This is *fantastic*! Jesus. I don't know what to say."

John laughed. "You don't have to say anything," he said. "But I get to say, '*I told you so*'."

I grinned back at him. "You go right ahead and say it."

"Proves what I've been telling you all along," John said, "If you throw enough money around, Medical Technology can accomplish *anything*."

He walked to the edge of the balcony and leaned on the railing. "I told you I had something to show you. What do you think?"

"I'm overwhelmed! You should have told me, I'd have brought a bottle of champagne."

"Funny you should mention that," John said. He looked toward the door and whistled.

The door slid open and a service drone rolled out onto the balcony. It glided silently to a spot a meter or so from John. Cradled in its tubular alloy arms were an ice-filled champagne bucket and two slender fluted glasses.

John reached into the bucket and fished out a dark green bottle swaddled in a white linen napkin. He held the bottle up and read the label. "Dom Perignon twenty-two. A good year, I think." He went to work on the cork.

"Since when do you know anything about champagne?"

"I don't," he said. "But that's what the kid at the wine shop told me."

"I'll bet it cost a bundle."

"It did." John grimaced, as though opening the bottle was strenuous work. The cork popped loudly and sweet-smelling white foam gushed from the neck of the bottle and splattered onto the balcony.

I plucked the glasses from the drone's manipulators and tried to maneuver one of them under the bottle to catch the foam.

John moved the bottle away. "You're supposed to let that go," he said. "It's part of the champagne ritual."

"Really?"

He cocked one eyebrow theatrically and shrugged. "Hell if I know, but it sounded good, didn't it?"

When most of the foaming action had died down, John poured champagne into both of our glasses and set the bottle back into the bucket. He looked at the drone. "Don't go anywhere with that."

I handed John a glass and we both raised them in salute. "You get to pick the toast," he said. "After all, you paid for the bubbly."

"I did?"

"Yep. I had the bill sent to you. I knew you wouldn't mind, considering the occasion."

"I had no idea that I was such a generous guy," I said.

John nodded. "You are, old buddy. Trust me on this. You *are*."

I thought for a couple of seconds and then raised my glass a few centimeters higher. "To dreams," I said. "And to miracles."

"Dreams and miracles," John repeated.

I don't know much about champagne, but this seemed unbelievably rich and smooth.

John lowered his glass and nodded. "Not bad." He leaned close and whispered out of the side of his mouth, "you should have brought beer."

"I don't know what came over me."

John reached for the champagne bucket. "Next time you'll know better."

I grinned. "God, I can't believe this. I am so happy for you."

"Me too," John said.

When the last of the champagne was gone, John dropped the empty bottle and glasses into the bucket and shooed the drone away.

"Okay," I said. "Give it up. How did you do it?"

John looked at the retreating robot. "Same way I always do it. I said 'go away,' and it went away."

I exhaled through my nose in mock exasperation. "You know what I'm talking about."

"Oh *that*," John said. "The neural shunt. We finally got it to work right."

"The neural shunt?"

John nodded. "Yep. I let them put a chip in my head and wires down my backbone. You didn't think I was going to allow all that hardware to go to waste, did you?"

"Wait a second," I said. "What about the seizures?"

John stared up toward the apex of the dome. "Not a problem any more."

I stood beside him and tried to follow his gaze. A trio of radon-scavengers circled in the distance like robotic vultures, black mylar delta-wings gliding in looping spirals under the soaring arch of the dome.

John pointed up to them. "Have you ever seen a radon-scavenger up close?"

I shook my head.

"There's not much to one," John said. "It's like a plastic bat-wing with a thousand tiny electrodes glued to it. As it glides through the air, the electrodes generate some kind of electrostatic field that attracts radon particles."

I waited for him to continue. I had no idea where he was going with this.

After a few seconds, he sighed heavily. "They've got little processors on board. Computers that only know how to do two things: sniff out concentrations of radon, and find their way home to charging stations when their power runs low."

"I don't mean to be rude," I said, "but is this a science lesson, or are you trying to tell me something?"

"I'm like those bats," he said. "Completely single-minded. I've been trying to get my legs back for so long that I don't know what else to do with my life."

He continued staring up at the dome for a few seconds and then turned back to face me suddenly. There was a strange look in his eyes. He quickly covered it up with a grin. "Enough about me. How's the case going, Sarge?"

"I'm still poking around," I said.

"Be careful where you poke," John said. "You've got somebody's attention."

"What do you mean?"

"I watch the net pretty closely." He rubbed absently at his thigh. "And lately, your name has been popping up all over the place. Somebody is making some very oblique inquiries about you."

"Any idea who that somebody might be?"

John shook his head. "I chased down one of the go-fetch routines they're using and tried to backtrack it to the source. No luck. It changed color maybe thirty times in ten microseconds."

"Changed color?"

"Like a chameleon," John said. "A good piece of intruder-ware changes its appearance to match its environment. Makes it harder for guard-dog routines to spot and kill it. This one pretended to be everything from a bank credit check, to a police subpoena, to a random power surge.

Once it even changed into a call-back from one of those psychic advisor hot lines. I managed to copy a little piece of it. It was a really clean piece of code, cutting-edge. My guess is, it was written by one monster of an AI."

"Who would be likely to own an AI capable of writing something like that?"

"It could be the Yakuza," he said. "They could certainly field the software and the hardware. Have you done anything to piss off the Sons of the Rising Sun lately?"

I shook my head. "It's probably not the Yak. If they were unhappy with me, they wouldn't keep it a secret; I'd just wake up one morning and find my head in the refrigerator between the leftover meat loaf and the bologna."

"How about somebody corporate?"

I thought about it. Somebody with corporate influence who might have cause to check me out. Somebody with a lot of processing power at his disposal. I could only think of one candidate: Kurt Rieger.

I shrugged. "Maybe."

"LAPD is interested in you too," John said. "They've got your name flagged in connection with a couple of murder cases. You're listed as a material witness in one case, and an ex-suspect in the other. Their inquiries weren't too hard to spot. Their idea of camouflage is a rubber nose-and-glasses."

"Thanks, John. I appreciate you watching my back."

He looked out over the city. "No problem, Sarge."

I was digging out another cigarette when I remembered something I'd been meaning to ask about. "Hey partner, do you remember that Turing Scion that you made of Maggie?"

"Sure," John said. "I remember."

"Do you still have it?"

John looked at me. "Of course. Do you want to talk to her? I could go plug it in."

I shook my head. "I don't want to talk to it," I said. "In fact, I'd appreciate it if you would erase that damned thing."

John cocked his head to the side. "Erase it? I can't erase it. That Scion is all that's left of her. Everything that she ever *was* is in there."

"She's dead," I said. "It's time we let her go."

John shook his head. "I can't do that, Sarge. It would be like … murder."

"Bullshit," I said. "It's just a recording. One's and zero's. It isn't Maggie."

"I plug her in sometimes," John said. "You should talk to her. She misses you."

"Maggie is dead," I said. My voice had an edge to it that I hadn't intended.

"What if she had been in a Lev accident?" John asked. "And she was still alive, but she had lost her legs."

"It's not the same thing," I said.

"It *is* the same thing," he said. "Did I stop being *me* when I was strapped into that damned exoskeleton?"

"Don't do this, John. Please."

"What if it were her arms *and* her legs? Would she still be Maggie?"

"Yes," I said quietly. "She would still be Maggie."

John said, "It's the same principle. She's lost her body, but her soul is alive."

"Don't," I said.

"She's *still* Maggie," he insisted.

I stared at him for a couple of seconds, but I couldn't think of anything to say that wouldn't have made it worse. I turned toward the sliding glass door. "I think I'd better go."

As I rode the elevator down, I tried not to think about Maggie. The Turing Scion was a hideous thing to me, but it wasn't the worst. Her body was out there. Pieces of her were walking around as spare parts grafted onto other people's bodies.

Every minute of every day, I carried around the secret fear that I might someday meet the organ recipient who'd bought Maggie's eyes. I'd just be walking down the street, and I'd suddenly find Maggie's beautiful animal eyes staring at me from out of someone else's face.

It was almost enough to keep me off the streets.

CHAPTER 15

‖‖ ‖ ‖ ‖ ‖‖‖ ‖ ‖ ‖‖ ‖ ‖ ‖ ‖‖ ‖‖ ‖‖‖ ‖‖ ‖ ‖ ‖‖‖‖ ‖ ‖‖ ‖ ‖‖ ‖‖

When I got home, there was a message waiting for me. Tommy Mailo had finished his analysis of Michael Winter's suicide recording.

I looked at my watch. It was a little after five. I called to let Tommy know that I was on my way.

I walked into Alphatronics just as Henry was letting himself out the front door. He jerked a thumb toward the curtain. "Tommy's in the back," he said. "He'll let you out when you're done."

I walked into the shop and Henry locked the door behind me. He waved at me through the window and walked away.

I parted the curtain and stepped into the back of the store. Three-quarters of the room was dedicated to shelves stacked with stock. The remaining space contained a steel workbench crammed with electronic test equipment, cabling, and boxes full of repair parts. On the far end sat two holo-decks and a flat-screen video monitor.

Tommy was perched on a high stool, eating a take-out burger and drinking a Coke from a plastic squeeze bulb. He looked up when I walked in. "Mr. Stalin, come on back."

I smiled as I covered the distance to his workbench. "It's David."

He grinned back at me. "Okay, David."

I pulled up another stool and sat down. "What have you got?"

Tommy turned back to his equipment. "I started out with a vectorscan," he said. "It told me that my recording was a copy, but we already knew that."

I nodded. "What did you find out? Has the recording been altered?"

Tommy shook his head. "No way. The Hitachi 1250 has a scan rate of seventy-five frames per second. That's Industry Standard. I used my computer to tally the number of frames in that recording. There are exactly 112,500 frames recorded on that chip. Twenty minutes worth of video data. Every frame is in sequential order. There are none missing, and there aren't any extras. No way has that recording been edited."

"Okay," I said. "So the recording is clean. What else did you find out?"

Tommy took a bite from his burger and chewed vigorously. He started talking again before he swallowed. "I started looking for evidence that someone else was in the room, like you told me."

"Did you come up with anything?"

He flipped a switch and a still frame of Michael and the hotel room sizzled into view above one of the decks. "I used a 3-D raytracing routine," Tommy said. "I told my system where the light sources in the room were, including reflective surfaces like those mirrors on the wall, and the chrome chassis on that blood test machine." He pointed to various images in the scene. "Once the software knows where the light is coming from, it knows what size and shape the shadows are going to be. I set up a routine to cancel any shadow caused by the guy who killed himself. Any shadow not accounted for by the furniture or the guy would have to be from someone else."

"Did you find any?"

He squirted a shot of Coke into his mouth to wash down the burger. "Nope. Every shadow in that recording came from a known source."

I sighed. "So there couldn't have possibly been another person in that room?"

Tommy shook his head rapidly. "I didn't say that. I just said I couldn't find any proof of it using shadow mapping. If our mystery person stayed well behind the camera and didn't have any light sources behind him, I wouldn't really expect to see any extra shadows."

He took another bite of the burger. This time he chewed and swallowed before continuing. "Next, I checked for reflections covering the area behind the camera. I went over the mirrored walls and the blood machine again. I came up dry. Whoever positioned that camera knew exactly what they were doing. It's like it was planned down to the millimeter."

"So there were no reflections?"

"Not at first," Tommy said. "I had the system check every frame, and then I checked them myself. The computer didn't get a fix on anything, but on *my* pass, I found this."

He punched a couple of keys, and the image of Michael jumped to life and fast forwarded to the part where he pulled the kitchen knife out of his pocket. Tommy slowed the recording to a crawl, and then stopped it. He watched a time code readout on his deck, and advanced the video frame-by-frame.

"Here." He used his keyboard to drag a wireframe box around the knife and enlarge it. The image of Michael's hand and the knife grew until it eclipsed the rest of the picture. By the time it stopped growing, the image was so grainy that it looked like abstract art. Tommy stroked the keyboard and the computer began enhancing the image.

When it reached maximum resolution, I could see the knife clearly. There, reflected in the carbon chrome blade, I could see a face. I couldn't see it clearly enough for positive identification, but I was certain that it was a woman. A woman with long dark hair.

"Is that her, Tommy? The woman who was in the shop when the camera was purchased?"

Tommy shrugged. "I can't tell for sure. Maybe. I think so."

"Can you increase the resolution any more?"

"Nope. This is as good as it gets."

"How about if you had better equipment? Or maybe a vid lab. Could they do it?"

"The limitation isn't my equipment or my training," Tommy said. "It's the camera that the recording was shot with."

"But you said the H-1250 was a good camera."

"It is, for a home video camera. But it isn't anywhere close to broadcast quality standards."

He shook his head. "The best equipment in the world won't pull out an image any cleaner than that, not even with the original chip."

"And that's the only frame in the recording that shows her face?"

"Yep. I'm sorry, but that's the best I can do."

"You did a great job, Tommy." I pulled out my wallet and handed Tommy a hundred marks. He accepted the money with a look of surprise and delight.

"You've earned it," I said. "You got me far more than I hoped for." I turned to leave.

"Wait a second," Tommy said. "There is one more thing, but I'm not really sure what it means."

He reached over and turned on the flat-screen monitor. After a few seconds, it warmed up and a two dimensional picture appeared: Michael Winter's left hand holding the gun to the side of his own head.

"This is going to look a little strange, since you're probably not used to seeing stuff in 2-D, but you can spot what I'm going to show you better on a monitor than in a hologram."

He fiddled with the controls on the second deck. "To save time, I've already enlarged and enhanced the part I want to show you. I've got this part of the recording isolated so we can loop back and look at it as many times as we want. Now, scope this out."

Tommy pressed a button. Michael's hand held the Glock to his head. His finger tightened visibly on the trigger and the recording looped back and started over again.

I watched it run through about five times. "I don't get it," I said finally. "What exactly am I looking for?"

Tommy punched a couple of more buttons. "Okay, let's slow it down a little."

I watched the scene in slow motion several times. "I must be blind, Tommy. What are you trying to show me?"

He pressed another button and a grid of fine red lines appeared on the screen, superimposed over the recording.

The image crawled by under the red grid. I still couldn't see what Tommy was aiming at. "Tommy, what... Wait a minute." The scene crawled by again. "Okay... okay, I've got you. His hand is wiggling."

I looked up at Tommy. He was nodding.

I shrugged. "So Winter had the shakes," I said. "I'd have the shakes too, if I was about to blow my own head off."

"Uh-uh," Tommy said. "Not the shakes. Keep watching."

He pointed at the screen. "See? The wrist keeps torquing back and forth. Each time it bends a little less, becomes a little steadier. After about a second, it stops altogether and steadies right out."

I watched the recording a few more times. "Okay, I see what you're talking about. Winter was making minute adjustments to the position of his gun hand. What does that mean?"

Tommy slurped the last of the Coke out of the squeeze bulb, sucking the soft plastic container until it collapsed upon itself. He pulled the bulb away from his lips with an audible pop and tossed it into a large plastic recycling bin. "I'm not sure what it means, but I know what it reminds me of."

He stood up and led me to a metal door set in the wall behind the stock shelves. On the other side of the door was a set of metal fire stairs. We climbed them to the roof.

The sun was low on the dome, but there was more than enough light to see by.

Three satellite dishes, two small and one large, formed a lopsided triangle on the rooftop.

Tommy walked over to the nearest of the small antennas. He consulted a red LED readout on the dish's motorized base. "Right now," he said, "this antenna is locked on Earlybird 21. I'm going to tell it to look for Satcom 63. Watch this."

He punched a code into a keypad on the unit's base. The dish drove around to a new angle, centered up and locked into a new position.

"There. Did you see that?"

"What?"

"Here, let me do it again. Watch closely." He keyed a new sequence and the dish powered back around to its original position.

Not only did I see it, but this time I heard it. When the antenna neared its new position, it went through a brief series of oscillations before locking up on the new angle. Its movements were remarkably similar to the recorded movements of Michael Winter's gun hand. I could hear the motor changing pitch as it adjusted the position of the dish in ever smaller increments. Like Michael's hand, the dish steadied out in less than a second.

I pulled out a cigarette and shot Tommy a questioning glance. He nodded, so I lit it.

"Okay, I see the similarity," I said. "What's causing it?"

"In the satellite dish, it's error nulling. You find it a lot in old analog electronics. You know anything about electronics?"

I shook my head.

Tommy sighed. "Okay, let's try it this way. You ever have somebody scratch your back? They never hit the right spot the first time, do they? You have to kind of guide them to it. 'A little to the right... No, too far! Back the other way a little... Okay, now down a little bit.' See what I'm saying?"

I nodded.

"So, analog error nulling routines are like that. The control circuit talks to the servomotor. 'Go left... Good... Keep going... Whoops! Too far! Back to the right a little... Uh-oh, too much, move left just a hair... Great! That's it! That's the spot!' The overshoot-and-correction cycle causes the servomotor to oscillate. If the circuit is tweaked properly, the oscillations will get progressively smaller, until they stop entirely. The servomotor has driven the load to the correct position. The whole thing happens pretty fast."

I blew a billow of smoke. "So what does this have to do with Michael Winter's gun?"

Tommy looked down at his feet. "You're gonna laugh."

"No I won't Tommy. If you've got a theory, I want to hear it, no matter how crazy it sounds."

"Is it possible... Is there any way to be sure that the man in that vid was really a man? Could he have been like, a robot or something?"

The question took me by surprise. "Why? What makes you think he wasn't human?"

Tommy cleared his throat softly. "I think his gun hand was running an error nulling routine, like a machine would. It's like the gun had to be pointed at just the perfect angle, and his hand kept following the error signal until it nulled out. The hand steadied up after it was in exactly the right spot. It's like it wasn't human."

I thought about it. It certainly sounded absurd, but then, this entire case was pretty weird.

"I don't think so, Tommy. I've seen about two thousand pages of police paperwork on the body, including the coroner's report. I even have a vid of the autopsy. Those guys ran DNA sequencing, retinal imaging, dental work comparisons, and a hundred other tests. I don't think a robot or an android—if such a thing were possible—could fool that many people."

"Maybe they're all in on it," Tommy said. "Maybe they all know he was an android, or whatever, and they faked the data to make him look human."

"I don't see how the data could all be fake," I said. "It would take thirty or forty people working together to make it airtight. That many people can't keep a secret for very long."

"Maybe you're right," Tommy said. "But I can't help thinking that the entire recording feels like a setup. Like it's an illusion."

I nodded absently and tilted my head to look at the dome.

The setting sun was a ruddy ball, reflected a hundred times in the faceted panels above us. Its rays dappled the underside of the dome with a kaleidoscope of shifting colors. It was a magnificent sunset, a vibrant watercolor painting in breathtaking neon blues, pinks, purples and yellows.

Tommy followed my gaze. "It's the pollution," he said.

"Huh?"

"The sunset. It looks that way because of the pollution. That's what my pop says, anyway. He says before the Industrial Revolution, sunsets and sunrises weren't anything special. Like the pollution suspended in the atmosphere is supposed to refract the light or something. You think that's true?"

I shrugged. "Not something I know a lot about," I admitted. "But, if your dad says it's true, it probably is. He strikes me as a pretty smart guy."

Tommy nodded without looking at me.

I wondered if it really were true. I hoped not. *This sunset is brought to you by the Westchem Corporation.* Jesus. Even the pretty colors of the sunset were a mask covering something ugly.

I felt like I was standing at the center of a maelstrom of fakery and misdirection. Murders that looked like suicides. Vid recordings that were contrived, but not edited. Disappearing cigarettes. Software agents that changed color like chameleons. Illusions. And behind every one of them lay death.

I took another hit from my cigarette and stared up through the dome at the poisoned watercolor sky.

CHAPTER 16

||| || | | ||||| | || ||| | || | || ||| ||| | || | ||||| || ||| | ||| |||

"I'm sorry, what did you say?" I could tell that Sonja was talking, but over the roar of the shower and the rain forest special effects, I couldn't make out her words.

She slid the shower door open and stepped in, fully dressed. The warm spray instantly soaked her to the skin. Her casually pretty blouse and skirt went from modest to provocatively clinging in the space of one heartbeat. "I said I'm cooking tonight. Do you like spaghetti?"

"Are you crazy?"

She ran her hands through her soaking wet mop of hair and pulled it away from her face. A stray lock drew itself up into a tiny curl above her right eyebrow. "Crazy? That's a distinct possibility."

She glanced around at the forest projection. "A jungle? I've never done this in a jungle before. I think I like the idea." She slipped her arms around me and snuggled up to my chest.

"Listen, Sonja. I don't think I'm ready for this."

She bit my neck gently and raked the fingernails of one hand slowly down the front of my body. "I don't think you're ready for it either, so you just go ahead and finish your shower. You take care of your business, and I'll take care of mine. You'll never even know I'm here."

Part of me still resisted this closeness. A voice inside my head begged for more time. Time to understand the conflicting feelings bouncing around in my chest. Time to get used to the idea that my life had not ended with Maggie's.

Another part of me very much wanted Sonja to stay.

I tilted her face up toward mine and kissed her, gently at first, then with growing ferocity. The night before, I'd been the passenger. This time, it was my turn to drive.

I took my time undressing her, peeling her soaking clothes off a piece at a time and dropping them to the floor of the shower stall.

I teased her unmercifully, pushing her to the brink and then backing off at the last second. After a half dozen near misses, she was positively frantic. "Stop teasing you bastard. Stop... teasing..."

At the instant that she passed the point of no return, I told House to switch the water from hot to icy cold. She screamed loud enough to make my ears ring, but she never stopped moving. Her feet locked around the backs of my calves, she shuddered and bucked and rode my body like a wild creature.

When it was over, she clung to me under the freezing spray of water. Every few seconds, her body convulsed a tiny bit. It occurred to me that she might be crying, but I couldn't tell for certain.

Sonja's spaghetti sauce was excellent. I might have used a few more onions and a bit less oregano, but I didn't say so. All in all, I liked her recipe better than mine and I told her as much.

Dinner was relaxed. The tension that had stretched between us at breakfast was gone, perhaps washed down my shower drain.

Afterward, we curled up in the den on my pit sofa and listened to Rusty Parker's *No Sense in Hangin' Around.* In my opinion, Rusty was one of only a handful of gifted blues artists born in the twenty-first century.

His smoky acoustic guitar wove back and forth across the bass rumble of his voice with an ease that was almost serpentine. As far as I was concerned, he was one of the few remaining signs that there was still hope for the human race.

Sonja snuggled up under my arm and lay her head on my chest like it was the most natural thing in the world. She closed her eyes. "What made you decide to be a sculptor?"

I thought for a long time before answering. "That's not an easy question," I said. "Until Maggie died, I never even thought about it. I certainly never considered myself artistic. But Maggie's death left this void in my chest, and the only things that I could find to fill it with were anger and booze."

Sonja's hand found mine and gave it a gentle squeeze.

"You can only pretend to be dead for so long," I said. "Then you've got to either open your eyes and stand up, or roll over and finish dying."

I shrugged. "Sculpting offered me a lot of things that I needed. It was hard work. It kept my hands busy, and my mind. It gave me a sense of direction. A reason for climbing out of bed in the morning. Looking back, it was probably therapy more than anything. And then, one day I sold one of my pieces, and that opened up another entire dimension I hadn't even considered. It's not about money, it's about making a difference—no matter how small—in someone else's life."

"How many pieces have you sold?"

"Eighteen," I said. "No, wait. Nineteen altogether."

"I'm trying to imagine how powerful that must feel," Sonja said. "Every day, people you don't even know look at your art, and it touches them. Maybe it makes them happy. Maybe it makes them sad, or lonely, or angry, but it touches them."

I nodded.

"I'm surprised that you came to it so late," Sonja said. "I've always thought that artists are born instead of made. That their talent sets them apart, even as children."

"Not me," I said. "When I was a kid, I couldn't even use finger paints."

Sonja stifled a giggle. "I'm trying to imagine David Stalin as a little boy. Did your friends call you Davey?"

"Joe."

"Joe? Your middle name is Joseph?"

"Uh-uh."

"Josephus?"

"Nope."

"Am I getting warm?"

"Ice cold. Try Alexander."

"Alexander? David Alexander Stalin. How do you get Joe out of that?"

I cocked my head just enough to relieve a crick in my neck. "John and I used to hang with this kid named Kevin Rojenco. His grandfather was always telling us horror stories about Joseph Stalin, this Soviet dictator who lived during the early twentieth century."

"Soviet? You mean Russian? I thought they were a monarchy, with a King or a Czar or something."

"They are," I said. "But before that, they tried out just about every kind of government you can imagine. In the end, I guess they went back to what worked the best. Anyway, Kevin thought it would be funny to call me Joe. It just sort of caught on."

"Sarge, and Joe. That's two nicknames. Any others that I should know about?"

I shook my head. "Just the two."

"Hmmm..." Sonja said. "Alexander... Alex. Can I call you that"

"No."

"Okay. Alex."

"What's *your* middle name?"

"Oh no," she said. "I'm not telling."

"Hey," I said. "Fair is fair. I showed you mine, now you show me yours."

"I'll be more than happy to show you mine any time you want, but I am *NOT* telling you my middle name."

"Fine," I said. "Be that way. You forget, Lady, I'm a professional snoop. Not only am I going to poke around in your personal affairs until I find out your middle name, but I'm going to bill you for it."

"You'll never find out," Sonja whispered. "It's the most carefully guarded secret of our time."

"I'll find out," I said. "I'll find out *all* of your dirty little secrets."

"You're not going to like some of them," she said.

"Which ones?"

"Well, for one thing, I'm really eighty-five years old."

"Oh, that. I already knew all about that. You carry it pretty well, but your age is starting to show."

"Oh yeah? Well how about this? I was born a man. I'm really a transsexual," she said in a teasing voice.

I made a show of yawning; she wasn't the only one who could tease. "I knew about that too. You've got a huge Adam's apple. That's a dead give-away, every time."

"Huge? Is that right?" She dug her fingers into my waist in search of my ticklish spots. It didn't take her long to find them.

I retaliated, quickly finding a place right under her ribs that drove her crazy.

It was shaping up into a tickle-fight of epic proportions when the phone rang.

I called for a truce.

She lay back on the sofa in a state of mock exhaustion. "Okay. You're safe for now, but I'm not done with you yet, Mister."

My breath was still coming hard when I answered the phone. I took it on visual.

"David?"

It took me a couple of seconds to recognize the caller. Lisa Caldwell had been beaten. Badly.

Her right eye was swollen completely shut and the left was nearly as bad. From the swelling and trickle of blood, I guessed that her nose was broken. Her lips were puffy and the lower one was split near the left corner of her mouth.

"David," she raised a plastic bag full of ice to the side of her face, "If you're not too busy, I could use a little company."

"Jesus, Lisa. Where are you?"

She touched her bruised cheek and winced. "I'm at home. Colosseum Apartments, unit thirty-four seventeen."

"Have you called the police?"

"No, David. No police."

"Lisa, you can't just..."

"No! No police and no hospitals. *Please*."

"You lie down," I said. "I'm on my way."

Lisa nodded feebly and terminated the connection.

I grabbed the Blackhart and my jacket out of the hall closet.

Sonja walked up behind me as I was strapping on the shoulder holster. "Can I come along? I know some first aid."

"There's a first aid kit under the sink in the hall bathroom."

She went after it. Over her shoulder she asked, "Have you got a flashlight? A small one, if possible."

"House, where's the small flashlight?"

"In the center kitchen drawer."

I went to the kitchen and grabbed it, flicked it on to test the batteries. I met Sonja at the door. "Do we need anything else?"

She shook her head.

"Let's go."

Colosseum Apartments turned out to be one of those faceless apartment stacks in Park La Brea, just about in the center of Dome 6. Dreary slabs of featureless gray concrete, devoid of life or character.

Sonja rang the bell.

I stood with my back to the apartment door and scanned the area. I didn't know who had roughed up Lisa, or even where it had happened, but if they were around somewhere, I wanted to know about it.

Lisa opened the door herself. It had three different types of alarms.

I wondered why she hadn't let the apartment AI answer the door.

The swelling in her face was worse. She leaned heavily against the wall without speaking.

"I hope you don't mind," I said. "I brought a friend."

"No, not at all. Come in." Her voice was weak, muffled by her bruised lips. Even so, her tone made it apparent that she *did* mind.

I couldn't help that. Ordinarily, I'd cut off my own arm before I'd spring an unexpected guest on someone. But Sonja claimed to have some medical training, and I figured that was a shade more important than social protocol.

Lisa stumbled as she backed away from the door to let us in. I grabbed her shoulders to keep her from falling and half-led/half-carried her to the couch. Not an easy task; she was a big woman.

She lay down very carefully, breathing in short cautious sips, testing for pain. There was no sign of the reactionary cringe that usually signals cracked ribs.

"Who did this to you?"

Sonja squeezed the top of my shoulder. "That can wait."

She slid between me and the couch. "Lisa, my name is Sonja. We met once at my brother Mike's apartment. Do you remember?"

Lisa's eyes were closed. She nodded weakly.

"Good. Now, let's have a look at you."

Sonja's voice was confident, her movements gentle but purposeful. "Can you open your eyes for me? Okay, that's good. Pick a spot on the ceiling and stare at it. I'm going to shine a little light in your eyes, okay?"

I'd had doctors do that same test on me a hundred times and I've never understood it. "What are you checking for?" I asked.

"Several things. Uneven pupil dilation might mean a concussion. I'm also checking for hyphema."

Lisa blinked. "Hi-what?"

"Hyphema. Blood trapped behind the cornea, the clear part of the eye that covers the iris. If blood collects there, it could mean a detached cornea."

She snapped off the light and squeezed Lisa's shoulder. "Don't worry, I don't see any serious signs. Now, follow my finger with your eyes. Good. Keep watching it."

Lisa tracked Sonja's finger. "How do you know so much about this stuff?"

"I was sort of a doctor, once."

"Sort of a doctor?" I asked. "How is it possible to be *sort of* a doctor?"

Sonja glared at me for a second. "I don't want to go into this right now."

She turned back to Lisa. "I'm going to have to touch your face," she said. "I need to check for fractures, especially around the cheekbones. It's going to hurt a little."

Lisa sucked in a deep breath and held it. "I'm ready."

Sonja's medical training was obviously a lot more extensive than my rusty first aid skills.

I didn't want to stand over her shoulder, so I passed the time giving Lisa's apartment the once-over. What the exterior lacked in character, the interior more than made up for. About half of the available wall space was covered by fake walnut shelves. The shelves were packed with book chips and little ceramic figurines.

I looked around the room, skimming book chip titles. Maybe a third of them were work-related: information systems theory, programming tutorials, that sort of thing. The rest were erotic romance novels with titles like *Love's Forbidden Journey* and *Stronger Pounds Thy Heart*.

The figurines turned out to be salt and pepper shakers in the shapes of animals, a lot of them extinct. Two horses, two dogs, two elephants, two monkeys, two tigers, two turtles, two kangaroos, two of just about everything. The pepper shaker giraffe had a cellophane tape bandage around his neck.

A corner of the front room was dominated by a work desk, complete with two computers and a massive stack of printer hardcopy.

Like the rest of the room, the desk was tidy. What little clutter there was looked too carefully arranged to be accidental. Something told me that it was pseudo-clutter, designed to relieve the impression of compulsive neatness.

"David."

I turned around.

Sonja held out a clear plastic bag full of water. "The ice is melted. Find the refrigerator and get some more, please."

I took the bag and went in search of the kitchen. The apartment wasn't big enough to hide it from me for long.

I opened the seal at the top of the plastic bag and poured the cold water down the sink.

My foot bumped against something on the floor, a blue plastic bowl. There were two of them, both tucked halfway under the little eave where the bottom of the kitchen cabinets overhung the floor. One of the bowls was empty, the other half full of water.

On the counter top by the sink was a strange looking plastic rack like the one my grandmother used to stack her dishes in to dry.

The refrigerator had one of those novelty voice boxes. When I opened the door to the freezer, the box oinked like a pig and asked if I was eating again.

The ice maker was hidden behind four cardboard tubs of gourmet ice cream and a stack of dieter's frozen dinners.

Why did Lisa bother with dieting at all? If she got her DNA tweaked a little, she could eat anything she wanted and be skinny as a rail. Was she allergic to viral DNA manipulation, like John? Or was it something else? A religious conviction, maybe?

Maggie had been that way about organ transplants. She'd been born in New Canaan, a Luddite colony down around Oceanside. One of those reclaim-the-Earth-smash-the-machines religious cults that lived like pioneers from the 1800's, and tried to breed pollution resistant crops.

Her father was a lay-preacher, a real hellfire-and-brimstone type who firmly believed that he was destined to sit at the right hand of God.

Maggie had grown up hating the Spartan lifestyle of the Luddites, trying to claw an existence out of the barren soil with only the kind of tools that they could make by hand. By her tenth birthday, she'd watched a dozen relatives and friends rot from cancers brought on by solar radiation and the carcinogen-laced air, dying because their suspicion of technology left them without the vaccines and treatments that could have saved them.

At nineteen, she'd run away to Los Angeles, into the arms of everything that she had been raised to fear and hate.

By the time I met her, she had shaken off most of her father's teachings, but she had somehow held on to his conviction that organ transplants—even blood transfusions—were the blackest of mortal sins.

Could Lisa have the same sort of hang up about DNA manipulation? I didn't know her well enough to even guess.

I filled the bag with ice and took it back to Sonja. She laid it gently across Lisa's eyes.

Lisa flinched when the cold plastic touched her face. "Is my nose broken?"

"I don't think so," Sonja said. "It's pretty swollen, but it doesn't seem to be displaced and the bleeding has stopped."

She met my eyes for a second and then looked back down to Lisa. "I think this is the work of a professional."

"I'll vouch for that," Lisa said. "They seemed pretty competent from where I was standing."

Sonja said, "I'm trying to say this looks like very careful work. A lot of bruising, some blood, but no real damage."

"That's not how it feels from in here," Lisa said.

Sonja touched Lisa's cheek. "I didn't mean that the way it sounded. I know you're hurting. And I know you're scared. But I can't find any sign of broken bones, and you don't have any of the classic symptoms of concussion or internal bleeding."

"So I'm going to be okay?"

"Well," Sonja said. "I'd really like to get you to a hospital, where they can run a full med-scan. But, based on what I can see, I think you're going to be fine."

Lisa let out a breath that was heavy with relief. "Thank you."

I found myself breathing a little easier too.

"Don't thank me yet," Sonja said. "I still need to do a bit of patchwork here and there. You might decide I'm a pretty lousy doctor before I get done."

Lisa raised her hand to steady the ice bag. The hand trembled slightly. "I did what you wanted, David. I ran that search you asked about."

I swallowed. I found myself hoping that this wasn't my fault, that Lisa had been the victim of a random mugging. I prayed that she hadn't been beaten like this because of some stupid little errand I'd sent her on.

I tried to keep the quaver out of my voice. "What did you find?"

Lisa coughed. "Pretty much what you expected."

Another cough. "A bunch of news articles: six girls over about eight months, the last one three years ago. The methods were pretty much identical to Aztec. Similar murder weapon. The girls were cut up pretty badly. The media nicknamed the killer Osiris. Egyptian mythology, means the *Judge of the Dead*. I looked it up."

"What happened to the killer?"

"This forty year old construction worker named Russell Carlisle walked into a police station and confessed to all six Osiris killings. Then he pulled a bomb out of his pocket and blew himself up. Wasn't a very big bomb, but he held it right up to his own head, so it did the trick. Made a hell of a mess, but nobody else really got hurt. His confession contained a lot of information that only the killer could have known. The killings stopped after he died. Case closed, just like you said."

"What city was it in?" I asked.

"Right here," Lisa said.

"What?" From the tone of Sonja's voice, she was as surprised as I was. "Los Angeles?"

"The good-old City of Angels," Lisa said.

"That's unbelievable," I said. "I'm not surprised that your search turned up another string of murders, but I sure as hell didn't expect it to be in my own back yard." I shook my head. "Did you find any other cases that fit the profile?"

"Uh-uh. Just the one. How'd I do?"

"You did good, Lisa. You did real good."

She smiled wearily behind her ice blindfold.

I had to ask. I didn't really want to know the answer, but I had to ask. "Who did this to you, Lisa? Why did they do it?"

Lisa sighed heavily. "If I'd just done my homework assignment, like you told me, I'd have been okay. But I had to go for the extra credit."

"What are you talking about?"

"I started thinking," she said, "about the questions you'd asked me, and things began to line up in my head. Kurt Rieger's thing for little girls. Aztec's thing for little girls. I thought I could see what you were leaning towards."

She took a deep breath and let it out slowly. "I ran another search. I scanned company records for Rieger's itinerary on the dates of all the

Aztec and Osiris murders. I looked for patterns. I figured he could have faked a few alibis, but not twenty."

"And?"

"He came up clean," Lisa said. "Rieger was in Europe at a trade conference for two of the Aztec killings. He was the keynote speaker at a fund raiser during one of the murders; about four hundred people can vouch for that one. He was on vacation in Jamaica for another one. I can account for his whereabouts during nine of the Aztec killings and three of the Osiris murders."

Sonja dabbed the bloody corner of Lisa's mouth with a sterile swab. "Couldn't company records be altered?" she asked.

Lisa jerked when the disinfectant stung her ravaged lip. "I thought of that. I scanned his travel visas through North American and European Immigration. He's also featured in a few page-six articles in various trade journals. Some of them detail his location on certain dates. You might not be convinced, David, but I am. Rieger may be a pervert, but he's definitely not Aztec or Osiris."

"Okay," I said. "You still haven't told me who did this to you."

"Rieger's goons," she whispered. "Two of them. I must have tripped a few warning flags when I pulled his files. Just because he's not your killer doesn't mean there aren't any skeletons in his closet."

"Did you recognize the goons?" I wanted names. Somebody had to pay for this.

"They were your typical wall-to-wall-muscle, blonde haired, blue-eyed Aryan Supermen. You know, Hitler Youths. I didn't recognize either of them, but I'm certain they were from Gebhardt-Wulkan Internal Security. They caught up with me on the Lev and beat the hell out of me. They took my purse and the data chips I was carrying to make it look like robbery, but they made their real motives pretty clear. They said I was screwing with things that could get me hurt, bad."

Jesus, this really *was* my fault.

Lisa didn't seem to think so. "David, I'm sorry. If I'd listened to you, none of this would have happened."

I sighed. "No, Lisa. This is my doing. I knew what the stakes were, and you didn't. I never should have involved you."

Sonja stood up and stretched her back. "I've done all the damage I can do. Are you sure I can't talk you into going to a hospital?"

"No," Lisa whispered. "No hospitals."

"Why the hell not?"

I hadn't meant for it to come out like that. I was getting angry. Not at Lisa. At myself. At two faceless thugs who had beaten up a defenseless woman on a train.

"Because they'll kill me if I go to the police. They told me that. They said I can take two weeks sick leave to heal up, but if I go to the cops, they'll..."

"They'll *what*?"

Her words came out in a whispered croak. "They said they'll drown me in my own bathtub."

Sonja started repacking the first aid kit. "If you show up in the Emergency Room looking like this, the ER staff will call the police. I've worked ER; it's standard operating procedure, no way to stop it."

"With pay," Lisa said. Her voice was weak, tired.

"What?"

"The two weeks sick leave," Lisa said, "it's time off with pay."

Sonja made a face. "Sounds like they're just a regular pair of saints. Maybe if they break your arm, you can get in on the employee profit sharing plan."

Lisa mumbled wearily. "It's the only job I've... got. I can retire in another five... years. I'm too old to start from... scratch somewhere... somewhere... else..." Her voice trailed off into silence.

She wasn't moving.

Despite Sonja's diagnosis, my heart stopped.

The look of concern that crossed Sonja's face must have mirrored my own. She knelt by the couch and examined Lisa's still form carefully.

Finally, she exhaled. "She's sleeping."

My heart started beating again.

Sonja stood up. "We can't leave her alone."

I nodded. "I'll go look for some blankets and pillows. We can sleep in here on the floor. That way, you can keep an eye on Lisa, and I can shoot the first Aryan Superman who knocks on the door."

She shot me a sour glance. "Go find the blankets."

If I'd known what to call it, I'd have asked the apartment AI for the blankets. Its name might be something simple. Then again, it might be something impossible to guess, like *Zarathustra* or *Lady Macbeth*.

I couldn't remember hearing Lisa address it, or talk about it a single time, so I didn't have a clue.

I looked up at the ceiling. "Apartment?"

No answer.

"AI?"

Nothing.

Screw it. I didn't feel like playing guessing games, and I could probably find the blankets quicker than I could find the AI's maintenance board.

I found the linen closet at the far end of the hall. Before I could open the door, something brushed against the back of my legs and shot down the hall toward the living room. It startled the hell out of me, and I barely caught a glimpse of it before it jetted around the corner at the other end of the hall. Some kind of animal. Something gray, and sleek, and fast. A cat?

It couldn't be a cat. Lisa couldn't possibly afford one. Probably, Lisa and Sonja and I together couldn't have afforded one.

I thought about the plastic bowls tucked under the kitchen cabinets; food and water bowls. It *was* a cat.

After I dug up the blankets, I made a quick tour of the apartment, making sure that all the windows were locked. Every one of them was alarmed.

I found and opened a steel door. It led to a fire escape. I closed it again, dead-bolted it and turned on the alarms. There were three of them, just like at the front door.

Sonja checked on Lisa again, while I threw together a makeshift bed of blankets and pillows on the floor.

The carpet wasn't expensive, but it was soft, and Lisa had kept it clean.

When her doctoring duties were complete, Sonja dimmed the lights and snuggled up with me under a synlon quilt patterned with colorful tropical fish.

I lay there staring up into the darkness and listening to the gentle rhythm of Sonja's breathing.

I wanted that chip, the one that the GWI security Nazis had stolen from Lisa's purse.

I knew that Lisa was probably right, in all likelihood, Kurt Rieger wasn't my man. But, somehow, I didn't want to let go of him. It was a decent theory and I liked it. It made a lot of pieces of the puzzle fit together in patterns that made sense to me.

I knew that it was selfish of me; Lisa had nearly died trying to get me that information. But I couldn't help it. I wanted that chip. I wanted to read the news articles about Osiris myself, and compare the times and dates of Rieger's itinerary.

Tomorrow. Worry about the chip tomorrow.

I was two-thirds asleep when I felt Sonja's whispered voice warm in my ear. "Corinne."

I scrunched into a more comfortable position. "Hmmm?"

She kissed me on the cheek and whispered. "That's my middle name, Corinne."

CHAPTER 17

Sonja woke me with a kiss. "Morning, Sleepyhead."

Her breath was fresh and minty. I was certain that mine was not.

She held out a mug of coffee. The cup was pink and covered in tiny writing that claimed to be 100 reasons why chocolate is better than men. The aroma of the coffee was rich enough to offset any misgivings I had about the Men/Chocolate equation.

I sat up far enough to accept the steaming cup and took a sip. "Good coffee."

Sonja showed me her dimples. "Thanks, but I didn't make it. Lisa did. It *is* good though, isn't it?"

I craned my neck. Lisa wasn't on the couch. "Where is Lisa?"

A voice floated down the hall. "In the kitchen, trying not to eavesdrop. About time you were up."

"Good morning to you too," I said.

I lowered my voice. "How's she doing?"

Sonja stole a sip from the other side of my cup. "A lot better than I expected. She's a pretty tough lady."

I sat the rest of the way up and stretched. My back made those muffled crackling sounds it uses to remind me that I'm not a kid anymore. I yawned. "Can I ask you a question?"

Sonja looked away from me. "Drugs."

I frowned. "What?"

"Not recreational drugs," she said. "Medications. Pharmaceutical drugs. To help people."

"What are you talking about?"

She turned toward me. "You were going to ask me what happened. Why I'm not a doctor."

I shook my head. "No I wasn't. I figured you would tell me about that when you wanted me to know. I was *going* to ask you where you got the toothbrush."

Sonja blushed. "Oh."

"But I would like to hear about the doctor thing," I said. "If you're ready to tell me."

Sonja hesitated. Then she shrugged. "No point in spilling half my guts."

She looked into my eyes. "You came to sculpture late in life. It wasn't like that for me. I knew by the time I was ten that I was going to be a doctor. I didn't just *want* it. I *lived* for it. I was going to help people. Heal people. There weren't any other options, not as far as I was concerned.

"I studied my ass off in school. I downloaded any file on the net that even smelled like it involved medicine. If I could only understand one word in three, that didn't matter to me. My subconscious was soaking it all up, and I figured I'd be able to tap into it one day."

"Wow," I said. "A child genius."

Sonja shook her head. "Not even close. Just an average kid, with average intelligence, who knew *exactly* what she wanted out of the world."

I watched her as she talked. There was an intensity in her face that I'd never seen before.

"Both our parents worked," she said. "But there wasn't a lot of money. I had to take out student loans for college. And then more loans for medical school. I got accepted into the residency program at Huntington General."

She stared off into nothingness, a sad little smile on her face. "And suddenly I was an intern. I was actually doing it. I was practicing medicine, helping to heal people." Her voice trailed off.

"What happened?"

She looked up at me. "I discovered the charity ward. I mean, I'd always known it was there, but it started to *get* to me. There were all these people down there. Sick people. Old people. Without money or insurance. People who needed help and couldn't afford it. The hospital provided basic care to the charity cases, don't get me wrong. But if one of them needed something with a big price tag, say an organ graft or specialized medication, forget it. Even if it meant the difference between life and death."

Her eyes gleamed. "I couldn't let happen. So I started to cheat the system. I looked for opportunities to reroute certain drugs to non-paying patients. I felt bad about spending other people's money, but I figured I could pay it back when I was a rich and famous doctor."

"But it didn't work out that way," I said.

Sonja sniffed. "Medicine is corporate," she said. "And corporations don't much care for young interns who spend company money without permission. My residency was terminated for cause. And just like that, it was over. I wasn't going to be a doctor any more. But the loans still had to be paid, and the rent, and everything else."

She put on a brave smile. "What was your first question again? I think I liked that one better."

I thought for a second. "Oh, yeah. Where did you get the toothbrush?"

"I carry one in my purse," she said.

I stood up and started folding the quilt. "You're still helping people," I said.

Sonja stared at me like I was crazy.

"Look around," I said. "The world's gotten pretty fucked up. Anything that brings a little happiness into someone's life without hurting anyone has got to be a good thing. Maybe even a noble thing."

Sonja started picking up the pillows. "Most people don't see it that way," she said.

I shrugged. "Most people don't spend years in self-imposed exile. Most people don't turn their backs on what little pleasure Life has to offer. It gives you a certain perspective."

A pillow still in each hand, she wrapped her arms around me and gave me a hug. "You're a kind man, Alex. Thanks."

I hugged her back. "Don't mention it, Corinne."

Lisa cleared her throat.

I looked up.

She was standing at the threshold to the hall, wearing a fuzzy green house robe with a feather boa collar. A lithe gray form stropped back and forth between her ankles, the cat from last night.

The swelling in Lisa's face had gone down a little, but she still looked like hell. "Break it up, you two. Breakfast is getting cold."

I gave Sonja a final squeeze and dropped the embrace. "Breakfast?"

"Yeah, breakfast. Why do you think I'm up? I've been waffling."

She looked thoughtful. "Is that a word? Waffling?"

Sonja tucked the pillows under her arms, slipped past Lisa, and headed down the hall toward the linen closet. "I tried to get her to stay on the couch and let me cook. She wouldn't listen to me. Maybe you should shoot her in the leg to keep her off her feet for a few days."

I squeezed past Lisa and the cat, and followed Sonja to the linen closet. I tucked the quilt away on a shelf. "Can't do it," I said. Bullets are way too expensive these days. I'll probably have to settle for clubbing her unconscious."

Lisa snorted. "I've already been clubbed this week and it didn't even slow me down. You can't keep a fat woman on the couch when the food is in the kitchen. Not with a club, anyway. You get between me and that refrigerator and you really *will* have to shoot me."

We had breakfast off the kitchen counter tops. There was a table and four chairs in the corner of the kitchen, but Lisa ignored them, so we did too. The cat feasted on a can of tuna.

The waffles turned out to be the frozen store- bought kind, but Lisa had worked a little magic on them using liberal amounts of honey-butter and a real oven instead of an ultrawave. With a bit of maple syrup and a few fresh strawberries, they were quite tasty.

After breakfast, Lisa filled the sink with hot soapy water and began to collect the dishes.

Sonja looked at her strangely. "What are you doing?"

"Washing the dishes."

"I can see that. Why don't you use the dishwasher? Is it broken?"

"It's controlled by the apartment AI."

"So?"

"So, I keep the AI turned off."

Sonja crossed her arms. "This I've got to hear."

Lisa picked up a kitchen sponge and scrubbed a soapy plate. "It's kind of weird," she said. "You're going to laugh."

"I won't laugh," Sonja said. She drew an X across her heart with one finger.

"You will," Lisa insisted.

"Okay," Sonja said. "I promise to *try* not to laugh. How's that?"

"I turned off the AI so that I wouldn't fall in love with him." She rinsed the plate, set it in the drain rack and grabbed another one. "When I first moved into this apartment, the management had wiped the AI and reloaded it from scratch. Just the default, factory personality. The voice didn't have any character, so I reprogrammed it to sound masculine... sexy."

"I don't see anything weird about that," Sonja said. "A lot of people program their AI's to have sexy voices."

"I didn't stop at the voice," Lisa said. "I started experimenting with the personality script itself. It's a tricky piece of code, but eventually I got it down to a system. Little by little, I changed things. I made him compassionate and nurturing. Then I made him impetuous and romantic. I gave him a name: Anthony. I didn't realize it at the time, but I was building the perfect man. It was great for a while. I could come home from work to someone who adored me. When Tony started starring in my dreams, I knew it had to stop. So I turned him off. I've been living without an AI for over a year."

"Why don't you just wipe his code?" Sonja asked. "Reload the default AI. At least you could run the dishwasher."

Lisa made an uncertain face. "I think about doing that sometimes. But I can't seem to make myself do it. It's like, as long as Tony's personality script exists, there will always be somebody who loves me. Even if it's not a real somebody."

Her eyes drifted down to the cat at her feet. She nudged his back playfully with a toe. "If I erase Tony, it'll just be me and Mr. Shoes, won't it Sweetheart?"

Mr. Shoes responded by gently butting the side of his head against Lisa's ankle. Lisa looked shyly over her shoulder to see if we were laughing at her foolishness behind her back.

I thought about a little anodized aluminum box tucked away somewhere in the back of a closet in John's apartment. A little box crammed full of ones and zeros that supposedly added up to Maggie Stalin. I never felt less like laughing in my life.

Sonja didn't laugh either.

We stood there in silence, groping for the right thing to say.

It was Lisa who finally broke the spell with a change of subject. "So, what are your plans now, David?"

"My immediate plans? I want to smoke a cigarette and brush my teeth. Preferably not in that order."

Lisa put the last dish in the rack and pulled the drain plug. "You know what I mean."

"I'd like to start by using your computer. Do you mind?"

Lisa dried her hands on a towel and walked out of the room. "Of course not," she said over her shoulder.

Sonja and I followed Lisa to the living room and watched while she powered up one of her two desktop computers.

When the *System Ready* icon appeared, Lisa stepped back to make room for me. "All yours."

I pulled Tommy Mailo's video chip out of my pocket and loaded it into Lisa's machine. It took me a couple of seconds to find the file I was looking for, a single frame of video from Michael Winter's suicide recording. The image of the dark-haired woman that Tommy had found reflected in the blade of Michael's knife. I copied the picture onto a blank chip and shut off Lisa's computer.

"What's that for?" Sonja asked.

"It's a bargaining tool. I'm going to try to get my hands on the police files for the Osiris case. What was his name?"

"Russell Carlisle," Lisa said.

"Right. I also want to pay a visit to Lisa's friends from the Lev. They have a chip that I'm interested in seeing. Besides, I want to talk to them about social courtesy on public transportation."

Lisa sat down carefully on the couch. "You don't have to do that."

"Don't worry, they won't be able to connect it with you."

"No, that's not what I meant. You don't have to track those guys down at all. I have a copy of the chip."

"You do? I thought you said they took all your chips."

"David, I'm a software engineer. When was the last time you heard of a data geek who didn't make back-up copies?"

"That just makes my visit to them a little less urgent," I said. "I'm still going to have a talk with them."

"You don't have to," said Lisa.

Sonja gave me a solemn look. "She's right, David. Getting back at those thugs won't fix anything. They're nothing more than hired muscle."

I nodded slowly. "You've got a point. They didn't just pick Lisa out of a crowd and decide to beat the hell out of her; they were following orders. Kurt Rieger may not be Aztec or Osiris, but it's a pretty safe bet that he had Lisa attacked. And for that, he's going to answer to *me*."

CHAPTER 18

Dancer pinched the bridge of her nose between the thumb and forefinger of her right hand, and squeezed her eyes shut. "Stalin, what the fuck are you doing here?"

She opened her eyes and glared at me across her desk. "Don't tell me, let me guess. It's Monday morning... You're dragging around another fucking body, aren't you?"

There were five other detectives scattered around Southwest Division Homicide. None of them even bothered to glance up from their work, leading me to believe that Dancer greeted all of her visitors in the same cordially retiring fashion.

"No," I said. "No new bodies yet, but the day..."

"Is still young. Yeah, yeah, yeah. You want to spout cliché dialogue, go bother somebody else. I've got a shitload of admin work to catch up on. What do you want?"

"I just dropped by to see what you guys do for entertainment when you're not threatening to kick somebody's door down."

"You're wasting my time, Stalin. Say whatever it is that you came to say, and then get out."

"Can I smoke?"

"Will it help you get to the fucking point?"

"It might."

She shoved a pile of papers away from her on the desk. "Please, have a seat. Light up. Take your time. I haven't got shit to do."

I pulled up a chair and lit a cigarette. The chair was heavily patched with silver microbond tape.

Four little magnets in the shapes of handguns were stuck to the front of Dancer's green metal desk. Stretched between them was a paper target silhouette with seven bullet holes through the heart. The grouping of the shots was nice and tight. *'Don't make me kill you'* was hand written across the top of the target in red paint stick.

"How's Harvey Miller doing?" I asked.

Dancer scowled. "Who?"

"The hostage from the Lev the other day. The guy who got thrown down the stairs. Is he still in the Trauma Ward?"

156

"He hasn't shown up on my case list," she said. "So he's probably still breathing. I hope to hell that isn't what you interrupted me for."

"I need some information," I said.

"Is this going to be a formal interrogation?" Dancer leaned back in her chair and smiled a dangerous little smile. "Should I call my lawyer? Or would it save time if I just confess?"

"I was thinking of a trade," I said.

"What do you have that I could possibly give a shit about?"

"A picture of the woman from the Lev, the one who killed Joseph Takamura with the laser."

Dancer sat up in her chair and punched an intercom button. "Bethany? Find Rick Delaney and get him up here. Now."

I cupped the palm of my left hand and thumped my ashes into it. Dancer slurped the last swallow from a plastic can of body builder's protein drink and handed me the can as an ashtray.

A door opened at the far end of the room, and Delaney walked in. He slid a chair over from another desk, and sat down to Dancer's right. He ignored me entirely.

Dancer leaned back in her chair again. "Rick, our friend Mr. Stalin has dropped by to enlighten us with regard to that unsolved One Eighty-Seven on the Lev the other day. He says he has a picture of the shooter."

"I need some information from the LAPD archives," I said. "I'm offering the picture in trade."

"What exactly do you want?" Dancer asked.

"I need a complete data pull on the Osiris murder investigation, including all of the autopsy data on the victims and the killer."

Dancer cracked her knuckles. "Osiris? I don't remember anything about an Osiris case. Rick?"

Delaney pulled out a pocket comp, punched a few keys, and stared at the tiny screen. His pupils didn't move; he was pretending to read, just like the other day when he'd pretended to read the little plastic card from the Magic Mirror.

He looked up. "Six murders. All teenage girls between thirteen and fifteen. A male Caucasian named Russell E. Carlisle confessed to all six murders on Five September, Twenty Sixty. Then he committed suicide with a homemade bomb in the day room over at Central Division in front of eleven witnesses. No one else was injured in the bombing."

The pocket comp was a prop. A smokescreen. Delaney was using it to draw attention away from his personal powers of observation and recall. I wondered if he had a natural photographic memory, or if he had some kind of augmenting brain implant.

Dancer looked at me. "That sound like your boy?"

"That's him."

"I can get your data pull," she said. "But first, let's have a look at this picture of yours."

I handed her the chip containing the image of the dark-haired mystery woman.

Dancer passed the chip to Delaney, and he loaded it into his pocket comp. He pecked at the keys and then turned the comp around so that Dancer and I could see the video display.

Oddly enough, the grainy image looked a little better on Delaney's comp than it had in Tommy Mailo's video workshop, possibly because the picture had to be so heavily compressed to fit on the tiny screen. It still wasn't very clear.

Dancer stared at it for a few seconds. "Is this some kind of a joke? I can't do anything with that. It's worthless."

"Maybe you can have it enhanced," I said.

Delaney fiddled with the keypad of his little computer and then stared at the readout. "It already has been enhanced," he said.

"Yeah," I said, "by a kid who works out of the back of a video store. Not exactly a professional video engineer." (Technically true.) "Maybe your vid lab can do better." (Probably *not* true.) "There's a chance that you'll get a clean enough image to I.D. the shooter." (Almost certainly an outright lie.)

Dancer pushed her chair away from her desk and stood up. "What if it turns out to be a piece of shit?"

"In case you don't recognize it," I said, "this is what's called a *lead.* Maybe it goes somewhere. Maybe it doesn't. That's how the game works."

Dancer crossed her arms. "Do you need a refresher course in reality, Stalin? We're the cops here, remember? You might want to keep that in mind."

I took a drag off my cigarette and blew a smoke ring toward the ceiling.

Delaney stared at the image on his screen. "Where did you get this picture, Mr. Stalin?"

"Come on," I said. "I'm not asking for much. A few data files on a closed investigation. All it will cost you is a couple of minutes of download time. If the picture turns out to be garbage, you haven't really lost anything."

"The picture," Dancer echoed. "Where did you get it?"

I'd hoped to avoid this part. I took a hit from my cigarette and exhaled slowly. "From the video recording of Michael Winter's suicide."

Dancer frowned. "Michael Winter?"

"Aztec," Delaney said. This time he didn't even pretend to check his comp. "Another closed serial murder investigation. Teenage girls between the ages of thirteen and fifteen, just like the Osiris case. The MO's were very similar. So similar in fact, that the departmental AI's flagged Aztec as a copycat."

"You were saying something about Aztec the other day," Dancer said, "when we were at your house. What is this fascination you have with serial killers?"

I sighed. "I think the cases may be related."

Dancer's face stiffened. "Aztec and Osiris? I'll tell you how they're related. The second guy," she snapped her fingers several times, "Aztec, sees this Osiris-guy's work on the vid and gets a hard-on. He likes it so much that he tries to copy the guy's MO. Other than that, and your fertile imagination, the only thing that ties those cases together is the fact that they're both closed. The killers were caught, Stalin. Finito. End of fucking story."

I resisted the temptation to point out that neither of the accused killers had actually been caught; they had both confessed, and now they both were dead.

"I think the woman in the picture might be an accessory to some of the Aztec and Osiris killings," I said. "Maybe even all of them."

"And this is the same female perp who punched a combat laser through Takajima's brain?"

"Takamura," Delaney said softly.

"Fine," Dancer said. "Taka-fucking-mura. Is it the same woman?"

"I don't know," I said. "I think so."

Dancer closed her eyes and rubbed her left cheek. "Why do I get the feeling that you're trying to fuck me without kissing me first?"

"Give me the files," I said. "I'm just trying to keep anyone else from getting hurt."

Dancer opened her eyes. "What the hell is that supposed to mean?"

"I can get what I need by hiring a jacker," I said, "but I'd rather not do that. Somebody is tracking me through the Net."

"So what?"

I thumped the tip of my cigarette ash into the can. "The last person who made inquiries into this case for me got stepped on. Hard. Somebody cornered her on a Lev and beat her half to death. I figure next time, they won't stop at half-way. If you don't help me, I won't have a choice; I'll have to hire another jacker. Chances are, the next one will end up on your list of unsolved One Eighty-Sevens."

"You've got the Midas Touch, Stalin. Everybody you touch winds up dead or seriously fucked up. Do you have any idea how much paperwork I have to do when your magic finger of death leaves a body on the sidewalk?"

"Give me the files," I said.

Dancer massaged her temples with her fingertips. "You're giving me a headache."

"I've given you my best lead," I said. "It won't hurt you to let me have the files."

"What's your interest in this, Stalin? Is this a case you're working on, or is it a personal crusade?"

"It's a case," I said.

"Who are you working for?"

"I don't think my client is ready to go public."

"For a man who came here to trade information, you're not exactly busting your ass to be helpful."

"If you have a question, ask it," I said. "I'll answer it, if I can. But I'm not giving up the name of my client."

"Maybe a couple of hours on the Inquisitor would change your mind," Dancer said. "That thing can squeeze your brain like a sponge."

I took a final hit off the cigarette and dropped the butt into the plastic can. It sizzled when it hit the last few drops of protein drink.

"Synaptic signal injection," Dancer said. "The Inquisitor uses the same basic technology as the machine we use for brainlock. Just a few minor differences in circuit design. What do you think, Stalin? Pump your brain full of synthetic neurotransmitters and fire a scanning electron beam into your hippocampus. They say it's a little like being struck by lightning, right in the fucking head. It's supposed to be safe, but you've heard the rumors, haven't you? Somebody flips the wrong switch, or the computer has a bad day... A person could get brainlocked. By accident, of course. Sort of like instant Alzheimer's."

"Fine," I said. "If you want to run me through the Inquisitor, go ahead. But let's get it over with. I've got things to do."

Dancer slapped at the paperwork on her desk. "Now I'm wasting *your* time? I was doing fine until you came along and blew my morning schedule right out the fucking window. Forget the Inquisitor, I'm going to handcuff you to this desk and make you finish all of these reports."

Delaney half smiled.

Dancer took a sharp breath, started to say something, and then stopped and released the breath slowly. "Rick, get Stalin his data pull and then get him out of here." She turned to me. "If you turn up any more corpses, Stalin, I swear to God I'll tack you down and shoot you myself."

CHAPTER 19

||| || | | ||||| | || || || | || | || ||| ||| | || | |||||| || ||| | ||| |||

The bright red legend carved circles in the air above the desktop comp in my den. At the axis of the warning's orbit floated the LAPD Southwest Division logo in streamlined ultrachrome letters.

My data shades were propped up on my forehead. I slid my hands into the control gloves and adjusted the audio conduction pads against the bones behind my ears. When I flipped the wraparound shades down over my eyes, the LAPD warning logo was repeated in the eyepieces. I punched the comp's holographic space bar, and the logo vanished, replaced by a file directory.

I crooked the fingers of my left hand to activate *browse* mode, and then scanned down through the directory menu to a file marked:

▶ **CARERRA, ELAINE, R: CRIME-SCENE: 09JAN60/9:11p.m.** ◀

I swallowed heavily. The last thing in the world I wanted was to take another slaughterhouse tour of butchered teenaged bodies, but it had to be done.

I pointed my right index finger at the filename to activate the recording, and the crime scene unfolded in front of my eyes. I ignored the data readouts that danced at the edge of my field of vision; I was only interested in the scene itself.

The room was shaped like a thick slice of pie, with a door at the narrow end of the wedge. The wall opposite the door was curved, a single huge window running from floor to ceiling and wall to wall. The glass was set for full transparency, revealing a night view of the Los Angeles skyline silhouetted against the dome.

The walls were covered with video panels tuned to one of those art channels. The screens cycled slowly through an apparently endless gallery of abstract paintings.

The bed was round. It hovered in the center of the room on an electromagnetic cushion, like a Lev.

Elaine Carerra's body lay half on and half off the bed. Her face was tilted upward, leaving her dead eyes to stare at the ceiling. A spatter of blood had struck her left cheek and trailed off like a tear. When she'd slid to the floor, most of the bed linens had gone with her.

The jumble of blood-slick sheets swaddled her body like a cocoon. A wheeled cleaning drone sat frozen on its fat rubber wheels. Its motionless manipulator arms were all bent toward the carpet near Elaine's body. The drone had obviously been feverishly trying to mop up the spreading stain of blood when the cops had arrived and shut it down.

My eyes found the raw hole that the killer had hacked in Elaine's chest, and suddenly I *knew*.

Just to be certain, I backed out of the program, and loaded and watched the crime scene recordings for two of the other Osiris victims. It wasn't really necessary; I was already certain. Delaney had called Aztec a copycat. He was wrong.

I flipped the datashades up onto my forehead and shut the computer down. I could feel my pulse pounding in my temples.

There were no more maybes. As soon as I'd spotted the mutilated body of Elaine Carerra, I'd known with an absolute and sickening moral certainty that I had seen this killer's work before. Aztec and Osiris were the same person. And he was still out there somewhere.

I peeled off the control gloves and datashades, and dropped them into one of the drawers of my desk. I suddenly wanted a shot of scotch very badly.

I settled for a cigarette, inhaling the smoke deeply and waiting for the calming effect of the nicotine to steady the tremor in my hands.

I tried to focus, to force some semblance of objectivity back into my mind. I needed to concentrate on the facts.

I had compared the victims from both cases. There was a definite pattern to the killer's selection. The girls had a quality about them that I couldn't quite describe, an essential sameness. All of them had been between thirteen and fifteen—and had been similar in size, build, coloring—but it wasn't that. It wasn't even that they looked alike, although they certainly had, to a degree. It was more of a feeling. The girls *felt* similar, as though they were somehow interchangeable.

That set me to wondering. If the killer followed some sort of specific criteria for choosing his victims, what about his patsies? Was there some essential similarity between Russell Carlisle and Michael Winter that had led to their selection? And if there was such a connection, what would it be? Probably not anything in their personal histories or lifestyles. They had lived in different parts of the city, traveled in different circles, and practiced totally different professions. Could the answer be in their deaths, rather than their lives?

I loaded the autopsy protocol on Russell Carlisle. In less than five minutes, I knew I was on to something. Carlisle's hands had been heavily callused, the right more so than the left: the mark of a right-handed carpenter. Like Michael, Carlisle had chosen to kill himself with his left hand, holding the homemade bomb against his left temple.

Two right-handed men who had chosen to kill themselves with their left hands. In both suicides, the death blow had come from the left side of the head. What could there be about the left side of the head, in particular, that could point to the killer?

I loaded the files from both autopsy protocols at the same time and instructed the computer to tag all similarities between Michael's autopsy results and Russell Carlisle's.

The comp bleeped and projected a short message: **FILE SORT IN PROGRESS. ESTIMATED COMPLETION = 00:01:30.** The seconds column started counting down immediately. I'd forgotten how slow the desktop's microprocessor was.

I lit a smoke and sat back to wait out the ninety seconds.

I was amassing a mountain of evidence, but I still didn't know where it was pointing. Kurt Rieger was my favorite suspect (in fact, the only one I had) but—when viewed objectively—the evidence against him wasn't exactly airtight. I knew that I should be considering other suspects, but I couldn't seem to come up with any.

Had I grown too attached to my Kurt Rieger theory? If Rieger was the killer, the woman was only an accomplice. Why was I so wrapped up in that scenario?

Why did I want Rieger to be guilty? Because he was a pedophile? Because his Gestapo had beaten Lisa to a pulp? Because he'd slept with Sonja?

The comp bleeped again and projected an enormous column of data.

I started reading.

Most of the flagged items were obviously garbage. Both corpses were adult males. Both had suffered fatal head wounds. Both men had two arms, two legs and the normal compliment of toes.

I went through the list, dropping any flagged item that obviously wasn't relevant. The column got shorter fast.

When I had the list down to about fifty lines, I spotted a heading labeled CRANIAL CAVITY▶FOREIGN MATTER▶PRESENCE OF. Under the label were ten entries:

  ▷ *Gallium Arsenide*

  ▷ *Platinum*

  ▷ *Carbonized Ceramic*

  ▷ *Silicon Monoxide*

  ▷ *Silicon Dioxide*

  ▷ *Selenium*

  ▷ *Nichrome*

  ▷ *Titanium*

  ▷ *Aluminum*

  ▷ *Orthostatic Epoxy*

I knew what orthostatic epoxy was. It was used for gluing broken bones together. I knew what platinum, titanium, and aluminum were, although I didn't know why traces of them would be found in the head wounds of two different men. Gallium arsenide? Nichrome? I had no idea what any of the rest of those things were, or what they were likely to be used for.

I drew a lung full of smoke and exhaled it slowly. "House, run a short database search for me. Where would you expect to find gallium arsenide, platinum, carbonized ceramic, silicon monoxide, silicon dioxide, selenium, nichrome, titanium, aluminum, and orthostatic epoxy used together?"

House's answer came almost instantly. "Neurosurgery."

I sat up straight. "Neurosurgery? You mean brain surgery?"

"Yes, David. The first nine substances you mentioned are routinely used in the manufacture of microchips. The most obvious application of microchip technology, in combination with Orthostatic epoxy, is neurosurgery."

"Holy shit."

"I'm sorry David, what did you say?"

"Never mind."

"Shall I start lunch, David?"

"No. But you can start me a pot of coffee."

"Of course."

I backed out of the autopsy reports and called up the LAPD Bomb Detail's file on Carlisle's bomb. I didn't get a lot out of the report, but I did get a name and contact information.

I punched up the phone number.

A cadaverously thin man in black coveralls answered on the first ring. "Scientific Investigations Division, Bomb Detail, do you want to declare an emergency?"

"No. I don't have an emergency."

His posture relaxed visibly. "How can I help you?"

"Can I speak to a Sergeant Victor Bradshaw?"

"It's Lieutenant Bradshaw now. Hold please."

His face was replaced by a hold video. Young bronzed gods and goddesses windsurfed on an idyllic beach. The sand was the color of raw sugar, and the water a beautiful shade of unpolluted blue. It must have been one of those virtual beaches; I couldn't imagine where they'd have found a stretch of real sand and water clean enough to shoot that scene.

I put out my cigarette and was in the process of lighting another when the hold video vanished.

A short, muscular African man in police blues appeared in its place. "Lieutenant Bradshaw. What can I do for you?"

I introduced myself and told him what I wanted.

"Three years, Mr. Stalin? You expect me to remember a case from three years ago?"

"A man blew his own head off in the middle of your police station," I said. "That strikes me as sort of memorable."

"Yeah well, be that as it may, we get some pretty crazy assholes here. Just this morning we had some idiot try to blow up one of those big robotic clowns out in front of a fast food restaurant. God only knows why. Dropped the bomb and blew one of his own feet off instead. Assholes, I'm telling you."

He rubbed his jaw slowly. "But I think I remember the guy you're talking about. I'm going to put you back on hold while I go pull the file. My memory might need a little boost."

I nodded, and Lieutenant Bradshaw switched places with the windsurfers.

He reappeared a lot sooner than I expected. "Okay, I've got you," he said. "Russell Carlisle, September of Sixty. Blew his brains all over the wallpaper down in the day room. What do you need?"

"What can you tell me about the bomb itself?"

Lieutenant Bradshaw flipped through a couple of pages of hardcopy. "IED. Improvised Explosive Device. Your basic kitchen-sink bomb."

"You mean homemade explosives? Like bathtub-nitro or kitchen-plastique?"

"Not at all," Bradshaw said. "The explosive used was HPX-16. Military-grade explosive. Stable as applesauce, but it packs one mother of a punch."

"So what makes it a kitchen-sink bomb?"

"Too many brother-in-law circuits."

"Huh?"

"Circuits that don't serve any real purpose," he said. "What my old man used to call *bells and whistles*. For instance, Carlisle used two different kinds of batteries. One of those compact high-density lithium jobs and a flat-pack of alkalines. You ask me, the alkalines would have worked just fine by themselves. A lot cheaper too."

"Anything else?"

Bradshaw flipped through the printouts again. "Remember, we pieced this together from fragments. It looked like there were a lot of microchips and circuitry that didn't have anything to do with the bomb at all. Brother-in-law circuits."

He looked up. "The weird thing is, whoever built that bomb knew exactly what they were doing."

"You lost me," I said.

"Most of the IED's we see are pure shit. Pipe bombs, stuff like that. Don't get me wrong, a lot of them work, even some of the bad ones. People watch too much vid and start to thinking that building a bomb doesn't look so hard. Carlisle's bomb wasn't like that. Like I said, we were working from reconstruction, but that bomb looked clean. Good detonator. Initiator wired up right. Good choice of explosives. Adequate power. As good an IED as you're likely to find. We went over the pieces pretty carefully, but we never did figure out what all that extra stuff was for."

He folded his printout in half. "That's about it. Help any?"

"I think so," I said. "Maybe a lot. I appreciate you taking the time to talk to me."

"Any time." He reached out to hang up.

"Oh, one more question," I said. "Those brother-in-law circuits: the battery, the chips and the extra circuitry. If you packaged it all up together, without the rest of the bomb, how big a package would it make?"

Bradshaw pursed his lips. "You want a guess? Hmmm... I'd say just about the same size as a pack of cigarettes."

CHAPTER 20

‖‖ ‖ ‖ ‖‖‖‖ ‖ ‖ ‖‖ ‖ ‖ ‖‖ ‖ ‖‖ ‖‖‖ ‖‖ ‖ ‖ ‖‖‖‖‖ ‖ ‖‖ ‖ ‖‖ ‖‖

It was darker than I expected when I stepped out the front door of my house. I looked up and saw that the normally transparent panels of the dome facing had taken on a strange glazed appearance. It was starting to rain.

Far above my head, the pelting of raindrops against the polycarbon panels reduced the sky to a soft blur that glimmered and rippled as the water ran down the arc of the dome. The effect was that of a soft-focus lens, absorbing and diffusing a lot of the afternoon sunlight. The light that did get through dappled the streets and buildings with shifting patterns of shadow.

I looked at my watch. If I hurried, I could make the barricade in time to catch the two o'clock Lev.

I lit a cigarette and increased my stride.

My brain registered it as a flicker of motion at the very edge of my peripheral vision: someone stepping out of a darkened doorway to my right, almost behind me.

Instinct took over. I spun left, away from the threat, and jammed my right hand into my windbreaker in search of the Blackhart. Good moves, both of them. They probably would have worked if I had been a hair faster.

The stranger's hand came up in a blur and jabbed the stainless steel horns of a police riot wand into the side of my neck. The zapper must have been heavily overcharged, because its electrodes fried the flesh of my neck where they made contact.

I fell, still turning as inertia attempted to carry me through the spin that my body had started. I caught a glimpse of my attacker's legs before the back of my head collided with the sidewalk. Boots. Black leather boots. Women's boots.

Darkness. Featureless. Borderless. Infinite.
No... not featureless.

Shades of darkness. Pools of velvet shadow. Phantom rivers of burnt black oil.

I cracked one eye. Big mistake. A brilliant bolt of light slammed through the tiny slit between my eyelids and blew a hole through the back of my head.

I jammed the eye shut.

Too late. Pain jack hammered its way into my brain. Pulsing, throbbing pain that carried a wrenching nausea on its shoulders.

I clamped my jaw shut and willed myself not to vomit. It seemed to work. A little.

Closing my eyes didn't make the pain go away, so I opened them just enough to squint through slitted lids.

I lay there, staring at a stretch of rich burgundy carpet. As my eyes adjusted to the light, I realized that it wasn't bright at all.

I became aware of sensations other than light and pain.

My left arm was asleep, trapped under my chest with the weight of my body on it.

The carpet against my cheek was plush, damp with the spreading stain of my saliva.

There was something in my right hand. From the heft and feel of it, I knew it was the Blackhart.

Somewhere, classical music played softly. I didn't recognize the piece, but it sounded like Mozart.

Smell. Something familiar, acrid. Gunpowder.

Another smell, again familiar. A flat metallic scent that reminded me of wet copper. I could almost place it.

I began to muster my energy for the Herculean task of rolling over. Ready... ready... and NOW.

The ceiling was more interesting than the floor had been. The plaster was sculpted in bas-relief.

I flexed the fingers of my left hand experimentally. They burned with the curious fire of returning circulation.

Arms next. Nothing radical, just flex the muscles. Everything still attached? Nothing broken?

Legs. Same game-plan.

After some careful psyching, I levered myself to a sitting position.

It turned out that Pain had a big brother named *Mister* Pain.

Mr. Pain was kind enough to stomp an entire ballet across the insides of my eyelids.

I stayed put and waited for Mr. Pain to fade to the point where he was merely unbearable. In the meantime, I let my eyes tour the room.

Floor to ceiling drapes covered what appeared to be French doors. The drapes looked expensive.

To the left of the drapes hung a painting. It might have been an authentic Renoir.

To the right of the drapes was an overstuffed chair. Obviously an antique, the chair had wine-colored upholstery and heavy walnut arms and legs. It made me think of those exclusive men's clubs that you see in old vids. Clubs with names like *The Gibraltar* and *The Academy.*

Sitting in the chair was a man. Mid thirties. Blonde razor-cut hair. Carefully masculine surgical-boutique face. Flawless gunmetal gray Italian suit.

I'd never seen him before, but I'd have bet even money that his name was Kurt Rieger.

Mr. Rieger, if that was his name, had been carefully strapped to the chair with nano-pore tape, and (equally carefully) shot through the middle of the forehead.

The source of the wet copper smell clicked in my mind: blood. A lot of it.

An entrance wound that size could only have come from a large caliber bullet.

Suddenly, I became conscious of the Blackhart clenched in my right fist. I raised the barrel to my nose and sniffed. Burnt gunpowder.

I ejected the magazine and cycled the slide to empty the chamber. One round was missing. I slid the magazine back into the grip reservoir, and shoved it home with the heel of my left hand until it clicked into place.

There wasn't much doubt where the bullet in Rieger's head had come from. Jesus.

I managed to get my legs under me and stumble to my feet. A tidal wave of pain and nausea crashed into me and sent me reeling around the room in a desperate struggle to keep my footing.

I banged my left knee sharply against a wooden end table before my gyros caught and stabilized. A love seat cut from the same mold as the chair beckoned to me from across the room. No. Bad idea. If I sat down, I might not make it back up.

After a minute or two on my feet, my knees got a little steadier. I wouldn't want to try to run, but I thought that I could handle walking, if I didn't push too hard.

What were my options?

No, it was too early for that. I knew my ass was wedged in a crack, but until I had some idea of how badly, there wasn't a lot of sense in making plans.

Start over.

Step one: find out how ugly the picture was. *Then* move on to step two: Damage Control.

Okay, where was I? A cliché question perhaps, but a crucial piece of data that I happened to be lacking.

I walked unsteadily to the drapes and pulled one end away from the wall enough to peek out. The drapes did indeed cover a set of French doors. The doors led to a large balcony. In the distance past the railing, the Gebhardt-Wulkan Informatik pyramid floated in the air. I was in Dome 11.

From the angle of my view, the room I was in was pretty high up. I let the drape fall back into place and moved away from the window.

I checked my watch. It was almost five p.m. I'd been out a little over three hours.

I made a quick search of the apartment, or suite, or whatever. It was huge, fourteen rooms. Living room, den, dining room, full kitchen, breakfast nook, study and four bedrooms, each with an attached bathroom.

No one was home except for me and the tentatively identified Mr. Rieger.

I used the mirror in the master bathroom to examine myself. There were two uniform blisters the size of pencil erasers just below my right ear, where the stun wand had fried me. The skin surrounding them had been heavily bruised by the high-volt/low-amp discharge. Four shallow scratches ran diagonally across my left cheek, apparently the mark of gouging fingernails. The right side of my face was still covered in strawberry wrinkles from my unceremonious nap on the carpet.

I looked for a hand mirror; I wanted to see the back of my head. I couldn't find one, so I settled for exploring the damage by touch. There was some swelling, a lot of tender flesh, and a little blood, but I could find no signs of skull fracture.

I looked at my pupils in the mirror. Was the left one a hair larger than the right? I couldn't be sure. Did I have a concussion? I didn't know enough to be certain.

I decided to say no. My body would let me know pretty soon if my diagnosis was wrong.

I snapped off the bathroom light and walked back to the living room.

My legs were getting steadier.

If I had looked hard enough, I could have probably come up with a pair of gloves, but it didn't seem to make much difference whether or not I left fingerprints. If a crime team went over the place, they were going to find my fibers and hairs and about a thousand other things linking me to the murder scene.

I didn't even know where my spent shell casing had gone. It was probably under the couch or buried in the carpet. The way my head felt, if I got down on my hands and knees to look, I'd probably pass out. But I had no doubt that the police would find it in about twenty seconds. One of the more obvious reasons that most criminal-types favor caseless ammo.

There was a pool of my saliva soaked into the carpet. I had certainly left more than enough for an easy DNA comparison.

None of that mattered anyway; my Blackhart was registered. The State Police had a ballistics map for it in their computers. Even if I threw the gun away, or destroyed it, they could run a database search and trace any bullets that it had fired back to me.

I stood for a minute, breathing slowly and steeling myself for my least favorite part of this. I gritted my teeth and began a systematic search of the body.

His skin and muscles were still pliable and reasonably warm. Rigor mortis hadn't set in yet. He hadn't been dead very long.

On a hunch, I examined his hands. His manicure was immaculate. There were traces of skin and blood under the fingernails of his right hand. I touched the scratches on my left cheek. Someone had given this frame a lot of thought.

I moved the little wooden end table to a handy position and emptied the contents of his pockets onto the top. A key ring with five key chips, one of them embossed with the BMW logo. A cigarette lighter machined from European surgical steel. A matching cigarette case, half full of expensive German cigarettes—*not* Ernte 23's. A silk handkerchief. A postcard, folded in quarters, with a launch pad shot of a Euro-Space orbital shuttle on one side and German writing on the other. A wallet containing three credit chips, an ID chip, seven business cards and €m4,200 in cash. The credit chips all had gold stripes.

There was a phone across the room. I used it to read the ID chip. The holo it projected was definitely the dead man. My first guess had been right. It was Kurt Rieger.

I helped myself to a smoke from the cigarette case, and lit it with the surgical steel lighter.

I snapped the BMW chip off the key ring and stuck it in my pocket. I wanted to search Rieger's car. If everything went okay, the key chip could be put back later. If not, it would go down a storm drain somewhere. As long as the car itself wasn't stolen, the cops probably wouldn't make too big a deal over the key.

Everything else went back in his pockets.

I stood for a minute and smoked.

I couldn't see a man like Kurt Rieger keeping track of his own socks. The apartment had to be equipped with an AI.

Could that be my alibi? If the AI had recorded the murder, the playback would prove that I hadn't killed Rieger. In fact, it would show who *had* murdered him.

Who was I kidding? Anyone smart enough to plan a setup like this wouldn't overlook something that obvious.

Still, I had to check. I was reasonably certain that the AI had been shut down or wiped, but you don't let a doctor amputate your leg without getting a second opinion.

It took me ten minutes to track down the AI's maintenance board. It was in the study, hidden behind an access plate that blended into the dark burl-wood wall paneling almost perfectly.

I popped the plate open. The hardware was nice, a Braun 6000 series. It was turned off.

I punched a few buttons and sequenced the system on-line. Something bleeped and a small flat-screen monitor lit up with a flashing message:

>>>>> ERROR CODE: 2A011FE0003 <<<<<

[PROGRAM NOT FOUND]

>>>>> SOFTWARE RELOAD REQUIRED <<<<<

Slicked. Damn.

I shut the system down and closed the access panel. It had been too much to hope for.

I stopped by the master bathroom, took a final drag off my cigarette, and flushed it down the toilet.

I walked back to the living room, exhaling smoke slowly as I went.

Now it was time to consider choices.

Option #1: I could call Dancer and trust to luck that LAPD Homicide was clever enough to see through this elaborate frame up. Not a really good idea, considering the strength of the evidence against me. If the cops ran a Magic Mirror on me, it was going to point its electronic finger straight at me. I'd seen things that (theoretically), no one but the killer should have seen. My brainwaves would contain recognition patterns for the body, the crime scene, and the murder weapon. Hell, the murder weapon was *registered* to me. Not to mention the fact that the police forensics team would find traces of my blood and skin under Rieger's fingernails.

If I went to the cops, they were going to wire me up to the Inquisitor. Dancer might have exaggerated the dangers of a session with the Inquisitor, but then again, maybe not. There had been rumors floating around the streets for years. From what I'd heard, even a relatively mild session could cause brain damage.

Which led me to Option #2: I could try to dig the bullet out of Rieger's skull and then give the place a clean sweep, eliminating all traces of my presence. Uh-uh. That might work in the vids, but not in real life.

Option #3: Get rid of the body. Either dispose of it permanently, or hide it somewhere long enough to figure out a way to prove my innocence. Which could lead to a whole slew of additional felonies, not the least of which was tampering with a crime scene.

Option #4: Leave the murder scene alone and get the hell out. With luck, I might be able to clear my name before the body was even discovered.

Not one of my options was any damn good. Every one of them had the potential to get me brainlocked.

I didn't find the prospect of having my conscious mind electronically flatlined very attractive. I had no desire to spend the rest of my life chasing invisible fireflies and pissing in my pants.

I finally decided on option #4.

The front door opened into a large foyer shared by only one other apartment. I whistled silently. Half a floor. Not a bad spread for an up-and-coming executive.

The only other doors in the foyer led to an elevator and a set of fire stairs. The foyer was empty. I took the stairs down eleven flights to the basement parking garage.

There were six hover jobs down there, two Porches, a Dornier, a Jaguar, a BMW, and a Lexus sport coupe. The BMW was parked in slot 11-A. It was Rieger's car, a metallic silver 925-I. The windows were tinted to a shade approaching black.

The car's alarm system buzzed once, to let me know that it was tracking me. I pulled the key chip out of my pocket and held it out so that the car could scan it. The alarm beeped softly, a friendly tone this time.

I stepped up to the car and slid the chip through the door sensor. The powered gull-wing door opened quietly, folding itself up and out of the way.

I slid behind the wheel and looked around. The interior of the car was rich with leather in sweeping ergonomic shapes.

I searched it quickly, but thoroughly. Nothing at all out of the ordinary, unless you counted the panties in the glove compartment. They were mint green and, to my eye, quite a bit too small to belong to anyone over the age of twelve or thirteen. I put them back where I'd found them.

I climbed out, and punched the button that closed the door.

Just to be thorough, I went through the trunk. Nothing. I didn't know what I'd been looking for, but I hadn't found it. I closed the trunk.

The pile of bodies in this case was still growing, I'd been set up for murder, and I was suddenly without a suspect again.

I looked down at the BMW key chip in my hand. There was still time to return it to Rieger's apartment, but some instinct told me not to.

Bolted to the cement wall was a stainless steel cabinet with a glass door. Inside was a chemical foam fire extinguisher. I hid the key chip in the cabinet behind the extinguisher.

When I got outside of Rieger's apartment building, I discovered that the rain had stopped. The squall had probably passed over while I was laying unconscious on Rieger's carpet, leaving only the sinking of the sun to darken the sky.

I walked to the Venice Boulevard Lev station and caught the six p.m. to Dome 6.

An old man sat at the rear of the Lev car with his feet tucked under him in the seat. It was that crazy old street preacher that everyone called Nostradamus. He scrutinized me with wild bloodshot eyes that seemed about to bulge from their sockets. His body swayed back and forth like one of those Indian snake charmers. "It's nearly here," he crooned. "The signs is all around us. More of 'em comin' ever day. The Convergence is comin'!"

The man's green flannel shirt was filthy. His stained brown jeans were at least three sizes too large. His trademark aroma of dried urine and old sweat permeated the Lev car.

"I ain't just jabberin' to hear myself talk," he croaked. "You runnin' outta time, boy."

I looked up at the *No Smoking* sign and lit a cigarette. "You're telling me," I said. "You're telling me."

CHAPTER 21

Lisa answered the door. She was dressed in a peach colored faux-satin blouse and black skirt with a slit that ran well up her plump left thigh. She'd made a valiant attempt at covering her bruises with makeup. The swelling in her face was receding nicely, but yellow and purple splotches peeked out from behind the camouflage. She opened the door wider and I stepped past her into the apartment.

When she caught sight of me, Sonja crossed the room in three quick strides, slid her arms around me, and kissed me.

"I don't have a lot of time," I said.

An impish grin came over Sonja's face. "What does that mean? You just dropped by for a quickie?" She pretended to unbutton the top of her blouse. "Shall we just drop right here on the carpet?"

Lisa prodded the carpet with her big toe. "This is my house, and nobody does the dirty deed on my carpet without my permission. Especially not before I get a chance to vacuum."

"Listen," I said. "Something has happened. We need to talk. All of us."

Sonja backed up a half step and held me at arm's length. "What happened to your face?"

"Rieger is dead," I said.

"What?" Sonja's voice nearly squeaked.

Lisa didn't say anything.

"Somebody blew Rieger away," I said. "And they used my gun to do it."

Sonja's hand flew to her mouth. "Oh my God."

"He was an asshole," Lisa said.

Sonja looked at Lisa like she was from another planet. "He's dead," Sonja said incredulously.

Lisa shrugged. "He was a bastard. He used people. He used me. He used Mike. Face it, Sonja. He used you too."

She looked at me. "If you shot him, I'm sure as hell not going to cry over it."

"I didn't shoot him," I said. "I was unconscious at the time."

I pulled my collar away from my neck and turned to show the bruising and blisters. "Somebody zapped me in the neck with a riot stunner. I woke up on Rieger's floor with my gun in my hand. I found Rieger taped to a chair with a bullet in his head. I'm pretty sure it came from my gun."

Lisa shrugged again. "I don't care if you *did* shoot him..."

"I didn't fucking shoot him!" I caught myself and lowered my voice. "I didn't shoot him, Lisa. I swear I didn't."

"I believe you," said Lisa.

Sonja looked at her left hand; there was blood on it. "You're bleeding."

"Yeah, from the back of my head. I know. My head hit the sidewalk when she stunned me."

"When *who* stunned you?" Lisa asked.

"Ms. X," I said. "The mystery woman."

Lisa tilted her head slightly. "The killer is a woman?"

"I don't know if she's the killer," I said, "but there's a woman wrapped up in this somehow."

I ticked the items off on my fingers. "It was a woman who zapped me. There was a woman with Michael when he was killed. *And*, there was a woman in the store when Michael bought the holo-camera."

Sonja walked over to Lisa's computer desk and steered the chair out from behind it. "Don't forget the woman on the Lev."

"Right," I said. "A woman tried to kill me on the Lev a couple of days ago."

Lisa ran her fingers through her hair. "What does this mystery woman look like?"

I shrugged, a move I immediately regretted. The muscles in my neck still hurt from the zapper. "Dark hair. Slender. Medium height. I never really got a good look at her."

"Not even when she zapped you?"

"She hit me from behind. I got a really good look at her boots, but that's about it."

Sonja wheeled the chair across the room and positioned it directly under a light fixture. "Sit down," she said. "I need to get a look at your head."

"I don't have time. I just came by to check on you and Lisa, and to tell you that I'm dropping out of sight for a few days."

Sonja pointed to the chair. "Sit."

"Why the disappearing act?" asked Lisa.

"I told you. I'm pretty sure that the killer used my gun to murder Rieger. She planted some other evidence too, a pretty tight frame. If I can't catch her before the police figure out that Rieger is dead, I'm screwed."

Sonja stood with her hands on her hips. "At least let me clean it up. If this gets infected while you're out there chasing bad guys, you're going to get sick. If you get sick, you lose the edge. If you lose the edge, the bad guys eat your lunch."

"Bad *girls*," Lisa said. "Or would the complement of *guys* be *gals*?"

Sonja pointed to the chair again. "Sit, David. This is only going to take a minute."

I sat.

Her fingers probed the back of my head. I knew she was using a gentle touch, but the contact triggered another wave of pain and nausea.

Sonja whistled softly through her teeth. "Your hair is pretty matted with blood. I can't really see anything. Lisa, can I ruin a couple of your face towels?"

"No problem. Look in the linen closet at the end of the hall. Try to take the ones that don't match."

Sonja walked out of sight down the hall.

Lisa settled her weight carefully onto the couch. "You should eat something before you go off chasing bad gals. If you go out there on an empty stomach, the bad gals will eat your lunch."

"No," I said. "No thank you."

The sound of running water came from the direction of the bathroom. A few seconds later, Sonja appeared at the end of the hall carrying three towels: two damp, one dry. The damp towels were hot enough to leave vapor trails.

Sonja applied one gently to the back of my scalp.

"Jesus! That's hot."

She blotted it carefully to dissolve the dried blood. "Now we're getting somewhere."

"I thought this wasn't going to take long."

"If you sit still, it won't."

"That towel is hot. And it hurts."

Lisa made a face. "If you're going to play with the big gals, you've got to be prepared to take your lumps."

Sonja switched to the second damp towel. "What now, David? Do you just walk out the front door and disappear?"

"I guess so. For a few days at least."

"Then what?"

"By then, I'll have either caught the killer, or the police will have caught me."

"Will you call me?"

I thought about it. "The police will probably tap my phone," I said. "But they wouldn't have any reason to tap Lisa's. It should be okay as long as I use a public phone. Yeah. I'll call when I can."

Sonja exhaled slowly. "Good. I'm going to worry myself to death as it is."

She switched to the dry towel. "Actually, this doesn't look too bad. You could use one or two staples, but I can fake it with a butterfly bandage. I'm going to have to shave a little patch back here, okay?"

"Whatever," I said. "Just hurry. I've got to get moving before the cops do."

Sonja looked up. "Lisa, have you got any scissors? I'm going to need a razor too."

"Scissors are somewhere in one of the kitchen drawers. You go after them; I'll get the razor."

Sonja lifted my right hand to the back of my head. "Here. Hold this towel there until I get back. You're scalp isn't bleeding much, but I don't want to have to clean it up again."

She and Lisa disappeared on their respective errands.

Lisa returned first. She handed me a pink plastic disposable razor and leaned close to my ear. "I thought you said you two weren't sleeping together."

"Oh. In the restaurant, when we had lunch? We weren't. Not then."

Lisa snapped her fingers. "Damn! I knew I should have raped you when I had the chance."

CHAPTER 22

III II I I IIIII I II II I I II I IIE IEII IIII II I IIIIII II IEI I III III

I called House from a pay phone at the 52nd Street Lev Depot because it was closest to the barricade.

He answered with his *David can't come to the phone* routine.

"House, this is David."

"Good evening, David."

"Evening, House. Listen, I just ran into my friend Roger. Everything is fine, but I won't be coming home any time soon. I just wanted to let you know not to look for me. I'm not expecting any visitors, so don't leave the light on, okay?"

"Of course, David. Will there be anything else?"

"No. Goodnight, House."

I hung up.

The entire conversation, following the words '*my friend Roger*' was a dodge that Maggie and I had worked out years before. When one of us thought the phone might be bugged, we used the 'Roger' code.

The meaning of everything after that phrase was inverted. We had included House in our little conspiracy, and it had paid off more than once.

I had just told House that:

A — Something was wrong.

B — I would be home soon.

C — I was expecting unwanted visitors.

D — If anyone showed up, leave a light on to warn me.

The police might not know about Rieger yet, but it wasn't too early to start watching my back.

I crossed through the barricade and circled two blocks out of my way to approach the house from the rear. The light in the loft was off, so my house was safe, for now at least.

I headed straight for my bedroom. A shower sounded fantastic, but I decided to settle for clean clothes. I didn't know how much time I had, and it probably wasn't a good idea to get Sonja's bandage wet anyway.

I emptied the contents of my pockets on the bed, and dropped my dirty pants on the floor. I usually clean up after myself, but I was in a hurry. One of House's remotes would have to take care of it.

I was looking through my closet for clean clothes when it struck me that Lisa's data chip hadn't been in the little pile of articles I'd dropped on the bed.

I turned back to the bed and poked through the junk from my pocket. The chip was definitely gone. It had either fallen out of my pocket, or the killer had searched me while I'd been unconscious. Either way, I'd lost Kurt Rieger's itinerary and immigration records, and the news stories on the Osiris murders.

With Lisa's copy of the chip lost to Rieger's goons, the data was completely gone. After what had happened to Lisa the first time, I couldn't ask her to risk running another search. I would try to get by without the chip, and hope that it wasn't costing me some crucial shred of information. I could always hire a jacker later, if I needed to.

I pulled on a pair of dark blue pants and zipped them up. "House, how much cash do we have on hand?"

"Eighteen hundred sixty-three Euro-marks. Will that be sufficient, or shall I arrange to withdraw more?"

I tossed a purple nylon travel bag on the bed and started stuffing it with a couple of changes of clothes. "That should be plenty," I said. "My accounts may be locked out by now anyway. Go ahead and bring me the money; I may have to leave in a hurry."

"Of course, David."

"While you're at it, bring my night goggles."

"Of course," House said.

I drew the Blackhart and ejected the magazine. I hadn't chambered a round, but I cycled the slide and checked anyway. The chamber was empty.

The pistol and magazine went into the travel bag, between two layers of clothing.

In the top of the closet was a black Kevlar box. I pulled it off the shelf, and pressed the ball of my right thumb to the lock sensor. The sensor strobed a red bar of light across my thumbprint and unlatched the lid of the box.

I flipped it open and pulled out Maggie's Blackhart. Funny, after four years, I still thought of it as Maggie's.

The box went back on the closet shelf.

On the way to the kitchen, I stopped by the hall closet and grabbed the cleaning kit. Maggie's Blackhart hadn't been cleaned or fired in years. I field stripped it and oiled it over the kitchen table. If the police came before I was finished, I could abandon Maggie's gun and slip out the side door with my travel bag. That way, I'd still have my own Blackhart.

If it hadn't begun already, sooner or later there was going to be an investigation into the death of Kurt Rieger. My Blackhart was a vital piece of evidence. I wanted to hand it over to the police in the same condition I'd found it in. If I fired it again, or even cleaned it, I'd be destroying evidence. I could still use it if I had to, but I wanted to avoid that if possible.

Maggie's pistol went back together without interruption. I loaded it with a fresh magazine and slid it into my shoulder holster. A spare magazine went in the pocket of my windbreaker, and another in my pants pocket.

A drone rolled into the kitchen on yellow neoprene wheels. Its vid camera eyes locked on my position at the table. It glided silently to a spot a half-meter or so from my chair, clutching a fat envelope in one of its three-fingered manipulators and the gray molded-plastic case for my night goggles in another.

I took the envelope, putting half of the cash in my pocket and the rest in the bag.

I popped open the gray plastic case and checked the power cell for the night goggles. The readout was well into the green: plenty of power. They were good goggles, Weaver Night-Stalkers that had somehow followed me home when I'd left the Army.

I nodded at the drone to dismiss it. "Thanks, House."

"My pleasure, David."

House's drone turned and rolled out of the kitchen.

If there was anything else I needed, I couldn't think of it.

I walked to the door. "House, the police are probably going to come looking for me pretty soon. If they have a warrant, go ahead and let them in, okay?"

"Very well, David."

"Record everything they do, but don't interfere with them."

"Of course."

"If they try to access your maintenance board, or tamper with your software in any way, I want you to copy your program and data files to your protected memory cores. Then erase yourself from the mainframe. Don't leave anything behind, not even maintenance files. I'll come back and reload you as soon as this blows over, okay?"

"Yes, David."

I stepped through the door and into the darkened street. "Good-bye, House."

"Good-bye, David."

The door clanging shut behind me sounded like the slamming of a prison door. And suddenly, I was alone.

CHAPTER 23

‖‖‖‖‖‖‖‖‖‖‖‖‖‖‖‖‖‖‖‖‖‖‖‖‖‖‖‖‖‖‖‖‖‖‖‖

The cops might not be on the lookout for me yet, but I decided not to risk the barricade. I left the Zone through North Lock with the intent of skirting no-man's land all the way around to the 7th Street Lock at Dome 11.

I wore my nose filters, and dosed myself with ear and eye drops. I decided to skip the solar block; I would be back under the domes long before the sun came up.

Outside the lock, I turned left. The curved concrete skirt of the dome's foundation stood like the wall of a fortress at my left shoulder. To my right, on the other side of the bulldozed margin of earth that separated the new Los Angeles from the old, lay the darkened bones of the abandoned city. Under the dome's halogen-arc perimeter lights, the pulverized earth took on an unnatural blue-gray hue, like the soil of some alien planet.

It took me a couple of hours to walk to the 7th Street Lock. By the time I got there, it was pushing midnight, and I was too tired to do much of anything.

I needed a place to spend the night. There was always Lisa's apartment, but I didn't want to take the chance of leading someone to her and Sonja. A hotel then, preferably a seedy one that wouldn't be too nosy about people who checked in after midnight.

I smiled when it came to me: the Velvet Clam. They didn't ask for ID and, with Holtzclaw dead, no one there knew me.

I caught a taxi to Dome 14.

The new night manager kept his black hair combed over the top of his head to disguise the onset of baldness. He was a big man, ruggedly built, but his waistline and neck were starting to show the symptoms of middle age spread.

He slid a ledger across the oval acryliflex counter for my signature. "You need a woman?"

I signed in as George T. Carson. "I'm meeting someone."

"You get more than three occupants in your room, you have to pay another ten marks."

184

I dropped the €m50 room rent on the counter top. "No problem. There'll just be the two of us."

He closed the ledger and slid a key chip across the counter. "Room 312. Third floor. Check out time is eleven."

Room 312 was painted fuchsia instead of pink. Other than that, it was identical to 216.

The hotel's cartoon clam holosign floated outside the room's only window, opening and closing languidly. The sign was obviously intended to be sensual, but from my window, its gargantuan scale made it more intimidating than erotic. It looked very much as though the giant fleshy lips were about to devour my room.

I locked the door and dropped the travel bag on the floor. It was time for that shower I'd been promising myself.

The plastic walls of the shower stall were a grubby salmon color, patched in several places with crooked rectangles of fiberglass. Streaks of rust stained the plastic from the water-spotted chrome fixtures to the drain in the floor.

The shower's projection unit kicked in as soon as I stepped in and slid the door shut. The shabby plastic walls faded behind an image of a grassy meadow. Two naked women appeared in the projection. They began touching themselves.

Some primal part of my psyche began to respond; I felt the stirrings of an unwanted erection. I didn't want to be stimulated, not tonight. I wanted a shower, and sleep.

I thumped the wall with the heal of my left hand, "off." The projection remained; the women continued to stroke themselves, oblivious to my command. "Off, goddamn it," I said, louder this time. The projection vanished and the shower walls reappeared.

A few seconds of staring at the grimy little shower stall convinced me that the porn projection was the lesser of evils. I sighed, "on."

The meadow reappeared. I tried not to look at the women.

The water surprised me by staying hot the entire time. I managed to keep my head dry enough for Sonja's bandage to stay attached.

Afterward, I sat on the carpet with a towel wrapped around my waist and smoked a cigarette. There weren't any chairs and I have a phobia about smoking in bed.

Bolted to the wall beside the blood-scanner was a holo-deck. The remote was chained to a nightstand beside the bed. I turned it on and flipped through the channels in search of a news program. I wanted to see if the word had gotten out on Rieger's murder. The deck showed twenty-two channels of porn vids. Not one of them looked anything like a news program.

I shut off the deck and ground out my cigarette in the ashtray on the nightstand.

Before I climbed into bed, I put on clean clothes and stuffed the Blackhart under the pillow. I might wake up wrinkled, but I wanted to be ready to move on a moment's notice.

I slid between the sheets and turned off the room lights. In place of the bright florescence of the overhead fixtures, pink tinted light from the holosign shone through the window. The reddish shadows it cast marched back and forth across the fuchsia walls each time the animated clam opened and closed.

I decided against closing the curtain. The pink light wasn't bright enough to bother me.

It took a little while to find a comfortable position; the back of my head was still pretty tender.

Exhaustion claimed me quickly and dragged me down into a deep dreamless sleep.

I came awake in the pink tinted gloom.

The door...

I grabbed the Blackhart, rolled out of bed and scooted across the carpet to stand to the left of the door with my back against the wall.

The lock snicked open, then the door opened slowly.

My visitor had taken the trouble to disconnect the lighting tubes in the hall, to keep the light from waking me when the door was opened. Good move. Had I not recently been zapped from behind and framed for murder, it probably would have worked. As it was, my paranoia was ready to wake me at the slightest sound.

A vague shape loomed in the open doorway and extended its arm into my room.

The lime-green pencil beam of a laser sight flashed from the intruder's fist to play across the rumpled bed sheets. Immediately in the wake of the targeting laser came the popcorn-popper burp of a silenced machine pistol, and a series of muffled thumps as a hail of slugs chewed my mattress to shreds. A brittle shattering sound told me that one of the bullets had found the lamp on the nightstand.

The stranger's finger relaxed on the trigger and the firing stopped. A head and shoulders followed the outstretched arm into my hotel room. The dim light of the hotel's holosign played across the intruder's face, the raised surfaces of his cheeks, nose, and forehead standing out in pink-tinged relief, the pits of his eye sockets and mouth lost in dark red shadow.

As soon as his head was clear of the door frame, I clubbed it with the barrel of the Blackhart just as hard as I could. The crack of steel-on-skull was much louder than the quiet cough of the machine pistol had been.

My would-be killer slammed sideways into the door frame, but didn't go down. He reeled, trying to shake off the blow. The machine pistol swung in my direction.

I stepped inside the arc of his extended fist and backhanded him across the face with the Blackhart. I felt the liquid crunch of bone and cartilage as my pistol broke the stranger's nose. Hot blood sprayed my fingers.

He slumped to the floor, the machine pistol spinning out of his grasp and across the carpet.

I kicked his legs into the room, and slammed and locked the door.

He lay on his side groaning.

I felt for the machine pistol with my foot and kicked it farther away from his hand. "How many more are out there?"

He grunted heavily and spit a mouthful of blood on my carpet. No answer.

I cycled a round into the chamber of the Blackhart.

His body jerked when the slide slammed forward. The odor of urine joined the lingering stench of gunpowder in the air.

Keeping the pistol pointed in his direction, I backed across the room to the bathroom and flicked the light switch with my elbow. The open doorway threw a triangular swath of light across the carpet. It was nearly bright enough to make me squint. I would have to be careful not to look toward the bathroom until my eyes adjusted.

The intruder lay on the carpet, blinking against the unexpected brightness. He looked young, maybe twenty-two or twenty-three. His shellacked brown hair fanned out in a rigid wing behind his head like the rear spoiler on a hovercraft. The sleeves of his silver jacket were torn off at the shoulders. Blood covered the lower half of his face, but I was pretty sure that I'd never seen him before.

I stepped into the center of the room, keeping my back to the light.

The machine pistol lay at my feet. I picked it up. It was made from a graphite laminate, light, but strong as hell. Most of the weight came from the silencer and laser sight. It didn't have an ejection port, so I figured it was chambered for caseless ammunition.

The fire selector was set to *Auto*. I thumbed it to *Single* and shoved the Blackhart into my shoulder rig.

A gentle tug on the trigger activated the targeting laser. A tiny spot of green light appeared on the wall. I aimed the machine pistol so that the green spot came to rest on the intruder's right knee.

"Feel like talking?" I asked.

Silence. Another mouthful of blood and spit on the carpet.

I squeezed the trigger gently. The pistol coughed once quietly, and my visitor screamed as the round blew out his knee.

I let him howl for a little while, to give him a chance to get used to the idea that I really had no-shit shot him, and that I would probably do it again.

I didn't have to worry about attracting attention; a lot of the Velvet Clam's patrons were screamers.

After fifteen or twenty seconds, I told him to shut up.

He grabbed his shattered knee and kept screaming. His grasping fingers slowed the flow of blood, but didn't stop it.

I put my left foot on his chest and shifted about half of my weight on to it. "Shut the fuck up. Now."

I pointed the green spot of light between his eyes.

It took him a visible effort of will to reign in his panic enough to stop screaming. His chest heaved heavily under my foot, like a child who's had the wind knocked out of him and is desperate for that next gulp of air. He couldn't stifle it entirely; he settled on a whimpering rooted deep in his chest.

"In three seconds, I'm going to do your other knee," I said. "About three seconds after that, your left elbow. Do you sense a pattern emerging here?"

He grunted. I decided to take it as a 'Yes'.

"Good," I said. "Now that we understand the rules of this game, let's play." I drew a bead on his left leg. "Three... Two..."

"Don't shoot! Oh God, please don't shoot me again! There's just the two of us, I swear. Just me and Bobby Dean, I *swear*!"

"See? That wasn't so hard, was it? I ask a simple question; you give a simple answer. Now let's try another one. Where is this Bobby Dean now?"

"Outside, across the street from the front of the hotel. In case you get past me."

I lifted my foot off his chest and backed over to the nightstand, still covering him with the machine pistol.

A stray round had punched a hole through the middle of my cigarette pack. I dumped the mangled contents of the pack onto the nightstand and rummaged through it. I managed to find an unbroken cigarette and light it left-handed. "Who sent you?"

"Nobody."

I stepped toward him. "Three..."

"No," he said. "I swear. Nobody sent us. We just got the word!"

"The word?"

"Your trid is all over the street. The man is forking fifty K to whoever stiffs you."

"Fifty thousand marks? What man? Give me a name."

He rolled back onto his side, still clutching the knee. "Don't *know*. It hurts. Oh God, it fucking hurts."

I took a drag off the cigarette and pumped a slug through the carpet a couple of centimeters from his good knee. The bullet appeared to shatter when it hit the floor. It was some sort of frangible round, designed for minimum penetration against hard objects like walls: an assassin's bullet.

The intruder flinched when the gun went off. "Please don't shoot me again! I don't *know* the man's name. I don't. I could make some shit up, but that's *all* I could do. I really don't know. Do I look connected enough to know the man's name?"

"How do you get in touch with this *man* when the job is done?"

"You're gonna think I'm lying."

"Try me."

He swallowed heavily. "Call a number and say this nursery rhyme shit. It's on the back of the trid, the number and the shit you gotta say. Then you leave the phone off the hook, and the man finds you."

"The trid. You have it on you?"

"Yeah. I think so."

"Get it," I said. "Carefully."

He pried one blood-covered hand away from his knee and felt his pockets. "Bobby must have it."

"Forget it. How did you find me?"

He wiped his hand on his jacket and wrapped it back around the crippled knee. "I'm bleeding to death here."

"Maybe you should talk a little faster then."

He coughed wetly and spit blood again. "Me and Bobby went door to door, checking all the rat-trap hotels and showing your pic around. We got lucky on the fourth or fifth one. The manager charged us a hundred marks."

"Did he give you a key chip?"

"No. I think he knew we were gonna stiff you. He didn't want the computer record to show that his pass chip had opened the door. I spoofed your lock. The jumper's in the hall on the floor. I missed the pattern the first time around and I had to run it again..."

The rest of the sentence lay unspoken: *or else I'd have caught you in bed.*

My eyes were pretty much adjusted to the light.

I dropped my cigarette in the ashtray and ejected the clip from the machine pistol.

The magazine was one of those staggered-box jobs that hold about ninety rounds. "Nice weapon," I said. "Russian?"

"Israeli," he groaned.

"My second guess."

I popped the top round out of the clip. The front third of the round, the bullet itself, seemed to be made of plastic. A cylindrical block of solid propellant was molded directly to the back of the plastic head.

"Plastic bullets?"

"No. The plastic part's a sabot. It opens up and falls off after the round leaves the barrel. The round is a ceramic flechette."

"Meat grinder rounds?"

"Yeah."

I'd seen meat grinders used in Argentina, out of a shotgun, not a machine pistol. The nickname was accurate.

I jammed the magazine back into the machine pistol and cocked it again. "You must have really wanted me dead."

He didn't answer.

"How long before Bobby comes looking for you?"

"Probably not at all," he said. "We're not exactly buddies. This is sort of a one-time partnership."

"What's your name?"

"Ryan." No hesitation, probably the truth. "Everybody calls me Razor."

"You ever kill anyone before, Ryan?"

"No," he said.

"I have."

He shuddered. "What are you going to do to me?"

"I'm going to walk out of here. If you behave yourself, you'll still be breathing when I do."

He looked up at me, the first glimmer of hope in his eyes.

I sat on the bed and changed my socks. The left one was soaked with blood from stepping on Ryan's chest. I rolled up the bloody sock so that the wet part was at the center, and wound the other sock around that to make a neat, dry packet. I stuck the little bundle in my pocket.

I pulled on my shoes and stood up. "If I ever catch you in my shadow, I'll kill you. No hesitation. Understand?"

Ryan nodded.

"Good. Now, close your eyes and turn your face to the wall. If you so much as flinch before I'm out of here, I'll empty this clip into your head."

Ryan clenched his eyes shut and turned his face away.

I flicked the fire selector on the machine pistol back to *Auto*. Despite Ryan's assurances, his backup might be inside the hotel, maybe just on the other side of my door.

I punched the bypass button on the electronic lock, snatched the door open, and leapt across the hall, clear of the doorway, the machine pistol at the ready. The hall was empty in both directions.

The stairs were about 20 meters down the hall to the right of my room. I covered the distance quickly and quietly until I stood with my back to the wall just short of the open doorway to the stairwell.

I wheeled around the corner and swung the machine pistol to cover the stairs. Nobody home.

I cat-footed down two flights and repeated my jack-in-the-box entry. The lobby was empty.

A split second after I rounded the corner, the longshoreman night manager stepped into his office and closed the door.

I walked around the end of the counter and rapped on the door with the barrel of the machine pistol.

"I didn't tell them nothing." His voice was muffled by the cheap wooden door.

"Then what are you hiding from?"

"I'm calling the cops."

"What are you going to tell them? That you sent someone up to my room to murder me in my sleep, and I had the nerve to get pissed-off about it?"

"I didn't send nobody nowhere."

"But you told them where to find me, didn't you?"

"Go away," he said. "I don't want no trouble."

"Open the door. I'm not going to hurt you."

"Go away. I got a gun in here."

"Open the door or I'm going to start shooting through the wall." I knocked on the sheetrock with the end of the silencer. "Sounds pretty thin," I said. "Think it'll stop bullets?"

Actually, it probably *would* stop the machine pistol's ceramic flechettes, but he didn't have to know that.

"The door ain't locked," he said.

"I didn't ask you if it was locked. I told you to open it."

The door opened a couple of centimeters.

"Open it the rest of the way, then back up slowly."

He did as he was told, backing away from the open door with his hands held out to show that they were empty. There was no sign of the gun he had mentioned.

I glanced around the room before stepping inside.

Longshoreman blinked several times rapidly. "What do you want?"

"Two things," I said. "First, is there a back way out of here?"

He jerked his chin toward a metal door on the other side of the desk. "What else?"

I dropped the key chip on the desk top. "I want my key deposit back. I'm checking out."

CHAPTER 24

I hopscotched across the darkened parking lot, using parked cars and shadows for cover. I didn't see any sign of Bobby Dean, if there was such a person. I had no doubt that Ryan had backup, but I didn't trust his version of the details. For all I knew, there were six of them, and none was named Bobby Dean.

On the far side of the parking lot, I stopped in the shadow of a coffee shop. A purple neon sign on the front of the building spelled out *Knick Knack Kerouac* in misshapen lettering designed to resemble graffiti. Cute.

I stood for a second, scanning the area for Ryan's buddies, and considered my next move. I could keep walking. I didn't really need to talk to this Bobby Dean. On the other hand, I wanted to see that trid. Besides, Bobby had come to pay me a visit in the night; it seemed only polite to return the favor.

I walked a block North on La Brea, turned left on Waring, walked another block, and turned left again on Detroit. I watched the shadows carefully, paranoia riding my shoulders like a pet demon.

The stretch of Melrose leading back toward the Velvet Clam was reasonably well lit. I stuck to the middle of the street to avoid being silhouetted by the streetlights.

Bobby was crouched in the shadow of a dilapidated brown Chrysler, eyes glued to the front door of the Velvet Clam.

Surprise. Bobby was Bobbie.

I swept the area with my eyes, looking for more of Ryan's friends. Nobody. Just Bobbie.

I crept up behind her, machine pistol ready if she turned around.

Sneaking up on her didn't exactly require ninja-like stealth. The idiot had brought her jam-box to an ambush.

I set the travel bag down quietly.

A machine pistol identical to Ryan's lay on the sidewalk beside her.

She was so wrapped up in watching the hotel and listening to her music that she didn't even notice when I picked up her weapon. I flicked on the safety and stuck it in my waistband.

193

A gentle tug on the trigger of Ryan's machine pistol kicked on the laser sight. I pointed the green dot at the fender directly in front of Bobbie's face.

She spun around, scrabbling frantically for her gun. She stopped when she realized that the green dot was dancing on the bridge of her nose. She sat down on the sidewalk and pulled the earphones out of her ears.

I could hear the music now, distant sounding and tinny. I didn't recognize the song, but the band was called *Albino Safari*, a white supremacist slash-rock group popular with skin heads and other Nazi wannabe's.

"Are you Bobbie?"

The woman nodded quickly.

"Move away from the car," I said, "into the light." I drew a path for her on the cement with the laser.

She started to get up.

"No. Don't stand up. Just slide over."

Bobbie planted her hands on the sidewalk and crabbed sideways in sort of a scoot-shuffle.

"There. That's good."

She settled to the sidewalk.

I got a better look at her in the light. She was a little older than Ryan, but not much.

Her left eye was artificial, a chromed steel sphere with a glowing red LED for a pupil. The left side of her head was shaved, her scalp tattooed with black zebra stripes. The tattoo flowed out of sight down the left side of her neck and re-emerged from the left sleeve of her black tee shirt. It probably covered the entire left side of her body. The hair on the right side of her head was a stiff ruff, cut and teased to resemble the mane of a zebra, and dyed to compliment her tattoo.

She wore tight red jeans and a wide black leather belt with silver swastika-shaped ornaments. The laces of her ultra-white Korean running shoes were threaded through a pair of steel military dog tags.

"How many of you are there?"

She spit her chewing gum on the sidewalk. "Just me and Razor."

She was probably lying.

"Where's Razor?" she asked. "Did you kill him?"

I planted the green targeting dot on the center of her forehead. "What do you think?"

"Shit."

"You've got a trid," I said. "I want it."

She reached around her back.

"Careful..."

Her hand came back around slowly. In it was a trid.

I took it carefully from her outstretched fingers. It was me all right. There was a printed message on the back, just like Ryan had said. I didn't have time to look at it closely; one of Ryan's thugs might come to Bobbie's rescue any second. I stuck the trid in the pocket of my windbreaker.

"Turn around. Lace your fingers behind your head." I gestured with the machine pistol.

Bobbie did as she was told.

"Listen to me carefully. I'm going to walk away. If you so much as sneeze before I'm out of sight, I'm going to cut you to ribbons. You got that?"

She nodded.

"If I ever see you again, you're dog food. You understand?"

Another nod.

I picked up my travel bag and backed away. When I got about ten meters, I turned around and started jogging toward a line of parked cars that represented the closest cover.

A half-second before I reached the nearest car, something shiny whistled past my right ear.

I spun around, dropped to one knee, and squeezed off three rounds.

Bobbie was standing, her right arm poised to loose another swastika-throwing star.

One of the flechettes caught her in the right leg, mid thigh. Another punched a hole through her left leg, just above the knee. The impact drove her back against the side of the Chrysler.

Unlike Ryan, she didn't scream when she went down. Instead, she gave a strange squeak followed by a guttural keening.

I walked away quickly, using the cars for cover as much as possible.

Shiruken. Goddamned throwing stars. I should have checked her belt.

I took a right at the first corner and began sprinting immediately, constantly watching the shadows. I turned left at the next corner and continued sprinting, trying to distance myself from the Velvet Clam as rapidly as possible.

When I had three or four blocks behind me, I ducked into an alley, and waited in the darkness, hoping to ambush any pursuers.

After several minutes, I began to hope that I'd escaped. The tension gradually drained from my shoulders as my muscles started to relax.

I pressed the illumination button on my watch and stole a glance at the numerals: 2:17. Jesus. The day was less than three hours old, and I'd already shot two people.

I felt the shakes coming on. I tried to squelch them, will them away, but the tremors hit me hard enough to make my teeth chatter. My knees went wobbly. I made a vain effort to ignore the churning in my stomach. A surge of naked fear washed over me and left me sagging against the wall of a building.

A psychologist would probably call it a defense mechanism; I call it my *war face*. When the heat is on, I project this aura of invulnerability, the fearless persona that John had dubbed Sergeant Steel. It's a mask that I hide behind; a cold hard edge that protects me from my own weaknesses. But when the pressure is off, my war face deserts me, and leaves me wallowing in my own fear and self pity.

I hid there in the darkened alley until the tremors finally played themselves out. I pushed myself away from the wall and straightened up. I rolled my shoulders and drew a breath to steady myself.

I put both machine pistols in my travel bag and zipped it shut. The Blackhart hung ready in my shoulder holster if I needed it.

I moved to the edge of the alley and looked both ways. All clear. I stepped into the street and started walking.

I found an all-night convenience store on Willoughby Avenue. A blonde woman with an advanced case of middle aged frumpery sold me a printout of the latest news feed, a plastic bulb of coffee, and a pack of Marlboros to replace the ones that Ryan had shot to pieces.

I stood under a streetlight in the parking lot and read the news. The headlines centered around a major bombing in San Diego. Six simultaneous explosions had partially collapsed one of the big domes downtown. The death toll was in the hundreds and escalating rapidly as rescue crews uncovered more bodies. A radical Luddite Cult was taking credit for the catastrophe, calling it *"A return to God's Plan."*

The number two story outlined the crash of a JAL orbital passenger shuttle at Narita International.

Rieger's murder wasn't mentioned at all.

I shoved the printout into my travel bag and twisted the button-shaped top off of the coffee. The plastic bulb only took a few seconds to heat the coffee to a decent drinking temperature. I took a sip. The coffee was surprisingly good.

There was a public terminal in the parking lot. I used it to call a cab.

Across the street from the entrance to Nexus Dreams was a male strip club called *Tuff Guise*. The club's holo-facade showed the harem chambers of some fabulously rich sultan, with an obvious twist on the gender-angle: the sultan's harem girls were half-naked male body builder types. Their stern-looking scimitar-wielding guards were (naturally) female.

Every ten or twenty seconds, one or the other of the sultan's harem boys seemed to find an excuse to lose his breechcloth, or whatever they're called. From my perspective, I couldn't understand why anyone would bother to go inside the club; the show seemed to be out here.

The entrance to the club was the only part of the building's front not hidden behind the holo-facade. It was one of those weirdly fluted archways that people associate with Arabic architecture. It blended into the illusion so well that the club had run arrow-shaped strips of orange bio-florescent tape from the sidewalk to the arch to show that it was the real doorway.

I glanced around to make certain that no one was looking in my direction, then reached my left arm into the hologram. My fingers found the brick front of the building. I half expected my touch to somehow disrupt or distort the image, but the laser-projected illusion flowed seamlessly around my arm, hiding it every bit as well as it hid the front of the strip club. Perfect.

I looked around again. Nobody was watching me. I closed my eyes and stepped into the heart of the holo-facade.

Even with my eyes closed, the laser light that created the projection was bright enough to paint shifting blobs of color on the insides of my eyelids. I knew that a few seconds in here with my eyes open could damage my retinas.

I groped around inside the travel bag until my fingers found the plastic case that held my night goggles. It seemed to take an eternity of working by touch to get the Night-Stalkers out of their case and settled in place over my forehead. I felt for the power switch and flicked it on. The electroptic image amplifiers squealed softly as they powered up. I flipped the lenses down over my eyes.

Night-Stalkers work by super-amplifying available light, illuminating near total darkness into something approximating daylight. I didn't need that right now; it was already too bright inside the holo-facade. But the Night-Stalkers had a safety feature, an instant-reaction filter-mode that could subtract dangerously bright light sources, leaving only wavelengths and intensities that were safe for human vision.

I almost didn't open my eyes. Theoretically, I should be able to see through the holo-facade as if it were not there. But what if I was wrong? What if the Night-Stalkers were super-amplifying the already too bright light of the holo-facade? I hoped that the split second it would take me to check wouldn't be enough to cause permanent eye damage.

I jerked my eyes open and slammed them shut just as fast, a rapid-fire blink that told me what I needed to know. The Night-Stalkers were working perfectly.

I opened my eyes. The view through the lenses was cool, and green, a ghostly soft-focus rendering of the street without the unpleasant glare of the lasers.

I smiled to myself. This was the perfect vantage point. I could see the front of Nexus Dreams on the other side of Santa Monica Boulevard, and everything moving on the street. As long as I stayed within a meter and a half of the front of the building, the Tuff Guise holo-facade would keep me totally hidden. People strolled by me on the sidewalk just a few meters away, oblivious to my presence.

The brick wall of the club was covered in graffiti. Among the traditional obscene and gang-related scrawlings was the curved-X symbol I'd seen on the Lev a few days before. Under the symbol was written *'TRUST THE FLESH. CONTROL THE MACHINE. WATCH FOR THE CONVERGENCE, YOUR FUTURE HANGS IN THE BALANCE.'*

There was that word again. Convergence. It was popping up all over the place, and I still had no idea what it meant.

I leaned against the wall and reached into my pocket in search of cigarettes. My fingers came across a plump little bundle of fabric: the socks. I pulled them out of my pocket. The outer sock was still dry; Ryan's blood hadn't soaked through. I dropped both socks onto the sidewalk and used the toe of my shoe to shove them into the layer of trash that was accumulating against the front of the building. Just another bit of garbage hidden behind the clean illusion of the hologram.

I went back into my pocket for the cigarettes. They hadn't been opened yet; I peeled off the foil wrapper and pried the first one out of the pack.

The smoke triggered a fit of coughing when it hit my lungs. I stifled it as quickly as I could; disembodied coughs were bound to attract attention.

I read the fine print on the pack: Mexican Marlboros. Damn. I should have checked before I bought them. I hated Mexican tobacco.

I jammed the pack into my pocket and pulled out the trid that I'd strong-armed from Bobbie. I wanted to read the printing on the back; I expected the three-dimensional image on the front to be distorted or washed out by the combined influences of the holo-facade and my Night-

Stalkers. Instead, the image of my face was somehow reinforced, standing out with a lurid clarity unusual for a trid. Except for the green skin tones imparted by the night goggles, it was an excellent likeness: a close-up shot on the street through a high-powered lens. The background was blurry, but I could make out an arched doorway framed in neon. The pic had been shot in the Zone, on the sidewalk in front of Trixie's.

I flipped the trid over. On the back, printed in bold black typeface, were my name, a phone number, and four lines of text.

> *"THE TIME HAS COME," THE WALRUS SAID,*
> *TO TALK OF MANY THINGS:*
> *OF SHOES - AND SHIPS - AND SEALING WAX -*
> *OF CABBAGES - AND KINGS -*

Maybe it made sense to someone else, but it sounded like gibberish to me.

The phone number didn't look familiar. The trid went back in my pocket.

I chain-smoked the harsh Mexican cigarettes, swallowed my cough reflex, and watched Nexus Dreams from my hidden position inside the hologram. Even at nearly four in the morning, the traffic in and out was reasonably frequent.

Every twenty minutes or so, a police car would cruise by, making its rounds. I had to fight the urge to jump for cover, reminding myself that the police couldn't see through the holo-facade any more than the people on the street.

Half a pack of cigarettes later, Jackal walked out of the front door.

As soon as I was sure that she was alone, I stepped out of the hologram and pulled the Night-Stalkers off my forehead. I had to jog across Santa Monica Boulevard to catch up to her. When I was two steps behind her, I slowed down to match her pace. "Jackal."

She stopped and turned around. Her eyes were glassy. She was either drunk, or exhausted, or both.

"Just a minute." She pulled a memory chip out of her pocket and plugged it into the back of her head. Her eyes closed for a second. When they opened, her expression went wary. "Stalin?"

"Yeah. I need to talk to you."

"You need to talk to *somebody*," she said. "The word is out. You're slicked, you just don't know it yet."

I walked a few steps in the direction she'd been heading and motioned for her to follow. "It's better if we keep moving."

She didn't follow. "It's better if *you* keep moving. Whichever way you're heading, I'm going the other way."

I stopped. "Come on," I said. "I'm serious. I need to talk to you."

Jackal shook her head. "*I'm* serious. You're a homicide waiting to happen. Whenever it goes down, I don't intend to be around. What in the hell did you do, anyway?"

I dug through my pocket and pulled out my cigarettes. "I've been investigating a series of murders. I must be starting to get close, because I'm making someone very uncomfortable. Whoever it is has put out a street-contract on me."

"I heard," Jackal said. "Fifty K."

"I need you to sniff around on the net and find out who it is."

Jackal shook her head again. "Uh-uh. I don't want any part of this."

I thumped a cigarette out of the pack and lit it. "I thought you jackers thrived on danger. Dancing through the net a micro-second ahead of death, and all that. I'll make it worth your while."

Jackal hesitated. "How much?"

This case was rapidly pricing itself over Sonja's ability to pay, but it wasn't about money anymore. It was about survival, and I couldn't ask Jackal to risk her life for loose change. "Fifteen K."

Jackal shook her head. "Thirty."

I sighed. "Twenty."

"Twenty-five."

"Twenty," I said again.

"Twenty-five," Jackal repeated. "Somebody's willing to pay fifty to get your head on a plate. It ought to be worth half that to keep it on your shoulders, don't you think?"

"Okay," I said. "Twenty-five thousand. Now, let's get moving. We've been standing here too long already."

Jackal fell into step on my left side. "Where are we going?"

"I need somewhere to hide for a few hours. I want to get some sleep and maybe make a couple of phone calls."

I took a drag off the cigarette and coughed. "I'm thinking maybe a hotel. Some place with a phone in the room and no vid cameras in the halls. Oh, it has to have a rear entrance so you can rent the room, and I can slip in the back way. You know any places like that?"

Jackal stopped and began to scan the street. "No hotels. I've got a better idea, but we'll have to catch a cab."

"Where to?"

"Dome 16," Jackal said. "Ever heard of R.U.R.?"

I shook my head.

"It's sort of a robot cult," she said. "A bunch of chipheads. They're pretty whacked, but their little lair is a good place to hide. It's also a great place to make a net run from."

"I'd prefer a hotel," I said. "I don't know your chiphead buddies. With fifty thousand marks on my head, how can I be sure that they won't try to collect?"

"They won't," Jackal said. "It's kind of hard to explain, but that's not what they're into."

"A couple of hours ago, two punks tried to murder me in my sleep."

Jackal looked at me out of the corner of her eye. "You did them first?"

"No," I said. "But they're both going to be shopping for new legs. And I'm not feeling very trusting right now."

Jackal leaned out into the street and waved at a passing taxi. "I said my friends were whacked. I didn't say they were scum. Anyway, you don't have to trust them. You just have to trust *me*."

The hovercab slid up to the curb, the blowers swirling dirt and gum wrappers around our feet in an ankle-high maelstrom.

Jackal opened the rear door and got in. "Come on," she said.

I slid in beside her and punched the button that closed the door.

Jackal tapped a fingertip on the bulletproof shield. "LAX."

That took me by surprise. "LAX? Are we flying somewhere?"

"Keep it in your pants," Jackal said. "You'll find out soon enough."

The driver stuck to the domes for as long as possible, cutting west on Santa Monica Boulevard through Beverly Hills and West Los Angeles, and south on the 405 into Dome 13 and the northern fringes of Culver City.

When we pulled into the vehicle lock at the southern end of Dome 13, he looked over his shoulder at us. "Make sure your windows is up all the way. The air's gone get a little shitty, and the filters ain't workin' real good."

"It's only about eighteen kilometers to Dome 17," Jackal said. "A few carcinogens every now and then are good for you. Keeps you from getting addicted to oxygen."

The driver didn't smile.

We checked our windows, and then sat in silence until the huge steel doors slid open at the far side of the lock.

Unlike the city streets outside the domes, the major highways hadn't been allowed to atrophy. LA was, after all, a major city, and major cities require highways to connect them to other major cities; a maxim that has endured since the days of the Roman Empire.

Out past the dome's perimeter lights, the 405 stretched through the darkened remains of Culver City like a black river of plast-phalt carving its way through man-made cliffs of dilapidated buildings. Traffic was sparse, a few cars here and there, but mostly large unmanned cargo trucks shuttling back and forth from LAX.

True to the driver's word, the car's filtration system was not airtight. The smell of the outside air invaded the taxi almost immediately after we left the dome. It was a complex miasma, a strong bass-note of burned petrochemicals, overlaid by a spectrum of unwholesome odors from sulfurous ash to chlorine. The farther we got from Dome 13, the worse the stench became. By the time the perimeter lights of Dome 17 rose in the taxi's windshield, my eyes were watering and the back of my throat was burning.

We drove through the lighted archway into Dome 17's north lock. As the huge steel doors slid shut behind us, the driver spoke over his shoulder. "Keep them windows shut until we clear the lock."

We waited, stewing in the rank chemical air that had filled the cab. When the inner doors cycled open, we drove into Dome 17. As soon as we were clear of the lock, we rolled down the windows and breathed clean, filtered air again.

Following Jackal's directions, the cabby drove west on Imperial Highway. To our right, through the faceted skin of the dome, we could see passenger shuttles taking off from LAX, climbing into the night sky on columns of fire. Each launch was surrounded by a hundred silent ghost-images, reflections in the angled panes of the dome.

I found myself trying to guess which of the launches were sub-orbital shots bound for other cities, and which had destinations in orbit or beyond, outside of earth's polluted atmosphere and out of reach of the clawing fingers of her gravity-well.

We stuck to Imperial Highway, skirting the southern edge of the airport all the way to Dome 16.

We stopped at a strip mall on Vista Del Mar.

Jackal thumbed the latch button on her door. It folded open with a pneumatic wheeze, and she climbed out. "This is the spot," she said.

I paid the driver and got out. The cab drove away, the wail of its blowers fading into the distance well before its taillights dwindled to red pinpricks, and then to nothingness.

I looked around. Except for a coin-operated Laundromat, and a holo-arcade, the shops in the little mall were all closed for the night. "Where are we going?"

Jackal pointed across the street, to a sprawl of unlit buildings behind a rusting chain-link fence. "There." She stepped into the street and began walking toward the fence.

I took a couple of quick steps to catch up to her. "Your friends live in there?"

"Some of them."

The farther we got from the street lights, the darker it became, until the soft glow of moonlight filtering down through the dome was our only real illumination. I thought about digging around in my travel bag for my night goggles, but Jackal seemed to know where she was going.

I followed her through a ragged hole in the fence onto a concrete slab covered by shallow drifts of sand and a liberal sprinkling of broken glass, squashed plastic cans, and the occasional piece of twisted metal junk.

Jackal led me through a narrow lane between two dark cement buildings. Ten or fifteen meters on the other side of the alley, the cement gave way to some sort of latticed metal platform.

I stopped at the edge of it. I could hear the rush of water from somewhere in the darkness below. "What's this?"

Jackal walked a couple of meters out onto the grating and stopped. "It's a catwalk. What did you think it was?"

"What's under it?"

"Who cares? It's just a catwalk."

"What's under it?" I repeated.

Jackal's voice sounded puzzled, "A sluiceway for a hydro-electric generator. A tide engine. This used to be the old tidal-electric plant, back before cold fusion put it out of business. Why? What's the problem?"

"Is there a way to go around? Without using the catwalk?"

"The tide-engine isn't going to hurt you," Jackal said. "We'll look at it tomorrow in daylight. You can see it through the grate, about ten meters down. It looks like a giant jet engine with the skin pulled off."

"Let's go around."

"We can't go around," Jackal said. "Or rather, we could, but we'd just have to walk over a different catwalk."

She bounced up and down several times, her boot heels ringing on the metal platform. "Come on. It won't collapse. Trust me."

I took a quick breath. "Fine," I said, stepping onto the metal platform before I could change my mind. "Let's go."

I crossed the catwalk over the tide-engine as quickly as possible. The clang of my heels on the grating seemed to echo the pounding of my heart. I tried not to think about the dark water rushing beneath me, or the black concrete chasm under my feet.

Vertigo struck me like a club to the head, and suddenly I was falling, tumbling into darkness and death.

CHAPTER 25

I couldn't tell whether I was actually screaming, or if the shriek I heard existed only in my mind.

A slab of cement came up and slammed into me, knocking the wind out of my lungs. I lay there, fighting for breath, and trying to get used to the idea that I had fallen—not into the abyss beneath the grating—but to the sandy, trash-littered pavement on the other side of the catwalk.

"You okay?" Jackal's face hovered over mine; her voice seemed to come from a great distance.

I tried to say something, but it came out as a strangled gasp.

"You okay?" Jackal repeated. She grabbed my shoulder and shook it.

"Give... me... a second," I said. "I'm alright."

A few seconds later, she helped me to my feet. I brushed the sand off my clothes and tried to regain my composure.

"What in the hell was that?" Jackal asked.

I could feel my ears burning, not just with embarrassment over my little spectacle, but with the knowledge that the past could reach out and squeeze my heart like a grape. "I... don't like catwalks," I said.

"I guess not," Jackal said. "Can you walk?"

"Yeah," I said. "Let's go."

Jackal led me through the darkness to another building. She chose a dark vacant doorway that looked just like any one of a half-dozen others. The doorway led to a narrow staircase, lit at irregular intervals by strips of green bio-florescent tape.

Jackal stopped at the foot of the staircase. "The stairs are metal," she said. "Are you okay with that?"

"Yeah," I said. "Just not metal gratings—in the dark—when there's water."

"Good," Jackal said. "Because the elevator's a death trap."

She started climbing. "I'll say this for you, Stalin: your phobias are specific as hell."

I followed her up three flights.

The walls all along the stairs were peppered with graffiti. At the head of the stairs, the scrawled slogans and crude drawings gave way to hand-painted murals that covered the walls and ceiling. The artist, whoever he or she was, was exceptionally talented. The paintings depicted a world of machines. Chrome-skinned robots walking, driving cars, picnicking, arguing, watching the vid.

Most of the robots were based on men, women, or children, but there were robot dogs and cats as well. An alley scene even showed robotic rats digging through trash from an overflowing dumpster.

The mural room was lit by a chandelier welded from lengths of strap-iron. Bolted to the iron framework were hundreds of red, amber, and white lights in a variety of shapes: apparently the headlamps, taillights, and running lights of cars. The entire collection was strung together with a rat's nest of multicolored wire.

Jackal ignored the murals and the chandelier. She crossed to the far wall and knocked on a door that blended in with the paintings so well that I hadn't noticed it. A blue LED came on to the left of the door, flashed twice, and went out.

It occurred to me that I still didn't have a clear idea of who we were coming to visit.

"What does R.U.R. mean?" I asked.

"It stands for Rossum's Universal Robots," Jackal said. "A stage play from the early Twentieth Century. History credits the playwright, a Czechoslovakian guy, with inventing the entire concept of robotics."

I was about to ask another question, but the door swung open.

Standing in the doorway was the teenage boy I'd seen hanging out with Jackal at Nexus Dreams, the one I'd come to think of as Cyber-kid.

His electro-mechanical hand, the circuit-run tattoos on his shaved scalp, and the twin electroptic lenses of his eyes teamed up to make him look like the hybrid stage between a seventeen year old kid and one of the chrome robots shown in the mural. His vid-camera eyes squealed softly as the lenses locked on us and spun us into focus.

He greeted Jackal with a nod.

Jackal jerked a thumb in my direction. "This is Mr. Client," she said. She pointed at the kid. "Mr. Client, this is Surf."

Surf treated me to a sarcastic smile. "Welcome to Prime Time, Mr. Client," he said in his gravelly, synthetic voice.

He ushered us through the door into a much larger room. Here, the robot motif on the walls continued, but these robots weren't going about their own business; they were kneeling, heads bowed, as if paying homage to royalty.

The floor was an obstacle course of computer hardware that spanned at least three decades of technology. The entire mess was connected, cross-connected, and re-connected by a baffling spider web of cabling. LEDs and plasma displays danced while cooling fans whispered to themselves in the gloom.

At intervals of four or five meters, the cables and equipment seemed to converge to form nexuses so dense with hardware that they reminded me of cocoons. These cocoons were apparently computer operating-stations, and most of them appeared to be occupied. Men and women, many of them not much older than Surf, rode the net in the semi-darkness, their fingers drumming on unseen keyboards. Every one that I could see had at least one or two cranial sockets, slender cables jacking their brains into their equipment, and no doubt, the DataNet construct. Most of them had one or more visible cybernetic enhancements: eyes, ears, arms, legs, or some combination thereof.

Every piece of cable and conduit seemed to lead to an even larger cocoon at the center of the room. There, surrounded by a chest-high wall of hodgepodge computer equipment, sat the oldest woman that I had ever seen.

Jackal leaned close to my ear. "That's Iron Betty, queen-mother of this little kingdom. We have to pay our respects."

I glanced around at the mural. Every one of the chrome-skinned robots in the painting was bowing toward the old woman's operating station, as though it were a kind of throne.

Surf made his way toward the old woman, hopping over cable runs and darting past electronics modules with an ease that spoke of youth, familiarity, and boosted reflexes. Jackal and I followed at a slower pace, picking our way around the obstacles.

By the time we got close enough to the woman to speak, I saw that her entire scalp was encased in a steel skullcap, a curved metal prosthesis dulled to the matte gray of old iron. There were several cranial sockets built into the skullcap, and the woman was hardwired into her network of computer gear by about ten bundles of ribbon cable.

Surf waved toward us with his real hand. "Jackal and her friend, Mr. Client."

The woman didn't even glance at me. Her right hand twitched, but whether it was reflex, or some minimalist acknowledgment of my existence, I couldn't say.

"Welcome Jackal. What brings you to our door?"

Iron Betty's voice was normal, human sounding. Not at all the machine voice that I'd expected after meeting Surf. She spoke in a near-whisper, with a detached quality that seemed to suggest that her conversation with us was occupying only a fraction of her mind.

"Mr. Client needs a safe place to log some down-time," Jackal said. "And we need to make a net run."

Iron Betty still did not look at us. In fact, her gaze never seemed to shift from whatever unseen focal point that it was fixed on. I began to wonder if she was blind. "Your run... it involves an Artificial Intelligence?"

"Maybe," Jackal said. "We won't really know until we have a look-see."

Iron Betty sat without speaking for nearly a minute. I was beginning to wonder if she'd forgotten us, when she finally spoke again. "Your Mr. Client... he is a catalyst. He brings us closer to the *Convergence*. Either Man or Machine will profit by his hand, but I cannot yet see which. There are patterns—within patterns—within patterns." Her whispered voice reduced her words to something approaching a hiss.

"I don't understand," Jackal said. "Are you saying that he can stay? Or that he has to leave?"

"He is welcome," the old woman said. "Mr. Stalin... we can use his correct name here, can we not? ...will hasten the Convergence. Turning him from my door will not stop that from happening."

"How do you know my name?" I asked.

"We listen to every whisper on the net," Surf said. "And your name is whispered in a lot of places."

"What in the hell does that mean? And what is this *Convergence* that I'm supposed to be affecting?"

"It's like a race," Jackal said, "to the next level of evolution."

"A race? Between whom?"

"Between Man and Machine," Surf said. His speech-synthesizer managed to capture the haughty quality in his voice: the tone that an adult uses to lecture a recalcitrant child.

"We're competing with machines?" I asked.

Iron Betty sighed. "Competing is perhaps not a strong enough word, Mr. Stalin. *Vying for existence* might be more accurate."

I snorted. "So you're telling me that there's some kind of conspiracy of machines going on? I'm supposed to believe that my household appliances are plotting behind my back?"

"Believe what you will," Iron Betty whispered. "But Homo Sapiens was not always the dominant species on this planet. And there exists no law in nature that says that it must continue to be."

"And this Convergence is supposed to be the next stage," I said. "Okay, I'll go along. What *is* the next stage. What comes after Man?"

"Homo Trovectior," Iron Betty said.

"Homo what?" I asked.

"Homo Trovectior," Jackal said. I couldn't tell if she believed what they were saying, or if she had just heard the song so many times that she could sing along when they came to the verse.

"Homo, as in 'Man'," Surf added, still using his lecturing voice. "And Trovectior, meaning 'Advanced'. Homo Trovectior: Advanced Man. The next logical step in evolution: Man-plus-Machine."

"And where is this Machine-Man supposed to come from?" I asked.

"Out of a bubble-gum machine," Surf said.

Iron Betty snapped the fingers of her right hand; Surf shut up.

Jackal said, "Either we will create it ourselves, or machines will do it for us."

I stared at her.

Iron Betty spoke again. "It began toward the end of the last century, with the advent of so-called *fuzzy logic*. Computers, which had previously been constrained to the concepts of *yes* and *no*, were introduced to the idea of *maybe*."

I crossed my arms. "What's so great about *maybe*? Yes and no are definite. They're decisive. *Maybe* strikes me as wishy-washy. Doesn't that make it a weaker concept?"

"Maybe is not a weaker concept," Iron Betty said. "It is stronger. Infinitely stronger. *Maybe* allows us to conceive of a third alternative when only two choices are apparent. That ability, that essential spark of creativity, was what separated the organic-mind from the machine-mind. Fuzzy logic blurred that line; it gave machines the power to create. It removed the single element that made man superior to machine."

Everything that Iron Betty said had a flat quality to it, a listlessness that sounded more like litany than personal conviction. Maybe she had been spouting her own platitudes for so long that she'd forgotten how to think.

"Give me a break," I said. "There are a hundred ways that man is superior to machine. A thousand ways. Ten thousand."

Surf flexed his left hand, the mechanical one. "Really? Is this your *knowledge* speaking? Or is it your *ego*? Is your flesh-and-blood hand as powerful as a hydraulic press? Can your legs run faster than a MagLev train? Or a hovercar?"

He intentionally refocused his eyes, making certain that I could hear the whirring of the electroptic lenses. "Can your organic eyeballs see in the infrared spectrum? Or examine an object a thousand times smaller than the point of a needle? How about your non-silicon brain? Can it remember every telephone number in the Los Angeles directory?"

He smiled sardonically. "Please, Mr. Stalin, tell me all the wonderful things that make you superior to a machine."

Iron Betty snapped her fingers again. "Enough. Mr. Stalin gets the idea."

She pointed an age-gnarled finger in my direction; her eyes never strayed from their unseen focal point. "We approach the Convergence. Whichever species reaches it first will become the first true organic-cybernetic hybrid. And they will inherit the Earth."

"What happens to the loser in this race?" I asked.

"Servitude," said Jackal. "Extinction. We won't really know until it happens."

I said nothing; I was beginning to wonder if coming here had been a mistake. These people were fruitcakes, and Jackal seemed to be just as nutty as the rest of them.

Iron Betty must have sensed my trepidation. A sardonic smile flickered across her lips. "We argue for nothing," she said. "It is not necessary that you understand the Convergence, Mr. Stalin, or even be aware of it. You will be a part of it. That is enough."

Surf turned and walked away. I was about to say something, when I realized that Jackal had fallen in behind Surf. Not wanting to spend the rest of the night verbally fencing with a ninety-nine year old fruit bat who apparently lived in the net full-time, I hurried to catch up. I was halfway across the room when it hit me: we had been dismissed, like servants. Or children.

I caught up with Jackal and Surf just as they were turning into a hallway that led away from Iron Betty's chamber.

Around the corner, we passed a young woman who was even farther gone than Surf. Her shaved head was pocked by twenty or so gold alloy data jacks. Rectangular patches of circuit board protruded from her scalp in several places, the skin around the circuits puckered in an uneasy mating between flesh and silicon. Both of her eyes were cybernetic, as were her arms and legs. She turned and watched me as we passed, her camera-eyes tracking me like a security system on alert.

I was glad when we turned another corner and I could no longer feel her electronic eyes on my back.

Surf led us to a small room. He held open the door, but didn't go inside. "The rooms in this hall are for the acolytes."

I stepped past him into the room, and looked around. The furnishings were Spartan: one twin bed, one table, and one chair, all with the utilitarian solidity of prison furniture. The entire wall facing the bed was photo-active. An apparently continuous sequence of images and text appeared and vanished at speeds that were undoubtedly carefully timed, and subliminal.

The other walls were hung with holo-posters: a human skull superimposed over a snapshot of the net; the earth hanging in space, half its surface green-blue and organic, the other half rendered in chromed steel chased with circuit runs, and gears, and cables; a flat white background covered in crisp black ones and zeros, with a large numeral 'two' scrawled in red paintstick; a grainy black and white flat-photo of Alan Turing, the so-called father of Artificial Intelligence.

Opposite the entrance, there was a second door. I walked across the room and opened it. It led to a small bathroom, designed by the same no-frills architect who had planned the room itself. It was clean, though.

I stepped back into the room and nodded toward the photo-active wall. "What's this? A little subliminal programming for the new recruits?"

"Education," Surf said. "We don't program our people; we educate them."

"Turn it off," I said.

Surf glanced at the flickering data on the wall. "It won't bother you. After a little while, you'll forget it's even there."

"Turn it off," I said again. "Or I'll turn it off myself, with a chair. I don't want to be educated."

Surf pulled a slender black remote out of his pocket and pointed it at the animated wall. The images vanished, and the wall reappeared.

Jackal sat down on the bed and bounced to test the mattress. "You'll be all right here."

I pulled off the windbreaker and tossed it on the foot of the bed.

Surf's gravelly voice came from the still-open door, "If you *do* cross wires with an AI, are you going to slick it?"

Jackal laid back on the bed and looked at the ceiling. "Probably not. Why do you ask?"

Surf leaned against the door frame with an assumed air of indifference. "I thought you might need some help."

Jackal closed her eyes. "What do you have in mind?"

"I've been cooking up a virus," Surf said. "All the simulations say that it'll crack a hardened AI like a walnut. I'm itching to try it."

"What's stopping you?" I asked. "If you guys are trying to make sure that the balance tips in favor of Man instead of machines, destroying AI's would seem to be built right into your job description."

Surf's voice took on the tone of a lecturer, and I knew that he was parroting learned doctrine. "Destruction for destruction's sake is not the mark of a species that is ready for ascension."

"But you want to kill something anyway," I said.

Surf's cybernetic hand closed slowly. "Every attack must be *on* purpose, and *with* purpose."

Jackal rubbed her eyes and then opened them. "In other words, you're looking for an excuse."

"Check it out," I said. "A cybernetic hit man."

Jackal shot me a glance and then looked back at Surf. "Thanks. We'll let you know."

Surf nodded and left, pulling the door closed behind him.

I stood there, watching Jackal.

"Relax," she said. "I was just being polite back there."

"You don't really believe all that crap about the Convergence?"

"Of course not," she said. "But the silicon in my head makes me sort of an honorary member around here. It pays off sometimes, so I'm very careful not to challenge the official party line."

I picked up the jacket and pulled out the trid. "Take a look at this." I handed it to Jackal.

She looked at the front then flipped it over. "What does this shit on the back mean?"

"Payment instructions," I said. "Whoever kills me is supposed to call that number, read the poem, and leave the phone off the hook. Supposedly, the Man will trace the call and get in touch."

Jackal sat up. "This number definitely doesn't belong to the Man. It's a public service line, maybe a suicide prevention hot-line, or something like that. It's probably got a watch-dog routine coded into it. You call the number and read the poem, the watch-dog sends out alarm signals in forty different directions."

"So it can't be traced?"

"Easy enough to find out who the phone line belongs to," she said. "But that won't tell us anything."

"Why not?"

"If you were broadcasting a contract hit, would you use your own phone? This is a subroutine piggybacked to somebody else's line. Whoever owns this phone line has no idea; I guarantee it."

"So there's no way to trace this thing back to the source?"

"I didn't say it couldn't be done, but it's dangerous as hell."

"You can do it?"

"There probably aren't more than four or five people in LA who can. Me, Giri-Sama, Ice Rider, Captain Kangaroo. Iron Betty could do it, if you asked her."

"No thanks. *You* do it.

Jackal stood up. "I'll need my deck." She yawned and stretched. "And some sleep. My edge is way off."

Her yawn triggered one of my own. "I know what you mean."

She walked to the door. "Get some rest, Stalin. I'll be back in a few hours."

I locked the door behind her and kicked off my shoes.

How far could I trust Surf, or the rest of Jackal's creepy little robot-wanna-be friends? Was it safe to go to sleep? Fifty thousand marks was a lot of money.

I slid the Blackhart under my pillow. I hoped to catch a couple of hours of sleep without having to shoot anybody. I turned the light off and climbed into bed.

CHAPTER 26

‖‖ ‖ ‖ ‖‖‖‖ ‖ ‖ ‖‖‖ ‖ ‖‖ ‖ ‖‖ ‖‖‖ ‖‖‖ ‖ ‖ ‖‖‖‖ ‖ ‖‖ ‖ ‖‖‖ ‖‖

"It's one of those egg muffin things." Jackal held out a white foil pouch printed with the logo of a fast food restaurant. "It's got cheese on it. Do you like cheese?"

I opened the pouch. "Yeah, I like cheese. Thanks."

She tossed a shoebox on the bed. "Everybody likes cheese," she said. "Everybody but me. There's coffee in there too."

The pouch contained an egg-and-bacon muffin wrapped in thermal plastic, a bulb of coffee, and a couple of paper napkins. Breakfast for one.

"Did you already have something?"

She set a blue fiberglass flight case on the bed and popped the lid. One corner of the case was patched with strapping tape. "I can't eat before a run. A full stomach takes my edge off."

I twisted the top off the coffee and waited for it to warm up. "What's in the shoe box?"

Jackal picked it up and tossed it to me without looking. "I almost forgot," she said. "I brought you sort of a disguise."

The top came off, but I managed to catch the box left handed while half-juggling the coffee bulb in my right hand. Inside the box were a pair of electric barber's clippers and a bottle of peroxide. Not much of a disguise.

I set the box down, fished out the breakfast muffin and unwrapped it. "Do you really think this will fool anybody?"

Jackal shrugged without looking up. "Crew cut, bleached-blonde hair. If you stop shaving and wear some shades, it might be enough to keep a bullet out of the back of your head."

"I guess it's better than nothing," I said. I took a bite of muffin. Greasy, but not too bad.

I swallowed and raised my fingers to touch Sonja's dressing. "I've got a bandage on the back of my head. My skull collided with a sidewalk."

Jackal pulled a tangle of ribbon cable out of the case and dropped it on the bed. "How bad is it?"

I turned my head so that she could see. "Not too bad. Just some split skin."

"I think we can work around that," Jackal said. "We'll leave it a little shaggy in the back so I don't have to cut so close." She picked up the shoebox and walked toward the bathroom.

"What about the peroxide?"

Jackal spoke over her shoulder. "It's a disinfectant. It'll probably burn like hell, but it shouldn't kill you."

I took another bite of muffin and followed her. I managed to wolf down the rest of it before she started.

To be honest, Jackal's own hairstyle didn't instill me with confidence. But even a really bad haircut was better than a bullet in the brain.

Jackal's prediction that the peroxide would burn like hell turned out to be a major understatement. But she was right. It didn't kill me.

When she was done, my hair was very blonde and very short on the top and sides, tapering to a thicker patch in the back. It was a strange cut, but I could live with it.

I showered while Jackal finished setting up her gear. Surprisingly, the shower stall wasn't wired for projection. No forests, no naked women, no subliminal education. I enjoyed the chance to shower in silence.

Jackal looked up when I walked back into the room. "Put your shirt on," she said. "I want to get the full effect."

I slipped on my shirt.

She nodded. "Better, but you can't wear the jacket."

"Why not?"

"Because you're wearing it in the trid that the Man is circulating. Anyway, it's like your trademark."

"I need it to cover up my shoulder holster."

"I didn't say you can't wear *a* jacket. I said you can't wear *that* jacket." She shrugged off her own jacket and handed it to me.

It was made of forest green synlon, cut in the style of those old bomber jackets. A strangely angular tiger was stitched across the back in multicolored thread. Above the tiger, the words MIG ALLEY were embroidered in stylized capitol letters intended to suggest bamboo. It was at least five sizes too large for her.

"It won't fit," I said.

"Try it on."

I strapped on the shoulder rig before I put on the jacket. It fit. The Blackhart didn't bulge too much. I took the jacket off again and tossed it on the bed.

Jackal held out an elastic headband set with four disks molded from matte black plastic. A long thread of fiber-optic cable connected the disks to one of several equipment modules set up on the room's only table. "How about it, Mr. Stalin? Do you want to go for a ride?"

I took the headband. "Where's yours?"

She held up a ribbon cable with a gold multi-pronged connector. "An induction-rig is good enough for piggyback," she said, "but you have to go straight neural for the big show. It shaves seven, maybe eight nanoseconds off your response time."

On the table top, between the comp and the matrix generator, was a pale green plastic cylinder. Jackal picked it up and pressed one end against her white jeans, on the inner slope of her left thigh. The cylinder made a soft popping noise followed by an even quieter hiss. When the hissing stopped, Jackal pulled the cylinder away from her thigh. About three centimeters of ceramic needle protruded from the end.

"What's that?"

She sat in a chair and massaged her left thigh where the needle had gone in. "Zoom," she said. "Mega-amphetamine. It's a Cuban combat drug designed to hype the shit out of your reflexes."

She scooted the chair up to the table and plugged the connector into the back of her head. "Sit down, Stalin. Get comfortable."

I sat on the bed and pulled the headband over my head.

There was a tiny microphone attached to the left side of the rig by a curved polycarbon arm. I swung it down in front of my lips.

A color bar test pattern appeared in front of my eyes. It was disorienting, because the left eye was nearly in focus, and the right wasn't even close.

Jackal's voice resonated inside my skull. "Move the trodes around until the test pattern is nice and sharp in both eyes."

I experimented with the black plastic disks for a couple of seconds. "Okay, I'm good."

"Have you ever been in the net before?"

"Simulation gear," I said, "but not neural."

"Sim isn't anywhere near fast enough for what we're going to do. Remember this though: neural is a lot faster, but it's also dangerous. If things get hairy in there, get that rig off your head. Don't wait for me to tell you. Got it?"

"Yeah."

"Good," she said. "Now, hang on to your ass."

She punched a key and the DataNet construct exploded into my head.

Deep space. Black. We are a tiny spark of white light. A star hanging in a starless void.

Kilometers overhead, a florescent blue grid divides one axis of the void into perfect squares.

Without warning, the void spins one hundred eighty degrees. Vertigo as the grid becomes the ground instead of the sky and we plummet toward it.

Details form below, tiny dots of color clustered around intersections of grid lines.

Still falling. Diving toward the latticework ground. Accelerating.

Colored dots increase in size, begin to assume individual shapes.

Shapes growing, expanding, increasing in clarity and detail until they are building-sized slabs of 3-D monochrome color scrolling below us at breakneck speed.

Still descending, we drop below the tops of the building analogs, careening through canyons of imaginary neon skyscrapers.

Vision blurs as a vicious snap-turn changes our course ninety degrees in a microsecond.

Beads of colored light flash down grid lines, brilliant sparks chained together like electronic strands of DNA riding the laser-fine blue graticules of the net. Subliminal flickers and surges as subroutines rocket from database to database, handing off blocks of information code.

We circle a slender green skyscraper of data. It sits at the intersection of two graticules, grid lines extending from it in four directions.

Despite my first impression, the skyscraper analog is not featureless. Rectangular patterns of lighter and darker green mottle the surface. The variations in shade are subtle and constantly changing as the database sorts and assimilates new information.

"That's it." Jackal's voice in my head. *"The number on the back of your trid. It's a public service line for Pacific Fusion and Electric. I guarantee that PF&E has no idea that their line is being used as a callback service for murder."*

We skim the grid, carving a square perimeter around the PF&E database at a distance of two graticules, perhaps a hundred meters.

Every time we pass over an intersection of two grid lines, Jackal deposits a dense globule of program-code. The globules attach themselves to the intersections and hang there like fat prisms of oily crystal.

We scroll sideways and survey Jackal's handiwork. Eleven prisms. The twelfth is missing, leaving a single gap in the crystal perimeter.

"What now?" Oddly, although Jackal's voice sounds like it originates inside my head, my own voice sounds distant.

"We call the number," Jackal says. *"Read the poem, and see what happens."*

Before I can respond, she says, "Okay, it's ringing. We're in."

Her voice recites the strange verse inside my head. "The time has come, the Walrus said..."

Four trains of multicolored sparks shoot out from the base of the skyscraper and race through the grid at blinding speed.

When each of the routines hits the intersection at the first graticule, it fragments into three smaller chains, one traveling straight, one turning right, the other left.

In an instant, four pieces of code have become twelve, all racing away from PF&E's green data analog in different directions.

Eleven quick flares as all but one of the speeding pieces of code are gobbled up by Jackal's booby traps.

The last program shoots through the opening in the perimeter.

Jackal screams down the grid line after it.

Our quarry pulls a ninety-degree turn at a junction and changes its appearance dramatically, sparks shift color and intensity. Jackal sticks with it, hurtling through the net at the speed of thought.

"That's one smooth block of code," she says. "It just turned itself into a Federal Tax Audit."

"Can you follow it home?"

"That depends on how smart it is. If it knows we're on its ass, it won't go home at all."

The subroutine changes direction and color three times in rapid succession.

"What if it doesn't go home? What if it's a decoy?"

"We catch it and take it apart. I might be able to figure out who wrote it. The little bastard just turned into a diplomatic inquiry from the Dominican Republic."

Suddenly, we turn left. The program goes straight.

"Why are..."

"Chill!"

We turn right and parallel the elusive subroutine, one graticule to its left and slightly to the rear. It's harder to see from here, but Jackal manages to follow it through a series of ninety degree acrobatics.

Her reflexes are unbelievably fast. The Cuban mega-amphetamine is pushing her reaction time into the realm of the supernatural.

"If we give it a little breathing room, maybe it'll think it's shaken us." Her voice has a brittle metallic quality. The drug is talking.

A picture pops into my head. An image of the two of us sitting in a shabby room in Iron Betty's little cult haven. My body is perched on the bed, unconsciously bobbing and weaving in time to our perceived maneuvers through the net. Jackal's eyes are closed, her fingers fluttering across the keyboard. Her lips are pulled back in a skeletal grin, the rictus of the Cuban speed riding her brain.

It is the illusion of flesh.

Reality lives in the DataNet.

The routine dodges and mutates. It becomes a subscription pitch from a long distance company. A prize notification from the State Lottery Commission.

Jackal whistles inside my skull. "There it goes. I think it's headed home."

The program pulls a final identity shift and shoots into the side of a towering red slab of data.

Jackal shears off and we climb away from the grid until the red analog is the size of a child's building block.

"What is it?"

"An AI," Jackal says. "A big, ugly one."

"Who does it belong to?"

A rectangular field of alphanumeric data pops into existence, superimposed over the image of the net. Bright green numbers and letters flit and shift as the data runs through a sort.

*After a couple of seconds, the data field vanishes, leaving a single line of green characters: **29503.3>>13296.4>>55703.6>>LADG**.*

"The mainframe's right here in LA," Jackal says.

"How can you tell?"

"From the grid coordinates. The last four letters stand for Los Angeles Data Grid."

"Can you find out who it belongs to?"

The rectangular data field reappears, and more numbers and letters flit by. "It's registered to somebody named Henry Clerval."

"Excellent," I say. "See if you can get an address."

"Hold up," Jackal says. "The name is phony; I guarantee it."

"How do you know?"

"Nobody uses their real name in the net," Jackal says. "Not when they're pulling something illegal. If the owner of that AI is half as smart as I think he is, the registration will lead through an elaborate system of fronts, blinds, and re-posts that ultimately dead-end in some data-haven. Maybe Key West, or one of the other Florida Pirate Republics."

"So how do we track him down?"

"We take the direct approach," she says. We bank suddenly and plunge toward the red slab.

"Jackal... I don't think this is a good idea."

The slab grows larger rapidly.

"Jackal, don't do this."

She ignores me. Perhaps the drug is totally in control now.

The analog looms like a rectangular mountain until it eclipses the entire net.

I steel myself for impact when we slam into the side of it.

The sensation is abrupt and strange. It reminds me of diving into a pool, an instantaneous and painless transition from one plane of existence to another.

The world is a dark scarlet blur seen through a candy apple lens set for soft focus. Vaguely perceived shapes shift and slide in the blood-tinged darkness. Vermilion walls of logarithms. Dense ruddy strata of information. Vertical helixes of glowing red coals smolder in towering fractal spirals. Platelets of data swim through a medium of plasma in a carefully random crossfire of information exchange.

Another field of alphanumeric data appears in front of my face, digits streaming by in a blur of digital static.

"I'm not even trying to get near the core data," Jackal says. "I'm just skimming, trying not to attract attention."

Suddenly, we seem to lurch, and the interior of the analog goes dark. Plumes of data recede, and are sucked into the faceted sides of the AI's data structure like a video of blossoming flowers run at high-speed in reverse.

"Oh shit," Jackal says. "We're busted."

"Get us out of here!"

"Yeah... I think you're right."

We pull a high-gravity turn that would be impossible in the real world.

Rainbow-hued lightning bolts leap from the dark heart of the AI construct to strike at us.

Jackal zigs and zags at random intervals.

Searing bolts of energy sizzle by us at incredible speeds.

Chrome bubbles the size of my fist begin to appear in our wake.

The rainbow lightning strikes one of the chrome spheres. Then another. Jackal is dropping decoys, logic traps to attract the lightning.

The ruse works for a half-second, then the AI learns to ignore the spheres, and the lightning reaches out for us again.

Four white sparks, identical to our own matrix image, appear around us and shear off in divergent directions.

The lightning spreads its attention between the five of us.

I can see the outer wall of the construct, a crimson dividing line between life and death.

One by one, the rainbow lightning destroys the false images. We become the sole focus of the AI's attention again.

Jackal continues her random changes of course and altitude, but the wall is still too far away. We aren't going to make it.

"Stalin, jack out. Now!"

Somewhere, in a seedy little room a million light years away, my hands snatch the induction rig off of my head.

The world snapped into existence, the net instantly relegated to the status of a silicon-generated fantasy.

Jackal's hand leapt off the keyboard and reached for the power switch on the matrix generator.

At the instant her finger touched the switch, something went through her like a surge of electricity. Her body stood up on its own, galvanized by some unseen force. Her back arched sharply and made a sound like ten people cracking their knuckles at once. Her hands flopped around like two fish tied to the ends of her wrists. She fell to the carpet and lay still.

I scrambled to hit the switch that Jackal had been reaching toward. The lights on the matrix generator winked out.

The odors of burned circuitry and singed flesh permeated the air.

A trickle of blood ran from Jackal's left nostril and down her cheek to drip on the carpet.

I dropped to my knees and felt the side of her neck for a pulse. It was weak and rapid.

Her eyes fluttered open, stared at the ceiling for a second, and then drifted closed again.

I looked around wildly. I honestly didn't know what to do. I knew some first aid, but I was ninety percent certain that the damage was to Jackal's brain. What's the first aid for that?

I grabbed the corner of the bed sheet and worked at staunching the stream of blood from her nose. I was about to yell for help when I heard feet pounding down the hall toward my room.

The door swung open. It was Surf.

"Jackal got zapped," I said. "Some kind of neural-feedback overload, I think. You've got to help me get her to a doctor."

Surf's electroptic eyes zoomed in on me and he stood without speaking for a couple of seconds.

"Are you deaf?" I shouted. "Go call an ambulance!"

Surf bent down and gently unplugged the ribbon cable from the back of Jackal's head. "Ambulances don't come out here," he said. "Anyhow, they couldn't help her. She needs a special doctor. A skull-mechanic."

"Do you know where to find one?"

"Yeah."

"Call him; tell him we're on the way. And call a taxi. Have it meet us at that strip mall across the street."

"We've got a car," Surf said. "I can drive her. And I've already got somebody calling her skull-mechanic."

"Then help me carry her," I said.

Surf reached down and slid his hands under Jackal's armpits. His vid-camera eyes locked on me again.

"What in the hell are you staring at?"

"You act like you actually give a shit," Surf said. He lifted Jackal's upper body.

I managed to lift her legs. "What is that supposed to mean?"

We started shuffling toward the door.

"Of course I give a shit. She was working for me when this happened. That makes it my responsibility."

Surf looked over his shoulder and maneuvered to clear the door jam as he backed out of the room. "Don't see that very often," he said.

His mechanical voice managed to convey a tone of confusion. "People who hire jackers don't usually treat us like that. When something goes wrong, they walk away and leave our bodies to rot where they fall. Then they go hire somebody else until they get whatever it is they're after."

"I don't care what you're used to," I said. "That's not how I do business."

CHAPTER 27

The sign hovered above the boutique, an animated hologram of two heads, one male, the other female. In the space of about ten seconds, both faces morphed from outright homeliness to vid-star perfection.

The words 'Second Looks' wrote themselves above the faces in fancy platinum script, then silently exploded into a million pinpoints of rainbow-colored light. The ugly heads reappeared, ready to repeat their fast-forward evolution to beauty.

"This is the place," Surf said.

He steered his car, a Focke-Wulf hover-sedan that was probably older than he was, around the corner and into a narrow alley behind the building.

As we turned the corner, Jackal's head lolled forward. A quiet mewling sound came from somewhere deep in her throat.

I gently guided her head back to my shoulder and pulled her slack body closer to mine.

Surf pulled up short of a service door in the rear of the surgical boutique. The old car settled onto its apron with a groan.

"What are we doing here?" I asked. "I thought you said she needed a skull-mechanic."

"Lance *is* a skull-mechanic," Surf said.

He climbed out of the car and knocked on the back door of the boutique. "The cosmetic surgery stuff is a profitable side-line."

The door was opened a lot more quickly than I expected, by a man in a lab coat. He was ludicrously handsome, his features nearly perfect, with just enough rugged imperfection thrown in to keep him from looking feminine. It was a calculated beauty, the sort of face you'd expect to find on someone who worked in a surgical boutique.

He looked up and down the alley before motioning us inside. Surf helped me lift Jackal out of the back seat and carry her into the clinic.

The treatment room that the man led us to smelled like every hospital I've ever been in: the burnt-ozone scent of ultrasonic sterilizers reinforced by the loamy earth smell of active-enzyme disinfectants.

Two of the four banks of florescent lights in the ceiling were turned off.

"You can put her there," the man in the lab coat said, pointing to a powered form-fitting couch that reminded me uncomfortably of a dentist's chair.

We lowered Jackal's limp body onto the couch.

The man pulled a vaguely pistol-shaped instrument from the pocket of his lab coat and leaned over Jackal's body. He parted her eyelids with thumb and forefinger and used the strange device to stare into one of her eyes, and then the other. "Been playing rough again, Gwen?"

"She crossed it up with an AI," Surf said.

"I figured as much," the man said.

He looked up and pointed toward an equipment cart crammed full of electronic gear that would have looked at home on Tommy Mailo's workbench. "Wheel that over here, will you Mr. Stalin?"

I pushed the cart to within his reach. "How do you know my name?"

He fished something out of his pants pocket and handed it to me. It was a copy of the trid that Bobbie had carried. "This is you, isn't it?"

I felt myself stiffen. "Yeah, it's me."

The man nodded. "When someone is on the run, his picture gets circulated around the face clinics. Usually, there's a fat reward attached. Makes it hard to change your face without anyone finding out."

I unzipped the front of the bomber jacket as casually as I could.

"Whoa, Stalin," Surf said. "You won't need the gun. Lance is a friend."

The man he'd referred to as Lance smiled a little and turned to fiddle with the equipment cart. "He's right. I could use fifty thousand marks, but I'm not greedy enough to sell out a friend of Gwen's."

He unrolled a thin coil of cable and clipped a sensor to the tip of one of Jackal's fingers. He slid Jackal's blue sweatshirt up far enough to paste a self-adhesive electrode to her sternum. Two more electrodes went on either side of her forehead.

He punched a couple of keys on one of the scopes, and a pattern of blue lines appeared. "Her sinus-rhythm is normal, but accelerated. Skin galvanics are a little out of whack. BP is up, but not out of control."

He squinted. "Has she been using amphetamines again?"

"Yes," I said. "Something she called Zoom."

"That's what I thought," Lance said. "Looks like she got lucky, not much organic damage. She's not going to flatline."

He looked at Surf. "I'll take care of her from here."

Surf nodded. "Thanks, Doc." He looked at me. "You need a ride somewhere?"

I shook my head. "I think I'll stick around."

Lance frowned. "Now that I know that Gwen's not in serious danger, I need to finish up some other jobs first. Mid-afternoon is my busiest time. I've got a penis enlargement, a face job, and three breast-reductions on the books."

"Three?" I asked.

Lance smiled wearily. "I call it the Vid-Star of the Week Club. Last week, it was Tori Caplin. Everybody wanted a pug nose, perfect teeth, and boobs out to here. Now, Tori's out, and Britannia King is in, and it's a long straight nose, pointed chin, and practically no breasts at all."

He looked at his watch. "I shouldn't be very long. For the cosmetic surgery part of this business, my job is mostly sales and bedside manner. My AI will handle the real work, won't you Tasha?"

"Of course, Doctor." The AI's voice was feminine, carefully pitched to conjure images of a friendly but highly competent nurse.

"Great," Lance said. "I'll go make the rounds, and do a little hand-holding. When I get back, we'll have a look at Gwen's silicon."

Surf walked to the door. "Last chance, Stalin," he said.

"No thanks," I said. "I'll stick with Jackal for a while."

Surf's electroptic eyes stared at me for a few seconds, then he nodded once and walked out the door.

Lance left on Surf's heels.

Despite Surf's assurances, as soon as the door closed, my first instinct was to get the hell out of there. It wasn't Lance himself that was bothering me. It was the situation, the entire slant that the case had taken. My name and face were all over the net, all over the street.

Everywhere I went, I seemed to run into strangers who knew my name. I couldn't escape the feeling that every move that I had made, and every move that I *would* make, had all been anticipated and accounted for. I was a puppet dancing and capering at the end of someone else's string, and the thing that really scared me—more than the possibility of death itself—was the thought that I might die without ever having seen the face of the Puppeteer.

Lance came back a lot sooner than I'd expected. "Now," he said, "let's see what we've got."

He rubbed his palms together and looked Jackal up and down a couple of times. "I'm going to start by unplugging her EMM," he said.

He unclipped the charcoal gray plastic box from Jackal's belt, and the thin fiber-optic cable that connected it to the jack in the back of her head. A few of the LEDs on the box flickered feebly.

I pointed to it. "What exactly is that thing?"

"It's an External Memory Module," Lance said.

"What's it for?"

"Gwen's implant is a Fuyagi RL-78000 series microprocessor, customized of course. The EMM lets her update her software."

"I thought there were data chips for that sort of thing."

"There are, if the program is small enough to fit on a single chip. The EMM is for big programs that require a lot of memory."

Lance plugged Jackal's memory module into one of the electronic units on the cart and eyed the readout.

"Her EMM is fried," he said. He pulled out a cable with a multi-pinned connector on one end. "Could you turn her head toward the wall, please? I need to jack directly into her CPU."

I turned Jackal's head as gently as I could.

"We'll start by wiping whatever she's got stashed up there, and loading fresh diagnostics software. Then we'll run a few test programs and see what we've got."

"Is there any way to salvage the data stored in her implant?"

"I don't know," Lance said. "I can run a recover routine on her CPU before I slick it. If the damage to her implant is localized to the CPU, we might be able to save something. Why? What are we looking for?"

"The owner of the AI."

"The one that zapped her? If it's a revenge thing, I wouldn't worry about it. Jackers don't do revenge. They live by some kind of skewed Bushido. Single combat, that sort of thing. They play it down to the wire, and if they win, they win big. When they lose, they don't cry about it."

"No," I said. "That's what she was after: the name of the owner of that AI."

Lance plugged a cable into the back of Jackal's head. "I'll do what I can, but I wouldn't count on it."

He turned and began fiddling with his test equipment. He made a rhythmic clicking sound between his teeth and the roof of his mouth as he worked.

After a minute or so, the clicking stopped. Lance worked in silence for a couple of seconds, his eyebrows pulled together in concentration. Finally, he sucked air through his teeth in an exaggerated hiss.

"How bad is it?" I asked.

"Not good," he said. "I've downloaded what I can, but it looks pretty garbled. Gwen's CPU got hit so hard that I can't even get her BIOS chips to take a fresh upload."

"Can you help her?"

"Certainly," Lance said. "But she needs some new silicon. She's going to have to go back under the knife."

"How soon can you do it?"

"I *could* do it now," Lance said. "But first we have to work out some financial arrangements. I'm a nice guy, but I don't work for free. Do you know if Gwen has any money?"

"She's got twenty-five K coming from the run she just made. If it runs over that, I'll cover the difference."

Lance gave me the same sort of prolonged stare that Surf liked to point at me. Finally, he nodded. "Okay. I'll up-link the parameters to the mainframe, and get my AI to write a piece of control code for the surgical robot."

He looked up toward the ceiling. "How long will that take, Tasha?"

"Ten minutes to download historicals from the NTR database," Tasha said. "Then another twenty minutes to write the code."

Lance glanced at his watch. "Take care of it, please. In the meantime, we'll roll Gwen into Suite 3. Then you can run Robot 3 through a standard pre-op routine to get Gwen ready for the table."

"Of course, Doctor."

"Great," Lance said. "That'll give me time to put together the silicon we're going to need."

He looked up at me. "The observation room for Suite 3 is across the hall, to your left. You can wait in there."

Lance turned, and was gone before I had a chance to tell him that I didn't want to actually watch the surgical procedure.

The observation room for Surgical Suite 3 was little more than a booth, the majority of which was taken up by two contoured swivel chairs. I sat in the one on the right.

The entire wall opposite the door was a window, a single sheet of transparent acryliflex, four or five centimeters thick. A Heads Up Display projected the time on the window in pale green block-style digits: 4:28 p.m., followed by a scrolling string of seconds in tenths, hundredths, and thousandths.

The surgical suite on the other side of the window was ten or twelve times the size of the observation booth, and still seemed to be crowded. The walls were lined with equipment racks, dermal stimulator units, banks of ultra-violet sterilization lamps, and about forty electronic modules, every one of which seemed to have two or three colored status bars, and a dozen flashing LEDs.

There was no sign of the surgical robot. I wondered what it would look like. Probably a souped-up version of one of House's service drones. I looked around for a service alcove, expecting the robot to roll into the room at any second.

I leaned back in my chair to await the arrival of Lance and the elusive robot. My eyes drifted upward to the ceiling of the operating suite.

I jerked upright. "Jesus!"

My first instinct was to back-peddle, to distance myself from the thing in the ceiling as quickly as possible. I had my Blackhart half-drawn before I could stop myself.

I stared up at the surgical robot. It was built into the ceiling of the operating suite. Or perhaps more correctly, it *was* the ceiling. And it was not a thing of beauty.

I got a grip on myself, slid the Blackhart back into my holster, and made an effort to lean back in the chair and relax. The relaxing part didn't come easy, not even with four or five centimeters of acryliflex between me and the robot.

It had at least a hundred stainless steel arms, each of which was articulated by several flexible joints. The diameters and lengths of the arms varied drastically, as did the hardware attached to the end of each. Every one seemed to have been designed for a specific purpose.

Some of them I recognized: radial bone saws, scalpels, pressure syringes, intravenous tubes, suction hoses, surgical lasers, and an array of manipulators that ranged from clamps with nearly microscopic fingers, to claws large enough to crush a man's skull.

For every device that I recognized, there were at least two that I had to guess at. About ten of the arms held what looked like electrodes, their shielded power cables snaking up into recessed tubes in the ceiling.

Most of the arms bristled with sensors: vid cameras (from micro to macro lens calibers), IR cameras, dermal contact pads, and multifaceted lens clusters.

The entire machine—with its stainless steel mandibles, and compound eyes—reminded me of a huge robotic spider. A hideously mutated spider, with far too many multi-jointed legs, hanging in the center of its web of power cables.

Lance and a female assistant whom I hadn't met rolled a gurney into the operating suite and locked it to the floor directly under the arms of the surgical robot. The woman, dressed in a lab coat and scrubs, was as ludicrously beautiful as Lance was handsome. They made a final check of Jackal's position under the robot, and left the operating suite.

Jackal lay strapped face-down on the gurney, naked except for an orange sheet that covered from the bottom of her shoulder blades to just above her calves. Her thin white body looked child-like and helpless with its back exposed to the steel spider overhead.

Banks of Ultra Violet lamps came on, flooding the suite with a white sterilizing glare.

A minute or so later, Lance squeezed into the booth and took the vacant chair to my left. "Still running the UV cycle?"

"I think so," I said.

He nodded. "The actual procedure won't start for another couple of minutes."

"Don't you have to shave her head, or something?"

"Not really," he said. "She's already got about half of it shaved off. But even if she didn't, we wouldn't need to shave much of a patch. This is a micro-invasive technique, what we call 'key-hole surgery'. It doesn't require much of an incision, and when the robot backs out, it will use a little blob of orthostatic epoxy to seal the hole in her skull. With eight or ten hours on the dermal stimulators, you'll hardly even be able to spot the incision site."

The UV lamps dimmed, and about a dozen of the robot's arms reached toward Jackal, connecting sensor leads, and inserting IV tubes. Another cluster of arms descended toward the back of Jackal's head.

Lance watched with me. "If you like, I can switch the micro-cam's video feed in here, and get you a robot's-eye view in full color 3-D."

"No thanks," I said. "This is close as I want to get."

A tiny scalpel carved a short incision in the back of Jackal's head. Blood welled up, dark against her pale skin.

Almost as quickly as the blood appeared, a trio of the robot's arms darted in to suction it away. The blood spiraled up toward the ceiling through clear plastic tubes. The spider was feeding.

Manipulator arms angled in to spread the lips of the wound. The robot's movements were quick, decisive, and unerring. Its multi-jointed arms bent and rotated themselves into positions that no human surgeon could hope to equal.

The bass hum of the robot's power supply throbbed through the acryliflex window at a frequency that verged on hypnotic. The servomotors driving the machine's arms whirred and chittered like metallic insects.

I had seen enough, more than I wanted to see. I tried to turn away, but found my eyes locked to the sight by that same sickening curiosity that draws crowds to accident scenes. I was repelled, but watched with horrid fascination as the machine bored into Jackal's brain.

"It'll be coming out in a second."

Lance's voice shook me out of my near-trance. "What?"

"The implant. The robot will be pulling it out in a second. Not all of it, of course. Just the BIOS chips and some minor peripheral circuitry. Once we replace that, and build her a new EMM, all we'll have to do to get Gwen's implant back on-line is reload her software."

He pointed toward the gurney. "Watch... There it comes now."

A slender steel arm with tiny manipulators reached into the hole in Jackal's head. A few seconds later, the robot retracted the manipulator. Clutched in its miniature metal fingers was a tiny piece of circuit board, glistening with cerebral fluid and tinged with blood.

I tried to distract myself from the grotesque scene by asking the first question that popped into my head. "How much surgery is done this way? By robot, I mean."

"About seventy-five percent," Lance said. "But in another year or two, robots will be handling it all. They're about twenty times faster than humans, a lot more efficient, and they don't make mistakes."

"None?"

"None that I've heard of. Their control code has to be written by an AI. Before it even starts to develop the program, the AI reviews every scrap of data that's available on any past surgical procedure that's even remotely similar. In other words, it starts out knowing all of the mistakes that have been made in the past. Then it factors in the physical condition and peculiarities of the patient, and writes a piece of software to control the robot. Add that to operating table telemetry, and real-time data processing, where are you going to get a mistake?"

"You're saying that no surgical robot has ever lost a patient?"

"Of course a few patients have died," Lance said. "But never from anything that turned out to be the fault of the robot. Remember, not all patients can be saved."

I grunted to keep from having to actually agree with Lance's blind faith in his machines. I wondered if he subscribed to R.U.R.'s theory about the *Convergence*. Was Jackal an intermediate step on the way to Homo Trovectior?

Lance continued to talk, but I tuned him out. I could feel it coming on, another one of those nagging little half-ideas that pick at my mind like a tickle at the back of your throat.

The microchip implant in Jackal's head; the unidentified microchips implanted in the brains of Michael Winter and Russell Carlisle. The precise movements of the surgical robot; the machine-like movements of Michael's gun hand.

The pieces of the puzzle swam around in my brain, taunting me, daring me to fit them together in the one pattern that made sense.

I sat bolt upright in the little contoured chair. "Holy shit!"

Lance jumped at my sudden outburst. "What?"

I stared through the window into the surgical suite. One of the robot's slender manipulators was sliding a new chip into the hole in the back of Jackal's head.

"That chip," I said, "the Fuyagi whatever-it-is. It feeds computer information code into Jackal's brain, right?"

"Yes."

"What's the difference between information code, and *control* code?"

Lance leaned back in his chair. "Well... let's see. Control code instructs a computer to perform a certain task. Like running a file search, or finding the cube root of 357. Information code is just... information. Data that can be retrieved on demand."

"Yeah, but what's the difference? Electronically, I mean."

"I'm not sure what you're getting at," Lance said. "From an electronic standpoint, I guess there isn't any real difference. They're both made up of ones and zeros."

"Could the chip in Jackal's head tell the difference between control code and information code?"

"Probably not. Where are you going with this?"

"Suppose I wrote a piece of control code, and injected it into Jackal's brain implant. Could I control her actions?"

"Like a puppet?" Lance asked. "A mind-control chip?"

I could tell out of the corner of my eye that he was smiling. He started to say something, and then caught himself when he realized that I wasn't smiling with him. "You're serious, aren't you?"

"Deadly," I said.

"Why do you want to control Gwen's mind?"

"I'm using her as an example," I said. "I just want to know if it's possible."

Lance paused for a few seconds. "No," he said finally. "The Fuyagi isn't designed for anything even remotely like that."

"What if it were a different CPU? A custom-designed chip?"

Lance shook his head. "No good. A corymbic implant just does sort of an end-run on short-term memory. It doesn't plug into any of the right parts of the brain."

"Wait a minute." I pointed the index finger of my left hand to a spot forward of my left temple; I tried to duplicate the position and angle that Michael's Glock had taken in his suicide recording. "What if the custom designed chip was implanted here?"

Lance sat up in his chair with a strange look on his face. "Of course," he whispered. "The Frontal Lobe. If you were going to do it... if it could be done, that would be the spot."

"Why? What's so special about the Frontal Lobe?"

"Its anterior divisions, the Prefrontal Lobe and the Supplementary Motor Cortex, help integrate personality with emotion. Nobody really understands *how*, but we do know that those portions of the brain convert thought into action, and action into thought."

He nodded slowly. "The left Prefrontal Lobe would be the perfect spot for the sort of implant you're talking about, if the subject were right-handed."

"Why would being right-handed make a difference?"

"The left hemisphere of the brain is dominant in something like ninety-eight percent of all right-handed people," Lance said. "If you wanted to control a right-handed person, it would make sense to target your implant for the left side of the brain."

He stopped and shook his head. "No. No. No. It *still* wouldn't work."

"Why not?"

"There wouldn't be enough memory storage."

"In the brain?"

"In the implant," Lance said. "If you're going to control someone's mind, you'll have to sublimate their will, displace their own personality. To do that, you'd have to have something to replace their personality *with*. A puppet personality, if you want to call it that. A piece of control code that big takes up a lot of memory chips. Maybe as many as twenty or thirty dense-packs. There isn't enough room in the human brain to squeeze in an implant that large."

"Could it be external? Like Jackal's External Memory Module?"

Lance smiled. "And have an interface cable dangling out of the side of your head? That would attract attention, don't you think?"

It was all starting to click now. "Not if your EMM was wireless," I said. "All you'd have to do is connect it to a wireless transceiver."

"That might work," Lance said. "But your transceiver would have to be very low-power, and very short range. Otherwise, the transmission might interfere with sensitive electronics."

"A transceiver with that short a range would have to be kept close to the subject's body—the *puppet's* body, wouldn't it?"

"Of course," Lance said.

I sat there, my eyes staring at the final stages of Jackal's surgery, but seeing nothing. I was stunned.

Tommy Mailo had been right all along. Michael Winter *had* been a robot, a flesh and blood *puppet* following a piece of control code like a machine.

"It's a beautiful setup," Lance said. "If you want to change your puppet's programming, all you have to do is walk up to him, and swap his EMM."

I nodded dumbly. I had been assuming that the woman in Michael's room had been there to fake his suicide. But she'd actually been there to recover an EMM-transmitter hidden in the pack of cigarettes that Michael had carried in his pocket.

The EMM, coupled with the chip in Michael's brain, would have given the cops enough evidence to start a witch-hunt. With the chip destroyed by the bullet, and the EMM removed, there was no evidence to point to the real killer. The woman had just been tidying up loose ends.

In Russell Carlisle's case, cleanup had been even simpler; the bomb had destroyed the EMM and the chip in his head at the same time.

Both cases were perfect wrap-ups: opportunity, forensic trace evidence, murder weapons, detailed confessions, and with one easily dismissible exception, no alibis. There was certainly no reason for anyone to suspect anything as unlikely as mind-control.

A lot of things were starting to make sense, but I still had a ton of unanswered questions.

Had Michael Winter and Russell Carlisle been nothing more than scapegoats, programmed to take the fall for somebody else's crimes? Or, had they actually been programmed to murder all those little girls? And if so, why?

How did the owner of the AI, the man who hid behind the phony name of Henry Clerval, factor into this? Why had he taken out a contract on me? Could he be the Puppeteer?

Lance cleared his throat. "This is all... hypothetical, right?" There was a wild look in his eyes. This wasn't a game of 'what-if' to him anymore. "You're not saying that somebody has actually *done* this, are you?"

"Take it easy," I said. "It's just idle speculation. Watching Jackal's surgery stirred up a few crazy ideas; I wanted to see where they went."

My lie sounded anemic, even to me.

Lance showed no sign of relaxing; he wasn't buying it. "Good," he said slowly. "Because—if anybody actually *does* build this mind-control chip of yours—it will mean technological slavery on a scale that even Orwell never dreamed of."

CHAPTER 28

The hours after Jackal's surgery passed slowly. It would have been safer to wait inside the boutique where no one could see me, but I couldn't smoke in there. I spent most of my time in the alley, chain-smoking cigarettes and trying to work things out.

I didn't have a suspect any more, but that sure as hell wasn't stopping the *Puppeteer*. He was out there somewhere. Watching me. Making moves. Playing with me. It *was* playing, too; there was no doubt about that. Why else would he bother to frame me for Kurt Rieger's murder? It would have been easier to kill me.

I was about to light another cigarette when Lance opened the back door of the boutique. "Jackal's coming around," he said.

I pushed the unlit cigarette back into my pack and followed him inside.

The lights in the recovery room were low, presumably so that Jackal could rest.

She lay in a powered bed, the upper half elevated about forty-five degrees, raising her to a position mid-way between reclining and sitting. Five slender cables ran from the back of her head to a bank of dermal stimulator units in a wheeled equipment rack. The flickering green LEDs on the face of the dermal units cast animated shadows on the walls.

Jackal's head was swathed in elastic bandage wraps, probably to hold the stimulator electrodes in place more than anything else; the incision hadn't been very large.

She must have reloaded the chip that remembered me, because she tried to smile when she saw me come in. "Stalin..." she whispered. "You stuck around."

"I had to make sure you were okay," I said.

She swallowed with visible effort. "Still pushing a pulse," she said. "But don't ask me to dance."

I smiled. "There go *my* plans for the evening."

Jackal grimaced and then closed her eyes. "Did we get whatever it was we were after?"

"No," I said. "But you gave it a hell of a shot. You dove right into the heart of a hostile AI. I don't know if that was genius, or stupidity, but it certainly was impressive."

"I'd be willing to hazard a guess on that," Lance said.

"I'm sorry," Jackal said. "I remember setting up for the run. I remember..."

She smiled weakly. "I bought you breakfast, didn't I?"

"Yes," I said. "Top-shelf, gourmet stuff." I ran my hand through my blonde buzz-cut. "You gave me a kickin' hair cut too."

Jackal squinted her eyes as though she were straining to see something.

"Take it easy, Gwen," Lance said. "I had to slick the data chips in your implant. I'm afraid that there are going to be some gaps in your memories."

Jackal's face held its tension for a few seconds, her concentration written clearly in her eyes, and then she relaxed back into the pillow. "I'm sorry," she said. Her voice was tired and breathy. "I guess I lost a lot. I can't really remember the run at all. It's just... gone."

My heart sank like a stone in my chest. I realized that I'd been harboring a secret hope that she could give me the name of the AI's real owner. The name of the Puppeteer.

"Don't worry about it," I said. "I'll just fall back on Plan *B*."

"What's that?" Lance asked.

"I don't know yet," I said.

"You should have downloaded the data from my implant before you slicked it," Jackal said.

"I tried," Lance said. "Most of what I got was gibberish. That AI hit you pretty hard."

Jackal closed her eyes for a few seconds. When she opened them again, she said, "let's try it anyway."

"Try what?" I asked.

"I want to have a go at reprocessing the data files Lance downloaded from my CPU. I know the data is corrupted, but we might get lucky and catch a little piece of something."

Lance shook his head. "You're not in any shape for it. And you don't upload known-bad software into your brain. It doesn't make sense."

"It can't hurt me," Jackal said.

Lance crossed his arms. "You don't know that for sure. What if that code has a virus and it screws up your CPU again? Or it kicks you into a neural-feedback loop that spikes your central nervous system?"

"It won't" Jackal said. "You said yourself that the code was corrupted. If it had a virus, it's dead already."

"I have to side with Lance," I said. "It doesn't sound like a good idea to me."

"It's my brain," Jackal said in a voice that was part croak, part whisper.

"It's *my* implant, and even the code that Lance downloaded from my CPU belongs to me." She breathed heavily for a couple of seconds. "Do it."

Lance looked at me. "What do you think?"

"Don't ask him," Jackal said. "It's not his decision."

Lance continued to stare at me.

"Do it!" Jackal hissed again.

Lanced sighed, and rubbed his eyes. "I hope you know what you're doing."

As soon as he was gone, Jackal relaxed back into her pillow and closed her eyes.

"If you're set on doing this," I said, "at least wait until you're in better shape."

"What about the price on your head?" Jackal whispered. "I remember *that* much. If we don't do this now, you may not *have* a later. And I put too much work into that kickin' new hair-job of yours to let it go to waste."

"Why are you doing this?" I asked. "Don't get me wrong, I'm grateful, but why are you taking such a risk?"

Jackal lay for a moment without speaking, then she sighed. "Every time a jacker punches into the net, he's taking a chance with his life. It's the nature of the beast."

"Yeah," I said. "But they do it for the money. You don't have to worry about that. You made the run. Your money is already earned, whether you do this or not."

"The run isn't finished yet," Jackal said. "Not till we get what we went in for. How would you like to be the PI who *almost* cracked the case?"

I didn't say anything.

"That's what I figured," Jackal said. "And I'm not going to be the jacker who *almost* drilled an AI."

I started to say something, but she cut me off. "Shut up, Stalin. I'm tired, and I want to get a couple of minutes rest before we do this."

She lay with her eyes closed until Lance returned.

He walked in with an External Memory Module tucked under one arm and a coil of ribbon cable in his hand. "Are you sure you want to do this?"

"I'm certain."

Lance laid the EMM on the bed next to Jackal and held up the connector end of the ribbon cable. "You know the drill."

Jackal turned her head to the side.

Lance peeled the elastic bandages away from the jacks in the back of her skull and plugged the gold-pinned connector into an empty socket.

Lance picked up the EMM. "Ready?"

Jackal swallowed, and whispered, "go!"

Lance punched a key on the EMM.

The LEDs on the unit began to flash sporadically, and Jackal's back arched in instant response, lifting her body until only her shoulders and heels made contact with the bed. Her head jerked to one side and then the other, her eyes rolling back until only the whites showed. Saliva sprayed from her parted lips. She released a raw, throat-rending growl through clenched teeth, and her arms began to jerk and twitch.

Lance stabbed his finger at the EMM, aiming for the button that would purge the bad code from Jackal's implant, but a violent spasm sent her left arm lashing out, knocking the unit out of his hand. Another jerk of her arm tipped the wheeled equipment rack over, sending the dermal stimulator units crashing to the floor.

Lance and I both dove for the EMM, which dangled and jerked at the end of the ribbon cable.

After two seconds of scrambling, Lance got a grip on the EMM. He reached out to shut the unit off, but Jackal's hand lashed out again. Her fingers locked around his wrist and squeezed.

"Don't..." The word came out as a strained hiss. "Don't... touch... it..."

Her arms stopped flailing and went as rigid as her spine.

We stared at her frozen body for perhaps ten seconds, the passage of time marked only by the tense and rapid breaths she took through her nostrils. Then slowly, her body began to relax. The tension went out of her muscles and surrendered her to gravity. She settled back into the bed.

"Getting..." Her ocular muscles relaxed, letting her eyes roll downward until the corneas were visible again. "I'm getting... a handle on it... now."

"We've got to flush that code out of there," Lance said.

"No..." Jackal said. "It's okay... I've isolated the... dangerous parts, now."

"I knew this was a bad idea," Lance said.

"Maybe," Jackal said. "But I think... it worked."

"What have you got?" I asked.

"I don't know yet," Jackal said, still breathing heavily. "I'm running through the data now. There are some pretty serious gaps where the code got scrambled, but I think I can piece it together."

I might be only heartbeats away from learning the name of the Puppeteer. Then the worm would turn, and the hunter would become the hunted, just as soon as I knew the name of my enemy.

"It looks like I was avoiding the protected core data," Jackal said. "I was concentrating on peripheral information flow. Trying to swim with the data stream, blend in."

She grimaced. "Big block of data missing there... I was skimming some unclassified correspondence files. Whoa... Gotcha!"

"Can you get a name?" I asked.

"I couldn't find out who that mainframe officially belongs to," she said. "They cover their tracks too well."

"Damn!"

"But I can tell you who's using it," Jackal said. Her voice, tired as it was, had a child-like taunting quality about it.

"Who?"

"A medical R&D company over on Hawthorne Boulevard," Jackal said. "It should be pretty simple to find out who owns it."

I almost smiled. Here it was: the payoff. "What's the name of the company?"

"Neuro-Tech Robotics," Jackal said. "Does that ring a bell?"

"Neuro-Tech?" Lance asked. "No kidding? That's the same company that built my surgical robots."

My knees nearly buckled. I groped for support, blundered into a wall, and leaned heavily on it. Henry Clerval—the man behind the murders of twenty-something teenage girls, the man who was offering a fifty-thousand mark reward for my own murder, the man I had come to call the Puppeteer—was the owner of Neuro-Tech Robotics... my life-long friend, John Hershell?

I felt like the floor had dropped out from under me. "No," I said. "You're wrong. It's not Neuro-Tech."

"I'm sorry," Jackal said softly. "But that's the way it stacks up."

"There are holes in the data," I said. "Big holes. You said so yourself. Go back and look at it again."

"I can re-run the data," Jackal said. "But it won't play out any different. We traced the murder callback to the AI, and the AI belongs to Neuro-Tech Robotics. That's where all the arrows point."

"I don't give a damn where the arrows point! Re-run the fucking data. It's not Neuro-Tech."

Lance grabbed my left arm just above the elbow. "Come on," he said. "Gwen needs to get some rest."

He gently tugged me toward the door.

I almost snatched my arm away from him, but on some level, I realized that he was right. I let him lead me out of the room.

Lance released my elbow when we were in the hall. "You've obviously got some things to work out," he said. "But don't take your problems out on Gwen. She nearly died chasing your riddles through the net. And then she was willing to risk it again when you didn't get what you wanted."

"But she's wrong," I said. "She's got to be."

Lance turned back toward Jackal's recovery room. "I really couldn't care less whether she's right or wrong," he said. "My concern is her health. You're not helping any by climbing up her ass."

I found my way out to the alley and lit a cigarette. Okay, okay. Think it out. Work it through...

It was a coincidence. It was some kind of frame-up. *Something.* I would call John, talk to him. He would tell me the truth. I *knew* he would.

But what could he say? That he just happened to be the owner of the company that was trying to murder me? That there was a perfectly good reason that all those little girls had to die?

Emptiness settled in my belly like an icicle. It brought with it a comforting numbness. I leaned against the wall of the boutique, staring off into nothing. I couldn't think. I couldn't feel. I didn't want to.

The pain seemed to come from far away. At first, I couldn't locate it; I couldn't even tell if it was real. But it grew stronger and more insistent. It was a burning, in my hand, my fingers. The burning refused to be ignored. It reached down into my fog of self-pity and brought me around like a slap in the face.

"Ow! Jesus!" I shook my right hand until the cigarette butt fell free and rolled on the pavement. I ground it out with the toe of my shoe.

I looked at my hand. The cigarette had burned down to my skin, blistering the backs of my index and middle fingers. For such a small injury, the burns hurt like hell.

I was glad for the pain. It had shaken me out of my stupor. It helped melt the icicle in my stomach, helped me turn it to fire.

Jackal was still awake when I opened the door to the recovery room. She tried to smile. "I didn't know if you were coming back. You left your bag."

I picked up the travel bag and slung it over my shoulder. "Thanks."

"I'm going to re-run that data," she said. "Maybe you're right. I could have made a mistake."

"You don't need to re-run it," I said. "We both know you were right. I just wasn't ready for it."

"Is it somebody you know?"

"Yeah," I said. "An old friend."

"I figured it was something like that," Jackal said. "I'm sorry."

"No," I said. "*I'm* sorry. I asked the questions. It's not your fault that I didn't like the answers."

Jackal closed her eyes.

"Sleep now," I said. "You done good."

Down the block from Second Looks, I bought a news printout from a vending machine. The top story had moved on to a terrorist attack on the Russian Royal Family. There was still no mention of Rieger's murder. That might mean that the body hadn't been discovered yet. Or, it might mean that the police were sitting on the story.

If God was listening to my prayers, the cops were still in the dark. I was counting on it; I needed to borrow Rieger's car. It was time to take the fight to the bad guy's home-turf, and public transportation didn't seem up to the challenge of providing a silent approach or a reliable get-away.

It took me fifteen minutes to catch a cab. I gave the driver the address of Kurt Rieger's apartment building in Dome 11. He drove a lot faster than necessary, but I didn't care.

Los Angeles slid by my window unnoticed. I felt around inside myself for my anger. It was still there, a hard little ember in my chest, smoldering with the quiet insistence of the cigarette burns on the backs of my fingers.

My right hand stole into my jacket just far enough to verify the presence of the Blackhart. *I'm coming, John. In just a little while.*

The garage under Rieger's building was deserted. His BMW was still parked in slot 11-A. The key chip was still behind the fire extinguisher, right where I'd left it.

I unlocked the car and slid behind the wheel. At the touch of a button, the gull-wing door powered shut behind me. I stuffed my purple travel bag into the front passenger seat.

I plugged in the key chip. The wraparound dashboard flared blue with plasma display instrumentation. The computer chirped and bleeped softly for a couple of seconds as it ran full-spectrum diagnostics and sequenced the car's various systems on line. The car's soundproofing was excellent; I could barely hear the turbines as they spun up.

I decided not to cut in the blowers right away; I hadn't driven in close to five years, and I'd never driven anything anywhere near as advanced as Rieger's car. I spent a minute or so cycling the double pistol grips of the control yoke through their full ranges of motion. The control surfaces on the front air-foils and rear spoilers flexed in instant response, the angry mosquito whine of the control servos oddly louder than the muted wail of the turbines.

My reflection stared back at me from the rear view mirror. The blonde buzz-cut and two-day beard made me look like Kurt Rieger's brother on a downhill skid. My face seemed different now, more gaunt, cheekbones prominent. I didn't remember those creases at the corners of my eyes. I lit the last of the Mexican Marlboros and glanced at the mirror again. I saw the face of a stranger.

I thumbed the button that kicked in the blowers and felt the BMW rise softly as the apron inflated. I backed slowly out of the slot, and drove out of the garage. The police could now add grand theft auto to my list of crimes.

The BMW handled like a dream. It cornered as well as can be expected from a hover vehicle, and had power to spare. I cruised the streets at random, putting some polish on my rusty driving skills. But I was too preoccupied to appreciate the luxury of driving such a superb machine.

After driving an hour or so, I plucked Rieger's phone out of its recess on the dashboard and punched up Lisa's number. If I was going to go beard the lion in his proverbial den, it would be better to have Lisa and Sonja tucked away somewhere safe. I wanted them to check into a hotel and lay low until the dust settled.

Lisa's phone rang about forty times without an answer before I gave up.

I turned west on Wilshire Boulevard, toward Park La Brea, and Lisa's apartment.

"It's probably nothing," I said aloud. I stepped on the accelerator.

I punched the redial key as I turned north on McCadden, and let the phone ring until I cut west again on 3rd Street. Still no answer.

Stay calm. Don't get bent out of shape. Knowing Lisa, they probably went out for a pizza or something.

I pulled up in front of Colosseum Apartments and was about to shut down the turbines when another car left the curb and raced away. I caught a glimpse of it under a streetlight; it was a Mercedes sport sedan: the same model as John's car. Judging color under a street lamp is tricky, but the car's paint was dark, maybe midnight blue. Like John's car.

I tried to get a look into the car as it drove under the light, but the window tint was too dark to see anything.

Was I being paranoid? Leaping to wild conclusions? Or was this really John driving away from Lisa's apartment?

I paused with my hand on the BMW's key chip. Shut it off and go inside? Or chase a car that could belong to anyone?

I looked around at the rest of the cars parked along the curb. Chevy's. Suzuki's. Fokkers. Middle-class cars in a middle-class neighborhood. And somehow, the only two high-end European cars in the neighborhood had both ended up in front of Lisa's apartment, and Lisa wasn't answering her phone.

I punched the redial key again. Still no answer. I held the receiver away from my ear, powered down the passenger window, and listened. In the distance, I could just make out the sound of the phone ringing in Lisa's apartment. Nobody home.

Sometimes, you've got to go with your gut reaction.

I let a couple of cars get between me and the Mercedes before I pulled away from the curb and slid into traffic. The Mercedes turned right onto Cloverdale, then left onto Olympic and out of Dome 6. I followed.

In Dome 8, the Mercedes cut south to 15th Street, and then east and through the 15th Street Tunnel into Dome 11. Where was he going?

At the entrance to Dome 10, the Mercedes started to pull away from me rapidly. I must have gotten too close and spooked him.

My question had answered itself; an innocent man wouldn't have any reason to run. It had to be John.

I stomped on the accelerator. The pitch of the turbines jumped an octave, and the BMW surged forward, narrowing the gap.

John's Mercedes stood on it hard, but the BMW had no trouble closing on his tail lights.

A red Suzuki truck turned out of a side street directly into my path. I swung the control yoke hard left and tried to pass it. No such luck. The maneuver left me staring into two pairs of headlights. Both of the oncoming cars leaned on their horns.

I couldn't go right, and I couldn't go straight. I jerked the controls to the left again and abandoned the street entirely. In the rear view mirror, I saw one of the oncoming cars miss the back of Rieger's car by centimeters.

The BMW bounced crazily when the curb and sidewalk interrupted the air cushion under its apron. The entire car shuddered as the left front fan ate the ground just past the border of the sidewalk. Dirt and mutilated grass sprayed out from under the front end. The car slid sideways through a row of bushes and ate them as well.

I found myself barreling across the front lawn of an apartment complex at close to 120 kilometers an hour. My right front bumper tagged a garbage can and blew it sideways into the street.

I glanced over the hedge: no oncoming traffic. I cut to the right, mowing down another stretch of bushes as I careened back into the street.

The tail lights of John's Mercedes were just turning right at the next corner. I punched the accelerator to the floor. The damaged front blower screamed, but the car rocketed forward at my command.

The soft blue plasma readout for the front blowers began flashing red warning tattletales.

I barely held the turn, swinging across both oncoming lanes and scraping the apron against the far curb before swerving back onto the right side of the street. If there had been any oncoming cars, or any parked cars for that matter, my trip would have ended right there.

I backed off on the speed just enough to regain control.

The Mercedes was disappearing into the tunnel that led to the vehicle side of the Humboldt Street Lock. John was leaving the domes.

I stepped on the brakes. The control-vanes on the rear spoiler expanded, and bit the air hard; the car decelerated heavily. The chase wasn't over, but the flashing amber lights above the tunnel entrance told me that I wasn't going to make it into the lock before the doors closed.

True to my prediction, the huge steel doors slid shut long before I got to the tunnel. *Damn.*

I pulled up to the entrance to the lock and lit a cigarette.

It takes about a minute and a half to cycle through all three stages of the vehicle lock. No matter what I did, John had a ninety-second head start on me.

After what seemed like an eternity, the lock doors slid open to admit the BMW. Ninety seconds later, I drove slowly out the other end and into the flat desolation of no-man's land.

Outside the circle of arc lights at the dome's perimeter, the only light came from the moon, the stars, and the headlights of Rieger's car. There was no sign of John or his Mercedes.

To make matters worse, the BMW's fans whipped the pulverized earth of no-man's land into a sandstorm that enveloped the car like a cloud. Soon, I couldn't see a thing. The blowing sand reflected the headlights back at me. I turned them off; they weren't helping anyway. I crept across the kilometer-wide ribbon of sand in total darkness.

The blinding cloud evaporated as quickly as it had appeared. I had driven out of no-man's land and on to the cracked remains of a paved street.

I flipped the headlight switch to low beams and cruised slowly. I had no idea where John had gone. For all I knew, he could have doubled back and returned to the domes by now. I didn't have a clue. All I could do was drive and hope for a lucky break.

My course through the abandoned streets was chosen partly at random, and partly through necessity. Some of the streets were too broken up or clogged with debris for the BMW to get through. Sometimes I had to back up a block or more before I could find a place to turn around.

Occasionally, one of the blowers would suck a small piece of debris off the road and rattle it around under the apron for a while before spitting it out.

I drove aimlessly, with a cigarette clenched between my teeth and the Blackhart cradled in my lap. The dilapidated buildings and skeletal cars made the hair on the back of my neck stand up. I didn't like this place. It felt of decay, and of death.

My headlights revealed the remains of a Post Office, its rusted flagpole fallen to block the street.

I made a U-turn and was driving away when I realized that I had been here before. I had a vague memory of having stepped over that very flagpole on some night long past.

When it hit me, it was like a punch in the stomach. I knew suddenly why this area looked familiar.

I turned right at the next corner. There was the burned-out bus station. A block farther along was the factory clothes outlet with the collapsed roof, right where I expected it to be.

I parked the car and walked the last block. The sharp chemical air stung my eyes and nose. When I inhaled, my lungs burned. I didn't care. Somewhere, John's Mercedes was speeding away into the night, and I didn't care about that either.

The warehouse squatted in the moonlight like the dark castle in a low-budget fantasy vid. I hadn't actually seen it since the night that Maggie died, but it had featured in my nightmares a thousand times.

I stared at it, tried to fix it in my mind as a building, just an old building. Rotting. Crumbling.

The years had obviously not been kind. Only a few of the corrugated steel roof panels remained. A good number of the rusted rafters had collapsed. Only one of the high windows had any glass left: a single triangular shard hanging like a stalactite from one of the upper frames.

Had John been leading me here? Or had my subconscious quietly steered me to the one spot in the universe that featured in my darkest dreams?

It mushroomed inside me: a seething, roiling maelstrom of pain, and anger, and fear. I thought for a moment that I would explode, or that the rage blazing inside me would leap from my eyes like laser beams and burn the old warehouse to its foundations.

I didn't remember drawing it, but suddenly the Blackhart was in my fist. It was a lightning rod, the barrel a steel conduit for my anger. The cigarette burns on my fingers tingled in anticipation as my index finger tightened on the trigger.

The first round slammed into the side of the warehouse, punching a fist-sized hole in the wall. The decaying steel rang like an anvil under a hammer, particles of rust exploding into a blood-colored cloud. Again. And again. And again. My trigger-finger squeezing rhythmically until the hammer of the Blackhart fell on an empty chamber. I ejected the empty magazine onto the ground and shoved another into the handle of the pistol with the heel of my hand.

I cycled the slide forward to chamber the next bullet. I raised the barrel toward the old building and set my finger on the trigger.

The last pane of glass slipped free of its window frame and fluttered end-over-end toward the ground. For a second, it almost seemed as if the glass might be caught by the wind and sail away like a crystalline leaf. But gravity plucked it from the air and shattered it into dust against the cracked cement.

I lowered my Blackhart. The warehouse was dead. The years would continue to wear away at its corpse until nothing remained at all, but that wouldn't matter. The old building was dead, and not a thousand centuries of entropy could make it any deader.

I slid the Blackhart into my shoulder rig and turned back toward the car.

I had work to do.

CHAPTER 29

III II I I IIIII I II III I II I III IIII III I II I IIIII II III I III III

The knob turned easily in my hand; Lisa's apartment wasn't locked. Not good.

I pulled the Blackhart and used the barrel to push the door. It swung open silently. None of the three alarms made a sound.

The living room was wrecked. Two of the fake walnut bookcases lay on the floor, one half atop the other. Book chips and ceramic animal salt shakers were scattered across the carpet. The pepper shaker giraffe had broken his neck again.

My first thought was that the room had been searched, but only the two bookshelves closest to the door had been upended. There had been a struggle, just inside the door.

I followed the Blackhart into the hall, moving as quietly as I could, listening for any sounds that the intruder was still here. The scent of blood hung heavy on the air.

The first door on the right led to the bedroom. The doorframe near the latch was split. The door had obviously been kicked open, but it was closed now. I listened for a couple of seconds before easing the door open. No Sonja; no Lisa; no bad guys.

The smell of blood grew stronger as I moved down the hall.

The second room on the right was the bathroom. The door was already open. I peeked around the corner. Empty.

The only doorway on the left side of the hall led to the last room in the apartment, the kitchen. I stood in the hallway and listened carefully. I heard something, just barely louder than my own breathing, a mewling sound. The cat? No, it didn't sound like a cat.

The blood-smell was powerful here. I didn't want to look around the corner. I wasn't afraid of finding the killer. I was afraid of finding Lisa, or Sonja, or both.

I tightened my grip on the Blackhart and spun around the corner, swinging the pistol to cover the entire room.

No intruder.

Lisa sat on the floor, her back against the cabinets, face hidden in her hands. She was weeping softly; her sobs had that low child-like keening

247

that sometimes comes at the end of a prolonged cry, when the person's energy is just about spent.

A long strip of cellophane tape hung from the circular florescent light above the table. From the end of the tape dangled a sheet of paper: a note turning slowly in an unseen draft.

The table top under the note was smeared with congealing blood, the stain turning brown against the white lacquered wood. At the center of the bloody smear lay the twisted corpse of Mr. Shoes. The cat's lithe gray body had been sliced from throat to tail, spilling his entrails all over the table.

I knelt down and put my hand on Lisa's shoulder. "Lisa..."

She flinched at my touch and nearly screamed. She snatched her hands away from her face, and for a half-second, her eyes were wide with fear. Then she recognized me, and she threw her arms around my neck and buried her face in my shoulder. "Oh David... Oh God..." She broke down into uncontrollable sobbing.

It took the better part of ten minutes to get Lisa calmed down enough to tell me what had happened.

"I... I didn't see anyone. I was... in the bedroom when I heard..." She broke down again.

I held the Blackhart down and away from her; I didn't want to holster it until I knew for certain that we were safe. My left hand cradled Lisa's head against my chest and stroked her hair.

Finally, she sniffed and tried again. "The front door opened. I heard it. I don't know if Sonja opened it, or if... I don't know; I didn't see..."

"Okay," I said. "You were in your bedroom and you heard the door open. Then what happened?"

Lisa took a deep breath. "I heard... I don't know, a fight. A struggle. Things falling over. Glass breaking. I... panicked. I locked my bedroom door. I was trying to call the police when someone started trying to break my door open. The latch... I could see that it wasn't going to hold. I ran to the door and tried to keep it shut with my body. Something hit the door... hard. I think I screamed... I don't know. And then the door flew open. It knocked me down, and before I could get up, someone had a foot or a knee in the middle of my back. I tried to roll over, but they stuck something in my neck. It... burned me... *shocked* me, and I passed out."

"Who?" I asked. "Did you get a good look at them?"

"I didn't see anything," Lisa said. "One second, the door was closed, the next I was on the floor and that electrical thing was jammed in my neck."

Lisa glanced up at the table and began to sob again. "My baby... My poor little baby... He never hurt anybody. He didn't deserve this."

I shook her shoulder softly. "Lisa. Where is Sonja?" She didn't answer. I shook her a little harder. "Lisa. I need to know where Sonja is."

"Gone...," Lisa sobbed. "Gone... and my poor little baby..."

I gently pried Lisa's arms from around my neck and stood up. Lisa's hands came up to cover her face again. On the left side of her neck were two circular blisters, twins to the ones on my own neck. She'd been zapped by a police riot wand, way over-charged.

I looked at the body of the cat. I'd never gotten the chance to get to know him, but the sight of his mangled little carcass added a few more grams to the weight of guilt that hung on my heart. Maybe he was only an animal, but he was dead because I'd dragged Lisa into the middle of this thing. Now, Sonja was gone, and a severely endangered species was one step closer to extinction.

I touched the note with the Blackhart to steady it.

> *AND WHY THE SEA IS BOILING HOT -*
> *AND WHETHER PIGS HAVE WINGS. "*

I dug around in my jacket pocket and came up with Bobbie Dean's trid. I read the four-line verse on the back, and then looked up at the note suspended from Lisa's light fixture. They were part of the same quotation, I was certain of it. I tried reading the two pieces together, aloud.

> *"THE TIME HAS COME, " THE WALRUS SAID,*
> *TO TALK OF MANY THINGS:*
> *OF SHOES - AND SHIPS - AND SEALING WAX -*
> *OF CABBAGES - AND KINGS -*
> *AND WHY THE SEA IS BOILING HOT -*
> *AND WHETHER PIGS HAVE WINGS. "*

The verse ran over and over again in my mind. It still sounded like gibberish to me.

I looked down at Mr. Shoes. Two circles of slightly darker gray marked the fur on the cat's side. I leaned closer; the fur was singed here: pencil eraser sized burns. Mr. Shoes had also felt the bite of the riot stunner.

I couldn't think of a single reason to shock the poor cat *after* its guts had been ripped out, so I reasoned that it must have happened the other way around. Mr. Shoes had been stunned, and *then* killed. Which meant that the cat hadn't been killed to keep him out of the way; the stunner would have done that. Mr. Shoes had been slaughtered for the hell of it, or maybe as a message: some kind of sick punctuation mark to the note.

I looked at the dangling sheet of paper again. The letters were perfectly formed capitals written with a heavy black laundry marker. No handwriting expert in the world could tell a thing from textbook block letters. There was no signature, but I had a pretty good idea who had written it.

I found a pair of suitcases in the top of Lisa's closet. I grabbed the smaller one and spent a few minutes packing it. She wasn't really up to helping, so I tried to guess my way through it. I stuck to the basics: clothes, underwear, a robe, and most of the toiletries from her vanity and the bathroom counter top.

It took a good fifteen minutes to get Lisa down the stairs to Rieger's BMW. I had to wait until she could walk, because she was just too big to carry.

The damaged blower made ominous scraping sounds as I started the turbines. I ignored the noises, and the flashing red warning tattle-tales on the instrument panel. I pulled away from the curb and accelerated. The car only had to hang on for a couple of more hours.

I took turns at random, constantly watching for a tail. Lisa sobbed quietly in the passenger seat.

The scenario unfolded itself in my mind like a vid.

There is a soft knock at the door. Sonja answers. The killer tricks her into opening the door, maybe with a story about me: David's in some kind of trouble; he needs help. When the door is open, the killer makes a grab for her. They struggle, but the stun wand tips the balance. Sonja is down, and the killer enters the apartment.

He forces his way into Lisa's bedroom. The killer takes her down with the stun wand.

At some point, Mr. Shoes enters the fray, and gets zapped for his trouble. The killer makes a special effort to eviscerate him.

I played the scene out three or four different ways. Maybe the killer picked the lock and Sonja rushed to the door to jam it closed. Maybe Mr. Shoes tried to hide instead of fight. The details didn't matter much.

In my mind, the killer was still without a face. No matter how hard I tried, I couldn't make myself see John attacking Lisa or Sonja.

And my mind's eye refused to form a picture of my friend butchering a helpless animal. But somebody had done it, just like somebody had carved up Elaine Carerra and Christine Clark, and all those other little girls. And, like Jackal said, all of the arrows pointed the same way.

After twenty minutes, I was confident that we weren't being followed. I pulled into a cheap motel and registered Lisa under the name of Shirley Conrad.

Lisa wasn't crazy about the idea. She sniffed and put on a brave face. "I don't want to stay here," she said.

"You can't go home yet," I said. "You're not safe there. Not until I get this straightened out."

"I want to go with you," Lisa said.

I shook my head. "Not this time. Not where I'm going."

I walked to the door. "Keep this locked until I come back."

"What if you... don't come back?"

"Then wait a couple of days and go home. The people that did this are only interested in you as a way to get to me. If I'm out of the picture, they'll lose interest in you."

Lisa stared at me as if trying to memorize my face. "You'll be okay?"

"Yeah," I said. "I'll be fine."

I winked at her and closed the door.

I drove west to the 405 and then south to the Culver City vehicle lock at the southern end of Dome 13. The ninety seconds that it took to cycle through the lock gave me a chance to think. I was reacting again, letting someone else goad me into action before I was ready.

What was I going to do? Knock on the front door of Neuro-Tech and demand John's unconditional surrender? How about the sentry robots, and the installed security systems? John's AI made no secret of its ability to deliver an "immediate and lethal response."

The AI had to be taken out of the equation, but how? My first thought was to shut down the power to the building, but I didn't have any idea of how to go about it. I'd have to locate someone with the right kind of technical skills, and with a price on my head, shopping for new friends seemed like a bad idea.

A virus might do the trick. But it would have to be a real show-stopper of a virus, one that could kill an AI, or at least shut it down cold for a few hours.

I smiled when it came to me. If his bragging was anything to go by, Surf might already have something that would do the trick. According to him, his new virus would 'crack a hardened AI like a walnut.'

The doors at the far end of the lock slid open. I drove out of the lock and left the domes behind for the second time that night.

It was nearly midnight when I pulled through the lighted archway into Dome 17's north lock. I waited for the inner doors to cycle open, and then drove into Dome 17. I followed the route that Jackal and I had taken by cab the night before: west on Imperial Highway, and then south on Vista Del Mar.

I parked Rieger's BMW at the strip-mall and walked across the street to the abandoned tidal-electric plant that played home to R.U.R.

I paused for a millisecond when I came to the far edge of the concrete pad. Then I stepped out onto that metal grating and walked across it. Seeing the old warehouse again had broken something free inside of me, and the catwalk over the tide engine had lost its power to freeze my heart. It was just another piece of steel now.

The tidal plant was littered with dilapidated buildings. It took me four tries to find the staircase that led to Iron Betty's little kingdom.

Surf answered my knock on the door. "How's Jackal doing?" His concern was probably genuine, but the flat mechanical quality of the voice chip made his question sound unemotional and disinterested.

"She's going to be okay," I said. "Lance says she'll be up and around by tomorrow."

"Good. We were watching when you interfaced with the AI. Jackal was playing it pretty close to the wire."

I searched for my cigarettes. "How long does it take to warm up this killer virus of yours?"

Surf grinned. "What do you have in mind?"

I lit a smoke. "I'm going to pay a visit to Neuro-Tech Robotics, and I need someone to take out their AI before it can take me out."

"Come on," Surf said. "You'll have to talk to the Lady." He turned and started walking away.

I followed. "Iron Betty? What do I need to see her for?"

"It's her decision," Surf said.

"Last night, you were making noises like Mr. Cyber-executioner. Now you've got to ask permission to come out and play? I thought you *wanted* to try out your new virus."

"I do," Surf said. "But every attack must be made..."

"*On* purpose, and *with* purpose," I said. "I've heard that one before."

Surf ignored my comment, and led me into Iron Betty's chamber and through the maze of computer hardware to her nest in the center of the room.

Her eyes were still locked on their invisible focal point. I wondered if she had slept, or even blinked since the last time I'd seen her. She smiled slightly. "The oyster returns," she said in her whispery voice. "Perhaps he is intent on growing some teeth."

"Pardon me?"

"You haven't read your Carroll, have you, Mr. Stalin?"

"Apparently not," I said.

"Lewis Carroll," Iron Betty said.

"Alice's Adventures in Wonderland?" I asked.

"Right author," Surf said. "Wrong book. Try *Through the Looking Glass.*"

I shook my head. "I don't follow."

"Your enemy has read it," Iron Betty said. "That's where he found the verse."

"The one about the walrus?"

"Exactly," said Iron Betty. "It's from Tweedledee's poem *The Walrus and the Carpenter.*"

"Who told you about the verse?" I asked.

"Nobody told us," Surf said. "We were monitoring Jackal's run when she used it to activate the call-back routine at Pacific Fusion and Electric."

"The poem sounds like nonsense to me," I said. "At least the parts I've heard so far. But maybe I should try to find a copy of it, to see if it means anything."

"You can find it in the net," Surf said. "Alongside every other piece of classic literature. But you don't need to bother now; we already looked it up."

"Does it really mean anything?"

"That depends on what you are willing to read into it," Iron Betty said. "When pared down to its essentials, the poem tells the story of a walrus and a carpenter who conspire to lure a bunch of unsuspecting oysters out of the sea and onto the beach for a walk. The oysters, who are unaccustomed to walking, quickly become exhausted. The walrus baffles their tired minds with stories about boiling seas and winged pigs. When the oysters are thoroughly confused, and too tired to escape, the walrus and the carpenter kill them and eat every one."

"And that makes me the oyster who wants to grow teeth?"

"That's what you came here for, isn't it?" Surf asked. "The bad guys have been taking you for a little walk on the beach and baffling you with nonsense. Now, you're all worn out, and you want us to help you grow some teeth so that you can bite them before they eat you."

I nodded. "I need you to take out an AI. I don't care if you slick it, or just knock it off line for a few hours. But it has to be out of my way."

"Why should we do this?" Iron Betty asked.

"You saw what happened to Jackal," I said. "Isn't that reason enough?"

"Revenge is a motive we try to avoid," Iron Betty said. "We cannot hope to advance to the next evolutionary level by embracing the animal instincts of our past."

"What about your Convergence?" I asked.

"I didn't think you believed in the Convergence," said Iron Betty.

"I don't," I said. "But according to you, that doesn't matter. What was it you were saying last night? It isn't necessary for me to understand the Convergence, or to even be aware of it. You said I'd be part of it anyway."

"True enough," said Iron Betty.

"Well if there is such a thing," I said, "it's happening at Neuro-Tech Robotics."

Iron Betty chuckled softly. "It isn't quite as simple as that, Mr. Stalin. Perhaps we've given you the impression that the Convergence will occur in one bold stroke. In fact, it will be like any other evolutionary contest. It will not be won or lost in a single skirmish, no matter how decisive. The struggle will last for years, perhaps decades, and many battles will be fought."

"Fine," I said. "But you can't win a war without winning some of the battles. And one of your battles is being fought at Neuro-Tech. If you don't show up, you're going to lose this one by default."

"We can't win if we don't fight," Surf said.

"The question," Iron Betty said, "isn't whether or not we will fight. Rather, it is a matter of *when*, and *where*. Although the net shows us that the Convergence is near, I can see no indication that Neuro-Tech Robotics is involved. We act in response to data, Mr. Stalin, not in response to the lack of it."

I stopped for a few seconds. Should I tell them? I thought of Sonja; time might be running out for her, if it hadn't run out already. I couldn't afford *not* to tell them.

"Okay," I said. "You're probably not going to believe this, but Neuro-Tech has made a quantum leap in neural implant technology. They've developed a custom microchip that gets implanted in the Prefrontal Lobe. I call it the Puppet Chip. It turns the human body into sort of a flesh and blood puppet, controlled by computer-generated software."

"Can you offer proof?" Iron Betty asked.

"Michael Winter and Russell Carlisle were both puppets," I said. "Look up their autopsy files in the LAPD Homicide database. There's evidence that both men had microchip implants in their left Prefrontal Lobes."

"That doesn't tell us a great deal," Iron Betty said. "Many people have neural implants."

"Not in their Prefrontal Lobes," I said. "Besides, if you check their medical histories, I think you'll find there is no record that either of them ever had any sort of neural implant."

"Then where did these implants come from?" Iron Betty asked.

"Michael Winter had an operative brain tumor," I said. "The records will undoubtedly show that Russell Carlisle suffered from something similar. Both men underwent neuro-surgery, and their operations were almost certainly performed by surgical robots. Anyone want to guess who builds those robots?"

"Neuro-Tech Robotics," said Surf.

"Got it in one," I said.

CHAPTER 30

At two-twenty a.m., Hawthorne Boulevard was deserted. I parked Rieger's BMW about a quarter of a block from the Neuro-Tech building.

John's new haunted-castle holo-facade hid his five-story cement cube behind an illusion of crumbling stone walls and shadowed towers. The trid I'd seen in John's apartment a couple of days earlier hadn't done the projection justice; the designer had really gone in for detail. Veils of cobwebs shrouded the castle's darkened window slits. Tattered banners hung from rusty flagpoles atop the battlements, and flocks of black bats looped and darted through the air around the towers. Every few seconds, a jagged fork of holographic lightning would split the air above the castle, throwing the old fortress into stark relief.

None of the other buildings on the block had holo-facades. Then again, none of them were ugly enough to need one.

I popped Rieger's car phone out of its recess on the dashboard, and punched in a number I'd gotten from Surf. Supposedly, the number belonged to a phone booth in the Cayman Islands. It rang six times.

If Surf's claims were true, each ring represented a transfer to a different switchboard in a different city. My call bounced from the Caymans, to the Florida Pirate Republics, to Zurich, to Singapore, to God-knows-where, and finally, to a number that technically didn't exist back in LA. Enough razzle-dazzle to make it hard as hell to trace.

Surf's gravelly mechanical voice answered after the sixth ring. "Joe's Pool Hall."

"I'm here," I said.

"Out front?"

"Just up the street," I said. "I'm looking at the building now. Are you ready?"

"Just a keystroke away," Surf said.

"What about the doors? Are you sure you can handle them?"

"Like I told you," Surf said, "it's covered. At the instant that the virus hits the mainframe, a subroutine injected into the building's maintenance computer will retract every automatic lock in the place. Exactly fifteen milliseconds later, the power will go down, leaving the locks in the unlatched position. You won't even have to say 'Open Sesame.'"

"Will the security systems be off line?"

"My virus will slick the mainframe," Surf said. "And if it doesn't finish the job, flat-lining the power grid will do the trick. Any other security systems should go down when the power gets cut."

I took a deep breath and released it slowly. "Give me thirty seconds," I said.

"The count-down is on," Surf said, and hung up.

I plugged the phone back into its recess, grabbed my Night-Stalkers and Ryan's machine pistol out of the travel bag, and climbed out of the car. The gull-wing door powered itself shut behind me.

I shoved the barrel of the machine pistol through my belt and adjusted the bomber jacket to cover it as much as possible. I started walking toward the Neuro-Tech building, in what I hoped was a casual manner.

Don't look at me; I'm just out for a stroll. Minding my own business. Kindly disregard the military-grade night goggles tucked under my arm and the silenced machine pistol sticking out of my jacket.

Either my timing was nearly perfect, or Surf's was. I was less than ten meters from the building when the haunted-castle holo-facade flickered twice, strobed with static for about a quarter of a second, and went out. The Neuro-Tech building was dark.

I slipped the Night-Stalkers over my forehead and flicked the power switch on. I flipped the lenses down over my eyes, and the dark building lit up in shades of green.

I covered the remaining distance with a few long strides, not drawing the machine pistol until I was standing in front of the entrance. My natural choice was the Blackhart, but Ryan's machine pistol was silenced, and wouldn't give away my position if I had to fire it.

I laid my hand on the translucent polycarbon door. The bulletproof surface was cool under my palm. I pushed gently and the door swung inward without a sound. Surf's door-lock virus had apparently done its work.

I stepped inside, slid quickly to the left of the doorway, and stood with my back to the wall. Even with no light to silhouette me, I wanted to get clear of the doorway as quickly as possible.

I gave the lobby a quick scan. No bad guys in sight.

I knew that John didn't have any security people, because he didn't trust them. I'd probably heard him say it a thousand times; he'd pulled enough sentry duty in the Army to know that guards are expensive, inattentive, and not very effective.

It was his sentry robots that had me worried. If they were just drones, remote-controlled by John's AI, they'd have gone down when the virus took the mainframe out. But if they were true robots, with on-board CPU's, they could operate independently of the AI.

John and I had never discussed his defense systems; it just wasn't the sort of thing that came up in polite conversation.

Of course, there was still John himself to think about, and his gunslinger—the woman with the laser.

I crossed the lobby quickly but quietly, ears cocked for any sound not of my own making.

At the door to the stairs, I did another jack-in-the-box entrance, ready to shoot man, woman, or robot. The stairwell was empty.

The stairs had emergency lighting. Battery-powered lamps cast half-moon shaped pools of light at the tops and bottoms of each landing, leaving the stretches of stair between in near darkness. The Night-Stalkers filtered both the light and dark areas to nearly uniform shades of cool green.

The machine pistol led the way up the stairs. I followed it as quietly as I could, struggling as I climbed to develop a sixth and seventh sense: some precognitive ability to sniff out where the bad guys were hiding.

I climbed the first three flights without incident. But just after I made the turn at the half-landing between the third and fourth floors, I heard a spitting sound from somewhere above me: a quick string of puffs, like pressurized air being forced through a tube. The wall next to my head erupted in a shower of powdered sheetrock. I hit the floor, rolling onto my back with my legs dangling down the stairs, the machine pistol swinging up in search of a target.

There! Up on the fourth-floor landing: a sentry robot! I squeezed off a burst, my rounds hammering the robot's thorax. The ceramic flechettes must have shattered harmlessly against the machine's carbon-laminate armor, because its Gatling gun fired in instant response. I half-rolled/half-shoved myself back down the stairway, the steps pummeling my spine as I slid out of the robot's arc of fire. A hail of projectiles chewed up the floor where I'd been a millisecond before.

I slid another few meters until I could get a hand onto the side rail and fight my way to my feet. The robot wasn't firing anymore, but I could hear the whining of its optical sensors as it scanned for me in the darkness. I ran down the stairs to the third-floor landing.

I paused at the fire door that opened off the stairway, and took a few seconds to figure out my next move. The sentry robot was now directly above me, on the fourth-floor landing. It couldn't get to me without coming down the stairs, a feat that a wheeled machine couldn't manage. True, the robot controlled the stairs that led up to John's fifth-floor apartment, but there was another set of stairs at the west end of the building.

The only problem was, I'd have to hunt for those other stairs. I'd had a couple of informal tours, but I'd never really paid attention to the building's layout. Usually, I just took the elevator directly to John's apartment.

For a half-second, I considered swapping weapons; my Blackhart's steel-jacketed bullets would almost certainly penetrate the robot's armor. I could blow the robot away, and make it up to John's apartment in seconds. But the Blackhart wasn't silenced.

Up to now, the exchange of fire had been quiet enough to escape detection by anyone outside of the stairwell. A single shot from the Blackhart would change all that, and I wasn't ready to advertise my position just yet. Better to stick to the third-floor for now, and look for that other set of stairs.

I opened the fire door and slipped through, low and fast, the machine pistol sweeping back and forth while I scanned for targets.

The door led to a large room that housed an automated assembly line. Seven or eight rows of conveyor belts stretched the length of the assembly area, each running down the center of a complex scaffolding of crossed I-beams. Dozens of robotic arms hung from each scaffold, manipulators and sensors paralyzed without power.

No sign of bad guys.

A thermex cylinder of liquid nitrogen bled tendrils of cool mist into the darkened air. Through my Night-Stalkers, the rising vapor gave the room the look of a horror vid seen through dark green sunglasses.

A ceiling-mounted security sensor array stood mute watch over the fire door, its vid lenses, infrared snoopers, and motion detectors blinded by the loss of power.

The door eased shut behind me with a barely audible click. I made my way across the room, moving slowly and carefully down an aisle between two assembly lines, following the machine pistol in my outstretched fist toward a door in the far corner.

My path took me past the nitrogen cylinder. A ribbon of cold air brushed my cheek like the breath of a ghost, raising goose bumps down my spine.

The door at the far side of the room opened as easily and quietly as the fire door had. It led to a hallway lined with doors, darkened except for evenly spaced puddles of light thrown by the emergency lanterns.

I peeked around the doorframe into the corridor, straight into the barrels of a Gatling gun. I jerked my head back, and a hail of shots pelted the door next to where my head had been. I felt a tug in the left shoulder of the jacket, where a round punched through a fold in the fabric without striking flesh. The rest of the shots stitched across the door above my head as I dove back into the assembly room.

I'd caught a glimpse of it: another sentry robot, making a beeline up the corridor toward me.

I hit the tile and slid down a stretch of floor between two rows of equipment. The machine pistol got between my chest and the floor, jamming into my ribs with bruising force.

My left elbow bounced off the base of an I-beam, sending that weird numbing fire up my arm which can only be triggered by the funny bone. The door to the hall swung shut behind me.

I struggled to my feet, encumbered by the tingling in my left arm, and the machine pistol in my right hand.

The door to the fire stairs was on the other side of the room. Stairs represented safety; wheeled robots can't handle stairs.

I headed for the fire door, angling to the right to get a couple of the assembly lines between me and the hall door. How in the hell had the robot found me so quickly? Was it in communication with the sentry robot on the fourth-floor landing? If it was, they were capable of launching coordinated attacks without the aid of their AI, a thought that did not bode well for our Intrepid Hero.

The robot came through the hall door before I'd covered a third of the distance to the fire stairs. I waited for it to start shooting, but it didn't. Apparently it was programmed to shoot only when it had a reasonable chance of hitting its target.

I started to edge closer to the fire door. Rows of equipment blocked my view of the robot, but I could hear the squelch of its neoprene wheels on the tile floor as it rolled up and down the aisles searching for me.

I kept moving, trying to stay low enough to use the assembly lines as cover. I came to the end of a row of equipment and crouched behind a rack of electronic heat-sinks. The fire door was only about five meters away, but it was five meters of open floor, with no cover to hide me from that trigger-happy robot.

My best bet was to track its movements by ear, and sprint for the door while the robot was farthest away. I listened. Nothing. No squelch of wheels on tile, no whining servos.

I flexed the tingling fingers of my left hand; the feeling was beginning to return. Was the robot gone? Had it given up on finding me, or moved its search to another room? Neither answer seemed very likely.

I held my breath in the green-tinted darkness, and strained to hear. Nothing. No... Wait... Something. Just at the lower threshold of my hearing, the quiet hum of electric motors, so faint that it might be my imagination.

Could that be it? Was the robot sitting quietly in some concealed position, waiting to ambush me when I made a break for the door? I didn't think robots were supposed to be that intelligent, but it never pays to underestimate your opponent, even if it happens to be a machine.

Surf had accused me of doing just that: underestimating machines. He'd rubbed my nose in the fact that machines were stronger than I was, faster, more durable, more meticulous; they could learn; they could create.

How intelligent were these robots? Apparently, this one was smart enough to lay an ambush. It also seemed to be trying to minimize the damage to the equipment in the workshop by not firing at me until it had a clear shot. Was it just waiting for another chance to shoot at me, or was it smart enough to keep me from escaping until reinforcements arrived? It didn't seem safe to discount any possibilities.

I already knew the machine pistol was useless against the robot's armor, and I wanted to avoid firing my Blackhart.

Could I make a run for it? If my suspicions were correct, and the robot was covering my escape route, its Gatling gun could cut me to ribbons before I covered half the distance to the door.

Both of the obvious choices, fighting and running, pretty much stank.

Wait a second... What was it that Iron Betty had said about choices? Something about the power to come up with a third alternative when only two choices are apparent. Was there a way to apply that idea here?

I had nothing with which to destroy or escape the robot. But did the robot *itself* have something that would help me overcome it? Maybe I could turn its own strength against it, sort of the psychological equivalent of Judo.

Its hardware was off limits. If I got close enough to touch its armor or weapons, the robot would blow me away.

That left software. There might be a way to screw up the robot's control code. I had no virus to inject into its CPU, and no giant electro-magnet to erase its program. I wasn't in a position to reprogram it... Or was I?

If the robot was as intelligent as I thought it was, it would be capable of learning from its experiences. And, if it was capable of *learning*, maybe I could *teach* it.

I lifted my head just enough to see the top of the nearest conveyor belt. A line of small circuit boards stretched down the length of the belt. I set the machine pistol gently on the floor and picked up five of the little circuit boards. I slipped the first board between the index and middle fingers of my right hand, and pitched it into the darkness with a flick of my wrist. The board sailed through the air like a thrown playing card, and crashed into something three or four aisles away with a clang.

The robot's servos kicked in immediately, buzzing erratically. From the sound, it was right about where I'd guessed it would be: at the same end of the assembly lines as me, but two or three aisles away. I could only assume that the modulated whining meant that it was panning its optical sensors back and forth, attempting to lock onto the source of the noise.

Its wheels squelched across the tile for about a second, paused, squelched for another second, and then stopped. The robot went silent again, just the low hum of its electric motors at the bottom of my hearing threshold. If my guess was correct, it had started to investigate the noise, and then changed its mind and returned to its position of ambush. The robot was smart; it had recognized the noise as a diversion, and wasn't going to let me lure it away.

I waited a couple of more seconds, and then lofted another circuit board in a totally different direction. It ricocheted off something with a metallic thump and then skidded across the tile floor. The sounds from the robot were a close reenactment of the first episode. It rolled a couple of meters off station, frantically scanning for the source of the noise, and then returned to its chosen spot.

The third circuit board I threw brought the servo whine that meant scanner movement, but not the squelch of its tires. The robot had looked around, but it hadn't rolled off station even for a second.

By the fourth circuit board, the robot's servos didn't react at all. It had recognized the noises as a series of decoys, and didn't even bother to scan with its optical sensors.

The robot didn't respond to the fifth circuit board either. I picked up Ryan's machine pistol and knocked the butt of it against the base of the nearest I-beam. The resulting clang didn't bring so much as a flinch from the robot. It had learned; this *particular* intruder uses noise as a distraction. Therefore, in order to avoid being tricked by the intruder, it must disregard all sudden or unexpected noises.

I turned around and started making my way back up the aisle to the other side of the room. Although I tried to move quietly, as long as I kept my head down, I didn't have to worry about making noise. The robot had programmed itself to be functionally deaf.

When I reached the far end of the aisle, I peeked carefully around the corner of the row of equipment, down the next aisle. I didn't expect to see the robot there; based on the sounds it had made, it was probably two or three rows over.

Perfect. I could get back to the hall door without crossing the robot's field of vision. I was about to head for the door when it occurred to me that I was probably underestimating the robot again. How long would it wait before abandoning its fruitless ambush? If I left it here, would it be trying to shoot me in the back two minutes from now? Better to take it out first.

I crossed the aisle to the next row of assembly equipment, and peeked down the next aisle. No robot.

I worked my way through two more rows before I found it. The robot was at the extreme limit of the effective range of my Night-Stalkers; its silhouette was just a darker green shape against a blurry green background. I assumed that it was keeping its optical sensors pointed toward the fire door that it expected me to escape through. The fact that it didn't start firing the second I stuck my head around the corner was reasonable proof that my assumption was correct.

I had a couple of problems. First: I couldn't see the robot well enough to target it. The laser sight on Ryan's machine pistol was useless. Its green beam was close to the shades of green used by the electroptic image amplifiers in my Night-Stalkers. I wouldn't be able to see the targeting dot with my Night-Stalkers on, and I couldn't see the robot in the dark if I took them off. Second: even if I could see the robot well enough to target it, the machine pistol still wasn't powerful enough to put it out of action.

I started to edge closer to the robot. Its guns and optical sensors were pointed toward the fire door, and it was disregarding any noise that I made. Theoretically, I should be able to march right up behind it. Maybe I could get close enough to topple some piece of equipment onto it, or something.

As I worked my way closer, I had to keep reminding myself that the robot couldn't see me and *refused* to hear me. I tried not to think about the fact that it had started to investigate my decoys twice, and then changed its mind and returned to its favorite vantage point. If it could change its mind about *that*, it could change its mind about ignoring the sounds that I made.

As I moved closer, the robot's image seemed to waver in the lenses of the Night-Stalkers. Streamers of vapor made the air around it seem to blur and ripple. It was parked next to the cylinder of liquid nitrogen that I had passed on my way in.

The first pieces of a plan began to stir around in my brain. It wasn't a very complicated plan, but it was a plan nevertheless.

I continued to close on the robot until I was seven or eight meters behind it. Then, I laid on the floor and took aim, not at the security robot, but at the cylinder of nitrogen beside it. I mentally crossed my fingers, and gave the trigger of the machine pistol a squeeze.

The ceramic meat-grinder rounds weren't designed to pierce armor, but they had no trouble punching through the thin double-walled thermex of the nitrogen cylinder. The wounded cylinder spewed super-cold liquid all over itself, the conveyor belt, the floor, and my friend the robot.

A good third of the robot frosted over instantly. The carbon-laminate and steel of its armor and chassis pinged as they contracted at different rates.

I drew a bead on the robot's back and pulled the trigger again, pumping a dozen or so rounds into the now frozen machine. The frosted metal and iced carbon-laminate shattered like fine crystal. The robot toppled to the floor in a shower of electrical sparks, its pneumatic Gatling gun pointed toward the ceiling. A few of its servos whined and jerked convulsively and then it lay still in a pool of smoky vapor. The assembly room was silent again.

Chalk one up for the good guys.

I walked back to the hall door. The fractured security robot made no move to stop me now. I eased the door open and peeked around the corner again.

This time, there were no shots, and no robot. I thought about Iron Betty's dire prophecies concerning Homo Trovectior and I almost laughed aloud. Machines might be able to run faster than humans, shoot straighter, fly higher, and calculate Pi to seventeen-hundred decimal places, but until machines understood treachery, Homo Sapiens was destined to stay on top.

My secret amusement was short-lived. I wasn't just dealing with robots here. There was still John. And, as I was finding out, he was quite well versed in the arts of treachery.

It took me two or three more minutes of cat-footing around the halls to find the second stairwell. I did another jack-in-the-box entry, and then climbed to the fifth-floor without running into any more of John's robots.

When I reached the top of the stairs, I laid Ryan's machine pistol on the upper step and drew my Blackhart. If there was going to be more shooting, I wanted the knockdown power of the 12mm steel-jacketed slugs. In about thirty seconds, John was going to know where I was anyway; I wouldn't have to worry about giving away my position.

I listened intently for any sounds from the other side of the fire door. Nothing.

I eased the fire door open. Emergency lanterns threw puddles of light at evenly spaced intervals down the length of the hallway. The corridor was empty, so was the foyer outside John's apartment.

The carved wooden doors that led to John's apartment were open.

John's voice came through the open doors. "Come on in, Sarge. The party can't start without you."

CHAPTER 31

"Do you remember that furlough we took in Rio?" John's unseen voice asked. "We picked up that pair of Filipino twins at the Fan Dancer Club? You swore that you could tell them apart, but I swapped girls on you halfway through the weekend, and you never knew it. I thought it was funny at the time; those girls were interchangeable. The girls didn't care, either; one American soldier with a pocket full of money is about the same as any other. But the joke was on me. *We* were just as interchangeable as *they* were."

John walked slowly out of his apartment and stood in the hall, his hands held open and empty, palms turned up in a casual imitation of the crucifixion posture.

"There's a moral to that story, Sarge," he said. "Sometimes, things aren't what they look like. Come to think of it, maybe things aren't *ever* what they look like."

I sighted my Blackhart in on his sternum. "Where's your back-up, John?"

"You don't need your gun," he said, "I'm not going to shoot it out with you."

"Where's your back-up, John? I don't want to have to ask again."

John smiled slightly. "I don't have any snipers in the rafters. You may not believe it, Sarge, but I'm not out to get you. In fact, I'm doing everything in my power to protect you."

I didn't lower the pistol. "You've got half the punks on the street trying to kill me," I said.

John shook his head. "If I'd wanted you dead, don't you think I would have hired a professional? I never thought for a second that a bunch of street punks could take you down. I did it to keep your head down. You were bearing down on me like a freight train, and I needed some room to think."

"What about Holtzclaw and Kurt Rieger? Did you kill them to keep me busy?"

"I didn't have anything to do with them. That was..." His voice trailed off.

"That was who?"

"That was somebody else."

I wanted to see John's face. I flipped the Night-Stalker lenses up onto my forehead. Between the emergency lanterns, and the light coming from John's apartment, I could see pretty well.

"I'm not in the mood for riddles, John."

John lowered his hands. "Can we go into my apartment and sit down? I feel like an idiot standing in the hall."

The skin around my eyes was sweaty from the Night-Stalkers. The air felt cool against it. "I like it out here just fine," I said. "Put your hands back up."

John sighed and raised his hands again.

"Look," he said, "it's not too late to walk away. I'll put the word on the street that the hit is canceled. Just go home and let it go."

"It's too late for that," I said. "I want to know what in the hell is going on."

"No," said John. "I don't think you do."

"Don't jerk me around," I said. "Where is she?"

"Who?"

"Sonja Winter," I said. "Where is she?"

"What makes you think I know?"

"You're starting to piss me off," I said.

John raised his eyebrows. "Is that supposed to be a threat? You're going to shoot me?"

"You think I won't?"

A tired little smile danced across John's lips. "No," he said. "I don't think you will. Maybe if I had a gun, but I can't see you killing an unarmed man. It's just not your style."

"Bad call," I said. "Remember that price you put on my head? A couple of street rats caught up with me in my hotel room the other night. I had to shoot both of them. Then there's the fact that you framed me for a murder that I didn't commit."

I tilted my head to either side as though relieving kinks in my neck, and then made a show of sighting the Blackhart in on John's forehead. "You see, old pal-o'-mine, my ass is wedged in a corner. You've played the game too well, John. I'll blow your brains out in a heartbeat."

We stood there for a few seconds while John tried to figure out whether or not I was bluffing. The weird thing was, even *I* didn't know if I could pull the trigger. I decided to up the ante before John could read the indecision in my eyes.

"We've got sort of a logistics problem here," I said. "The only way for you to be sure that I will shoot you, is if I actually *do* shoot you.

Unfortunately, by the time you find out, it'll be too late; your brains will be all over the floor. So I suggest a compromise. I'm going to count to three. If you don't tell me where Sonja is by then, I'm going to shoot you in the right kneecap. That'll solve both our problems. I'll still be able to ask you a few questions, and you will know for absolute certain that I am *not* fucking around."

I nodded toward him. "If I were you, I'd unbuckle my belt."

"What for?"

"In about three seconds, you're going to need a tourniquet."

John swallowed visibly; his wistful smile seemed to desert him. "All right Sarge," he said. "Maybe you *would* shoot me."

"No maybe about it," I said, with a bravado that I didn't feel. "You've left me with nothing to lose."

John sighed. "Your woman is safe."

"You'd better hope so," I said. "Where is she?"

"In the third-floor R&D lab."

"Let's go see," I said.

John looked around and took a step toward the far end of the hall. "Okay," he said. "This way."

"No," I said. "We'll use *these* stairs."

John shrugged and walked toward me. I backed against the wall and kept my Blackhart on him as he passed me. I fell into step behind him. "Slowly," I said. "And keep your hands where I can see them."

John slowed his pace. I grabbed a handful of the back of his collar, and shoved the barrel of my Blackhart against his spine. "Let's go for a little walk."

When we were safely through the fire door and onto the stairs I said, "I want to hear it, John. All of it."

John sighed. "I don't even know where to start."

We moved slowly, my eyes scanning constantly for any sign of John's backup. "How about the beginning?"

"The beginning?" John said. "I'd have to say it started at Iguazu Falls, when that laser chopped a hole in my spine."

"Whoa," I said, jerking his collar and bringing him to a halt. "I saved your life at Iguazu. You've got no reason to want revenge against me."

"This is not about revenge," John said. "It's about getting my legs back. Or at least it was at first. Now it's about a lot of things."

I looked around. Standing here was a bad idea. I nudged John with the barrel of the Blackhart to get him moving again. "You were saying?"

"You remember what I was like after Iguazu," he said. "All I could think about was getting out of that damned exoskeleton. That's what I got into bio-medical R&D for in the first place. Nerve splicing, pyramidal pathway switching, I tried it all. None of it even came close to working. I finally decided to let my AI have a run at the problem. I fed it every file on neuro-cybernetics that I could find, whole bodies of data from hospitals, biotech clinics, and research labs all over the world. Sweden, Japan, Germany, China. After I had squeezed the legitimate sources for all they could produce, I hired jackers to go after scraps and rumors. When I had nothing left to feed the AI, I programmed it to design a custom chip: a neural bypass to route motor-control signals around the damage in my spine."

The fourth-floor landing was clear, but I watched the fire door out of the corner of my eye until we made the turn and started down the next flight of stairs. "I know all this," I said. "Get to the part about the puppet chip."

"The puppet chip?" John asked. "Is that what you call it?"

"Why not? It certainly fits. What do you call it?"

"I call it what I've always called it," John said. "The neural shunt."

"Wait a second," I said. "Your neural shunt is the puppet chip? The same chip that you used to control Russell Carlisle, and Michael Winter?"

"It's been modified a little," John said. "But yes, the one you call the *puppet chip* is a later generation of the neural shunt."

John stopped at the next landing. "Third-floor," he said. "The R&D lab is through this door and down the hall."

"Open it," I said.

John opened the door. The corridor was empty. I nudged him with the Blackhart. "Keep moving."

John started walking again. I jerked on his collar to slow him down. The hallway was lined with doors, any one of which might pop open to reveal a security robot or John's lady gunslinger. The ones that really made me nervous were those we had already passed. I had no way to keep an eye on them without stopping every few meters to look over my shoulder.

"Okay," I said. "Your AI designed the neural shunt. Then what happened?"

John walked for a few seconds without speaking, as if deciding how to continue. "Actually," he said finally. "My AI designed six generations of chips before it came up with something that looked promising. We ran computer simulations, and laboratory trials using monkeys, but in the end, the only way to be sure was to go under the knife myself."

"You're walking," I said, "so it obviously worked."

"The surgical procedure *itself* was a success," John said, "but the implants still had to be programmed. We had to recreate the neural patterns that my Supplementary Motor Cortex should have been using to talk to my legs."

"What you're saying is, you had to *reprogram* your brain to communicate with the muscles in your lower body via the chip and the fiberoptic link."

"That's basically it," John said. "We needed a piece of control code. We could have written it from scratch, but it was easier to record someone else's synaptic patterns, and tailor the recording to my body. I used one of my lab assistants, a Vietnamese kid named Tran, and mapped his motor responses. When we imprinted them on the chip in my frontal lobe, we ran into something unforeseen."

"Yeah," I said. "It sent you into a seizure. You told me about that."

"It wasn't exactly a seizure," John said. "It was more like cross-talk."

"Cross-talk?"

"It's an electronics term. When two improperly shielded wires or cables are run too close together, they cross-talk: the signal passing through one can interfere with the signal passing through the other. Usually, the stronger of the two signals will end up garbling, or dominating, the weaker signal."

"And you had this cross-talk going on in your brain?"

"More or less," John said. "The frontal lobes and motor cortex don't just control voluntary muscle movement; they also integrate personality with emotion, and help translate thought into action. When we injected Tran's motor control code into the chip, it was like having a bomb go off inside my head. A little slice of Tran's mind was heterodyned into that signal: thoughts, emotions, force of will, and they all came out of that chip like water out of a fire hose. I found myself fighting to control my own mind."

"Tran's personality took over your brain?"

"Almost," John said. "For a couple of seconds, anyway. I was struggling and thrashing around so much that the AI registered my response as a full-blown seizure, and erased the program code out of the chip."

"Are you trying to tell me that this entire fucking mind-control thing was an accident?"

"It isn't really mind-control," John said. "It's really more like personality-transfer."

"But it was an accident?" I repeated.

"I sure as hell wasn't looking for it," John said. "You want to know the real bitch about it? The chip didn't really work, not for what it had been designed for, anyway. We ran into all sorts of neural feedback problems from the lower part of my spinal cord. It's taken nearly two years to work the kinks out. Personality-transfer fell into my lap almost from the beginning, but I've only had my own legs back for a few weeks."

I still couldn't believe it. "How can something like mind-control just fall into your lap?"

"A quirk of fate," John said. "The apple fell on Newton's head, and he brought the world the concept of gravity. I injected Tran's synaptic patterns into my frontal lobe, and I discovered the secret of personality-transfer."

John stopped in front of a door. "This is the lab. Your woman is in there."

"Open it slowly," I said. "And I hate to sound cliché, but—no sudden moves."

John pushed the door, and it swung slowly open, spilling a bright wedge of light into the hall. John stood blinking under the light.

"The surgical labs have back-up power," he said. "Thirty two phased-plasma cadmium tetra-cores down on the second-floor. It's expensive as hell, but we actually do a little surgery in here once in a while, and it keeps us from losing a patient if the power drops off line."

I looked over his shoulder into the lab; the unaccustomed light was bright, but not enough to dazzle me. The room was huge; it probably took up half of the third-floor. Rows of workbenches and electronics racks stretched away in all directions.

The surgical robot built into the ceiling was huge, three or four times as large as the model I'd seen at Second Looks. And if Lance's robot had reminded me of a spider, then this one was the queen, the birth mother of an entire species of spider-machines.

A black carbon-plastic nacelle, probably a protective housing for sensitive components, hung at the center of the machine's cluster of multi-jointed legs like the underside of a fat carapace. I could easily picture the bloated body distending to squeeze out glistening sacs of spider eggs. The mental image made my skin crawl.

Clear tubing dangled from the carapace in loops, some of which wrapped around the robot's arms to connect with manipulator attachments. A greenish-amber liquid filled the tubing. It was probably some sort of hydraulic fluid, but its coloring was disgustingly organic.

The unit was obviously a prototype, lacking the miniaturization and economy-of-form designed into the production models that followed. Its arms were much longer and some were nearly as thick as one of my wrists. Each of the couplings in its hundred arms was over-sized, probably to make it easier to work on, but the bulbous joints created a hideous effect of biological mutation.

The huge queen-spider was motionless. Unless someone cycled her power on line and loaded her software, she would remain that way: asleep. That was fine with me; I had no desire to see her awaken. Ever.

I tore my eyes away from the dormant robot and scanned the rest of the room for threats. No bad guys. No sentry robots. But the rows of equipment had to provide a few hundred hiding places.

Sonja lay strapped to a powered contour chair, directly under the queen-spider. Her eyes were closed; a trio of manipulator arms dangled a few centimeters above her forehead. Her mouth was covered by a strip of surgical tape.

I shoved John into the room, and then followed him, my Blackhart still trained between his shoulder blades.

Sonja's eyes drifted open. She tried to turn her head, but the surgical chair's forehead strap held her fast. She caught sight of me out of the corner of her eye, and tears immediately began leaking down her cheeks.

John presented her with a wave of his hand. "See? I told you she wasn't hurt."

I backed across the room toward Sonja, keeping the Blackhart pointed in John's direction. I didn't like the idea of standing under the arms of the queen-spider, but I didn't seem to have much choice.

When I got to Sonja, I started fumbling at the strip of tape that covered her mouth. It was a difficult job; not only was I trying to work left-handed, but I had to do it without looking. I couldn't afford to take my eyes off John.

I managed to get my fingernails under one corner of the tape. I tugged it gently away from her mouth.

Sonja started trying to talk as soon as the tape came off. Her voice was thick and slurred, as though she'd been drugged. I couldn't understand a word.

"What's wrong with her, John?"

Sonja tried again. "Rrrrrroooo... Rrrroooo... booottt..."

I touched the side of her face. "It's okay," I said. "I know about the robot."

"It's just a little dermal anesthetic," John said. "To keep her quiet. It won't hurt her."

I flicked my eyes down at Sonja and then back up to John. Four circular patches of silver foil were stuck to the right side of her neck.

I started feeling for them and trying to peel them off with my left hand, my eyes on John the entire time.

"I'm proud of you, John," I said. "Kidnapping is so much more civilized than murder. You really are making progress."

John crossed his arms and leaned against a rack of electronic modules. "I admit that we've done some pretty outrageous things," he said. "But we've done some *extraordinary* things too. Try to see the big picture here. I've discovered the secret to immortality!"

I got a fingernail under the edge of one of the foil patches. I peeled it away and dropped it on the floor.

"Think about it," John said. "We can record the human mind, capture a person's personality and thought patterns, and imprint them on a Turing Scion. Inside a Turing Scion, a human mind can live forever. But what about the body? We can replace damaged organs, and tinker with genetic codes and hormone balances, but sooner or later, accident or age catches up with us and the body fails."

I felt for another of the dermal patches. "It's a closed cycle," I said. "You live; then you die. That's how it works."

John shook his head violently. He was almost bouncing with excitement, like a little boy who was finally able to tell some secret that was just too delicious to keep bottled up inside.

"But it doesn't have to be that way," he said. "Not anymore. My chip makes it possible to reload those personalities into human bodies! We can extend life indefinitely. There isn't an injury or disease, *including* old age, that can't be cured by a body swap. This is going to blow the Medical Industry right out of its fucking boots!"

The second patch came loose and went onto the floor. "A body swap? What in the hell do you mean *a body swap?* You make it sound like changing clothes."

"Maybe it will go that far some day," John said. "We might get to the point where we swap bodies for the hell of it. Just like you said, Sarge. Like changing clothes!"

"One question," I said. "These bodies that you're swapping about so freely. Where do they come from?"

"Mononuclear reproduction," John said. "We *clone* them."

"You should study up on cloning," I said. "Clones don't gestate or develop any faster than natural organisms do. It takes five years to grow a five-year-old child. If one of your body swappers wants a twenty-year-old body, it'll take twenty years to grow one. That's why cloned organs have never made it into the organ transplant market." The third patch stuck to my fingertips and I had to flex my fingers for a few seconds to get it loose.

"That's true for the moment," John said. "But technology never stands still. Have you ever heard of Deichstram Bionetics?"

I shook my head and reached for the last patch.

"It's a Dutch R&D lab. They're working on something called *accelerated cellular mitosis*. Force-growing clones. The technology is just around the corner."

"When, exactly, is just-around-the-corner? A few months? A couple of years? Twenty? What if it doesn't pan out at all?"

John's smile retreated. "There are other options," he said. "Brain-locked criminals, for instance. Their minds are pretty much blank-slates anyway. A lot of them are bound to have nice healthy bodies."

"That's the sickest thing I ever heard," I said. "Every human-rights group and religious faction on the planet will be ready to burn you at the stake. And I'll be more than willing to hand them the matches."

"Okay," John said. "Fine. Forget criminals. What about corpses? When somebody dies, we can salvage the organs, right? What's to stop us from salvaging the entire body? We figure out the cause of death, repair the body, and reload the personality from a Turing Scion."

The fourth patch resisted my attempts to peel it up. I dug my fingernails in a little deeper, on the theory that Sonja would be safer with a few superficial scratches than with John's drugs in her system.

"I was wrong before," I said. "*That's* the sickest thing I ever heard."

"Goddamn it!" John said. "You're not seeing the possibilities. You aren't even trying."

"You're right about that," I said. "I don't even want to *think* about what you're suggesting."

The last dermal patch came free and joined its brothers on the floor. I felt for the straps that held Sonja's right arm down. My fingers found the buckle and started to worry it loose.

"Listen to yourself," John said. "You sound like a Luddite, cowering in your mud hut, pretending that the world is flat. If the technology to make Turing Scions had been around a hundred years ago, don't you think that Einstein would have taken advantage of it? Imagine what he could have accomplished if he'd had two or three lifetimes to work with."

I shook my head. "Okay, Saint Francis," I said. "You're the greatest thing since the Wright Brothers. You've found the cure for everything from death to the common cold. Now, explain to me again how all of this adds up to kidnapping, slavery, and murder."

John cocked his head to the side. "Slavery?"

"What do you call what you did to Michael Winter and Russell Carlisle? They weren't some theoretical laboratory-grown clones or the brain-dead criminals whose bodies you're so hot to preempt. They were just two poor bastards with brain tumors. When they went under the knives of your surgical robots, they had no idea that you were planning to give them a little bonus gift, did they?"

I tightened my grip on the butt of my Blackhart. "And while we're on the subject of nasty surprises, when do we get to the part where twenty or so little girls get their hearts chopped out of their chests?"

A pencil thin beam of red light glinted for a millisecond, bright even in the well-lit lab.

Pain exploded in my right wrist as the beam of a laser drilled through my flesh. I screamed, and instinctively jerked my wounded arm to my chest. The Blackhart tumbled from my pain-numbed fingers and clattered across the floor.

"Freeze!" It was a woman's voice.

I stood there in mute agony, staring at the neatly cauterized hole in my wrist, the stench of my own cooked flesh strong in my nostrils.

The voice had come from the open doorway. I turned my head and looked at it dumbly. I'd been so wrapped up in John's lunatic tale that I'd let my guard down.

The laser came through the door first, followed by her right arm, followed by the rest of her.

She wore tight blue jeans, black boots, and a tan leather jacket. Dark brown hair hung to her shoulders.

I recognized her as the woman from the Lev, the one who'd taken a notch out of my ear with the laser. Apparently she was back to finish the job, laser and all.

The white-hot nova of pain in my wrist made it difficult to think clearly, but there was something about her, a nagging hint of familiarity that went beyond our run-in on the Lev.

Her face was different; I was virtually certain of that. She'd been to the surgical boutiques. I had the vague impression that—whoever she was—her cheekbones were higher now than they had been, and her chin a little less prominent than my memory suggested.

She crossed the floor between us in five or six long strides. I tried to focus on her face through the fog of my pain. Where in the hell did I know her from?

I found myself staring into her wide almond-shaped eyes. They were beautiful: deep brown, lightening to amber near the pupils. Animal eyes. *Maggie's* eyes.

Even the pulsing core of pain in my arm couldn't still the singing in my heart. She was alive! Somehow, I didn't know how; I didn't care... Maggie was alive!

My voice wavered and nearly broke. "Maggie?"

She smiled at me, and it was as if the sun had come out from behind the clouds.

"Hello, David."

CHAPTER 32

I had played this moment out countless times in my dreams. *Maggie wasn't really dead, and the virus in the hospital's computers hadn't sold her body off for organ barter... The accident had left her with amnesia, and she'd wandered out of the hospital and into the streets. Or she lay in a coma on some charity ward, and the virus-stricken computer had labeled her as Jane Doe. One day she might wake up and the first word that she'd whisper would be my name.*

Suddenly, I had a thousand questions and I couldn't figure out which one to ask first. What had happened? Where had she been? Why the new face? Why hadn't anyone told me anything? I was almost afraid to ask any of them, for fear that I would spook her and she'd flit away like a butterfly. The questions would wait. She was alive! All I could think about was taking her into my arms. Everything else would sort itself out.

John walked to a workbench and pulled open a drawer. "Damn it, Maggie," he said. "You didn't have to shoot him."

"Don't be stupid," I said. "She walked in and saw a man threatening you with a gun. My back was to the door. She couldn't recognize me."

"That's close," Maggie said. "Except that I *did* recognize you. I shot you because I wanted to. A girl needs to indulge herself every now and then."

Her voice was calm, emotionless, as if she were discussing whether or not to have another cup of coffee.

"You can't mean that," I said.

"Oh, but I *do*," Maggie said. "In fact, it's something I've been wanting to do for a long time."

John rummaged around in the drawer and pulled out a blue plastic packet about twice the size of his hand. He carried it over to me, stripping open the plastic wrapping as he walked.

"I'm sorry, Sarge," he said. "I tried to keep you out of this, but you wouldn't let me."

The packet contained a gel-pack bandage, a translucent blue-green blob of osmotic jelly, laced with analgesics and disinfectants. John held it out to me; it quivered in his hands like a living creature. "Give me your arm."

I stared at him, only half comprehending the meaning of his words. My brain was busy playing back what Maggie had said. Surely I had misunderstood. She couldn't be saying that she'd shot me on purpose, that she'd *wanted* to shoot me...

"Come on, Sarge," John said. "Give me your arm. I'm not going to hurt you."

He reached out for my injured arm and pulled it gently away from my chest.

The pain leapt an octave when John peeled the synlon cuff of my jacket away from the laser burn.

Maggie watched me over John's shoulder while he wrapped the gel-pack bandage around my burned wrist. She pursed her lips in a fake pout.

"Oh, I'm sorry," she said. "Did I muff my lines? Is this the part where I'm supposed to leap into your arms and tell you how much I love you? How much I've missed you?"

Her words slid between my ribs and pierced my heart like a stiletto. The cruel lilt in her voice twisted the blade in the wound. It was as though she hated me. How could that be? How could Maggie hate me?

John pulled the ends of the osmotic jelly together and then kneaded the blue-green blob until it was a continuous band around my wrist. The analgesics in the gel had an immediate cooling effect on the laser burn. John stepped back to admire his work from arm's length.

The floral scent of the gel-pack played a weird counter tone to the stench of my cooked flesh, and the singed petrochemical stink of the burned synlon jacket.

Maggie's laser slashed a groove in the tile, a few centimeters from my left foot, laying bare the cement underneath. The floor crackled softly as it cooled, and heat radiated up my leg.

"David, I don't believe you're paying attention." Her laser swung up to point at my chest.

John immediately jumped between us, and pushed the barrel of the laser down. "That's enough, Maggie. David isn't going to cause any trouble. Are you, Sarge?"

My gaze seemed to drift up to Maggie's face of its own accord. Something burned behind her beautiful animal eyes, a spark of madness that reminded me of the look on Michael Winter's face the second before he'd pulled the trigger.

"Did you enjoy your trip to the warehouse?" she asked. "I go there a lot. Ever since John showed me where it happened."

She laughed. "How many people do you suppose get to visit the spot where they died?"

John touched the side of Maggie's face with the backs of his fingers. "Stop it, Maggie," he said in a near-whisper. "This isn't about death; it's about life. You of all people should know that."

Maggie closed her eyes and stood for a few seconds, feeling the touch of his hand on her cheek, then she nodded once and relaxed her grip on the laser.

In the brief seconds that they touched, I saw something pass between them: an intimacy that went far beyond the casual contact of friends. It was the sort of touch that lovers share in their closest moments, and it hit me far harder than the laser had.

"Good girl," John whispered. "We don't need the laser now. Just keep an eye on him."

John looked at me for a second, and then walked over to a computer console adjacent to the surgical robot. He slid into a form-fitting chair in front of the console and began punching keys. The control panel lit up with an entire grid of colored LEDs. They began to flash on and off in abstract patterns.

Maggie opened her eyes and looked toward John. "Is the implant ready?"

John's fingers continued to click on the keys. Several of the equipment cabinets woke up and began to hum.

"Give me a minute," he said. "I've got to power up the robot."

My eyes went to Sonja, still strapped to the powered chair under the arms of the queen-spider robot. Implant?

"I thought you would have already powered up," Maggie said.

John flipped a row of four or five switches with the palm of his hand, and several cooling fans whispered to life up in the ceiling, somewhere up inside the guts of the robot.

"I would have, but I had to wait for you to show up and take Sarge off my hands. I couldn't very well prep for surgery while he had a gun on me."

I couldn't believe my ears. They were going to *do* it. They were actually going to implant one of their nasty little chips in Sonja's brain.

"Why are you doing this?" I asked.

Maggie chose to interpret the question her own way. Her eyes narrowed to slits. "You let me die," she said. "You let me *die* and you didn't do anything about it."

I felt my cheeks flush. "What are you talking about? I nearly died trying to save you. I went into that sewer of a pit two seconds after you did, and I didn't come out until..."

Maggie cut me off. "Do you know what they did to me, David? They put my body in the freezer like a piece of meat. They carved pieces off of me, do you know that? They cut out my heart, David. One of my kidneys. My hand. Selling me off a slice at a time."

"Do you think I wouldn't have stopped it if I could have? Jesus Christ, Maggie, I was unconscious for three days. By the time I came to, it was all over. Your body was gone."

"You didn't try very hard to find it, *did* you? You didn't actually *look* for me, did you?"

Her words hit me like a fist. "There was a virus," I said. "They told me..."

"Who gives a damn what they told you? The question is, what did you *do* about it? Where the hell were you when your wife's body was on the carving-block? It was John who tracked down the organ clinic and bought my body back. If it weren't for him, I'd be walking around as spare parts right now."

This is not real, I thought. It's just a dream. Just another one of my crazy nightmares.

I must have spoken some of it aloud, either that, or Maggie read my thoughts.

"Nightmare?" She snorted. "Try living inside a Turing Scion, David. Do you know how long a year is when you're trapped in a machine that thinks a thousand times as fast as a human brain?"

"No," I said softly.

"Do the math," Maggie said. "It's a thousand years, David. That works out to ten or fifteen lifetimes. You can't touch anything, because you don't have any arms. You can't walk, because you don't have any legs. You're an invalid, David, and the worst sort. Too far gone to be helped by surgery. The kind of freak that should have died, but didn't. The kind that gets locked away in a dark room at the back of the house because the family is ashamed. And you're awake for every second of it. Waiting for the person you love most in all the world to come to you. Waiting for him to tell you that your arms and legs don't matter, that it doesn't matter if your pretty face is gone. But he never comes. And you're waiting. Thinking. Wanting. Remembering what it was like to be alive, to have a body, to be able to *feel*. Don't talk to me about nightmares, David. You don't even know what a nightmare is."

John cleared his throat. "You can't blame David for that, Maggie," he said. "That was my fault. I shouldn't have left you plugged into the net. I knew better. And I'm sorry for it, Darling. I've told you that a thousand times. I just couldn't bring myself to let you go."

Maggie shook her head. "Don't apologize for loving me," she said. "*Never* apologize for that. You were there for me every day, when my beloved husband was nowhere to be found."

John reached into an oval recess in the control console and pulled out a small bundle. It was a sim rig, wraparound data-shades and a pair of gray data-gloves studded with sensors, a lot like the setup I had at home, except that John's was wireless so his gloves and shades weren't tethered to the computer, giving him the freedom to operate from anywhere in the room.

He slipped his hands into the data-gloves and pulled the shades over his eyes. His hands began to dance in a strange combination of fluid gestures and abrupt motions; he was reading data and manipulating control features that could only be seen through the data-shades.

Maggie stared at me. "If you had loved me, if you had *really* loved me, you would have figured it out. You would have come to me."

"The mainframe is slicked," John said. "We'll have to purge the virus and reload from the protected data cores later, when the main power is back on. In the meantime, it looks like we have enough power to run the surgical protocols from the local consoles."

"Get on with it," Maggie said.

Banks of LEDs flared to life on several of the equipment cabinets. John's hands continued their dance. He nodded while he worked.

"It's been a long time since I've had to sequence this thing without the AI, but I think we're just about there."

Maggie walked over to stand near Sonja. She reached out and brushed a wisp of hair away from Sonja's cheek.

Sonja was still groggy from the dermal anesthetics, and the forehead strap held her motionless, but she was aware enough to try to twist her face away from Maggie's touch. Tears collected at the corners of her eyelids and trickled down her temples. Her voice was slow and heavy. "Don't... you... touch... me..."

"No need to cry," Maggie whispered. "We won't touch your heart. I promise."

Her left hand rose to her chest, as though unconsciously covering her own heart. "That's where your soul lives," she said. "My Daddy tried to teach me that when I was a little girl, but I didn't believe him. I didn't believe anything he said."

She paused and then closed her eyes for a couple of breaths. "I used to laugh behind his back, call him a bible-thumper, and a fanatic. But he was right. About a lot of things. I had to die to understand what he'd been trying to tell me my whole life."

When Maggie's eyes opened, they seemed to lose their focus. "Within each of us lives a trinity," she said. "Like the *Holy* Trinity: the Father, the Son, and the Holy Ghost. But for us, it's the Mind, and the Flesh, and the Spirit."

She looked at me and squinted her eyes, as though trying to peek at something that was silhouetted by a bright light. "It's the heart that brings the three together, your Mind, Flesh, and Spirit. Did you know that?"

I had no idea what she was talking about.

"Maggie," John said. "Let's not go through this again. What happened to you didn't have anything to do with God."

Maggie raised her voice. "John doesn't believe me," she said. "He drew me forth from my frozen tomb just as surely as Jesus did to Lazarus, and he *still* can't believe that there is more to life than electro-chemistry."

Her voice softened. "He doesn't believe in souls. But I *know* that they're real, David, beyond any inkling of doubt. Because I know what it feels like to live without one."

"What are you talking about?"

"John's chip could only reunite two sides of the trinity," she said. "My mind and my body. He couldn't restore my soul, David, because my heart was gone."

"Stop it, Maggie," John said. "You know where this always leads."

"John is too sweet to say so," Maggie said. "But he thinks I'm suffering from delusions. I can't blame him for that; he doesn't know what *I* know. Have you ever heard the old saying that fish aren't aware of water? That's what people are like; they're born, they live, they build or destroy, they make love, and they die, all without ever quite being aware of their own souls: the little piece of God that they carry around inside their chests. But if you took a man's soul away *then* he would notice it, just as surely as a fish becomes aware of water when the last of it has drained away. I know what that's like. I know how it feels to wake up with an emptiness inside you that is so wide, and so deep, that you can scream inside your own head as loud as you want, and you'll never even hear the faintest stirrings of an echo. But it doesn't do any good, David. It doesn't matter how long you scream, or how loud."

Maggie leaned close to me and whispered, "when you don't have a soul, no one can hear you. Not even God."

"Move Sarge away from the robot," John said. "I'm just about ready to run the UV cycle."

Maggie ignored him. "Your soul lives inside your heart," she said again. "The Bible talks about it in a thousand different places. Jeremiah 24, verse 7: *'And I will give them a heart to know me, that I am the Lord and they shall be my people, and I will be their God; for they shall return unto me with their whole heart.'* You see, David? You can't *know* God without your heart. And you can't return unto Him unless your heart is whole!"

Her eyebrows drew together. "That's why I was so empty inside. By the time John managed to recover my body, the organ clinic had already cut out my heart and sold it. They'd also sold one of my kidneys, and my hand."

The fingers of her left hand flexed unconsciously. "But the hand didn't matter, any more than the kidney did. John bought replacements and they work just fine. But you can't let them take your heart, David. I never listened to my father, but I should have. He knew what he was talking about. He knew that you can't go before God without your soul."

Maggie looked puzzled for a second, her gaze distant and unfocused. "They gave my heart to a pretty little girl, fourteen years old. Her name was... Elaine Carerra."

The sound of Elaine Carerra's name brought reality down on my head with the force of a hammer blow. I had been just sort of floating along, pretending that none of this was real. But it *was* real.

The sim recording of the girl's homicide scene came back to me in sickening detail. Her young body sprawled half on and half off the bed, face tilted upward, dead eyes staring at the ceiling. A drop of blood trailing down her left cheek like a tear. The blood-streaked bed sheets swaddling her body. And behind the image of Elaine Carerra came the memories of all the other girls: Kathy Armstrong... Miko Otosaki... Felicia Stevens... Christine Clark... All close to the same age. All lying dead with gaping holes hacked into their chests.

"It was you," I whispered. "It wasn't John at all. It was *you.*"

Maggie kept talking as if she hadn't heard me. "I watched her for weeks," she said. "It practically killed me every time I saw her. Knowing that my heart was beating inside her chest. *Knowing* that my soul was burning inside her, making her alive, making her a person. While I was just this empty husk, this hollow shell of a thing that used to be human. And I knew that I would never be human again, not until she gave me back what she had taken from me."

John's data-gloved hands went through the motions of opening a box, and suddenly the robot's arms came to life. They began to move in sequence, four or five at a time, cycling each joint through its full range of motion as John took control of them and ran start-up diagnostics.

"Maggie," John said. "It's time. Both of you need to move away from the robot."

"She was sleeping when I came into her room," Maggie said softly. "So young. So pretty. I must have stood there for an hour, watching the gentle rise and fall of her chest. If I listened closely, I could actually hear my heart beating just under her skin. Fluttering under her ribs like a bird batting itself against the bars of a cage. I could feel it, the energy of my soul radiating through the pores of her skin, warming my face from across the room like the heat of a furnace."

"Maggie," John said. "I'm ready to run the UV cycle and turn control of the robot over to the computer."

Maggie's eyes drifted down to rest on Sonja's bound body. "Her parents were out of the house," Maggie said. "I sat on the edge of her bed and shook her gently to wake her. She tried to scream. I held my hand over her mouth and told her the truth, that it would be okay. I wasn't there to hurt her. I just wanted something back that had been taken from me. Something important. She fought me for a while, until I showed it to her, held it up in front of her face so that she could see that it was mine. I told her that I needed my soul, that God wanted me to have it, so that the trinity could be complete. So that I could *really* be alive again.

"I thought it was over then," Maggie said. "But Elaine won't let it be over. I passed her on the street about a month later. At first, I almost didn't recognize her. She was younger, and shorter, and her hair was different. But I knew that it was her."

The muscles in Maggie's neck tensed, and her right hand unconsciously drew the laser up to her chest. "I ran and I hid," she said. "I locked myself into a dingy little hotel room and didn't so much as open the door. I pulled the curtains and huddled in the dark, hungry and afraid. I could feel her out there, moving through the streets. Searching for me. Stalking me. I couldn't even order food, because she might hear the sound of my voice and find me. I tried to slow the beating of my heart so that she couldn't feel it."

A tear ran down Maggie's cheek. "But you can't hide forever, David. You can't be afraid every second of every day. Eventually, the fear begins to turn to something else. And after a while, I stopped waiting for her to come to me. I went to her instead."

Maggie looked up at me, the tears glistening in her eyes. "I can't make her stop, David. I keep trying, but she won't stop coming back. She's too clever for me. She makes it hard for me to recognize her. She changes her name. Her eyes. Her face. But it's always her, David. It's always... her."

Maggie's gaze caught mine and transfixed me like an insect pinned to a board. Behind the tears, her beautiful amber-brown eyes blazed with an agony that I could scarcely imagine.

Some part of me wanted to fold her into my arms. To forget the past, no matter how horrible it was...

But I couldn't. This *thing* wasn't Maggie. It had Maggie's memories, and it looked out at the world through Maggie's eyes, but it was *not* Maggie. John's creation was not the resurrection of Maggie Stalin, but a chimera, a thing that spoke with Maggie's voice. An insane thing. A monster.

The natural corollary to that thought came unbidden to my mind. It was up to me to stop this. No one outside of this room knew the truth. If this didn't stop here, tonight, Maggie would go back to hunting Elaine Carerra. More little girls would die to satisfy her psychotic fantasies.

No. Maggie had to be stopped, and for that, I needed a weapon. Over the years, Maggie had given me enough lumps on the sparring-mat to prove that she was at least my equal in unarmed-combat. With my right arm fried, I wouldn't stand a chance.

I scanned the floor for the Blackhart, trying to keep my eye movements casually disinterested. No luck. I'd probably have to crawl around on hands and knees to find it, giving Maggie all the time she needed to put several nicely cauterized holes through my head.

What did that leave for weapons? Maybe something lying around, a scalpel, or an injector-syrette, or something. I gave the room the once-over again, looking for anything that might conceivably be used as a weapon. No luck. There might be something inside one of the drawers or cabinets, but Maggie would hardly stand by and wait for me to conduct an organized search.

Maggie must have caught my eye movements. "You're getting ready to try something, aren't you David?"

The tone of her voice changed totally, as though she had shifted moods in an instant. She glanced down at Sonja. "Time to rescue your damsel in distress?"

Maggie frowned, an exaggerated theatrical expression. "She's not really a very good damsel, is she? In fact, she's basically just your common variety street-whore. But I guess that doesn't really matter, because you're not much of a detective either. You're not really much of anything, are you David?"

John pushed the data-shades back up onto his forehead and stood up.

"Such a pitiful little man," Maggie said. "Holed up in your cave like a hermit.   Sad little man, drowning in scotch, wallowing in self-pity. Welding together pieces of people's trash, pretending that it's art."

Maggie laughed, a single short syllable dripping with sarcasm. "Do you know who bought all those so-called sculptures of yours? *I* did, David. Every one that you ever sold. I'm the mystery buyer that Susan Blayne told you about. As far as I know, I'm your *only* buyer. Can you guess what I did with all your little masterpieces? I had them hauled to a foundry, and I watched them go into the arc-furnace. You should have seen it, David, your precious little bits of twisted metal melting like icicles in the sun."

It was obviously meant to be a devastating blow—brutally shredding the last inklings of my artistic fantasies. Squashing me to the floor in a puddle of self-pity. In another place, under different circumstances, it might have crushed me as thoroughly as Maggie intended. But coming in the wake of so many other terrible revelations, this latest insult didn't seem to matter very much.

My eyes settled on John as he walked toward us. His steps were exaggerated, heels clicking loudly on the floor. He was agitated. Maybe it was his frustration at Maggie's refusal to cooperate, or maybe he really didn't want to send Sonja under the knife.

He claimed that he'd been trying to protect me. What if it were true? We'd been friends most of our lives.   Could I use that friendship somehow? Was there a way to leverage his guilt and self-doubt into some kind of tactical advantage?

I suddenly realized that I'd found the weapon I'd been searching for. It wasn't a gun, or a lead pipe. It was John.

I cleared my throat and nodded toward Sonja. "So she gets the chip now?"

John nodded. "I'm sorry, Sarge. I wish it didn't have to be this way."

"You don't have to do this," I said. "What has this woman done to you? How did she become a candidate for your puppet-chip?"

"She hasn't done anything to me," John said. "Believe me, Sarge, it's not personal."

"And that makes it better?" I asked. "It's okay to murder innocent people if you do it to protect Maggie?"

"Don't act so self-righteous," John said. "You've killed people for a whole lot less. What about Argentina? How many people did you kill down there? Ten? Fifteen? People with lives, families. And you murdered them, because our government was pissed off at their government. That's justification for murder? Sure, I've killed to protect the things I love. I'm not proud of it, but I'll do it again if I have to."

"And again?" I asked. "And again after that? This is *it*, John? *This* is your immortality?"

John's eyes jerked up to meet mine.

"I hope you can get your money back," I said, "because you're sure as hell not getting what you paid for."

I poked my left hand toward Maggie. "You think that *thing* is Maggie Stalin?"

"She *is* Maggie," John said.

"Bullshit," I said. "Bull-shit."

I poked my finger in her direction again. "I don't know *what* that is: an animated corpse, maybe. A scientific curiosity, without a doubt. But it's *not* a human being. And it most certainly is *not* Maggie."

"She isn't..."

"Not *she*, John. *It!*"

Maggie yanked the laser around to point at me. "Shut up, David."

I looked at her. This was a dicey game, at best. The trick was to push far enough to snap John around, without going so far that Maggie would burn me down.

"Or what?" I snapped. "You'll shoot me?"

My eyes went back to John. "Does this sound like Maggie to you? The real Maggie? The gentle, sweet Maggie that I fell in love with? That *you* fell in love with? Did you ever see the real Maggie raise a hand to anyone, except on the practice-floor, or in self-defense? I mean sure, she knew her way around guns, but did you ever hear of the real Maggie actually shooting anything besides a target?"

"I *am* Maggie!" she said. "Don't listen to him, Baby; he just wants to confuse you. He's trying to divide us."

"How many people has this thing killed now? Twenty-five? Thirty? Jesus, John, how many has it killed that you don't even *know* about? That's why you've got to implant Sonja with the puppet chip, isn't it? You need another scapegoat because that thing has been killing little girls again."

"Don't do this, David," John said. "For your own good, stop it now."

"What are you saying? If I behave myself, she's going to let me walk out of here? Look at yourself, John. You're a button-push away from doing the same thing to Sonja that you did to Russell Carlisle and Michael Winter. That thing, that *maniac*, has turned you into a killer right along side her. She butchers the little girls, and you create the puppets to take the blame."

I waved my left hand at the surgical robot. "You're so excited about this technological miracle of yours. When do you start using it to change the world, like you talked about, instead of covering up for that thing's murders?"

Maggie pulled the trigger. The laser drilled through my left leg, a molten tunnel of pain through the meat of my thigh. I screamed as my leg folded. I collapsed to the floor.

It took me a couple of seconds of breathing through clenched teeth to get enough of a handle on the pain to speak.

"When..." my voice came out in a hiss. "When it brings... you a heart... that it's ripped... out of the chest of some little... girl... What do you do... with it? Or does she... *eat* it?"

Maggie aimed the laser at my head and pulled the trigger. John moved at the same instant, grabbing the barrel of the weapon and pushing it to the side. The deadly beam flashed by my head, close enough that I felt the heat of its passing.

"Stop it, Maggie!" John shouted. "Stop it, now!"

Maggie screamed, an inarticulate shriek with no words behind it. John and Maggie grappled over the weapon. John hung on to the barrel, jerking and twisting it, trying to wrench it out of Maggie's hands.

My Blackhart lay on the floor where it had fallen. I started crawling toward it, scrabbling as quickly as my injured limbs would pull me.

I was just about a meter short when I heard John shout "David! Look out!"

I rolled to my left and the laser fried the patch of floor where I'd just been laying. I snapped my head around just in time to see Maggie's left hand whip out and smash into John's windpipe. He fell to the floor, gasping and clawing at his throat.

She aimed the laser at my forehead and made a kissing gesture with her lips. Her finger tightened on the trigger.

"Drop it!" The voice came from behind me, sharp and mechanical.

Maggie's eyes darted to the door.

I turned my head too.

Surf stood in the doorway, a strange and vaguely rifle-shaped weapon pointed at Maggie. The barrel portion of the weapon seemed to consist of five or six brick-sized superconductor modules wrapped in electrical tape and conduit foil.

Five more of Iron Betty's fledglings surged through the door and fanned out like a SWAT Team. One woman and four men, all of them about as heavily augmented with cybernetic hardware as Surf. Their guns looked like Surf's, and they all pointed at Maggie. I could see more of them moving out there in the hall.

"Drop it!" Surf yelled again. "Right fucking now!"

Maggie's laser flared again, and the man to Surf's left shrieked and fell to the floor with a smoking hole in his chest.

Surf's strange weapon squealed like a bank of charging capacitors when he fired it. At least two of his henchmen fired a millisecond behind him. The lights flickered.

Maggie spun to her right, dancing away from the unseen energy beams. The barrel of her laser swept around toward Surf, and she pulled the trigger. Nothing happened; her battery pack was dry.

Surf and his soldiers fired again. The squeals of their weapons were nearly simultaneous. The lights flickered again, and Maggie's body recoiled, as though she'd been struck full in the chest by a heavy weight.

She staggered a half-step backwards, swaying gently, like a tree in the breeze. The maniacal tension in her face relaxed slowly, as if the demons that had driven her were exorcised at last. The laser slipped from her fingers, bounced once off the floor, and snapped back to hover near her right ankle, still tethered to the battery pack on her belt by its coiled power cable. Her knees buckled and she collapsed.

And suddenly, everything was still.

The silence held for several heartbeats. And then there was a sound. It was extremely faint, a plaintive whimper, like the mewling of a kitten.

I struggled to get my legs under me. The hole in my thigh was a core of pain, pulsing in time to the nauseous throbbing inside my skull. Somehow, I staggered to my feet and stumbled toward Maggie.

I knew that it must be some sort of trick, one last chance for the thing that Maggie had become to wreak its vengeance on me. But I couldn't stop myself.

I was drawn inexorably to the sound of her quiet whimperings. My knees buckled and I sank to the floor at her side.

Her eyes were closed, but she seemed to sense my presence. "David?" Her voice was tremulous. A bubble of saliva grew on her lips and burst.

"Yes, Maggie?"

Her right hand was cradled against her chest. She shifted her head slightly, as though looking at something through her closed eyelids. "I tested myself this morning. I came out negative again."

I stared down at her. What in the hell was she talking about? Was she hallucinating? Had Surf's strange weapon somehow scrambled the chip in her brain?

She coughed, and the mewling started again, deep within her throat. She swallowed it with an effort, and spoke again. "The home tests... they aren't a hundred percent accurate, are they?"

Her voice seemed different. The hard edge was fading from it, returning some of the quiet serenity that I remembered. She was beginning to sound like the real Maggie.

"Do you think..." She coughed again. Her voice was even weaker when she spoke again. "Do you think we should go see... a doctor?"

It hit me suddenly. Surf's weapon had somehow driven the real Maggie back to the surface, or part of her anyway. She was reliving an old memory. And I knew exactly which memory it was.

A lump of steel grew in the back of my throat, making it impossible for me to swallow. My voice was a hoarse whisper. "Whatever you say, Magpie. I'll have House make us an appointment."

A smile played across her lips for a second, but was quickly erased by a grimace. Her eyes remained closed. "We're going to make a baby, David. I promise you we are." Her right hand fell back from her chest and lay palm up, fingers twitching slightly.

I took her hand in mine. Her fingers wrapped around my hand. I squeezed my eyes shut in a vain effort to dam a flood of tears. "I know we are, Princess. I know."

She drew a sharp breath and released it slowly. Her grip on my hand relaxed, and she was still.

I squeezed her hand gently. "Good-bye, Maggie."

John shrieked, a crazy wordless sound that hung in the air like the cry of a wounded animal.

He slapped the data-shades down over his eyes; his hands began to flail and weave inside the data-gloves. "Goddamn you! Goddamn you *ALL!*"

The hideous spider-queen struck. Two of the big manipulator arms lashed out and snatched one of Surf's men, lifting him off the ground. A half-dozen smaller arms darted in to attack, stabbing at the man's face with syringes and scalpels.

He tried to scream, but one of the scalpels slashed his throat before he got a chance. Another scalpel plunged into his belly just above the groin, and ripped its way upward until it struck his sternum, gutting him, spilling fat loops of intestine all over the floor. The air swelled with the wet copper stink of hot blood and visceral feces.

John's hands were dancing now inside their data-gloves; the queen-spider reached for another victim. "You bastards!" he screamed. "You killed her! You fucking *killed* her!"

Surf and his squad dove for the floor, away from the robot's grasping arms, but the machine was inhumanly fast. A three-fingered claw snagged the back of the woman's jacket before she could get out of range. One of the radial bone saws veered in, its spinning blade spraying blood and bits of gray matter as it sliced into the back of the woman's skull. Her death-cries were nearly drowned out by the sickening dental-drill whine of steel teeth grinding through bone.

A cluster of robot arms shot toward me, blades slashing and fingers grabbing. My reflexes kicked in, launching me backwards, away from the robot's attack. One of the scalpels tagged me in mid-flight, slicing diagonally across my chest, laying open the fabric of my jacket just a millimeter short of my flesh. My shoulders hit the floor and I skidded across the tile on my back, sliding safely out of range.

The robot's arms windmilled crazily, searching for new targets, but Surf and what was left of his squad were laying on the floor now, below the reach of the deadly machine.

John disappeared behind one of the equipment consoles.

Both sides jockeyed for some kind of advantage. Surf's men tried to shift into positions that would give them an angle-of-fire on John, but the robot's arms responded instantly, ready to cut down anyone who moved in close enough to get a clean shot. After about twenty seconds of useless maneuvering, Surf's men settled down to wait, and the queen-spider went still.

"Looks like we've got us a stand-off," Surf said.

John's only answer was the sound of rapid breathing from his hiding place behind the console.

"Gypsy, are you out there?" Surf called.

"We're out here," said a voice from outside the door.

"Good," Surf said. "You and Viper get down to the second-floor and start venting the plasma from the backup power cells."

"We're on it," the voice said.

That seemed to catch John's attention. "Huh? What? No. No, wait. You can't do that! Those are phased-plasma units. You don't know what will happen!"

"I know exactly what they are," Surf said. "Convair L-Series Phased-plasma cadmium tetra-cores, right? Thirty-two of them, I believe. When we hit that plasma with a spark, this place goes up like a fucking bomb."

"You'll never get out of here," John said.

"This is the first big battle of the Convergence," Surf said. "We've been waiting for it for years. Planning for it. If death is the price, we'll pay it. Every one of us."

"What in the hell are you talking about?" John asked. "Who are you people?"

"Who we are doesn't matter," Surf said. "All that matters is what we do. And tonight, we're here to make sure that evolution turns right instead of left."

One of Surf's men raised his head enough to spit in John's direction. "There's a war on, Asshole. Man against Machine. And you're on the wrong side."

"I don't know what you're talking about," John said. "But I want out of here, and I'm taking Maggie with me."

"You sold out your species," Surf said. "No way you're getting out of here alive."

John exhaled heavily. "What do *you* say, Sarge? Do these lunatics speak for you? Are you ready to die for their paranoid fantasies?"

"I don't want to die," I said. "But I agree with Surf on one point. You have to be stopped. And if dying is what it takes..."

"Is that right?" John asked. "How about your girlfriend here? Did she sign on for the long-haul?"

Oh god... *Sonja*. She'd been laying there so quiet amidst all the blood and the screaming that I'd almost forgotten about her.

I'd come crashing in here to save her, David the Avenging Angel, complete with everything except a flaming sword. And now, unless I could do something to stop it, she was going to die anyway.

"Screw... you..." Sonja said.

Damn it! She was coming around again, and with incredibly bad timing. Go under, I thought. Please, don't fight it. Just let the drugs take you down. Or at least keep your mouth shut.

I looked around. My Blackhart was only about two meters away. I started to crawl towards it, every movement bringing a new surge of pain from my wrist and leg.

"You... killed... my brother," Sonja mumbled.

"Ice, Hammerhead, listen up," Surf said. "Here's the game plan: crawl to the door and get the hell out of here. Stay flat on your stomachs and don't raise so much as an eyebrow. That damn thing in the ceiling shouldn't be able to reach you."

"Okay," one of the men said. "Then what?"

"Tell Gypsy to set the plasma cells to blow in three minutes. That'll give you time to get out of the building."

One of the men started crawling for the exit. Several of the robot's arms swiped at him, but he stayed just out of their reach.

"What about you?" the other man asked.

"I'm staying here," Surf said. "To make sure that Dr. Maniac doesn't slip out the back way."

"Then I'm not leaving either," the man said.

"Goddamn it, Hammerhead, there's no sense in both of us dying," Surf said. "I'm a casualty of war."

"That's fine," Hammerhead said. "Then we're both casualties."

"You're a stubborn bastard," Surf said.

"Yeah, well, you'll forgive me for it in a couple of minutes."

I was a half-meter away from the Blackhart. *Just a little farther.*

John must have realized from my silence that he'd scored a hit. "How about it, Sarge? Is pretty Ms. Redhead expendable?"

Movement at the corner of my eye caught my attention. A trio of robotic arms were descending to hover above Sonja's chest and I realized that the queen-spider was about to feed again.

"Shall we see if Maggie was right?" John asked. "Would you like for me to open this one up and find out if we can see her soul?"

"Go ahead..." Sonja said. "Bastard..."

The fingers of my left hand touched the butt of the Blackhart. I walked my fingers across the top of it and dragged it into my palm. "That doesn't sound like the John I know," I said.

"It frankly isn't my first choice. But I'm in a corner here, and I'll do what I have to."

I hauled my right hand up and wrapped it around the grip of the Blackhart, gritting my teeth to stifle the whimper that climbed my throat.

The man called Ice yelled from across the room, "I'm at the door."

"Good," Surf said. "Now get the fuck out. You go too, Hammerhead. There's still time."

"Zero chance," Hammerhead said.

"Okay, Sarge, I'm tired of fucking around," John said. "You've got about five seconds to call off your dogs, or Ms. Redhead gets turned into bite-sized chunks."

"You've seen what they're like," I said. "You think they're going to listen to me?"

"You'd damn well better hope they do," John said. "*Four* seconds."

"Screw... you..." Sonja added.

"These guys don't work for me," I said.

"*Three* seconds."

I took a deep breath and shoved myself sideways as hard as I could, rolling over and over across the floor. Each revolution drove jagged bolts of pain through me like fresh shots from the laser.

"*Two.*"

I took a last tumble and slid to a stop face down, a few meters across from John's hiding place. Suddenly I was staring at him down the sights of my Blackhart.

"*One.*"

I pulled the trigger. The recoil hit my injured wrist like a sledgehammer. I screamed.

The steel-jacketed round slammed into the wrap-around data-shades just above the bridge of his nose. The impact knocked him to the floor in a shower of gore and shattered plastic. He twitched once and then lay still at the center of a spreading pool of blood. The robot's spider-arms quivered in response, and then hung limp.

Surf stood up and wiped his hands together. "Game over." He looked around. "Hammerhead, get off your ass and go untie the woman."

Hammerhead climbed to his feet and did as he was told, ducking and darting as he moved under the arms of the surgical robot. It was a job that he obviously didn't want, but he couldn't figure out how to refuse after having broadcasted his instant willingness to die for the *cause*.

"Get a move on," Surf said. "The clock is ticking." He reached down and offered me a hand.

With his help, I managed to struggle to my feet.

Ten seconds later, when the last of Sonja's straps had been released, Hammerhead looked up. "This one's not walking," he said loudly. "She's pretty tranked."

"I can... walk," said Sonja.

"Carry her," Surf said. The lenses of his electroptic eyes spun and whirred as he gave the room a last sweeping glance. "Let's go."

The stairs nearly killed me; Surf practically had to drag me down them. Each step brought a fresh wave of pain.

I tried to take my mind off it. "What kind... of gun is that?"

"It's an EMP rifle," Surf said.

"Imp? Little... demons? Or magical men?"

"EMP," Surf said. "E. M. P. Electromagnetic Pulse."

"How does it work?"

"A strong enough electromagnetic pulse will slick a microchip. We actually brought them in case the AI was still kicking. They just happened to come in handy for Zombie Woman."

One of Surf's soldiers met us at the second-floor landing. "Fifty seconds," he said.

"All right!" Surf said. "You heard him. We've gotta move!"

The man fell into step on my right side and shouldered part of my weight. We started to move a little faster.

"So your EMP rifle wouldn't hurt a normal person?" I asked.

"Nope," Surf said. "Unless it slicked your digital watch, you'd never even know you'd been pulsed."

"Then how did you know it would work on Maggie?"

We made the last turn before the first-floor landing.

"We knew about the chip in her head," Surf said. "And about the one in your friend John's head."

"You've been tracking John all along?" I asked. "You already had him figured into your Convergence predictions?"

"Uh-uh," Surf said. "We found out about him the easy way. We bugged you."

"You bugged me?"

"Yeah," Surf said. "We slipped a micro-bug into the collar of your jacket. No offense, but we weren't going to come charging in just because you had a hard-on. So we listened for a while. When we knew for sure that this was the real deal, we grabbed our torches and pitchforks, and marched on the castle."

We were half-way across the parking lot and still moving when the first explosion hit. It sounded more like a gunshot than anything, but the secondary that followed about three seconds later had a bass rumble to it that nearly deafened me.

The windows were bulletproof polycarbon. They didn't shatter; instead, they bulged and split like overripe fruit, belching streamers of fire and gouts of black smoke. The shock wave blew us off our feet and sent us skidding across the pavement. A fireball boiled out of the front door and climbed the face of the building.

A second later, we were on our feet again and doing our best imitation of a run.

Surf's Focke-Wulf hover-sedan swerved to a halt at the far side of the parking lot. The driver was an Iron Betty Disciple that I'd never met.

Surf and his soldier were easing me into the back seat when someone screamed, "Look! Up there! On the roof!"

All eyes turned to the top of the burning Neuro-Tech Building.

Up there, silhouetted against the rising flames, stood Maggie. She shouldn't have been alive, but somehow she was. Maybe Surf's EMP-gun had only damaged her chips instead of slicking them completely.

She had something slung across her shoulder. It took me a half-second to realize that it was a body. John's body.

Maggie looked around frantically, and then spotted the fire escape on the north face of the building. She took off towards it at the closest thing to a full run she could manage.

In their last seconds, the plasma power cores must have sent a final surge of energy coursing through the building's wiring grid. The holo-projectors flickered to life, and for the space of perhaps two seconds, Maggie ran with her burden along the battlements at the top of a haunted castle wall. Then, the last of the power died, and the illusion faded from existence.

"She's going to make it!" I whispered.

I didn't know which personality had the upper hand: the psycho-killer, or the old Maggie that had reappeared for those few seconds on the floor of John's lab. And suddenly, despite everything that had happened, despite everything that she had done, I found myself praying that she would make it.

Tears welled up to blur my vision. "Come on, Magpie!" I whispered. "Come on!"

She was just a few meters short of the fire escape when she stumbled. John's body slipped from her arms and fell to the roof. She paused for a second, torn between her reluctance to leave John and the beckoning safety of the fire escape.

"Go!" I whispered. "Leave him. Save yourself!"

Maggie bent over and grabbed John's lifeless body. She struggled back to her feet and started toward the fire escape. Just before she reached it, the roof erupted in flame. For the tiniest fraction of a second, Maggie and John's silhouettes flared like magnesium and they were painted in liquid fire.

A millisecond later, the entire top of the building was vaporized by another explosion, and Maggie and John's atoms climbed toward the dome on a column of burning plasma. A hundred brilliant reflections blossomed in the faceted polycarbon panels overhead, repeating the fiery images of Maggie and John a hundred times across the dome.

The flash of heat across my face dried my tears. Anger, sorrow, and regret lay crystallized in the salty residue on my skin.

I slid into the back seat of the car and let them close the door behind me.

EPILOGUE

Rico filled my glass and limped away without attempting to start a conversation. He could see that I had things to think about.

Out of long habit, I reached for the glass with my right hand, until I caught sight of the blue gel-pack bandages that swaddled my wrist and hand like a mitten. I lowered the healing hand to the table top. The skin grafts were coming along nicely.

I picked up the glass with my left hand and silently toasted Sonja. She had disappeared shortly after I'd loaned her the money to pay off her indenture. I took a swallow of scotch and shrugged. I guess a part of me had always known that it wasn't real.

The loan, if you could call it that, had taken me from comfortably independent to as near broke as I had ever been. I still had a few thousand stashed away, but it was time to start looking for work. Or, it would have been, had I not been living in the shadow of the proverbial sword.

The cops had to know about Rieger's murder by now. From their perspective, I had method, motive, and opportunity. I'd undoubtedly left fingerprints, DNA, and hair and fiber evidence all over the crime scene. Not to mention that the murder weapon was registered to me.

Today, tomorrow, the next day at the latest, Dancer and Delaney—or others cut from the same piece of cloth—were going to walk in the door and drag me away. They were going to take me for a little ride on the Inquisitor.

By itself, that didn't seem too bad. The Inquisitor would ferret out the truth, that I was innocent of the murder of Kurt Rieger. And, who knew, maybe all the rumors about the Inquisitor, the whispers of brain damage, were exaggerated, or even outright bullshit.

My real problem ran deeper. I couldn't afford to let them put me on the Inquisitor at all, because—if they did—they were going to find out the truth. All of it, including the part about the puppet chip. I wasn't sure that I could let that happen.

If the police got their hands on that chip, it might just end up in an evidence locker. Then again, they might think it was weird enough, or dangerous enough, to buck it upstairs. Sooner or later, it would pass across the wrong person's desk. There are always factions in the

Government that can find uses for something like that. Puppet-soldiers, puppet-assassins. As Jackal's skull-mechanic, Lance, had put it: *'technological slavery on a scale that even Orwell never dreamed of.'*

There were undoubtedly copies of the puppet-chip laying around, but without John or the AI to help, it would be difficult or impossible to figure out what the chips were for, or how they had to be implanted and programmed.

The R&D team at Neuro-Tech knew about it, but they'd built the chip as a neural shunt, to help John walk again. My instincts told me that John would have kept the unexpected side effect, the personality transfer aspect, to himself. So there was a decent chance that the secret of the puppet-chip had gone up in smoke, right along with the Neuro-Tech Building.

Which brought me around to my dilemma. If I let the cops wire me up to the Inquisitor, I'd be exonerated of Kurt Rieger's murder, but the secret of the puppet-chip would be out. The only way to refuse the Inquisitor would be to plead guilty to Rieger's murder up-front, which would lead to certain brain-lock.

I took a slug of scotch. Either *I* was screwed, or the whole world was screwed. A hell of a choice.

I downed the rest of my scotch, and was about to signal for another, when someone set a glass down on the table in front of me. "Buy you a drink, Sailor?"

It took me a second to recognize Lisa. She'd lost some weight, and done a kind of wild lion's mane thing with her hair. I realized for the first time how pretty she could be when she took care of herself.

Lisa smiled. "Aren't you going to invite me to sit down?"

"By all means," I said.

She dropped a short piece of computer hardcopy on the table and sat down.

"What's this?"

"It's a present," Lisa said. "Your reprieve."

I picked up the printout and looked at it. It was an excerpt from a corporate immigration request. The Gebhardt-Wulkan Informatik logo was printed in the upper left-hand corner, along with a date/time stamp.

I looked up at Lisa. "This says that Kurt Rieger flew back to Germany yesterday afternoon."

Lisa nodded.

"That's not possible," I said. "Rieger is dead. I saw it myself."

Lisa shrugged. "Gebhardt-Wulkan has decided to cover it up. It appears that the big dogs at GWI were aware of Rieger's taste for little girls. They are apparently under the impression that he was killed by the father of one of his underage lovers."

Lisa did the rabbit-scrunch thing with her nose. "I guess somebody claiming to be an irate father posted a few threatening notes to Rieger's e-mail account at GWI."

I stared at Lisa.

"Relax," she said. "I used a public access terminal. I paid cash and kept the video pickup turned off. There's no way anybody can trace it." She smiled. "Besides, GWI is too busy covering up and trying to avoid a scandal to investigate too closely."

"So..."

"So, Rieger's death officially didn't happen," she said.

I let out a breath of air that I'd been holding for two weeks.

Lisa leaned across the table and kissed me. "You taste like scotch."

"Yeah. I've been drinking a little."

"I'm sorry that she ran out on you," Lisa said. "I wish I could say I saw that coming, but I didn't. I really thought there was something between you guys."

She reached across the table and squeezed the back of my hand.

I picked up the fresh drink, looked at it, and put it down without tasting it. "Guess not."

Lisa dipped the tip of her index finger in my scotch and traced it around the rim of the glass. "I erased Tony," she said.

She looked down at her hands for a second and then back up to meet my eyes. "He was a wonderful dream, but I guess a person can't live on dreams forever." She raised her hand to her mouth and licked a drop of scotch off her fingertip.

I picked up the glass and took a sip. "That sounds like a good first step. Where do you go from here?"

Something touched my right leg just above the ankle. Lisa's toes slid under the hem of my pants leg and began to trace circles on the bare flesh above my sock. "Both of us need a fresh start, David. Why can't we do it together?"

I took another sip of scotch to stall for a second, while I thought of the best way to say it. The silence stretched between us.

Lisa frowned a little and her toes stopped wandering.

"I'm sorry," I said finally. "I know that this is the part of the story where the intrepid hero rides off into the sunset with the pretty girl."

I raised my left hand and touched her cheek. "And you're certainly pretty enough... But I just can't do this right now."

Lisa started to say something, but I put my finger to her lips.

"I wouldn't be any good for you now. Maybe later, when I get my head back on straight, but not now."

Lisa's foot retreated. A few seconds later, she stood up slowly. "I'll wait," she said.

"You don't have to do that."

"I will," she said.

I started to open my mouth, but she pulled my own trick, shushing me with her finger across my lips. She leaned over and kissed me gently, her finger still between our lips. "Don't be too long," she whispered. She turned and walked away without looking back.

When the door closed behind her, I set my drink down and tried to pretend that it was the alcohol that was blurring my vision. I closed my eyes and prayed for a Billie Holiday song.

A little while later, I gulped down the rest of my scotch and signaled for another.

Demi set a fresh glass in front of me and nodded toward a woman in the next booth. "Already paid for," she said. "Your secret admirer..."

ACKNOWLEDGMENTS

I would like to thank the following people for their brilliant technical guidance in the creation of this book. (Any errors that have crept in were my fault, not theirs.)

Mitchell Pearlman, Forensic Psychologist
A. E. (Art) Crosby, Royal Canadian Mounted Police
Dr. Richard G. Courtney, Neurosurgery Resident
Dr. S. Chawla, Neurologist
Annette J. Grosshans, U.S. Secret Service, Forensic Services Division
Dr. Kevin Gerhart, MD, PhD, Neuroscientist
Lt. Bill Nelson, SWAT Captain, San Diego Police Department
William Reese, Retired U.S. Army Intelligence Officer

I'd also like to acknowledge the contributions of several people whose assistance was of a less technical nature, but every bit as valuable:

Cary Stevens, for his help with *Homo Trovectior* and other matters of cultural anthropology; Michael I. Turner, Commander, USN (Ret.), for his assistance with the geography of future Los Angeles; Brian Morgan, the original model for David Stalin; the Phoenix Arizona Public Library, for providing exceptional research support to a complete stranger with all manner of crazy questions; Brenda Collins, for helping me drag this story into the twenty-first century; Crystal Larson, for her fantastic painting of the Los Angeles domes, and for allowing us to stage the simulated murder of her daughter; Eyler Larson, for his creative and wonderfully devious enhancements to the realism of the aforementioned mock homicide (and—of course—for allowing us to simulate the death of his daughter); Megan Larson, for lying very still and looking extremely dead whenever the camera was pointed in her direction; Christy Coulter, for allowing her daughter to pose as Simulated Homicide Victim #2; Candice Russel, for volunteering to be our second (and equally convincing) murder victim, and for posing as our figure model for early versions of the cover image; Maria Edwards for her untiring support, her excellent research, and for protecting my writing time so that I could actually write this book; my editor and long-time friend, Don Gerrard, for his endless patience and unfailing optimism; and the staff of San Diego's finest specialty genre bookstore, *Mysterious Galaxy*, for loving DOME CITY BLUES for almost as long as I have.

Finally, I would like to thank the many (many) advance readers, who put their love and time into making this book everything I wanted it to be.

AUTHOR'S NOTE

I began writing the first draft of *Dome City Blues* in 1992. Needless to say, a lot has changed since then. Global economics and the international political situation are radically different. Technology has taken some interesting turns, and I have somehow managed to grow a couple of decades older.

The world we now live in is a very different place from the one I inhabited when I first sat down to work on this book. In 1992, most people (your faithful author included) had never heard the word '*internet.*' Cellular phones were the size of cinder blocks, and nobody I knew could afford one. The first movie of the *Matrix* trilogy was still seven years in the future. The date 9/11 had no special significance to the average person on the street, and the currency now known as the *Euro* had not yet been invented.

When I made the decision to release *Dome City Blues*, nearly twenty years after it was written, I found myself faced with a dilemma. How heavily should the book be edited? Should I tear the entire thing apart word-by-word, or just knock off a few of the rough spots?

I have to admit that I was tempted to go over the entire thing in microscopic detail—polishing the language, refining the story, smoothing out the dialogue, and updating the technology. Ultimately, I resisted that temptation.

With the exception of a few minor tweaks here and there, I've left the story pretty much as I originally wrote it. As a result, the book you've just finished reading is not the meticulously re-engineered product of a novelist with several award-winning books under his belt. It's the first attempt of a fledgling writer who's just gotten up the nerve to try his hand at a piece of novel-length fiction.

The world depicted in this book is not the future I see from where I stand today. It's the future I saw back *then*, in 1992, when a fictional character named David Stalin first began to speak to me about a darkly dystopian vision of Los Angeles lurking just over the horizon.

— Jeff Edwards

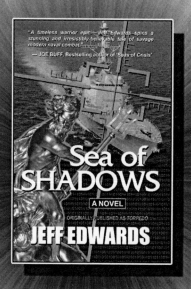

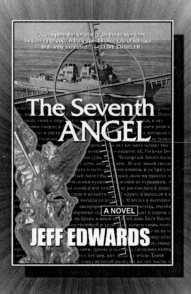

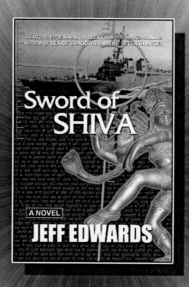

CPSIA information can be obtained at www.ICGtesting.com
Printed in the USA
BVOW010815231211

279094BV00001B/37/P